ARTIFACT

Artorian's Archives Book Eight

DENNIS VANDERKERKEN
DAKOTA KROUT

ACKNOWLEDGMENTS

From Dennis:

There are many people who have made this book possible. First is Dakota himself, for without whom this entire series would never have come about. In addition to letting me write in his universe, he has taken it upon himself to be the most glorious senior editor and keep straight all the madness for which I am responsible, with resulting hilarity therein.

An eternal thank you to my late grandfather, after whom a significant chunk of Artorian's personality is indebted. He was a man of mighty strides, and is missed dearly.

A special thank you to my parents, for being ever supportive in my odd endeavors, Mountaindale Press for being a fantastic publisher, and all the fans of Artorian's Archives, Divine Dungeon, and Completionist Chronicles who are responsible for the popularity allowing this to come to pass. May your affinity channels be strong and plentiful!

Last of all, thank you. Thank you for picking this up and giving it a read. Artifact is the continuation of a multi-book series, and I dearly hope you will enjoy them as the story keeps progressing. Artorian's Archives may start before Divine Dungeon, but don't worry! It's going all the way past the end of Completionist Chronicles! So if you liked this, keep an eye out for more things from Mountaindale Press!

Please consider giving us five stars on Amazon, Audible, and anywhere else you'd like to spread the word!

CHAPTER ONE

"You traitorous *plankton*! Cease your fleeing antics at once! That prisoner is property of the Octoid Authority. You cannot abscond with it!" The nasal irritation of the Arbiters in full chase fell on deaf ears. Not that the shadow sharks didn't hear them, they were just too busy giggling and flashing out of the underwater region.

The shark, Tear, lost all vestiges of amusement when he realized just how close those needle-teeth were getting to his tail. Not in the mood to get hooked, he created a shadowy duplicate of his friend to try to lead a few of the pursuers away. "Rip, ravine or coral reef?"

"Achlwaleon!" Tear wasn't certain what Rip had said, but then again his mouth was currently doubling as a dubious storage compartment. Artorian, the luggage squeezed within this toothy space, had little say in the matter. It was either this, causing Rip's mouth to glow, or be an easily trackable beacon that the Arbiters weren't going to have any issues finding. Mouth travel was a go! ...So long as the old man didn't think about it too much.

Rip tried to repeat himself, but when Tear clearly didn't

understand a second time, Rip veered off by himself with a stubborn grunt. The noise could be understood, at least! This time, Tear clearly caught the 'come on, this way'!

Tear created more shadowy duplicates of them both, letting those continue on the path they'd been going before the mostly hidden originals sharply angled off to a new direction. He thought the ruse had succeeded, but a stinging pain stabbing his dorsal fin told him otherwise. "Ow!"

One of the Arbiters had caught up to him, not sufficiently led astray by the simple trick of distracting shadows. "You shall not escape from me! I, Unexpectus, shall never let my quarry go. You two shall be added to the trial, judged as accessories! Cease your rampant swimming and—"

**Bphu*!*

Rip had gotten annoyed at the monologuing, turning about to powerfully tail-slap the unexpecting wordsmith that loved the sound of his own hubris. Froth garbled from a dazed Unexpectus as he was rung like a bell and sent away, and Rip made another spiral turn to resume their wild escape. The vibration from the impact was no doubt going to alert the rest of their pursuers. The tiger shark did not like being the one that was chased.

Tear experienced a flash of inspiration. "Beacon! That's what you were trying to say. We're going in the direction of the beacon!"

Rip mumbled out words that roughly translated to 'About time! Hurry up!' The passenger just wished he'd stop talking. It was so *awkward*...!

"You cannot escape from me!" The shadow sharks both looked over their fins at the sudden reappearance of a familiar voice. That inkquisitor was back? So fast? How? "I have you marked on my map! You will never escape me!"

Tear glanced at Rip, and nudged forward with his nose. They were going to have to split up. Or they'd never have the time to make it to the beacon. Rip's expression was pained in response, clearly not wanting to split their party. "*Ow*!"

A rogue needle grazing his dorsal fin forced him to adhere to priorities. Rip relented, nodding at his hunting brother. He sped forward as Tear spiral-twisted and smacked Unexpectus with his tail.

It didn't have the desired impact as the octopus recovered quickly. Unexpectus's shouting monologue quickly picked back up, but stifled under the sudden assault of a mouthful of teeth. Rather than run away as Unexpectus had come to expect of these quarries, this one had turned to fight. Or eat him, given all those dang teeth around him. He needed to use all his tentacles just to prevent that maw from crunching down on him when it tried. He had resistance to bludgeoning abilities active, not piercing for Authority's sake!

Tear, as a novice Shadowmancer, didn't fare so well against a seasoned Arbiter. No amount of tail or fang was going to best a member of the Red Inkquisition. Winning hadn't been the point. Every moment he could delay this Arbiter, the Arbiter after that, and the one after that as they all began to flock toward him, was another moment Rip had to make it to the beacon.

In holding them off, he was stabbed many times.

Many more than a shark could ordinarily survive, yet his divine boon kept him in the fight. The water around him was cloudy with his blood by the time he could no longer move his tails or fin. Unable to keep fighting and buying time. Tear knew he'd done all he could. This was the end of the line.

Ahh. What a beautiful, dumb, fun idea this had been. A final fin-slap to the face of the society that had treated them so poorly. He hoped Rip had made it to the beacon by now, but wished he could have gone with.

"Arbiters! Detain this monstrosity! I shall see it rot in the coldest of shells." One of the octopi began blaring orders, but his voice vanished as a sudden darkness bit away the source causing all the hubbub. It silenced the other Arbiters, fixing their attention on their surroundings as securing a half-dead prisoner didn't seem as important as deducing what the new threat was.

A single lantern light appeared above the position the talkative Arbiter used to be, an oversized anglerfish illuminating his terrifying face. "Hello, boys. Get lost on your way through the boss's territory? **Tsk tsk*. You know the Authority's influence doesn't extend here."

Tear found his bonds loosened when his jailors were forced to join their brethren, as several more lantern lights illuminated the dark.

Another anglerfish became visible close to the first, his tone just as amused. "You're in the depths now, Squiddy. You think we're just going to let you take what you want, and let you go on with your tides? Oh *no*. That shark? You don't seem to like him. That means we do like him. We like him a lot. Swim off and get ebbed."

The Arbiters huddled, fully aware of the several abyssal grenadiers lurking just out of sight behind the anglerfish. They'd been encircled in their fight against the shark, which had clearly been a distraction in hindsight. The verdict was decided on when Unexpectus drew his strongest nail, the imposing weapon aglow with enchantments. "You shall not stand between the Inkquisition and their goals, you translucent school of krill. I will not suffer a second jailbreak within the span of a single tide. Have at thee!"

The anglerfish bellowed with laughter. "You fool! The slipstreams have changed everything. Can you not feel it? The movements in the depths. How they pull and make the waves above soar high. Yes, come feed me, little squishy snack. I shall chew you until all your flavor has become bland. Just for fun."

Tear was vaguely aware of a fight raging around him when it started. He was dipping in and out of consciousness from his exhaustion. There were a lot of blinking lights moving and zipping around, but nothing specific that he could discern when he wasn't experiencing a moment of clarity. What he did notice was the difference in the Inkquisition's abilities when the limitation to capture dropped away. They were vicious monstrosities. Their red ink was caustic, their nails biting and puncturing through shells as if those protections were little more than loose sand.

He knew a grenadier had bit him in the fin to drag him away, but events were spotty at best by that point. When he came to a significant portion of time later, his wounds were bound in opaque white kelp. Blood loss had ended, and a reactionary swallow made a mouthful of food that had been shoved into his maw make its way down to his stomach. Tear the hammerhead blinked painfully, too hazy in mind to speak or think clearly.

Tear saw an entire school of injured sharks just like him nearby, lying on a bed of coral that enjoyed a constant stream of filtered water. The flow allowed his gills to keep him breathing even though he wasn't moving. It felt nice. He'd been transported a good distance, but couldn't place where. Since he seemed to be fine, he had another look at the sharks. Sharks were a good sight. Though they were massive, with white underbellies.

A dolphin nudged the side of his face before clicking at him. It got Tear's attention, which made the dolphin mighty pleased. "You lived! Thank the kelp. You're probably feeling very lost? You're in the boss's territory."

Tear didn't have an immediate response, and just half-glared at the dolphin who was trying to be helpful.

"You don't seem to know what that means. Well to begin, you're safe. Always good to be safe, right? Any enemy of the Authority is a friend of ours. I heard you had an entire pack of Arbiters on your tail! The named retainers are going to want to know all about that when you're better."

Tear attempted to move. A mistake, as all the wounds on his body didn't flex so well. The kelp was all that was keeping him together. He spoke through his pain. "...Who?"

"A word! The shadow shark speaks! The tide to your recovery will be swift indeed." The dolphin performed an underwater flip, clicking in joy. "You mean me? I forgot to introduce myself. Call me Flipper. I have a habit of… flipping fish above the water ceiling. Don't worry! I eat them! I only play with the food I'm going to eat. If you meant the retainers, they're on their way and you'll meet them soon enough. You focus on getting better."

Tear grunted, wincing as he did the best he could to lay more comfortably on the coral. This dolphin was too chipper for his liking, and he wasn't used to being immobile. That was usually the end of a shark. Tear instead had a sudden flash of insight, spurred on to ask the pertinent questions. "Who's the boss?"

Flipper snickered. "You wouldn't believe me if I told you. None ever do when we first recover them out of the Authority's jaws. The boss is a grandson of the ancient Daimyo. His excellency is named 'Breach,' and he is a cavitation caster!"

Tear understood… the name. That was it. The rest was garbled nonsense. "Am I… supposed to be impressed?"

"I'd prefer it if you weren't." The large creature in question silently crossed above Tear's resting position, the boss flanked and followed by several impressive and imposing whale sharks. Each was loosely wearing matching attire that didn't at all suit their natural forms. "Flipper, if you could be so kind as to allow a retainer to do the introductions, that would be favorable."

Tear's mouth gaped when the coloration on the 'boss' became clear, failing to remain unimpressed. Breach was an *orca*! The reaction on the hammerhead's face told Breach enough. "Whale, whale, whale, I see we have another addition to our school. Eat well, young shark. I look forward to hearing your tale from my retainers."

The shark was speechless as the entourage passed, having dropped by to check on other injured within what he now realized was a nursery. Several coral reefs each had a stationary or prone injured seafaring child upon it. Several dolphins went about to check on them, a few applying fresh kelp. Tear just about broke all his medicinal bonds when he saw who the group stopped at. "Rip!"

With a loud snarl from the wrecking jolts of pain, Tear wounded himself to move, to the great distraught displeasure of the nurse dolphin nearby. That didn't stop the hammerhead from wildly beating his tail through the water. No matter how many rocks his face crashed into on the way to his hunting brother. "Rip!"

Two of the whale sharks bodied him when he got too close, mushing Tear between their forms both for his own safety, and that of their Daimyo. Breach looked behind him with interest. "You know this one? Well too, it seems. Good."

The hammerhead was trapped. Tear felt solidly stuck in place, barely able to wiggle a fin as he saw the horrible, life-threatening wounds on his friend. Even the special kelp was barely having an effect. Only the soft, warm internal glow of their alignment boon seemed to be keeping him stable. No! He hadn't made it to the beacon? Had it all been for nothing?

Breach turned to address a retainer. "Where is the fish that brought this survivor?"

One of the retainer whale sharks swam a few feet closer. "Boss, that manta ray is still nearby. We can fetch her if you wish?"

The quick response in the form of a curt wavelength from Breach made two retainer whale sharks take off. When they returned, a bleeding Tear had been installed and placed on the coral bed next to his brother, since attempts to remove him resulted in the hammerhead making his way back there regardless. He wasn't going to leave Rip. Not after what they'd been through together.

When the manta ray arrived, the whale sharks around the boss shuddered. The creature approaching them was deceptively small, but it bothered them greatly that unless they were looking right at her, they could not detect her. She gave off no information to their electrosenses, as if she was shrouded. The two whale sharks that had gone to get her trailed behind, leaving a sizable distance between them to keep the manta flanked.

Breach couldn't prevent himself from being interested. Why was a small manta ray such a fright?

Her voice was smooth, teasing as she spoke. "Such fear. Is my appearance not to your liking, Breachy?"

Breach was starting to get irritated that this fish just threw his name around. He knew they were going to know one way or the other, but all the gossip just wasn't for him. The part that bothered him was that the manta ray thought he was scared. He wasn't scared.

The manta ray stopped short, choosing not to fully close the distance. After a cursory check of the creatures in her vicinity, she seemed pleased with something. "Perhaps this will help."

Obscuring clouds swirled around the manta ray, her form swirling and collapsing inwards before water displaced at her sudden, explosive size increase. A great white shark now took the place of where the ray had been, stunning most of the onlookers. Breach remained stoic, unaffected by the display while his retainers formed a close shell around him. "A krill trick. Who are you that brings the fallen to my territory?"

The great white lowered herself to the altitude where she could nest between Rip and Tear, experiencing no visible breathing issues from stopping her movements. Rather than reply to Breach right away, she studied Rip with invasive sight, then nodded in approval. "He will pull through. Good."

Her attention turned, shifting to Tear, who felt violated as the great white seemed to look right through him. "Oh, another one? I suppose there will be two of the old man's little ones that I am looking after, for a little while."

She floated up, having no need of her fins to make the vertical movement. That unsettled the retainers, and Breach was starting to feel a pinch of apprehension. Here was someone who truly didn't give an abyss that he was an orca. That was normally enough to shush even the sharpest-toothed deep dweller.

Her smooth voice spoke with intentional tenderness. "I am here to support a friend of mine. These little ones have received his interference. So he must care for them. Given they are both unwell, I will remain until they are."

Breach tried not to sound snappy, but she wasn't answering the question. "I do not take kindly to intrusions, stranger."

The dark great white smiled in response, showing a set of teeth that each far surpassed the sharpness of even Inkquisitor blades. "You're amusing, grandchild of Halcyon. In the search for my friend, I found Rip here. Too late for my liking, while accosted by nasty piranhas. It seems my friend was moved via beacon, and this little one was on his way back to assist his brother. Which I surmise is this hammerhead, who cannot help but stay by his brother's side. Such loyalty. How I prize such things."

She widened her smile, feeling like answering his question. "I have a bone to pick with a few tentacled nobodies, and will help remove this pesky Authority that has so foolishly let power go to their heads. I am the silent edge. The Queen of shadow and mist. You may call me Brianna."

Tear felt immense relief at the news.

Rip had done it! Plus, he seemed to have made a friend along the way. A very protective friend… that could change size and shape at the drop of a tail, and couldn't begin to give a shell about local circumstances. Huh… where had he seen that before? His relief spread from his stomach to his face. The great white had said she was here to care for them, and that knowledge set him at indescribable ease.

They were going to be alright.

They were *both* going to be alright.

CHAPTER TWO

Artorian wanted to complain.

Not about his rescuer, but about the sequence of current events. His rescue had taken a few odd twists and turns. Rip had done a fantastic job of getting him to the beacon. Unfortunately, Tear was the smart one. Rather than take the tiny dragon with him to a different beacon, Rip had sent him off to a random location in the beacon network before hurrying back to his brother. So on arrival, Artorian had popped out and fallen right on top of an unsuspecting dancing Goblin's head.

The Goblin screamed at first, but rejoiced when realizing that the mystery fire-snake hadn't burned it in the slightest. After which the green creature lifted him up and paraded him about the Goblin encampment like some cheap trophy. Artorian made note that these were original model Goblins, the ones he remembered from written Skyspear accounts.

Not the work of art Bob had been.

Now he was part of an abyss-blasted hat cobbled together with vine and twigs. The Goblin he'd fallen on had clearly become a Shaman due to his mystical find, just because the creature wore the Wololo snake-crown of foosh-foosh, as they'd come to call him. That bothered him ever so slightly. He wasn't a snake, he was a Long! *Ah*... who cared? This Goblin tribe sure didn't, and sweet celestial mercy were they stupid.

Rip was a loquacious genius in comparison.

While stuck as a makeshift crown, Artorian had plenty of grumble time. Trapped in the unpleasant position that he couldn't do or say a thing with his mana and stamina perpetually in the dumps. A terrible fate. So after a few weeks of watching a Goblin tribe just about backstab itself into extinction to wear the burning noodle circlet, he checked out and considered a nap, since this pass-the-hat game wasn't going to end. If anything, some other species was going to pick it up and up the ante.

Entering his mental space for a reprieve, Artorian strolled his human form around his bonfire room. Flopping onto a big silver root, he pressed his hands onto his face and brushed them back into his hair. "Something went wrong here. Now what am I supposed to do for a year? A full year? Abyss, Eternium!"

Scilla **fwopped** into being, appearing as a far less smoky variant of her usual self. Her limbs moved properly, and she actually used her feet to walk around. Was there a special occasion? Artorian straightened his back, sitting up some more as he wrung his hands together.

She just sat down next to him, then copied the way he was sitting. Hand-wringing included. Scilla seemed uncertain, her eyes narrowing as she turned her chin. "Can I make a comment?"

Artorian didn't see why not, but wasn't certain why she asked. "I don't think I could stop you if you did? You've never asked before. You're also walking about like a normal person. That's unlike you. Feel free to comment?"

Scilla inhaled, the breath sharp. "I'm angry. At a very specific person. Can Eternium be considered a person? He can, right? I'm badly tempted to call him a dumb rock. No activity for a year? *I'm* furious! How are you supposed to grow if you're forcibly kept in an inept state?"

Artorian reached over a hand, softly taking Scilla's so she could squeeze. "Do you mind if I ask why you are far more upset at this than even I am? I'm not happy, but I can understand the vengeful stab from Eternium. I stabbed him first."

Scilla squeezed his grip, happy to vent. "You need fresh experiences. New sights and new thoughts in order to help you cope with the old. You're never going to want to tackle a regret if you're stuck in the mire of the material you don't even want to look at! That tyrant!"

Artorian could understand that. Scilla was looking out for him, rather than caring about the circumstances of his current situation. He snickered at the last mention in her outburst. "A tyrant? Oh, no. No, no, no. He's fairly benign, just incredibly salty that I keep breaking his toys. I think Eternium is finding a part of himself that he's long forgotten about, and is just lashing out."

He made a circular motion with a digit. "The way I see it: After uncountable eons of being untouchable and residing at the pinnacle of power, he's vulnerable. As you so eloquently confirmed, he's a person. A person has flaws, and I think that triple S-ranked being had long forgotten what it was like to be anything other than a seeker of **Order**. Yes, he's done us an inconvenience, but only in pursuit of trying to stick to his desired ends. He was a mighty being and, in Cal, he was made to give up the majority of his power to survive the old world. That makes anyone who is used to a certain level of comfort with power… grumpy. Would you expect anything else of a petulant child with cosmic, world-changing power?"

Scilla was torn, visibly unhappy as she fussed mumbles under her breath. "Well I don't like it. He can grow up and stop throwing his whiny little attitude around. It was fine when it was just cheeky little poking, but as soon as he tasted what he could do with Karmic Luck, it was like he became obsessed with using it."

Artorian remained quiet for a moment, but nodded slowly as he mulled her words over. "Yes… Yes, I think so. I think you've stumbled on something, my dear. What do you think of this? Here we have a person that has lived for a single purpose so long that they have forgotten what it has been like to peek over their shoulder. Seeing the lives that occurred behind him."

He began making a circle with his digit again as he talked it through. "Stuck in Cal, Eternium has become malleable. Having made a world with Cal that is ripe for him to express his **Law** upon. Wouldn't it be wonderful for a scion of **Order**? All you could wish for at your fingertips. The movements of the world yours to balance as you think it right in your eyes. Then the living appear and start to muck it up. Your perfectly planted fields. Your well-ordered rivers. Awful."

Artorian held his own hands to cease his fidgeting. "However, they are people that live and exist in your system, so it's only right they become part of the order. That takes a little doing, but now Eternium is paying attention to the small lives he has for so long ignored. Who wouldn't, when you have such a high purpose to dedicate yourself to?"

He leaned back, narrowing his gaze at the ceiling. "I recall Oberon telling me that, up until my intervention, he had successfully prevented Eternium from dabbling with the karma tool. How does one make 'order' if they don't know what the broken state of something is? You can't make something correctly if you have not also made it incorrectly."

Artorian mused on Eternium's use of the karma attribute. "So he takes his first bite of the pie, and sees that I can handle his little back-clap of irritation."

Amused at the thought, he smiled coyly to himself. "I don't know what he was thinking. Though, if I had been in such a small box, seeing I could prod at the world and finding that it would react with such vigor, I would feel akin to having the lid removed. I would want to prod at it again, and again, and again. And who better to prod at than the piece of the puzzle I knew could take it? Especially when that piece keeps mucking about, giving you headaches while breaking all your well-made toys. I'd be upset with me if I did that."

Scilla scowled. "Stop defending the thing that ensured you turned into a long newt."

"I'm not!" Artorian's hands waved ahead of him. "I'm just saying I understand what might have turned a dungeon once wise and revered into a bit of a child. He's allowed to play. None will scold him. He hasn't had fun in ages, and he's in a position of discomfort. Anyone would lash out under conditions like that. I know I would. I mean, I *am* breaking things."

Scilla growled, having upgraded from a scowl. "I will bite your nose if you don't quit."

His hands went up into the air. "I yield. I take it the certainty of your form has to do with being spear-point focused on your irritation? You're usually more flighty, and your form follows."

Pouting, she crossed her arms and looked away. "Am *not*."

Artorian gently rolled his shoulders, one of his legs settling above the other. "Well, are you going to stay mad the whole year?"

She glared vehemently at him, her fingers drumming impatiently on her bicep with force. "I sure am!"

He couldn't help but break down and laugh, hand slapping his knee from her burning attitude. "Oh, you're a treat. I won't keep babbling about empathy then. Alright. I'll share in your anger. *Bad* Eternium. Bad! How dare you trap me as a tiny noodle! I have become a hat!"

Scilla punched the air. "Yeah! Bad Eternium! Burn it to the ground!"

"Maybe that's a bit much to just—" Artorian was cut off by her sharp glare. Right, they were *angry* today. "Yeah! Burn it all! Take that mountain. Throw it on the ground!"

Scilla got up and pretended to hurl something. While nothing left her hand, some shadows split on the ground regardless, as if she had smashed something heavy. "Throw it on the ground!"

He cleared his throat. "Scilla, honey, you forgot to manifest the thing you were breaking."

Blinking, she looked at her hands and then the floor. Realizing she had, in fact, forgotten to make the vase in her anger. She formed the vase this time, jumping in the air just to bring the pot crashing down. Shattering it into a hundred shards. She screamed at the ground for a moment afterwards, her fists balled up as she tried that whole breathing-to-relax thing. It didn't work so well, and a few more vases perished in the process. "Tyrant!"

"No, we covered that. Not a tyrant." Artorian pressed his hand to his face, letting go to press a finger into his own chest. "*I* was a tyrant. I know what that feels like. I know the weight of the guilt you carry around afterward. Eternium is lashing out; I did it on purpose."

He crouched and bent forwards, holding both sides of his head to ruffle his own hair. "What a mess that was. They all hated me."

Scilla slowed her rampage, cocking her head. "No they didn't?"

Artorian remained crouched, his elbows coming to rest on his knees. "Of course they did. I remember the whole battalion shouting at me in the Wilds. They despised me, saddled me with that horrible title, and made me live with that abyssal weight. Then I made some truly stupid decisions, and I lost all those beautiful fools."

Scilla crouched down in front of him, copying his pose. "I had a hunch you thought that was your fault. Listen, in regret land, your next stop is the Wilds. Do you want to go see why you're wrong?"

"I…" Artorian fell back and sat on his butt, holding his face with his hand. He sighed and needed a moment. "I don't particularly want to, Scilla, but it's not lost on me that I'm bloody stuck. Worst thing that happens is… what? I die while a useless noodle? Going up a rank doesn't help anyone this time around."

The pink-haired girl pressed her fingers together, amonsteepling them with a grin. "Well… *technically*, the influx of energy on successful resolution might be the equivalent to a nice, firm, kick to the keister."

Artorian perked up. "Are you saying that going up to A-five might do to Eternium what my upper B-ranks did to Cal?"

Scilla's fingers drummed together, her sly smile widening. "*Ma~aybe.*"

She waited for his gears to click to a decision, gleefully watching Artorian slap his knees before getting up. "Why not? After all, we're angry today. Right?"

"Yeah!" Both of Scilla's fists punched the sky. "I don't think it will help with getting out of being a hat, but I have doubts that anyone is going to try to damage a flaming crown that looks so neat."

He looked taken aback, with a hand playfully pressed to his chest. "Are you saying I make a good hat?"

She nodded, making a clicking sound with her mouth while pointing at him with both hands. "I'm saying you make a fabulous hat."

Artorian flattened his expression, the Tibbins line heavy and present on his face. "Just send me in."

"Hehehe. See you when you're back!" Scilla waved her hand as if she was an all-powerful soothsayer, watching Artorian vanish from the bonfire space, his mind now elsewhere. She stood in place after he was gone, her hands wringing one another. Scilla looked over her shoulder, staring at the void. "Was that good enough? Why are you in such a rush?"

A pink bloom answered with a wavelength. Coronas of color and sound replying without the use of actual language. Scilla understood regardless, and nodded. "I know… I know. I'm trying. We have to go at his pace. We have to. Just hold on the best you can. If you can't bear it and need to interfere, just come and be here. You know you're welcome."

Her tone softened. "You know he wouldn't turn you away."

Scilla's offer received a reply of silence. It lasted longer than she liked until the pink bloom formed a string and reached out, escaping from the wall of void. Crossing the empty space and connecting to the sapling Silverwood Tree that had replaced Artorian's bonfire, it found both harmony and warmth. Several new stalks grew upon the Silverwood's vacant branches, causing whole bouquets of cherry blossoms to form and open wide. The tree emboldened, growing in size for a moment as it appeared to take a freeing breath.

The Liminal being smiled, opening her arms. "See? Even if it's quiet outside, and even if it's unbearably lonely, the door here is always open for you. Don't you Tower people know that? I know the planet outside of Cal is barren, and there's nothing to latch on to, as you can't stop telling me how vacant the world feels. But…"

Scilla spread her arms further, as if inviting a hug. "**Love**, tell them to come to Cal. Reach out with more than just tiny strings. There are uncountable souls here that would adore the presence of their **Laws**. Closer than they have ever known them. Come. You are welcome. *Come.*"

CHAPTER THREE

When Artorian re-lived his memory, he was in the form of Tzu.

Tzu got off his horse. Not because he needed to, but because of how painful it was to ride in such an old, hard saddle. As far as his butt was concerned, there wasn't a dang difference between saddle and no saddle! Why even bother.

Pressing his hands to his hips, he rotated his middle with a grunt, trying to make those aches go away. The other commanders in the same retinue of course found this a perfect opportunity to make fun of him. "Oh, look, another thing Tzu can't do. Need a nice tent to nap in? What about a fat pillow for that saddle!"

Laughter broke from the mounted party. Those self-important sharp-chins and their fancy half-plate. They were just tiring their horses out, in Tzu's opinion. A breastplate was all you needed when you already had padded protection underneath. Even that was something he told his troops to remove when going towards the Wilds. Tzu had been laughed out of the strategy tent for his suggestion they travel lighter, but he remained adamant about the choice.

Tzu patted his hip, walking the rest of the way to camp.

They'd erected it on the cliff at the edge of a small plain which overlooked the region known as the Catakan Wilds. These lands experienced a tropical rainforest climate all year round, yet seemed to be perpetually stuck in the fall season. Given all the yellow and reddish-brown canopy colors. Expected rainfall was daily, and by the *Phoenix* was it heavy. He flicked his own cheek at that thought. He wouldn't start thinking like that.

Give *no* credit to the Kingdom. *Blast* them for sending people to the Wilds!

Here it was hot at night, and cold during the day. The sticky, wet kind of hot that resulted from swamp gasses which didn't like to disperse or rise unless the sun was out. His least favorite; though *everywhere* he'd been that wasn't a pile of pillows had become his new least favorite. The wet haze hung as a thin mist around the canopy, and no amount of staring was letting him get more information out of the impenetrable cluster of endless, tightly packed trees.

He wasn't even sure how to breach the place. There was thick foliage regardless of where he looked. With vines interconnecting certain trees and the fog obscuring any details past a few hundred feet. He spotted at least twelve snakes, and he didn't want to think about the spiders that he hadn't.

He'd only seen the webs.

A hard shudder struck him. Abyss, he could not stand spiders. Insects were just not his thing. Speaking of bothersome insects, his counterparts were just as wet behind the ears as him when it came to the campaign trail. They thought their reading and drills were going to see them through as if this was a leisurely trek over calm seas.

If only the truth were so convenient. Taking a knee on the cliff, he studied the land they were about to invade. That's right… invade. The reports of the Wilds breaking from their borders to assail the Kingdom were nothing but abyssal lies. This was a resource grab. An insulting, obvious one. If anything, Tzu was confused as to why most other commanders didn't notice it. Then again, half of them had been bought with gold and gifts to look the other way on so many occasions that he doubted this would be any different.

Only a handful of other commanders also studied the scene nearby, but the number was paltry. A milk-run of a campaign, they'd been told. Tzu would believe it if it happened, since the numbers in the ledger didn't add up. The provisions were supposed to cover fifty thousand troops. The budget had been set for the same amount. So what were they doing here with a measly fifth of both? A scant one hundred commanders, each leading a hundred troops.

Whoever had put this mission together hadn't done it for gain. Someone was purposefully trying to make the Phoenix Kingdom incur losses. Through competition, strife, or otherwise. The troupe of local commanders had already broken into factions, each under their own chosen mob-rule leader by method of popularity. Nobody was surprised that Tzu ended up being neither leader nor follower. As if they wanted him after hearing word on the kinds of demands he had for the people under his banner.

Abyss. Tzu couldn't call the people under his banner a group.

He ended up with the strays nobody else wanted because they requested too many transfers, or were too hard to work with. Figured he'd get the trouble pack. He did smirk a little at the thought that he was responsible for most of said transfers. These people weren't soldiers by choice. They were conscripts, people given ultimatums, prisoners given a redemption chance, or the few who simply had nothing left and nowhere else to go.

Most just couldn't keep up with his training regimen, thinking it was unnecessary. They were strong enough, fast enough, good enough. They didn't need to strive for more. Though the few that understood why it was necessary, saw the use of it, or actually were professed soldiers that had chosen this life also ended up not staying under his banner. Tzu's ways were too much.

Unfortunately for them, Tzu had promised he'd come home

alive and in one piece. Academy slacking measures weren't going to cut it, and he had maybe a handful of troops that seemed to understand what he and his plans were about. Out of his misfit bundle of one-hundred, he had seven warriors he could count on. Only seven. Two of them because his ridiculous tactics and orders had gotten them out of an ugly trap once before. Sure, they were both out of breath and couldn't walk right for a day from the mad dashes he'd made them do with tight turns and even tighter orders, but they'd made it.

He counted them out on his fingers.

Those seven were named Zho, Ming, Yoshe, Aki, Hong, Ichiro, and Miki. Aki and Miki were women that had snuck into the military for the pay, and pretended their best not to be what they were. Tzu had won them over when he didn't reveal their secret during those annoying inspections. Pointless things, meant purely to irritate and unsettle the force. So what if there was a little contraband? You had to let people be people.

They'd been nervous that their banner commander knew, but Tzu had merely smiled at them, covering the matter up by saying he'd personally checked the tent they were in when his superior came by. Nothing out of place. Nothing strange. Then he'd narrowed his eyes at the inspector that accompanied his superior, and nudged his head a few tents down.

The inspector had beelined for the tent, of course, just to throw the flap open and start yelling at nothing. Tzu's guess had been… unlucky. He hadn't known the troops in that tent had started to play cards and gamble after he'd poked his head in earlier. That tent squad wasn't happy with him either, and they were out from under his banner a week later.

Ah well. Lose five average mooks, retain two quality runners. Or he had, when they'd tried to sneakily confront him about it after the inspection passed. Surprising what the words, 'I know your genders, and I don't care. You're welcome under my banner,' could do.

It seemed that with their income secured, and a commander that had no qualms letting them keep up the flow of earnings, they also didn't mind the insane training regimen. Aki even started a rumor that only a real soldier could handle the Tyrant's training, which Tzu did nothing about. They disliked him anyway, what was a little more pitch on that fire?

That rumor was how he had met Zho and Ming. Two veterans of war, covered in scars, with mouths full of expletives and spirits so hardened you could sharpen your swords on them. Zho and Ming didn't care about the war. It was just another fight they were in. Instead they cared more about competent leadership and people trying to push them. So in their eyes, they'd rather deal with Tzu than some two-copper new blood who didn't have enough hair on their face to even pretend to have a beard.

Their only downside? Zho and Ming were snappy. They complained about every little thing, until it was action time. Then you could count on them to be in position, on cue, with weapons ready, in formation, when you needed them to bloody be there. Tzu had given them one of his plans to read over when they loudly complained he was just another nobody. Their complaints had dropped to quips, then to mumbles. Their words softened to the occasional pointed bit of commentary, then fell to silence as they held their chins and spoke in hushed tones about the listed tactics.

Zho snarkily addressed Tzu. "You must play Kings and Castles. This is some seven grasshoppers ahead of the jump kind of plan."

"You must play Peons if it took you that long to notice." Tzu grinned at them, his reply equally stabby. Though it was in their vein of comedy and they visibly appreciated it. Zho and Ming laughed to themselves, putting the plans down to engage in a battle of glorious insults.

They liked this one.

Yoshe and Hong had been the ones he'd broken the flags out for, since they had been stuck in a training exercise that the opposing team had decided to take too seriously. Possibly because Yoshe and Hong had cheated them out of a tiny bit of coin—or maybe all of it. Yoshe and Hong had been professional thieves before they'd been given the choice of, 'You can join the legion, or you can hang.'

Couldn't call that a choice.

This duo was quick on their feet and, to Tzu's enjoyment, quick on the uptake. They realized his display of tactical flags was for them when they got trapped behind a berm and didn't know if their opponents were going to burst in from the left or right. Overlooking the scene from the high ground, Tzu saw all the movements well and responded with haste. The rapid change of directions had let them escape from the field, bolting right up the hill and over to the set of flag bearers that had gotten them out of that mess.

They were glad to meet a fellow schemer! Tzu was glad to have them.

Lastly there was Ichiro. Ichiro was special. In the sense that he was literal in all things, and neither understood, nor grasped even the smallest strings of nuance. If you used a regional colloquialism, such as mentioning that the pheasants were numerous today—meaning that people you didn't like were about in great numbers—Ichiro thought it was time to go hunt for food, and got his bow. When people tried to make clear to him that they had meant some of the other soldiers, Ichiro took that to mean they were pheasants in disguise and opened fire on them.

The camp despised the man that couldn't recognize friend from foe, but Tzu adored him. For all the faults in how he understood things, Ichiro was amazing at one thing in particular: The ability to follow orders with a perfect sense of timing. If you needed him to cross a field in ten seconds, then by the Phoenix, he would have that field crossed regardless of how dead he was when he got there.

When Tzu told him: "I need this flag, on that hill, before anyone can catch you," Ichiro had accomplished it on the first try, and was abyss-near reduced to tears when the people in the banner group he was under cheered for him with wild abandon. It was the first time he'd been lifted on the shoulders of others.

His name repetitively shouted for being the sole reason they got first place in a capture the hill game. Other commanders had thought about complicated back and forths on the field of battle, blocking forces, cutting off avenues, clever positioning.

No. Not Ichiro.

Tzu had said take this and put it there. So he did, and it was amazing. The enemy team had laughed at Tzu's banner group when they saw Ichiro run at full speed over to them, like he was on the wrong team and the flag needed to be on the other side. Since it happened right at the start of the battle before troops had been settled in their planned positions, he had that flag on the hill moments before the horn blew to start the event. After which Ichiro slammed that flag down, and collapsed right next to it. The horn then blew again, signaling Tzu's victory.

When commander Watdis on the opposing team realized that win was legal, he loudly accused Tzu of cheating, since this apparently counted as an official win as far as their commanding General was concerned. The heavily armored, long bearded man had laughed with his arms crossed when informed about the display. The win was fairly awarded. In the General's words: "In battle, if you can seize victory before your enemy is prepared… you have won well."

CHAPTER FOUR

Artorian re-lived those days in the camp. Following Tzu around to watch his younger self be just as embarrassingly sneaky as he recalled being. It hadn't been so bad when he'd done it as Tzu, but watching it all over again was cringy. Did he always have such a penchant for irritating the living abyss out of just about anyone? It sure seemed like it. The thought made him smile after a while, enjoying the slow meander along his own memories. Experienced again in vivid detail, with one difference. A difference he was becoming quite keen to.

It wasn't just his memory he was limited to.

In this tribulation, he also heard words spoken that he otherwise would not have. A replaying of events, enhanced. A conversation Artorian had never known before could be experienced in full detail, so long as he was standing close enough. Without any loss of clarity, he watched two soldiers from an opposing camp talk black abyss about Tzu after the commander had passed out of earshot.

He knew not to interfere. Not physically. That would cause another weird not-event to occur like with Grant, the Beast Core that had stripped him of his initial corruption. That memory had been a strong lesson in how he should be tackling these tribulations. He was to take it on the chin, to accept the blows as they came, processing them anew all over again.

Artorian stopped wondering and wandering when he reached the cliff Tzu once again sat at, for the fifth day in a row. He held his beard, slowly nodding in understanding at his younger self's struggles. Even now, he couldn't figure out a good solution to the questions from back then. Not a one.

The problem was threefold.

The invading force had not properly been informed of its goal. Even if they assailed the Wilds, they had no clearly defined order for what they needed to take, or defeat, or do. The interpretation was left to the commanders who each took a batch of troops in.

There lay the second problem. After what must have been political embezzlement, the force arrived at one fifth its planned size, with one fifth of the supplies. Then split up again into small groups. Why? Why did they need to split up at all? A hundred troops under a banner was going to lead to disarray and confusion in a location so dense with environmental difficulties.

Which introduced the third problem. How were they going to plan and react when they could not speak with flags? He could barely see through the mist when above the forest, and it was guaranteed to be far worse when he was in it.

Tzu might not know how bad it was going to be yet, but Artorian did. It was an awful experience. The entire troop would be blind, suffer communication failures without end, and be entirely unable to coordinate larger assaults. Their voices didn't carry as far in the swamps of the Wilds, and they had not yet discovered that some of the swamp gasses were lethal. Some troops died just from inhaling.

Artorian squeezed the bridge of his nose, knowing full well Tzu was stuck, and needed to make some questionable decisions. The old man gritted his teeth, squeezing his eyes shut as his face turned away from the scene. He didn't want to remember the next few days, but he was unable. Here was where it had started. The regret. Before it had all gone to the abyss.

He didn't want to ride along inside of Tzu's perspective for this, and followed along as the days passed, watching Tzu's reputation being slandered and slathered in ever darker paints. An army stuck in a stagnant camp fought only itself, and every grievance loved a scapegoat. Who better to blame than the banner of rejects?

He should have put a stop to that before it got out of hand, and Tzu had failed to. He was distracted entirely by the task in front of him, rather than who was behind him. Unaware how their words had already started to stab at his heart. A lesson Tzu was not soon to forget when the day came to press on into the Wilds.

To begin, all the horses had to be left behind. There was just no way in for them, and the horses had no interest in proceeding to such a place regardless. They grew tense and defiant, stamping and huffing. Tzu should have been as a horse that day, and also refused to go in. What a lovely feature hindsight was. A shame one had to make the mistakes before they realized their choices had been a bad idea. Not even a thinker like Tzu was immune to making dumb decisions.

It just happened to be the case that some dumb decisions cost lives.

Their first big mistake? Entering during the day. It made the slow, creeping buildup of gasses remain entirely unnoticeable. Anyone that bent low enough to tie their shoes passed out from lack of oxygen, and didn't last much longer than that. The tight growth of the Wilds made traversing the place as difficult as Tzu expected. Anyone in heavy armor was going to get sucked into the swamp, and the entire ground was made of said swamp.

The only time troops felt hard solid ground beneath their boots, it was a tree root of some kind. A slip could break an ankle, and if anyone ended up in the murky water then they were gone. Friends had no chance to pull you back out. Most soldiers were just too heavy even without their armor.

Then there was the blissful hope that they would have some silence. Not because there were many insects, or the bubbling of the swamp was distracting. No, it was because several banners had decided to bring their abyss-blasted *bagpipes*! Their lung capacity expended at the great inconvenience and frustration of the others. Who thought it was a good idea to bring those? That provision allotment was wasteful!

Tzu wanted to cover his ears each time that blaring **pwiiiiip** started up again. Unfortunately, he needed them. With sight and flags out of the equation to speak to your entire group at once, yelling had become the go-to solution.

The second big mistake, bagpipes of blaring doom not counted, was that they had forgotten they were here to invade. The Wilds had natives. Natives that were very good with blowguns and numbing poisons. Numbness was the only weapon needed when the Wilds themselves gobbled invaders up like candy if they so much as sneezed the wrong direction. Some lucky Phoenix troops merely became delirious. It was easy to tell when they spouted newfound wisdom, such as: "Do not sneeze on a snake pretending to be a branch. Repeat. Do not sneeze on a snake. They can and will take offense, and their reply comes with a bite to the face."

"Take cover!" Tzu shouted his order, but it saved maybe a sixth of the troops under his banner. Which was currently being lost in the bubbling swamp slop below. They'd dropped his banner? Those awful little— **Ftock**! "Those darts are getting too accurate for my liking. Retreat back to the camp!"

Many people that heard him didn't find the order to their liking, and voiced their dissent. "The Phoenix does not retreat! Our Kingdom's mighty warriors only rise!"

Tzu rolled his eyes, but not as hard as Aki and Miki did. Taking stock of the situation, it seemed that a good number of those under his banner had outright ignored his original order to take cover. They had listened to other commanders instead, who had yelled something far more foolish in the rough vocalized shape of "Charge!"

Tzu rumbled out his words with a growing headache. "Realize when you can't win, you fools!"

This was where it had dawned on Tzu just how many of his soldiers despised him. Those in cover were looking for opportunities not to be. Aside from maybe fifteen of them that kept in close vicinity to their commander, the rest were all about that assault life. What happened to these people? Did they hate him so much that they would gladly pretend they were no longer farmers, and throw their lives away for the glory of some dumb little Kingdom name? They weren't soldiers! Why did they suddenly think they were?

"*Fine.* Fools, the whole lot of them." Tzu ducked for better cover and yelled loudly. "Ming! Any chance for a flaming distraction?"

Ming did not give him good news. "Snake eyes on that dice roll, Commander! I can't get anything to make a spark. It's too wet here, and from the rumbling of those clouds above, we're all going to be very wet soon!"

Tzu gritted his teeth, forced to make a bad decision. He bellowed loud: "All troops who do not want to be under my command, charge the enemy! Find your glory! I release you! All troops who want to live, fall back!"

He tried not to think about the screams of dying from the men he sent forward. How cruel intelligence could be. He knew that any with resentment in their hearts would jump on the chance for a free release from Tzu's banner without needing to use one of their extremely precious transfer tickets. They jumped at the chance, thus also jumping right in front of the volley of darts, and making themselves targets while the fifteen remaining loyal troops extracted themselves from a losing situation.

Nine survived getting back to the opening where they'd breached into the thicket of the Wilds, but Tzu put his hand up before they went through. He had a terrible gut feeling.

Riram, a short man who made up for it with ego, didn't listen to that command, having solely desired to flee from his death. He pushed through the opening, and Tzu's unpleasant feelings were confirmed to be reality when an arrow of the Phoenix Kingdom's make plunged through Riram's throat.

The short soldier gargled and fell to the swamp, his thrashing ignored. They all knew there was no saving him, as they'd lost six on the way here to slips, falls, the swamp, and wildlife.

Cursing under his breath, Tzu made a hand motion to take cover from incoming arrow fire. Even if he had to do it against what should have been safe home terrain. His back pressed against a tupelo tree, thumb bitten as he tried to scrape together ideas. Ichiro was at his side, hoping Tzu had some kind of plan. The commander glanced at his soldier only to sigh and release his thumb. "I know, Ichi, I know. Zho! Ming! I need you."

While Tzu only called over two soldiers, the entire huddle of nine got themselves within easy earshot. Artorian saw their desperation even if Tzu didn't, who was far too occupied trying to put a plan together. This was a terrible game board, and he was short on pieces. He was rushing, and not fully seeing what he had around him. The betrayal of the majority of his banner hurt more than expected, even if it was he who'd just sent people to their deaths. Farmers. Abyss-blasted outcasts with nowhere better to go. He thought himself a monster.

Tzu pressed his hands to his forehead, whispering under his breath. "This must be what it's like to be a King. How I despise it."

Yoshe softly punched his commander in the shoulder. "Pull it together. That was a Phoenix arrow that did Riram in. Are we being shot for trying to leave? What's going on? Hong and I hung back because we knew this was a little fishy, but this whole 'invasion' has been a slaughter. Why are you mumbling about Kings? Did we get set up? This feels like a setup."

Tzu bit his hand, glancing around the bend of the tree at the opening. Nobody was entering, but he knew there was at least one archer waiting for them. *Think, Tzu, think.* Why did this all look so out of place? Why didn't this make sense? "Just… give me some air."

Yoshe backed away from the commander as sweat ran down Tzu's forehead. His fingers starting to bleed from how bad he was biting them. His eyes flicked between the people around him. All of them huddled behind whatever tree was close enough to put a wall between their backs and 'friendly' arrows. "Maybe they just thought we were natives. May…"

The commander shook himself. "No, our archers are far too good for that, and the majority are under the General's command. It doesn't add up. I need… I need someone with a good memory."

The group immediately pointed to Miki, who scowled at them all, wanting very much to have remained a wallflower. She half-spat her words, cross from recent circumstances. "What do you need?"

Tzu was counting on his fingers. "Tell me what happened when we entered the Wilds. When we breached. I don't mean that we did. Tell me how. Where were troops placed? Who moved? Who did not?"

Miki rattled it off as if she was pruning her Sunday flowers, a task done with practiced ease. "One hundred banners of one hundred men lined up along the forest's edge. I remember overhearing some of the other commanders ordering 'for maximum breach.' I don't know what that means."

Tzu filled in that bit. "It means they wanted a large number of troops to enter the Wilds simultaneously. They wanted a wide line of troops all in at the same time. Please continue?"

Miki did so. "The General remained behind with two retinues of one hundred troops each. Words around the camp were that those commanders are his favorites. When the horn sounded, all commanders moved their troops so they could breach. Two soldiers from the banners of the General's favored commanders remained behind them."

Tzu nodded, asking the pointed question: "Did they have bows?"

Miki understood now, glancing at the breach point. "They did."

The commander grumbled. "A hundred breach points, two hundred troops to spare with bows. Two archers per breach point. That's not insurmountable, but we're at a disadvantage. Don't know for sure if it's still just two after Riram took one for the team."

Ming threw a small branch in their direction for attention. It was enough. "Tell me you're not going insane first. It's getting hard to breathe in here, and it's getting dark from the clouds. That rain is coming down any moment. What's this King nonsense? You didn't seem the type to want to be one."

Tzu nodded in heavy agreement. "Oh, I don't, Ming, I don't. It's something they told me when I was signing up as a commander, and it's been eating at me ever since. As a commander, your job is to send your troops to die. You just have to hope your plans, tactics, and strategies are good enough for losses to remain minimal while you accomplish the Kingdom's goals."

He bit his thumb again at the irritation. "However, when it comes to proper soldiers, those are men that chose that life. They're willing. They throw themselves into the fray of their own choice. I can live with it, if my soldiers are willing. It's much harder when I know for a fact they did not choose this life, and that they're stuck here. Forced to see to the desires of a place that couldn't give two coppers about them."

He stabbed his bleeding thumb over his shoulder at the breaching position. "That's the job of a King. According to them. As a King, you have to make the unwilling moves on the board as you need, regardless of what others want. Both as a commander and as a King, each death weighs on your consciousness. You remember their faces, their voices, the way their nose twitched or how their eyes smiled when the rest of them couldn't."

His gaze met Ming's. "That's why I don't think I ever want to be a King, Ming. If the person didn't choose the fate themselves, I want no part of it."

Ichiro was confused as could be, and shoulder nudged his commander in the ribs. That brought Tzu back to his senses. His mind snapped to how Ichiro needed the world formed for him to understand it. An idea started to come together, as speaking to Ichiro allowed for no distractions. "Yes, Ichiro. I have a plan. Aki, you're good with weather. Does thunder boom loudly *before* rain falls, or after?"

Aki just shook her head. "Neither, it has to do with the light that comes down, I think. If we have not heard any by now, then there won't be any."

Tzu sharply exhaled. "Then I've only got the bad options. Everyone pry off some bark, or use anything you can find that would work as a shield. Aki, Miki, you have the bows. Stay behind Zho and Ming's shields and pick off the archers outside. Start with the ones you can easily see if there's more than two. Yoshe, Hong, flank to the left side, in the direction of camp. Axe any hiding archers some questions, don't let them respond. Ichiro and… Valka?"

Valka, an injured soldier just doing his best, nodded when the commander guessed at his name. Tzu nodded back in acknowledgement, and finished giving his directions. "Do the same, but veer off to the right. Do not go out and start hunting. If you find any troops hiding in the close vicinity, kill them and regroup right away."

They all gave him a decisive nod, gathering what they needed before readying themselves near the breach. Tzu took a deep breath, squeezing the spear in his hands. "On three."

CHAPTER FIVE

Artorian watched as his old squad went through archers with clockwork proficiency. They lost Valka, but Tzu's wounded people made it to the camp's edge. Or what was left of it. The place had been packed up, the provisions stolen, and the guard nowhere to be seen. Neither the General or his favorites were present when Tzu's few scavenged their way through the camp's remains.

To Aki and Ming's complete befuddlement, Tzu found all the best goodies, particularly when it came to food. "How do you *do* that?"

Tzu just shrugged and bit into a peach that was still good, slurping his mouthful down before answering. "Don't know. Just comes easily. I considered writing a book on the topic one day. Fantastic foods, and where to find them. Sounds nice, doesn't it?"

His troops dropped the matter, getting back to gathering the little they could find as it became increasingly clear they had been betrayed; sent into the Wilds to die. There was so little left of the camp that any survivor returning with more than a minor wound just wouldn't make it.

Miki ended up thrashing a tent left behind just to vent her frustrations. "They lied to us! They left us to rot! We are going to die out here!"

Aki was swiftly at her side, but there just wasn't any calming Miki down when she was right. Any archers that decided to come back to camp would without the orders to do so. Meaning they'd be shot as both groups would see the others as deserters. Anyone still in the Wilds would be dead during the nighttime, when the heat and gasses rose. Or when the wildlife actually woke up. This had just been a slaughter; a culling of mouths that the military couldn't feed.

Tzu still didn't understand. Why would the Kingdom do this to itself? An idea stabbed him like a bad hangover. What if it didn't? Clues pointed to the General being a turncoat. If the General was fighting for another flag, this suddenly made much, much more sense. How did he not see this coming? No. Wrong question. There was no point in burdening himself with the reality that had occurred, and he could never change. The right question was what to do from now on.

Tzu had a wonderful thought. "Say, how do you all feel about… I don't know… backstabbing the people responsible for doing this to us? We might fail. We might die. Or we might blow open a big plot and possibly buy our freedom out of this abyssal army."

Miki stomped in his direction, her tone still plenty miffed. "If you have a way to stab that overly-muscled General in the spine, I am going to need knives. Lots and lots of knives!"

The scene paused.

Movement stopped when Artorian extended his hand, needing a moment to collect himself and stroll over to Tzu. He wanted to look at his old self for a while. Up until that point, Tzu had not realized the weight that lived on his shoulders. The old man mumbled to himself, then waved his hand the other way to let time move once more. "About here, I think?"

Tzu the Tyrant held his head. This was the moment he

made a critical mistake, his mouth saying the worst possible thing before his mind was ready. "Yes."

Artorian laced his fingers, sitting on a fallen log to watch the realization of that word come alive in Tzu's eyes. Because it had been a lie. A terrible lie that he now needed to make a reality. The old man was attentive to the events around him this time. As Tzu, this was where the world had melted away. Tunnel vision blocked off his peripheral sight, both his hands holding the sides of his young head as the voices broke through the wall like maddened warriors storming during a siege.

Tzu didn't hear Miki demanding explanations and plans, or Aki failing to calm her down. Zho and Ming also lingered nearby, interested in what the clever one had to say. It was Ichiro that recognized the signs of mental strife in his commander. Signs that not all was well. When he dropped his weapons to sprint over to Tzu, Yoshe noticed Tzu's nosebleed when the first red drop of it fell from the edge of his stubble.

Ichiro caught Tzu when the man fell to a knee, the commander's head swimming while his vision and comfort went sideways. Tzu lost his lunch, but Ichiro had water and helpful advice at the ready. "Breathe, breathe deep. It will pass. Breathe deep."

Tzu's head felt like a throbbing abyss. The attempt to make the mental leap from their current situation, to one where they came up top was too much. Right as he began his attempt to create a grounding platform to start, the carpet was pulled from under his feet in the form of unwelcome memories. The scathing commentary from other troops, and behind the tent vocal stabs at his passing. A person just never knew when they were going to be slammed with terrible thoughts, and in this case it happened to hit him at a bad time.

The little words wormed into his heart, whispering their venom every time his mind grasped a thread to try to pull him out. It was just enough to break his concentration and increase his headache, but Tzu kept trying to force his thoughts to keep working.

He had to put a plan together. They needed to get out of the Wilds. They needed to get back and have a good reason not to be marked as deserters on arrival. They needed to not get caught. They needed to live and find a route to victory. Flashes of insight and pieces of scenes came only to be muddled by indecision and uncertainty.

Had it not been for Ichiro repeatedly telling him to breathe, things might have gone differently. Instead of a worse fate, Tzu just passed out with three people ready to catch him. Ichiro had told them he was likely to fall. The commander actually falling was what shut Miki up, her hand worriedly shoved against her breastplate. "Tell me I am not responsible for nagging him to death."

Aki was about to tell her no, but Zho and Ming cut her off in unison with a very loud, "Yes!"

She chased them through the camp with her scavenged knives at their outburst, Zho and Ming too busy laughing the entire way, playing parkour through and around the abandoned tents to avoid Miki's fury. What a fun game that was. For them, it cut the tension.

Ichiro and Yoshe laid their commander down, and confirmed he was still breathing. The small group didn't understand why Tzu just collapsed like that, but Ichiro of all people had their answers. "Overthinking. You know why people tell you getting too smart is bad, and to work in the field instead of reading books? This is why. This happens to me as well. You think too hard, and your head starts to hurt. Do it too much and you can just keel over. Commander will live; that plan Miki asked for wasn't simple."

Yoshe and Hong grimaced and hissed between their teeth, sharing a look of 'I'd rather not suffer that fate.' Hong looked visibly uncomfortable. "I guess this is why commanders are paid more. I can't complain. We're out of the greenery, and made it back here. That counts for more than the commander might think. That swamp was a deathtrap and almost nobody saw it.

I've been in heists with more ways out than the mess we were just in."

Yoshe grabbed his shoulder. "I know, I was there with you for the majority of those. You take one of those deep breaths too. You look pale, and one person collapsed on the ground is too much for me. Especially when it's the one who I hope has the answers."

Yoshe turned his overly round head to address Ichiro. "Something I hope he has the chance to do. Is he going to collapse each time he tries to make the plan to get back home? Or out of here at all. I don't know what to do. Leaving is desertion, and that means arriving at the Phoenix Kingdom loses me my head. We can't stay, either. There's nothing here to survive on, and abyss if I go into the Wilds for food."

Ichiro had some difficulty, so he just answered the question he could handle. "The commander is likely to go through this again. Yes. If it's anything like mine, anytime he tries to think too hard. His version might be different from my malady, but I have faith. He did, after all, tell Miki 'yes.'"

The group was collectively surprised Ichiro could handle the concept of faith without getting terribly confused, but they were in no position to question the man's hold on life. Anything to hold on to was good right now.

Aki held her own arms, frustrated rather than frightened. "He did say it, but this might be slow going. What about the short term? The right now. What do we do right now?"

Zho and Ming pushed their way into the conversation, one arm around the neck of the other while they were both out of breath. Miki was far behind them, her hands on her knees as she was far too tired to continue yelling and chasing. "We put up camp! We wash up. We eat. We all get sleep. We continue in the morning."

Ichiro nodded. "Nothing to do right now but wait. Commander needs rest. Commander also has a bag full of nicer food."

"Mine! For sharing, I mean." Aki swiped the bag up before

the thieves could get their grubby hands on it. The bag went behind her back, his smile showing a suspicious amount of teeth. "Yes. *Sharing.*"

Artorian laughed hard.

So this was what had happened after he spiraled into darkness. That… honestly wasn't nearly as bad as he remembered it. During the moment it had been horrible. Looking at it again… they didn't hate him at all, and the troops that hadn't wanted to stick around weren't worth his attention. Those people had made their choice, and he shouldn't beat himself up for the decisions others had made. Not unless they were his adopted children.

"Overthinking, Ichiro? How well-worded." Artorian nodded, wringing his hands. He paused the scene again, knowing it was over. He chose not to leave this time, remaining seated to live in the memory. He knew he shouldn't linger. It wasn't healthy. "Just a minute. Just for a minute."

Artorian stayed for more than a minute, having decided to let the scene play after all, even if nothing interesting happened. His small group put up a large tent. They got Tzu inside. Made a fire. Noisily enjoyed the scavenged food. Which Artorian supposed explained why they'd mentioned the bag had mysteriously gone missing.

Scilla stepped into the memory, looking around with a frown. "There you are! Why are you still here? The regret part of the memory ended hours ago!"

Artorian shrugged. "I suppose I didn't think I had many other places to be. Besides, I was sort of hoping to see the follow up. I remember the abyss I ended up giving that General, even if it's how I ended up in the Socorro. I ended up alright because of these seven minds that wouldn't let me quit, and I didn't want to let them down. Some days, they carried me for hours when Tzu was too exhausted trying to get the next step of the plan together. It was hard going for a while. I don't suppose you have the memory of when I had to give my report in front of the Senate? That was a thing of beauty."

Scilla sat down next to him, but shook her head no. "I filter memories. I don't have an easy 'pick and place' power like that. I didn't take you for the lingering kind, but in this case, I understand. Wololo vine and twig noodle-hat of observation isn't the best career."

Artorian nodded, then smiled softly. "Maybe I should try being a candle. Like Ember."

Scilla poked him in the ribs. "You are on fire out there. Not much difference, just hope you end up in a jar and you're all set."

The old man let out a half-hearted 'Ha!' as the memory around him dissolved away, placing Artorian and Scilla back into the bonfire space. They were sitting right back on the root they'd been before starting as Scilla confirmed her earlier claim. "Told you. Just filtering. I can't make them go on forever."

Artorian raised his hands, trying to let it go. "It was nice while it lasted. Can't live in memories. They'll keep a hold of you forever. Their claws will sink into you and happily keep you mired there. Reliving your heyday, and times that were better. Or worse, in this case."

He motioned to the memory that had just concluded. "I don't feel particularly different after that one, Scilla. I just understand what you meant with them not hating me. They were all people, making their own choices. Some chose to stay; most chose to leave. That there was some bad press between the cracks… well, that's just not a burden I need to carry. I take it that I end up seeing those seven again. One last time?"

Scilla made an unpleasant face. "You know how I feel about being cruel, Sunny."

Her naming convention caught his attention, looking over his own hands to see they were old. "Oh. I can be my proper age again, or is this more of an in-here-only thing?"

"The latter." Scilla leaned back, resting her weight on her arms. "Sorry, Sunny. You'll still be what you are out there. Maybe in Cal you have a shot, but you have to get there first.

Speaking of, I'm ready to pull the lever if you want to give Eternium the boot."

Artorian smirked, leaning back like she was. He spotted something interesting. "Actually, before that. Are those petals? Since when does this tree have flowers? Or have I been a blind fool this entire time?"

"Told you he'd notice! Yes!" Scilla shook with giddy affection, her face contorted in victorious happiness as she shot upright. "Sunny. We have a visitor!"

CHAPTER SIX

Artorian looked around, but was fairly certain it was just him and Scilla. Abyss, there being someone other than him in this space alone was an unexpected feat. Now there was another? He had almost thought that the amount of growth on the tree correlated to his rank, but he was no longer certain now. Artorian didn't see anyone, to pressed his hands to his hips and looked at Scilla.

"You may have jumped the shark on the noticing bit. I'm fairly good at it, but I don't think that this time y—"

The **plink** of a kalimba silenced him entirely. Celestine light shone from the fresh leaves and flowers that had grown from the silver branches. How he'd missed that light, thus becoming quickly aware of who the visitor was.

He remained quiet when the kalimba kept playing its relaxed melody. It was soothing. Comforting. He liked it, even if he had no reply. Thinking about it, he'd never really directly spoken with his **Law** after he'd gone up the Tower. Spoken to it, yes. With it… not so much. He'd known his **Law** could send back emotions, feelings, and intentions. Using ways of speaking that involved no pictures and no words. Though he doubted they were unable to do so? He just didn't have information on the limitations of Heavenlies.

Scilla leaned over without bending her body, whispering so as to not break up the good mood. "She says hi."

The kalimba hadn't stopped its melody, but Artorian leaned back towards Scilla, his voice a hushed whisper to match. "How do I say hi back?"

Scilla waved her hand dismissively. "She heard you. She *knows*. She'd hear you even if you hadn't said anything. We're in your head, remember? Thoughts are loud here, even if you can control the more rampant wandering ones while you do this."

Artorian nodded in acceptance, following along as he returned to enjoying the performance. "Translate for me, dear? I don't speak plink-plink. Scree-scree, sure. Not plink-plink."

She involuntarily went, "*Pffffft*."

Getting a good reaction out of Scilla made the old man's day. Easing one hand over the other, he gently swayed to the sounds of the music. A transient, gentle little pleasure that he took the time to enjoy. The tune from his small Silverwood felt kind, warm, and welcoming. Perhaps he was being short-sighted when it came to communication? Thinking spoken, written, and other words out loud had been the best way to convey things. Yet, saying nothing, he felt that he grasped the inherent meaning of this tune just fine. This was a heartfelt thank you, in melodious long form.

"Who needs words, when emotion speaks in such volumes?" The kalimba's song was synesthesia of the heart. Rather than tasting or smelling when engaged with another sense, this was an auditory layer that became a feeling. How quant and pleasant such an experience was; to grasp the feelings of feelings. Philosophy at its finest. How crude he had been for only considering the surface sounds. How *lost* he became when he melted away into the tender melody.

Artorian passively lost his defined shape as the song continued, the old man becoming little more than a man-shaped cloud of fog where some of his defining features were all that remained. In this fogged state, rather than be limited to the kalimba, he now also heard the caring string of a violin. First one, then two, then followed by many more as they accompanied the kalimba.

His mind wandered to pleasant memories, where he lingered when lost. For a moment he existed on a tiny bench under a tiny tree. Holding a broken cup while watching life at the end of the known world. Solemn, yet providing contentment. There was nothing to do here. Nothing that needed doing here. Save to watch small sproutlings tumble over themselves as the days faded away.

It ached. How the memory ached. How had his life come to this? So convoluted, messy, and confusing. He'd gone from a simple life to dealing with dungeons and carefully Wisp-curated Cores. Seated at tables where he counted old Goblins as friends, and sat with Kings and Queens from lands of yore. Him, the little troublemaker from Morovia. With his mouth around a pie and a smile plastered on his face.

Those were the easy days. His supposed final days. How nice it would have been had the world kept on turning, even if he'd left it. How was it that this recollection was so painful? Especially when the fifth regret had seemed so… minor. Tzu had suffered at the time, but Artorian was a person grown from painful experiences. He was past this, and supposed he had to just had to see it to believe it.

A-rank five? What a novel concept. Even now, it just seemed so… fleeting. All that self-inflicted pain, just to kick a rock. That was what his rank ups were good for, it seemed. Kicking rocks. He watched the horizon in his memory while leaned against a birch tree. One of his favorites in the Fringe. Back in those early days, when the village had been small and had many Elders, he could just watch the sunset like this anytime he wanted.

Artorian felt drained as he lingered in the memory. Speaking to nobody but himself as some strain caught up to him. "I'm tired. I'm so, so very tired. Maybe a nap. Just a tiny nap. A bit of sleep to this lovely melody sounds heavenly. Yes. I think that would be… that would be…"

The kalimba continued playing as Artorian's hazy form reduced entirely to mist and fizzled out of being. His mind had fallen asleep, along with the rest of him. Scilla held her knees and continued the sway he'd started, listening to the **Law** speak through that gentle song. "I know… that regret was devious, and hits slow. Thanks for helping him sleep. He's been choosing not to, for too long a time."

The instrument didn't stop, the notes just changed, altering to ones no longer meant to help a mind ease into a place of comfort. Scilla replied, her tone low. "Halfway. Halfway home. Do you think he'll miss me, when I'm gone?"

The notes responded with some sharp trills, which made the Liminal creature nod. "You're right. You're right. See it through to the end, and find out then. I'm just… gaining more wisdom as time goes by. My awareness of myself is increasing. I'm starting to worry about things. Will I be as loved as Caliph, or am I just the voice one hears when pain needs to happen?"

Petals fell from the Silverwood Tree in response, reforming as Artorian's favorite robes. They fell slow, miraculously settling perfectly on her shoulders before squeezing Scilla tight. The pressure exactly that of a good hug. She grabbed the hems and squeezed, biting her cheek so she didn't cry. "I know, **Love**, I know. I just want to hear it said. Can't a girl be selfish once in a while?"

Scilla stood, her feet lifting from the floor. "Stay as long as you want. I'm going to check out for a little while. I think I need to go and talk to people too, and someone who will not judge me for what I am should be nearby."

The robe tightened by itself to say something, then harmlessly fell to pieces. Scattering into individual petals that returned slowly to the branches they had come from. Scilla understood, but couldn't reciprocate the kindness. "Back in a bit."

The Wisp in charge of keeping tabs on the Seed Cores

shrieked when a pink-affinity human appeared out of the topmost Core on the Silverwood Tree in Cal's Soul Space. He flickered a panicked rainbow of colors, dropped his clipboard, and sped off.

Scilla watched the Wisp dart between branches, bashing into one on the way only to awkwardly backpedal with an amusing wobble. Then zip right back off again. She turned, crouching down next to Artorian's Seed Core. Her chin rested on her arms, which rested on her knees as she hunched down. "So that's what you look like now? You may have been onto something with those thoughts about kicking rocks. Stop kicking yourself, old man."

"He has a tendency to do that when he thinks nobody is looking."

Scilla peeked over her shoulder, where an unexpected sight awaited her. Iridescent flames roiled from Dawn's form, but they carried the same tender sway as the kalimba from before. Not the expected purgatory flames that lashed out freely from one Scilla knew to be a creature of war.

Scilla replied with a weak smile, knowing full well that the Incarnate could see her for what she was. A mess of Liminal energy. Temporary in this world. She did not expect a hand to be extended toward her as a greeting.

"He also has a tendency to make people worry, and I don't need to know what you're made of to see you're in that boat."

Scilla took the hand, which didn't burn in the slightest even if it was wrought with iridescent, fractalizing flame. "Priscilla, daughter of Shamira. Child of Chasuble. Hidden memory of regret. Tribulation tracker. Liminal being of Artorian, Ascended of **Love**."

The Incarnate's grip closed with hers, and shook in welcome. "Ember, of war. Dawn, of fire. Corona, of **Sun**. S-ranked Incarnate of my **Law.** Family of Artorian. Friend of his friends. Foe of his foes. Caretaker of his many, many messes. It is pleasant to meet you. Would you be my friend, Priscilla of

Chasuble? You may feel free to call me any of those names, or Soleille. Whichever strikes your comfort."

Scilla was glad she was already on her knees, because she would have fallen had it not been for the stability. Her voice betrayed that she was a child, no matter how grown up she tried to sound. "That would make me very happy."

Corona opened her arms while lowering herself to a knee, her expression motherly. "Would you like to be held?"

Scilla pressed herself into the Incarnate's chest. Unaware how she'd managed to get up so fast and move her position to one enveloped by Corona's arms. "That would also make me very happy."

"You're just like Caliph. If you knew him." Corona picked Scilla up like a weightless bundle, carrying her while walking in a loose circle. The back of the child's head was gently tended with soft rubs as she paced. "Does our old man even know you're just a baby, or have you pulled the wool over his eyes? Made him believe you're something else so you could do your job? You don't need to tell me you're lonely, dear. I can just see it. You hold on as long as you'd like. We can talk after. Okay?"

Scilla silently nodded into the crook of Corona's neck, where her face remained buried.

Tatum void-stepped in out of curiosity since he'd felt a disturbance, as Dawn rarely moved one of her spare bodies away from work. When he saw the bundle being held, followed by the shake of Dawn's head that confirmed he couldn't help, he just made a motion with his fingers to his forehead that he understood, stepping back out to resume work.

"I know only of Dawn." Scilla managed to get her words in after a few more minutes of being held. "Who's Corona, or Soleille?"

Corona eased back down to a knee, as the Liminal one seemed okay enough to be put on her feet. "I will tell the whole story to Artorian, when we can once more spend some time. To sate you until then, I'm the same person, mostly. Different reasons for actions, with mostly the same outcomes. Again, call me Dawn if that's easier for you. It no longer makes a difference to me. Say what's comfortable. You say you knew of me when I was at my prior first step? Well, the story is short, and easy. A friend helped me with a problem, and I found that I was needed elsewhere in the Tower. When I re-Incarnated, I took several new names that I'm now trimming down. Soleille fits me better, now that I am more… whole. While Corona is the word that refers to the stellar Aura that surrounds the sun, and is the outermost part of the sun's atmosphere. I've been testing out Corona as a namesake lately, just to see how it feels."

Scilla reached her hand up, Corona taking it so they could walk. "What would you like to do?"

The pink-haired girl bobbed her head lightly from left to right. "I want to make more friends."

Corona smiled in reply, knowing a thing or two about that desire. "We can go do that. I know many that would love to meet you. All of the chosen would be elated to see you. Especially Sunny's. We will have to leave the Seed Core behind if we go. Is that okay?"

Scilla looked to her left. Watching the motionless Core just sit there. Nestled and asleep. "I think I'll be okay."

Her gaze moved from the Core to Corona, a worry manifesting on her face. "I'm not used to walking."

The Incarnate easily picked her back up before soul-stepping out through a burning portal of fractals. "Then… I'll carry you."

CHAPTER SEVEN

Event notice!

Message from Eternium:

Did you just rank up while in my system? That's forbidden! Where is your Wisp? How is your observer Wisp not with you? This should have been all under wraps, and now the back of my Core feels sore. Fine! I'll give you the ability to allot a complicated quest, so you can at least do something with your time. Though I am not removing those recovery penalties. You will have to get through that difficulty the hard way.

Artorian woke up as an ultramarine noodle crown. He was on a human's head this time. Much larger village. Maybe a solid town? He was still waking up and wasn't sold on the first impressions. Still a hat though. Oh, wait! Upgrade! He was part of a real crown now. Fancy. What had he missed?

He tried to pull up notifications, but had none. He must have been asleep for some time, but that was fine. He was up now, refreshed and with new mental sleeves to roll up so he could get to business. Once he figured out what that business was.

Currently, he was in some kind of procession. Or parade? Hard to tell. He couldn't see what was behind him, but there was a cobblestone path in front, and he kept bobbing as he was on some kind of horse. Yes, definitely a horse; the clip-clop sounds were starting to come to him. Along with the roaring of a crowd. Happy crowd? He'd chalk it up to that. They were headed to some large building where a person in suspiciously clerical robes awaited.

Oh, *fantastic*. He was in a coronation. Wasn't that just so *nice*. His thoughts oozed sarcasm, but he was along for the ride. Might as well start prodding at things. Alright, so. From the top. No stamina and no mana. Check. What about his mana pool in general? Was that still a feature he could play with?

He slotted in Electrosense without any issues, and watched his status sheet make his mana bar smaller. No strain. No fuss. Just an easy on or off kind of thing. Oh, he was still paying for the Resplendence Field? Well… that was fine. Leave it on. Omnibreath, on. Mapping, on. Hey, he could see the route he'd traveled! What a mess.

How did he end up in the west of Midgard? Long naps are long. Very well, just take it at face value and move on. West of Midgard. Some human regency, a far cry from the Goblin days. Back to work. Electrosense, he'd already turned that on. Sustenance? Never deactivated. What about Empowerment? He tried, and it flared to life without issue, removing his mana bar entirely as he invested all of it. Neat!

A wet cough got his attention. He couldn't see it with his eyes, but Electrosense was vision in its own way. He was definitely in a procession, with a long line of horses. Possibly a cart, and some troops? Right behind the ride he was hitching was a smaller horse. A young girl was on it based on the outlines. Why the cough? That was of interest. The climate they were in was serene, and didn't lend itself to such a cough. Sickness perhaps? Shame he had none of his tools.

A consideration struck. Inspect required line of sight. Would Electrosense count as sight? He *sort of* knew where she was. *Dale* it! Inspect!

Name: Katarina
Race: Human
Character Level: 5
Class: Noble
Profession: Princess in waiting

Noble was a class? Seemed like a waste. This wasn't enough information to go by. The mechanics of inspection and why it didn't always show him the same information were foreign to him. Or maybe the Pylons just didn't… Never mind. A lot could be wrong. What if he tried Cra's properties command? He technically didn't have it. Did he? Properties!

Properties:

Katarina is a human Princess in the lands of Goa'yuld. She is currently afflicted by Waterlung, a disease that causes the lungs to slowly be filled with water. This disease was inflicted by Crown Prince Herranoia, upon which head currently rests the Everburning Crown.

Katarina is the rightful heir to the throne of Goa'yuld. Currently qualifying as Queen if she takes the position, or is assigned it via regency council. Whoever takes her hand in wedlock shall become King, as she has no living parents. Both were assassinated in a secret coup by Herranoia in his bid for increased power. Waterlung will kill Katarina in four days, eight hours, three minutes, and one second.

Had he kicked Eternium in the rocks yet? Could he do it again just for this? He despised things of this nature. Political abyss was a matter he loathed. Someone had taken a girl's parents from her. For a title and some power? The head of which he was currently resting on? Oh no. Nonono. This would not do. Meddling fully engaged!

Swiftly looking over his options, his eyes locked onto Omnibreath. Turning off his Empowerment since it didn't do a lick of good, he threw open the extra lever on that ability. Specifically turning the effect into a field so Katarina could instantly breathe easier in his presence. That would put a temporary stopper on that disease, even if it wasn't a cure.

Looking over the rest, he felt a bit downtrodden. That was it? That was the breadth of his options? Abyss that! How did he make the pink sparkly zap happen? Could he do it on cue without demons around that needed a solid thrashing? Could he pretend he was on the head of one?

No helpful results were forthcoming.

On arrival at the big building, he was taken from Herranoia's head by the cleric, who put the crown on some glorified silk-covered pedestal. Silk? These humans had gotten some advancements in, at least. Artorian immediately ignored the bluster and pomp spilling forth from the cleric's mouth the moment it began. He wasn't in the mood! Instead he was berating himself for new ideas. "Come on, old boy. You must have something. You always have something. No matter how unreliable or crackpot insane the thought."

He had statistics. Great. What else did he have? His wit. Wit was good. What else? A spare body currently of no good to him. Off the table. What else? He was a Long. What did a Long have? No bonuses to anything he could recall, except…

A Nixie Tube popped into being above his head with a wondrous mental drumroll. At least he imagined it so, as a thread of hope wrapped itself around his hand. The Long had no bonuses, but it did have downsides. Spell Runes on his bones kind of downsides. Which worked by themselves and sent him splattering around the place, and into trees where he played flag.

Did he still have those? Electrosense said yes when he

looked at himself and ignored the flesh. Though the bone-scripting was inactive, they felt… lesser. A far diminished amount seemed to be present as well! *Oh, Eternium, you really botched this…* Bob had made the original scripting a work of art. This rendition was the work of crayons. He missed Bob. That Goblin may have done things to purposefully stab him in the keister, but by Cal, was he passionate about his craft.

Bob must have worked for years on this Long. Or the original model that went through endless alterations and tweaks. Had Eternium just… taken such craftsmanship and botch-copied it, then crammed it down to size? The insult. Bob wouldn't have accepted this, and neither did Artorian. This body was a passion work from his friend, though why Bob had put in a control scheme that he couldn't use was beyond him.

Wait. No, no it wasn't.

The control scheme had been Bob's prank. Bob's beautiful, final prank. Artorian was good at thinking, so he tried to think his way to a solution. The Runes didn't work like that, so he needed to discard the old ways he'd tried to affect them. What if how the Runes worked wasn't important at all? A shocking concept, but what if? What did he have to lose by trying other methods?

The Nixie Tube above Artorian's head gained a friend, and they shook as maracas when the ideas struck him. "Don't think like a human in a Long. Act as a Long, and forget the human. Do not think. Merely do. Merely do. One must flail before they walk. So flail, Artorian. Flail!"

The cleric's head snapped to the pedestal when he was done with the anointing rites. Katarina had been named Queen. The regency council was concluded, and the wedding could commence. However, the loud clatter the crown had made as it removed itself from the pillow and loudly hit the ground was difficult to ignore. It forced the thin, long man in oversized robes that made him appear chunky to swallow his words rather than seamlessly continue with proceedings.

"Well? Get on with it!" Herranoia was impatient. He needed this done and over with so he could be the official King, and commence his rule. That the Queen's life would be short didn't matter to him in the slightest. It especially irked him that she was rubbing at her sternum in confusion. Her breathing troubles had mysteriously stopped. A disease didn't just go away! "Get on with it!"

The cleric scrambled to pick up the crown. The item didn't seem odd, save for the visual effect it always had. He began his loud speech before all the people gathered. Speaking well-rehearsed words about the impending marriage and its meaning. He was cut off again as the crown shook in his fingers, like it didn't want to be there. The nervous, sweat-beaded cleric pretended he'd stuttered, but continued right away.

He raised the item up high. "Therefore, whosoever weareth this crown, shall be the sovereign of Goa'yuld. With the placing of this royal icon, I declare the wedding complete, and Lord Herranoia the offici—Whoops!"

The crown flailed from his hands, spinning clear out of position and launching right over Herranoia's head. Only to land squarely on Katarina's head with a loud **plopf**, as if a pillow had softened the landing of what could have been a very painful impact.

Bilmun the cleric hurried over to the smaller throne, as the Lord was no doubt about to gut him if he didn't see this corrected. The crowd uttered a mixture of gasps and laughter. Some thought it was a nervous fumble. More keen-eyed individuals had noticed that the cleric had made no motion that would have allowed that crown to move the way it did, and devolved into gossip.

Katarina knew better than to move as the crown was removed, but the flailing item twisted from the man's grip with another violent spin, forcing the cleric to let go and stumble back as the crown just… hovered there. It awkwardly tried to rotate and right itself, but appeared to be having significant difficulty, like a small animal rolling around while its head was stuck in place.

When the crown got horizontal and adjusted to be nice and even above Katarina, gravity once again took hold. When the crown softly plopped back down onto her head, laughter in the crowd stopped completely. Replaced by gasps, whispers, worries, and even more delicious gossip. Artorian had no clue as he was paying attention to his scheme, but the crowd was fully aware that the crown needed to be placed on Herranoia's head for the ceremony to be complete and official.

"I'm sorry, my lord. I'll get that on your head right away." The cleric swiftly stepped forward, taking the sides of the crown and tugging up. To his dislike, it didn't move an inch off her head. Far more stubborn than the cleric, Artorian was. Not. Moving. A big ol' no! Complete with tongue sticking out of his mouth to **nyeh** at the cleric. "I need some help!"

Artorian found that handling the cleric by himself was... manageable. One cleric and five warriors from the Lord's retinue that all tried prying the crown from Katarina's head at once? Not as manageable. He moved against their will, but went suspiciously motionless when the retinue succeeded, now back in the cleric's hands. "I think... I think I have it. Yes. Just... just a set of flukes. That's all."

The Lord's men looked at Bilmun as if they were going to string him up if this was a bad prank. One of them growled at the cleric. "It better have been, Bilmun."

Artorian had a far worse scheme in mind already. Who cared that he didn't have skills or abilities? He could flail! Specifically, he could flail in desirable directions. The trap was set.

Bilmun, thinking his days were numbered if he didn't get this done and over with, hurried closer to the Lord while he quickly rattled off the rest of the required ceremony. He tried to shove the crown down in a hurry, but while it stopped mid-motion, Bilmun did not. His face smashed against the back of the crown before he rolled onto the ground with a bloodied nose. "*Ow!*"

Herranoia looked up at the crown floating above his head after he saw the cleric fall. "What in the name of the Ancients is—"

His words were cut short as the crown turned and seemed to empower itself. It gained a soft radiance in any case. The problem Herranoia had was that it gained that radiance shortly before zipping down at incredible speed and bashing him squarely in the face. Repeatedly! Though he didn't hear Artorian yell at him each time there was an impact.

Artorian felt miffed as he delivered his improvised strikes, not caring that nobody could hear him. "Strength? Who cares about strength! I have *health*! I will break this health bar off this sheet and smash in your face! Then keep bashing the living abyss out of you until you learn not to be such a horrible git. Get back here, you miserable excuse of a book spine! I'm not done clobbering you!"

The Lord had more than a mere bloody nose as the crown meant for his coronation bashed the snot out of him. Some of the blows missed, but the crown seemed to have no intention to stop turning his face into a piece of abstract art painted entirely in the purple color scheme.

Medium used: Bashing!

The crowd was never going to accept this coronation after that display. Not a soul in attendance believed the Lord was ever going to be King. The crown itself had a 'big mad.' When Herranoia finally fell to the dirt after an itemized beat down that was going to make for one celestial tale; the crown hovered back over to Katarina, and harmlessly settled in place on her head.

The clerics had nothing to say after that event. That was divine providence at work, or hexery beyond their wildest dreams. The Lord's men divided on the spot. Several who knew what was at stake strode forth, and lined up in front of the crowned Queen, deferentially kneeling. "Loyalty to the rightful heir!"

Katarina was too young for this, but the drop of Herranoia's blood that fell from the crown and stained her cheek didn't even budge her emotional needle. She was uncertain how to proceed, but a prompt appeared in her vision from the Voice of the World. One with a divine, shimmering gold outline.

Event notice! You have been offered a quest by a Divine! Sunny, Sovereign of the Sun, has extended to you the following Quest:

Quest: To be the best there ever was.

Become the first of a long series of rulers, who rule right, rather than with might.

Information: A Divine has offered you a legacy quest. This quest is difficult to complete, and may be rejected at no penalty. This quest has multiple offers and stipulations. A legacy quest is meant to be completed over multiple steps of lineage. The rewards for completion are great, but hidden.

In addition to this quest, you have been offered alignment with Sunny. Either via direct contact, or by touching an artifact under his domain. So long as you are in the vicinity of the Everburning Crown, you will be provided occasional assistance with this quest.

Requirements: As both a person and a ruler, strive to be the best you can be. Act in the best interest of your people, and see them flourish and be merry.

Katarina's hand moved to press accept. The message mentioned help. No matter what else this quest might entail, it offered *help*, and she was desperate. Celestine light squeezed around her frame, fading within seconds as information and new additions to her status filled her vision.

A new prompt hanging in front of her dropped aching weights right from her heart as she read it, but the new presence standing next to her made it all feel like a dream. In front of her was information on the crown, and next to her stood an old man. Visible only as an outline through this new electrical vision she possessed. He smiled at her, supportive and happy. Like a grandfather pleased to see his youngest.

Name: Everburning Crown
Material: Varied
Rarity: Unique
Special Quality: Variable
The Everburning Crown is a unique item, not meant to exist in this world in the capacity that it currently does. While aligned to Sunny and nearby, this crown extends control of certain abilities of which you will not pay the cost. These abilities can be altered so they affect yourself, or yourself and all of those in close vicinity. Information on these abilities will be triggered upon the first time they are used.

Abilities:
Sustenance—Be Well Fed and Well Hydrated.
Electrosense—See electrical fields, and your occasional helper.
Omnibreath—Breathe anything.

Special:
Note that these abilities use your own mana pool, rather than the crown's.
Divine Shell—Create a protective shield around yourself.
Empowerment—Improve your personal might. Self only.
Resplendent Obliterator—Test me.

Katarina's sight blazed aglow with life. Her breathing eased further. She was aware of everything around her, even what she could not see behind her throne. She also noticed nobody else was aware of what was happening. She looked to her right, where a robed old man made a motion to the frightened people that were looking at her. Her bloodied crown had, after all, just about bludgeoned a man to death.

She had no difficulty reading the words that fell from her

new advisor's lips, and she nodded to the directions. The elder's words had been simple, but clear. It was what she would have wanted in the position of all those attending. It was what she still wanted for herself. She squeezed her armrest, and spoke the words to herself to affirm them. "Love them."

CHAPTER EIGHT

Artorian performed the wiggle-dance of great success. Still, it was thanks to Eternium that he'd gotten to make something of this entire debacle. At best, his wiggles made the crown on Katarina's head hover and spin in place above her hair. With the occasional bobbing to match what he wanted to be his arm movements. "I call that a win!"

Speaking of arm movements, perhaps if he grew up naturally, the Long body would do a better job with the appropriate relevant sizes for the rest of his frame. Those tiny arms and legs were still too small. He'd try to influence growth this time around, since he was doing it from scratch. On the big plus side, slow growth allowed a far more natural and convenient method of learning how to be a Long.

This time, he'd get it right.

Additionally, he'd successfully applied the quest he made to Katarina, who was currently doing her best to give a speech. Now, she did have just a pinch of help. When Katarina saw his line-shape mouth words at her after that initial suggestion, the young Queen replied with a very verbal: "Advise me."

The knights around her initially assumed that had been

directed to them. They gathered in a small huddle to convene and speak in hushed whispers on what to do about the current situation. Artorian instead made a minor bow as his line-shape, letting it wink out since it was rather difficult to keep active. The shape was also draining Katarina's mana rather than his to maintain, and he wasn't too fond of that.

The young Queen received another divinely-colored prompt.

Quest notice!
Point at ten individuals and assign them as council members to serve as your advisors. Don't be too concerned with who you choose, you can always replace them later. Point at an individual and assign one of these keywords: Trade, Health, War, Infrastructure, Commerce, Building, Faith, Safety, Agriculture, Law.
Reward: None! This just makes it easier to talk.

Katarina didn't waste a second of time, starting that speech in the format she'd seen her mother perform. Her words didn't travel very far, but those in her vicinity had no issues grasping them when they realized she was assigning court positions on the spot.

Once all titles were assigned from the bundle of loyal people that had gathered nearby, she fell back in her chair and improvised. "Councilmembers! You will strive to do the utmost in your assigned field, and you will consult with me on the direction these matters are to take. You start immediately! Secure this region!"

Artorian thought the rulership skill must be in her blood. That had been pretty good! The assigned ten yelled in unison. "All hail Queen Katarina!"

Confused crowds finally had a grasp on the situation. They had a Queen, and that was it. They all began to cheer after a few people picked up the baton to set the celebrations off. Sparking the wildfire in the others as news spread equally fast.

Herranoia had been rebuked! Slapped by the crown itself as the rightful heir was pulled up to the pedestal.

Herranoia himself was anything but pleased when he came to. Barking out orders that they were going to do this the hard way. "Kill everyone in the way! Take the crown by force! The country will be mine!"

An archer in his retinue drew his bow, chilling Katarina to her stomach when she saw the arrow was aimed right at her. Without much thought, she yelled out in panic, "Divine Shell!"

The arrow loosed, but didn't pierce her skin. The wooden shaft snapped against a glowing field that sprang into being around her with a **vwum**. The shield hummed loudly when struck, but remained unharmed and intact even if the new shield value listed on her status sheet went down by a few painful points.

A few lost points were nothing when compared to the surge in confidence she felt. Katarina's shocked expression gawked at the location where the field became visible, watching it fade while knowing it was still there. She could feel the shell linger, like a warm sweater in winter time.

A small war broke out near the procession location, the raised theater used for more than mock fights as real swords clashed over ownership of the crown. Herranoia and his men were beasts on the field, but they made scant headway when the crowd determined their own loyalties and chose to butt in. Pots and pans were hurled at those under the usurper's flag, angry words yelled ceaselessly.

A pan to the head was just as lethal as a mace when swung hard enough, so the townsfolk didn't particularly get many replies. Just more dead under their feet, which they walked over while focusing on the prize. Herranoia was captured a bare few minutes later, and his bound form was dragged before the still-seated young Queen.

People thought she remained seated because she was regal, but Katarina just felt scared. She was rooted to her seat while a prompt in her vision told her to breathe. Just breathe. She was given several prompts to read, and dismissed them when she didn't want to see the prompts anymore. That hadn't prevented them from being helpful. By the time Herranoia was at her feet, she had a list of advice visible only to her on what she could do, in the event that she didn't know what her options were.

She didn't yet know how to feel about the fact that the prompts never chose for her, nor seemed to suggest that one choice might be better than the other. One of the prompts had specifically stated that it was important she make her own decisions. Decisions she could own. Decisions she wouldn't regret. Katarina was stuck between two choices at this moment.

To let the man live. Or to kill him.

Swallowing, she rose from her makeshift throne to hold her own hands. After a breath, she spoke loudly. "Councilmen. Citizens. Countrymen. Before me kneels the man who slew my parents, and all I loved. Only to gain the crown now resting upon my head. While I am your new Queen, I am young. Can you respect me as you did my father? Can you serve me as you did my mother? I see from the pain in your hearts that most of you wished it had not come to this."

Another breath, and Katarina's confidence began to show. "So I will declare this now: Until I am of age, I hereby re-institute the regency council. So I may learn to be a Queen who you can respect. So I can learn to be a Queen you are happy to serve. My council will advise me, and I will steer them. My council will enact my will, and I will trust them. If you find any in my council act against the public interest, let your Queen know, and they shall be replaced after trial."

A third big breath, and now her voice was steady. "So say I, Queen Katarina, third of my lineage. The ten before me shall decide the Lord's fate, and the ten before me shall rebuild this Queendom. Though not here! Here we will find our bearings, but we will not remain. While this was our homeland, this place has become barren, riddled with strife. New homes and castles will be erected to a location even further west, near an ancient beacon that brings great prosperity and luck. This is my decree."

She fell down rather than sit down. That speech had taken so much out of her. She felt incredibly tired when knights dragged a screaming Lord away. When she remembered a shield existed around her, the feeling of safety came to rest on her shoulders. Katarina drifted off to the land of slumber shortly after, having looked for, and then seen, the old man when she wanted one last inch of certainty.

Artorian smiled at her, and watched her finally get some rest.

The Queendom moved on around the young Queen, a ten-man guard posted nearby ensuring that Her Majesty's sleep went uninterrupted. While Katarina didn't know how to run things, the knights she had assigned were in full swing of figuring it out. Her decree had given them power, and they needed to create the power structures that would let them use it.

While a few dissidents were rooted out over the hours that passed, in general, the majority of the Goa'yuld Queendom started off on the right foot. Citizens understood what was expected of them at the mention that they needed to report to the council. It was their task to make sure information went around if those above them were doing a good job.

The knights and council understood that until the Queen was of age, they would be running the show. With occasional input from the Queen who wore a crown that had abyss-near bashed a usurper to death.

It was the clerics that were in the fire, trying their best to gain an audience with the sleeping Queen. Surely, she could be woken to answer their divine questions! The guards were having none of it, and more than one proselytizer was thrown out of the theater. If their Queen was asleep, it was because she needed sleep.

It had escaped the notice of no clerics just which words she had yelled out to protect herself from that arrow. '*Divine*' Shield. An ability unheard of since before the time of their namesake.

Only legends existed of the before times, where impossibly powerful beings walked and reshaped the lands, surrounded by living orbs of shining color while they went about their tasks of creation.

This became a hefty additional reason why the clerics were in such a panic. This undermined their entire source of authority! If the Queen wasn't amicable to their existence, and she had a *real* connection to the beyond, that posed an incredible issue for all of the people who merely believed that they did. Some believers were already spreading the gossip of the Queen's newly discovered defensive ability. She would be a legend in her own right within days, and the clergy could not spare days.

Katarina herself was lost to this sea of political turmoil. She was suffering a nightmare; a terrible recollection of events where her parents had been removed from the cycle of life right in front of her. Except that this time, the scene was different. When she burst into the hall where she would normally see Herranoia's men apply the skill of their blades, there instead stood the luminous specters of her parents. Another figure was with them. Someone old, bald, and with a long beard.

The Ancient said nothing as her glowing parents swung their arms around Katarina to pick her up. They showered her with praise for doing so very good in staying alive. They told her she would be a great Queen. That she should listen to her people and her heart in equal measure. Katarina heard them, but was too busy weeping to properly respond. There was a pain in her heart, while more weight dropped from her chest as her tears spilled over.

Instead of suffering through repetitions of awful dreams, she sat with the minds of her parents, sneakily retrieved by a wily old man. He was bathed in green light, when she paid a bit more attention—though that became an irrelevant detail as she delved into the presence of her loved ones, who spoke to her as if they were completely real, yet knew they had passed. They were supportive, doing their best with one dream's worth of time to pass as much legacy knowledge to their youngest as they could. Since their youngest was all that was left.

Near the end of the dream, which Katarina could feel coming, her parents looked at the old man who'd remained silent the entire time. He merely smiled at them, soundlessly whispering his soothing words, even though their ears heard it regardless. "Have five more minutes. If she wakes up, then she wakes up."

Katarina now recognized the old man as the outline of the advisor as she got closer to waking. As her dream increased in lucidity, her awareness of it also caused her surroundings to fracture. One could not, after all, dream like this when they were awake. By full choice, she dove into the arms of her mother. If she had five more minutes, she would spend it squeezing them close.

The young Queen slept far longer than people anticipated. Yet her slumber was peaceful, and none dared interrupt when silent tears rolled down her smooth cheeks. She woke at the dawn of a new day, when the seventh shifting of guards traded positions around her stilled form. Though they all quickly became loud from excitement when she rose from the seat. "My Lady! Everyone! The Lady is awake. Guard formations! Formations!"

The councilman of Trade was closest. He could be seen running from the top of the hill all the way down to the theater without missing a stride, severely out of breath on arrival. **Wheeze**! "My…" **Cough**! "Lady! Are you well?"

Katarina felt fresh, though in need of a bath as well. She was neither hungry nor thirsty, and breath came smooth and easy. Her senses extended to touch the electric fields, and the feeling of her shield being in place became a quick comfort. "I'm well, Councilman Zacharias. Please convene the council. We have much to discuss concerning the Empire."

Zacharias was taken aback. She had such spark in her eyes, no longer remotely the broken girl she'd been from before she had gone to sleep. Fresh knowledge and parental advice swirled in her thoughts, causing Katarina to extend her hand in expectation as she answered his silent question. "Yes, Councilman. *Empire*. We are expanding."

Zacharias, a large, portly man with a love for moustache grooming and art, took the Queen's offered hand and gladly took the lead. The guard group moved with them while the councilmember supported the majority of the young Queen's weight. To his surprise, he had nothing to say in retort to her clarity. If anything, the directness was refreshing. In fact, he felt extremely good in her presence, as did the guards. So when he responded, he did so with matching grace. "At your will, my Lady."

CHAPTER NINE

Artorian felt a green knock on his Forum space. *Oh, hey!* The Forum was usable? News to him. Accepting the incoming request, he expected the connection to collapse immediately. The connection didn't seem to sputter when he and Yvessa suddenly occupied the marble structure that the Forum now represented. The scenery within was small, but appeared cozy with its large stacked plinths and multiple loungers. The current Forum offered enough room for about six people to sit.

Yvessa popped in as a Wisp, then swiftly formed her human guise, and sat down like she'd been defeated and desired three whole months of sleep. She said nothing until prompted, groaning in response when Artorian asked if she was alright. "No. I would rather stay locked on your shoulder than go back out *there*. Wisp politics can burn in the abyss. Is there fire in the abyss? Can we make there be some? It took me weeks to free myself from that awful death-trap when Dani left. I thought I was just going to be able to leave and head out, but *no~o~o~o*."

"Do you want to talk about it?" Artorian leaned back against a pillar, reaching to see if he had his long beard. He did! Success. A soothing few squeezes and grooming motions later, he felt mighty content. This was the right of it. "Or is that going to cause trouble for you?"

Yvessa shook her head regardless of it being mushed against marble. "Nobody is going to so much as peep after your sneaky information-nibbling from Invictus. There's been an entire mess outside around that that you don't know about. To be clear, you don't *want* to know about it. Not unless you like headaches."

Artorian nodded, looking at the space around him. "How is this working? Shouldn't a Forum connection have collapsed?"

His caretaker made an unpleasant whine, but the noise didn't appear to be because of anything he'd done. "I'm paying your end of the mana costs too. Which is how I made the knock work at all. I was so confused as to why things haven't been working. So much isn't working, and a chunk of it is the Wisps' fault."

Artorian raised an eyebrow, both curious and hungry for this gossip from outside Eternium. "Is there more to that juicy goodness you just dropped on the table?"

Yvessa picked up her head, glaring at him through eyes that screamed they were in dire need of rest. "You gossip-loving… Never mind. Yes. Much more. Wisps and Gnomes are having a… disagreement. It's an ongoing disagreement, and we honestly need Cal. We don't have Cal. So we're doing the best we can with what we have. Also, we finally had the Pylons to put these together. So here you go. The effect has been active, but only now can I slot it into your page. Just read the prompts while I work."

You have gained a title!
Title gained: Horizon Walker.
You walk the line between dreams and reality, existence and fantasy, the realms and layers. As the first Horizon Walker to tread freely through dreams, you are considered the progenitor of this ability line. All costs relating to movements between dreams, and the shaping thereof, are nullified.

You have gained a title!

Title gained: Speedrunner.
Your exploits and critical need for speed have been noticed. You have been awarded this title for breaking the speed of sound while on foot. While this title remains slotted, your jog and run speeds can be strained to double their normal maximum. This will drain significant amounts of additional stamina, but you will be able to go faster! Nobody with this title does not want to go faster.

Notice!
You are at the maximum allotted 10 titles. If you gain another one, you must choose to replace an existing title. This will cause the chosen title to be lost until the conditions are met for it to be regained. Should we manage to get title-combining functioning, you will be able to combine existing titles to accomplish a greater effect. Opening up slots for new titles.
Note that some titles simply cannot be combined. Titles that can be combined will be updated to show as 'broken titles' with dots on the side of the title to show in which fashion it can be placed in a sentence for alteration. More information will be revealed about title combining when we get it to work.

Artorian dismissed the prompts, waiting a moment for more to appear. "More title nonsense so far. Little conveniences I can appreciate, but nothing earth-shattering."

Yvessa stretched, dropping her human guise to become an orb. Just so she could drop to her seat and roll against a pillar. Her light dimmed as she spoke. "It works. It's done. It's in place. Tell me you aren't going to enact some massive scheme anytime soon and I can go take a nap."

The old man pressed his fingers together. "*We~e~ell...*"

The primal noise that erupted from the dim green orb was best explained as the sound one made when they did not want to get up in the morning, badgered by people they did not like. "Tell. *Now.*"

It was so good to have Yvessa back. Artorian had done that entirely on purpose. "It's not pressing, if you'd like to nap. My plan comes down to my particular difficulties. If you happen to know how long I'll remain stuck in baby Long form, I can give you better information."

His Wisp grumbled and rolled back to the middle of her seat, pulling up a plethora of information screens. "I'm not being monitored right now, so I'm just going to gush and tell you things you're not supposed to know. Don't go gabbing. Got it?"

He smiled and shoved two thumbs up in her direction. "Got it!"

Rifling through menu after menu, the orb gained some red on the edge of her luminance the deeper she dug. "What the abyss. Unguent of Youth? How did you even…? This is a restricted item. These should have all been confiscated. Oh… it was. Well, you've been *busy*."

Artorian remained quiet as Yvessa caught up on recent events. 'Recent' meaning anything that had occurred since she'd last checked out for a while. "You and Eternium are like an old couple. Look at all this endless bickering. Here it is. Dragon growth patterns."

Yvessa moved some screens around to have a better grasp on the information. "Alright. I'm seeing that nasty all-attribute demerit. That's rough, buddy. Your Long form will grow depending on the amount of food intake, sleep, and activity it gets. That sustenance ability of yours caps out the first metric, so at the moment we're looking at a year for the next size category increase. Sleep will cut that down further, but activity? That's going to be difficult in your current state."

He nodded, pensive about his limitations. "Sleep is something I vastly enjoy. Sleep is for the week after all. All week. All the time. Don't get up, just be cozy in a pillow mound. Given the current circumstances, I would rather keep busy rather than be bored out of my mind and sleeping my days away. I must thank you for turning my Administrator title on earlier. That *was* you, right?"

Yvessa wanted to rub at her face, but lacked the hands to do so. "In the dream you cobbled together for that girl? Yes, that was me. How did you notice? I wasn't going to mention it."

Artorian winked. "Well, I can't turn it on myself, and that green glow in the dreamscape was hard to miss. Thank you for that, dear. It helped. Can you flip that to be active again? I think I may dig around using this… What is it called? *Deep System Access* option? See if I can't help or otherwise find solutions. I'm immobile anyway, unless I feel like flailing. I'm getting good at flailing."

Yvessa snorted. "It's a low bar."

"A bar I am successfully crossing! Honestly, I'm not going to pretend I'm *all that* when flailing is the best I've got." He huffed in reply, crossing a leg over the other and looking away. To his caretaker's great amusement, which her chuckle gave away. A sudden golden glow surrounded him, making him look at his own being. "*Hmm*? What just happened?"

Checking his page, Yvessa informed him. "You leveled up. Based on the log, you've done that a few times already, but it doesn't seem to be affecting that latent penalty of yours. To explain: The sun came up recently, and DE points are calculated shortly after dawn. We actually want it at dawn exactly, but we ran into the problem of dawn happening at a different time depending on where you are. Let's see how many of those DE points you're getting. I'm going to use Gnome metrics to actually understand what I'm looking at. Also, I don't like mushed notices so I'm going to space this one out a bit."

Deity: Rank 5
Follower count: Sixty-one thousand two hundred and forty-four.
Followers generate up to 25 DE a day.
DE gained per day: 1,531,100
Altar count: Twenty-two.
Altars generate 50 DE a day.
DE gained per day: 1,100
Shrine count: Four.
Shrines generate 100 DE a day.

DE gained per day: 400
Temple size 1 count: One.
Temple size 2 count: Zero.
Temple size 3 count: Zero.
Temples generate 250, 500, and 1,000 DE daily in order of rank.
DE gained per day: 250
Total DE Gained per day: 1,532,850
Conversion experience gained instead: 15,328

Yvessa blinked at the information. "You… uh… you're going to start having that happen more frequently. I believe. That ridiculous experience conversion play you made early on—which seemed minor at the start—is no longer so minor. You are one *popular* deity to follow. I *have* to know why."

His Wisp poured through log files, her color gaining luminance as she went. "Interesting. It's been barely two weeks since you were last 'active' and worn by a Goblin shaman. Looks like you were 'acquired' by Midgardians, gained some fame on the way as a crown without realizing it, and now you're level 19. I was wondering if there was more than one reason for the Speedrunner title. Now I have it."

Artorian hummed with interest. "Any chance that can turn into some specialization experience instead? That's my bottleneck."

His caretaker reached out with some of her glow and just pinched him. "No. This is all general experience. For your specialization, you will need to specifically do things with those abilities, and in that mindset. You currently can't lift a toothpick, much less a whole bow. Your level is going to skyrocket, but the bonuses are still going to be trapped behind the Asgard attribute gain blockade."

The old man pulled the deity information up for himself. "Whohoho! Look at that! Multiple millions of points to get something done no longer looks like such a pipe dream. Well, alright then. Should I stop converting them and start stockpiling to have a small hoard of interference goodies?"

Yvessa had to give up the convenience of being an orb, deciding to exist in her human shape, since it gave her so many more options to express herself. She pressed her hands together, fingers easing against her lips as she sat cross-legged. "I'm not sure… Tell me of your actual plans. Or I'm not going to be able to advise squat. Speeding up your Long growth is not in the cards."

The old man got up to stretch, rolling his shoulders. "Alright. Here's what's going on. The goal has not changed. I need to punch Barry in the nose. Barry the dessert fork. Actually, I'll just start calling him Forky for short. Sheerly out of spite. Forky has a lot of friends, and I don't like Forky's friends."

Artorian's shoulder went pop, but it was a good one. "I've cleaned up Midgard, but not without cost. That gives this realm some time to build up against the inevitable return of annoyances I've kicked off. I also know their numbers are limited, so they will try to be smarter about it this time. That means I want to be giving them plenty of distractions until it's time for me to storm the castle. Because of course I'm going to storm the castle."

He took a big breath, counting on his fingers. "For that I need several things. A buffet of allies, infrastructure to slow down invaders, and tools for the job. The hardest part is going to be getting the word out."

Yvessa perked up with interest. "Getting the word out?"

Artorian nodded, packing back and forth. "It's time. I need other willing people from Cal to get in here and start causing a ruckus. My absence as an offensive force is going to hurt a painful, painful amount. I need a spearpoint of trouble to keep the information-gatherers distracted while I recuperate."

A Nixie Tube sparked above his head. "How is my old disciple doing?"

His caretaker shrugged. "Last I knew, he started a life with Minya. Got reacquainted with his old friends Hans and Tom. There was some fuss about the full story concerning Killer of Her Loneliness, but I don't have the details."

Brand new plans jumped for attention in Artorian's brain, each falling over the other like a group of Dark Elf couriers each trying to deliver their news first. "Is that so? That group… that group would do wonderfully if they were willing. Yes. Dale. Minya. Tom. Hans. Rose."

He nodded to himself a great set of ideas coming together. "Yes. If you can get word out to that group that I need them, that would be helpful. Tell them it's only for a year, as I'm in a pickle. Tell them it's to practice for their Guilds and organizations, and that they can set up in… wherever it is I currently am. Katarina would benefit from competent Guild-based leadership secretly operating on a higher purpose under her nose. Plus I'll be able to vouch for them. Minya can even get started on acquisitions."

Artorian smiled wide, his hands steepling in delight. "That's a smooth five, but I think… I think I could make it *six*. They're short an old friend. Yvessa, once my level reaches twenty, turn off the experience converter. I'm going to need to use some *points*."

CHAPTER TEN

"He wants us to do *what*?" Minya sounded upset before Yvessa had finished relaying her message. The Wisp had successfully gathered them all in Niflheim with a little help, in the normal gathering circle usually reserved for the supervisors. Though that seemed to be the end of her success as Minya did not appear to be remotely on board with the proposed idea. She was a complete opposite of Dale, who was bouncing on his toes from excitement at the prospect.

Yvessa swiftly dropped her planned retort on the table. "It's a request. Nothing more. You can decline if you want. If you need motivation, Artorian said that it would double as an opportunity for you to stock that store you want to erect. Plus it would really help Cal by not being demon-slapped."

"Oh, can we gooooo?" Dale pleaded. "It sounds like so much fun. There's so little to do in Cal now that reconstruction is ongoing. Eternia has stuff we could *do*."

The outburst reminded Minya of Cal's antics rather than Dale's, and sighed with exasperation.

Hans balanced a knife on his finger, a cheesy grin wide on his face. Oh, he was going to capitalize on a childish outburst like that. Hans would tell tall tales of Dale's embarrassing behavior. Well embellished with floral language for extra cringiness. "Well, I was going to decline on principle. But if Dale keeps being a bunny, I will have to go just for my own entertainment."

Rose's reply was right to the point. "I'm bored. I miss hunting. I miss adventuring. Even if it's dealing with the numbers, I say we go. Or, at minimum, I will go. Where we live in Cal is currently a paradise, but sweet celestials above are my fingers itching for something meaningful to do. Lounging about all day and attending to my grapes is fine and all, but it lacks the chaos I crave. Stomping grapes to make wine only goes so far."

"Awww. Shnookums. I thought you liked living at our winery?" Hans stuck his lip out at her poutily. His stomach was rounder than before from his newfound love of drinking their own supply. An assassin knew better, but Rose wasn't wrong. Life in Cal was idyllic for them, but it was rote in its boredom and lack of threats. They had all been forged in fire, but now they were getting fat. Or at least he was.

Rose pinched him in the weenus, making her husband yelp. "I love my orchard, but I crave more. I'm *bored,* sweetheart. We used to go dungeon delving, and nothing has gotten my heart to race in panic since. Also, my dresses are starting to become a bit… tight."

"You look great in all your dresses and nothing is wrong, ever." Hans rattled that off so fast, the entire table looked at him with worry.

Dale was going to sass back from the quip, but even he was concerned at his friend's immediate meekness. "You alright there, buddy?"

Hans quickly nodded when Dale asked, his hands already shaking the mention off. There was no problem. Rose looked fantastic. He leaned to Dale, whispering in a rush. "Do not mention her weight. Do not dare. She will snipe you like a fly on a rabbit's ass from five hundred yards."

Dale got the hint, having someone himself now. "Well, I

don't know any of the downsides, and would obviously like to go. Tom, what do you think?"

The Northman sat with his arms crossed. His big face was an open book, a red mixture of consternation and concentration. "I am torn."

Hans quipped, "No, you are Tom! **Ow*!"

Rose was far less gentle with the pinching this time.

They motioned for him to continue, which Tom took as leeway to go ahead and put his worries on the table. "For me it is like so: Last time, I could not discern the difference between 'real' and 'not real.' It was all the same in some ways, yet I could not enjoy the thrill of battle. Nothing was a challenge. I held this opinion until I left Eternium. To live in Cal."

Tom's consternation replaced itself with discomfort. "Like you all. My life is perfect here. It is as wonderful as I could hope it to be if I enjoyed being a domestic, spoiled housecat. My hands ache to hold my hammer in a meaningful way. My strength is worthless where I am! There are no challenges. There is nothing to fight. Life is dull, yet filled with drinking and merriment."

Tom's concentration was the next expression to go, replaced by a mixture of guilt and anxiety. "The longer I linger, the more I feel a hole in my heart. A hole that tells me something is missing. Like the fire in my berserker soul is slowly being quietly smothered by sedentary life and an excess of daily comforts. We have everything we could possibly want. So why am I so unhappy?"

He released a heavy sigh, the Northman's face going neutral. "Now I think of the fights in the other Core, and I quietly yearn for the soft release it might offer. Even diminished as they are, with fights I couldn't care less about. It would give me the satisfaction to swing Thud, my prized hammer. He currently rots away on a shelf, even if he cannot rot."

Tom bit his inner cheek before speaking more, his temper rising now that he'd repressed the fleeting earlier feelings. "I wish to feel my blood boil. I wish to let my fire rage. I wish to see the sun and challenge it by burning with my spirit alone. I wish to earn my victories, rather than languish in them day after day. I dread the 'morrow, for I know it will be but a repeat of yesterday. That is not to say I do not love my time with you all. This longing is just… A phantom pain. I am missing a limb I did not know I had."

Silence fell a moment after. Yvessa could see that everyone except Minya felt this particular experience. She seemed to be the only one thoroughly enjoying the excess downtime and lack of work. Her gaze didn't escape the acquisition expert's notice.

Minya worked thumbs into her temples, sighing. "I'm the holdup? What an awful feeling. Fine. You get the chance to sell me. Pitch me your goods."

Yvessa nodded, creating some diagrams for them. "Currently, Artorian is in Eternia. He has cleared Midgard of all the demons, but got himself locked in a box as a result, one that will keep him stuck behind its lock all year long. Meaning that the demons that come back in are going to get a chance at takeover, and—"

Hans shoved his hands forwards to interrupt. "*Whoa*, whoa there! Are you telling me there's *more* of those things? I thought we killed all the ones in Cal? We had whole war councils about them. I thought that was all wrapped up and over. Those things were horrifying!"

Deep interest fell on Yvessa's words after that news, causing her to shrink back a few inches from the pressure. "Ah. Erm. Yes, well. The short answer is no. The rest are in Eternium, and so far, Artorian has been single-handedly keeping them all back. Preventing them from leaking out since the gazebos they need in order to seep out into Cal's Soul Space are there."

Tom smashed his mug on the ground. "Single-handedly? Dale! Isn't this man your teacher? From the Academy you spoke about owning. Why are you letting your mentor go at this alone? That is disrespectful for a disciple. No Northman would abide by such conduct."

Dale shot his hands up. "I didn't know! I found out just

now! I didn't know he was still alive, much less that he was doing all of *that.*"

The rest of the party realized Dale had never gone game testing with them, and had never been subject to Tiny-torian's healing. Minya quirked a brow, laying a hand on her husband's shoulder for support. "Dale? Artorian was your mentor? Why is this the first I'm hearing of this? He's kind of, you know, a big deal here."

His hands remained in the air. "It never came up! How was I supposed to know? Nobody tells me anything! It's just like it was in Mountaindale. All I get when I talk about the old days is seeing everyone else suffer discomfort."

Dale looked to Minya with concern as his hands came down. "So far when I notice, I've just been telling you: Don't worry about it, because you hate talking about anything related to work. So I won't bring it up around you. You get this awful crease on your forehead, like you're in pain from the topic. I don't like seeing you like that."

He took Minya's hand, giving it a thoughtful squeeze. "I don't even know what the strange mirror-shatter marks hanging in the middle of some fields are, when they are rampantly strung all over this place. I was just told not to touch them. When the tiny war broke out without warning, I was told it was 'just a fluke,' but I didn't like being reminded there's still creatures or people that want us harm. This is the first time I'm told about 'demons,' and I feel rather out of the loop. So I'd really like some answers."

Minya's expression softened in response. That crease vanished as she warmed from hearing the reason Dale kept trying to lessen her burdens. "Daww… you sweetie. I forget how much you care when you don't talk to me like this. Thank you, dear. Well… I won't be upset then. Though I wish you'd told me. Or did you, and I just forgot?"

She shook her head. "It doesn't matter. Let's see about those answers for you after the meeting, *hmm*? I know Artorian decently well, and it's unlike him to need help. Given what I've heard and seen over the years. It is awfully rare that he wouldn't have some wiggly little scheme to…"

Minya blinked, her breath steadying as her grip on Dale made him wince. She slowly locked her gaze with Yvessa's. "Are *we* the plot? Is it so bad there, that we are *directly needed* for things not to go awry?"

Yvessa pulled up a chair as she created her human form. Not having normal emotive capacity felt too limiting. Sitting down with them so Minya could see the Tibbins expression plastered on her face, Yvessa ditched the sales pitch. "It's that bad. In truth, if you didn't accept, my immediate plan was to go back and say you all declined, so we could plan out who else to ask and how else to solve the problem. Because he is truly, truly landlocked. Artorian is trapped in an item, and already using significant schemery just to get this much done."

Yvessa counted on her fingers. "He has no mana, no stamina, and will be killed on sight by any demon that finds him. All while he tries his best to guide some new-blood youngster into setting up a small empire, in order to deter the incoming force that is inevitably going to assail that realm. If he was free, this wouldn't be necessary. Though if you know Artorian, then you know how much he's angered Eternium with his meddling. You can probably even guess why he meddled."

Minya inhaled deeply and slowly to calm herself. Her eyes closed as she could indeed, very easily imagine the kind of abyss involved. "Isn't the current version of the game in Eternium going to be wiped? Like iterations in Cal."

Yvessa assented with a nod. "If we successfully finish the cleanup plan, then most likely yes. If we fail, there will be another demon break, and they will once again flood the Soul Space. Then it won't matter, and we will have to recover Eternium from Barry's hand. That may be difficult to accomplish, but we have some serious powerhouses on our side. Currently, they're still limited by Cal's maximum power-level. They have to keep one step below him. That's the single S-ranks right now. We have a good chance of rebuking and getting back to where we were, but that's not a win. That's a return to status quo. Artorian is aiming for a win. I'm pretty sure he has a plan against Forky. Oh, sorry. Barry. Artorian has an infectious case of vengeance."

She smiled while the table snorted. Dale smirked and couldn't withhold his following sneer when he pictured the High Elf face on Cal's old statue. "That sounds nice and spiteful for him. I like it. My memory is a little wobbly, but I remember that 'Barry' person. It's accompanied by incredible hatred. Forky sounds fantastic, a full improvement. I'm adopting the use."

Minya tapped Dale on the shoulder, firmly nodding in agreement. "Horribly on the nose. It's great."

The Wisp continued now that the mood felt warmer. "Artorian's plan is for you to set up your organizations and Guilds. Both to practice running them, and to cause a nice big distraction so the demons look a particular way. I know from experience that they can tamper with map data, which is rather irritating until we can track down the cause. I dislike that they're making it look like they are places they're not, and vice versa."

Tom bashed his large fist on the table. "I am joining this fight. In fact, I would wager many others would gladly do so as well. That fight with the last incursion was my last, great accomplishment. I crave more! I will not rest on my laurels. I will go, but who else can we bring? For that matter, why not take everyone?"

Yvessa tilted her head left to right. That was going to need a lot of explanation. "There are… problems… on that front. Though I can certainly spread the word, and hope more people trickle in. Our powerhouses and realm supervisors may all need to stay behind. There is still work that needs to be done in Cal with the great restoration. Our S-rankers are working on secret projects, or turning Cal's Vanaheim into a copy of our old world."

Rose was putting things together. "So, if I understand this right, we have an active threat to our well-being that is barely being contained. With an actual, big chance that it can now make headway?"

Yvessa considered the statement. "That is correct."

Rose made her decision apparent. "Hans! Get my bow!"

The assassin winked at the table and tongue clicked at them while making finger crossbows. "Sounds like we're going regardless. Of course, sweetie! Do pack my daggers! All of them!"

Dale turned to Tom to ask something else, but the Northman was already jogging toward the beacon. A huge smile was painted on his face, and waking dreams of swinging Thud actively played in front of his eyes. So he turned to Minya instead, whose expression currently appeared dark. The sight made Dale think better of it, swallowing his question on if he got any new gear.

Minya's eyes flicked to Yvessa, her face unmoving. "We're going. But we're going to need weapons. Lots, and lots of weapons. Do my DE points still have value? I need to spend a few million on an information network, and a new toy for Dale. He's got that droopy puppy look going."

Yvessa smiled in response, knowing this meant everyone was on board. "They sure do, and I would be delighted to direct a Wisp over to you to help with purchases."

"Yes! Come on, tell your friends!" Dale punched the sky, excited as could be. He was getting new toys, a fight, answers, and time with his whole party all in one go. "It's adventure time!"

CHAPTER ELEVEN

When Yvessa arrived in Eternium's Midgard Queendom of Goa'yuld as it was being taken apart, she illuminated the throne room, bathing the whole area in a soft green glow. Even invisible, her Presence changed the room's colors, and she looked around to see if that was still being blocked by the perception filters. Since nobody noticed, she figured it worked fine and settled inside a lantern to get to work. Yvessa knocked on Artorian's Forum right away, entering his bonfire space right as the connection formed. "Old man, great news! They're on their way!"

His lack of immediate reply was strange, but it didn't take effort on her part to see the hundreds of screens floating around the room as Artorian paced between them. He was mumbling to himself about some numbers he was comparing. She caught a 'that can't be right.'

Yvessa trilled. "Alright. Now what? What are you doing?"

Artorian heard her this time, nearly slipping on the hem of his robe from the speed of his turn. He caught himself with an arm flail and an embarrassing undulation. "Whu—! Got myself. Alright. *Hmm*? Ah! Yvessa! Fantastic timing. I may have solved a problem and just need it confirmed. Is Dev available?"

Yvessa sped to where Artorian stood, looking over the information screens with apprehension and a hint of panic. What was he breaking this time? "What did you do?"

Artorian innocently pointed at a screen. "Oh, nothing. I just moved some numbers around and made—"

With a **scree**, the Wisp passed him by in a flash, causing his robes to flutter as she passed. Snatching the designated screen up to study it with intensity, Yvessa frowned while looking for problems. The bothersome part was that she didn't find any. She found… solutions? "Did… did *you* fix this?"

Catching himself for the second time in a minute, he strolled over and summoned up the Forum location so he could sit down on a lounger. Yvessa didn't seem in the mood to consider mana costs, so he just spoke. "Yes. I did. I was thinking about some of the things Oberon mentioned. Pylons not working right and such. One solution in particular came to me while I was snooping around for goodies—well, *two*, now that I have done said snooping—with pleasant side effects!"

Artorian beamed and rubbed his hands together. "One, I found out how to make Artifacts. I was just looking for something neat to use DE points for, but I stumbled on that mechanism by accident. It has some… *stipulations of interest.* Two, it was mentioned that attributes don't calculate right. So I pulled that information up. I found out what Oberon meant about my mana pool being too large. He's actually right; it's a bad connection in the Pylon system. Something isn't calculating right."

Shuffling through a few screens, he pulled the one he needed to the forefront. "Here we go. So, I am currently a Divine. Or rather, I am when the title is active. With the Administrator title's deep system access, I have discovered that this also gives you the cleric tag. Anyone with the cleric tag has their mana pool doubled so long as their Divine likes them. I don't dislike myself, so the Pylons applied this benefit."

He moved his finger down, pointing at his mana regeneration. "It also seemed strange that this number was so ridiculously high. So I looked into it. Turns out it was wrong. I've been getting double mana regeneration based on an error in the base formula. Both the Pylon for mana regeneration, and the backup Pylon for that same measure have been in effect. I should be getting half the amount. There was also a minor numerical error with stamina regeneration, when I had a peek."

Artorian made visible the screen which listed his fixed base formulas for all the values in his attributes. "Here's all the basics. The proper basics, without strange additions that make no sense or have no source. From these, I compiled a list of reasonable scaling. I found the logs for a growth-based system, and a flat bonus system, depending on what a person's base class had for 'preferred attributes.' Generalist didn't have any, so I had to look it up for other things."

Fiddling around with the information a moment, he pulled up the relevant example. "Here. Some of Tatum's handiwork. Perception, wisdom, and intelligence are the suggested characteristics for a Ritualist. Meaning that for those three attributes, the Pylons need to look at the 'growth' table. For the other values, they need to look at the 'flat bonus' table. I put them all together while you've been gone."

Yvessa thought this was a pretty worthwhile improvement. "You know we can't just roll this out, right? Bits and pieces maybe, but a big change like this is a full-on Pylon overhaul. We might even have to grow an entire field of new ones to activate, before we can turn off the old ones."

Artorian nodded sagely. "I'm well aware. It's been explained a few times. Dev, Oberon, or Eternium would be good candidates for review. I'm just playing advisor while working on things in the system. Now that I'm starting to understand how they work, I feel like I can start adding valuable help. It was a lot of reading, and Oberon was right with his Pylon mention. Abyss if I'm touching one of those again."

He grumbled and tried to poke at something. "Blast. This

still irks me. Yvessa, can I see what my own Administrator title does? It's not coming up with me tapping it."

Too distracted by going over the information of his suggested alterations, she missed the twinkle in the old man's eyes when she waved the information at him. "*Hmm*? Sure. I'm just reviewing this myself before I elevate it."

Title: Administrator
CAL Assigned
Cannot Combine
Cal Shop Access
Eternium Shop Access
Deep System Access
Bug-Fix Screens
Can Grant Titles
Can Remove Titles
If active as 'Administrator,' the user counts as an immortal object.
No actions cost energy.

Artorian's expression became flat and unreadable. There wasn't a chance in the abyss he was going to give away his true feelings of sheer giddiness he was currently experiencing. His Administrator title had *such* goodies. Oh, this was glorious! It was a shame he couldn't control if it was on or off, but celestials above. The power!

Though he knew about the title bit, the rest was a surprise! An extremely pleasant surprise. He didn't even know what to play with first. There were just so many goodies. No actions cost energy? Bug-fix screens like when he repaired broken items? *Cal* shop access? Oh, call him a child, because this was *the* candy store!

He needed to be sneaky when it came to playing with these options. Yvessa could realize this was a scheme at any moment and shut his title down. Thus he also needed to hurry to scooch his prior plan into motion. So he could do one thing. Just one teensy thing. His hands sifted through screens, throwing a few in between him and Yvessa to obscure her sight. One extra second could mean everything.

A glorious idea sparked in his mind as he worked, so he summoned up the panel that had to do with the beacon network. His beacon network. Or rather, it was his beacon network *now*. Tapping away at the connective tissues, he sneakily applied his Administrator access to mass select all the beacons in Midgard. Like throwing down a whole host of levers all at once, he flicked their control to him with a snap of the finger. Once he confirmed the change, he immediately closed the relevant screen to pull something entirely unrelated close. He was inspecting it with a satisfied smirk as Yvessa moved screens out of the way to hover over.

"What was that? You just snapped your fingers." Artorian looked surprised when he turned to the sound of her voice, acting surprised and moving the decoy screen behind him.

"Nothing! It was—" The screen was whisked from his control, pulled in front of his caretaker as she checked his dubious claim.

"Potions? What were you doing looking at potions? Oh no, mister. Were you trying to undo the Unguent of Youth's effect? *Tsk tsk.* I'm locking your access to this panel. No cheating your way out of that baby form. I know you got it through questionable methods, but countering cheating with cheating isn't going to fly!"

He put his hands up in the air, surrendering with a dramatic sigh. "*Fi~i~ine.*"

When she wandered off with his potion screen, he sneakily glanced at his status and summoned up the deity menu to view the altar portion. Just to confirm if it worked or not. Satisfaction scratched his back, but he questioned if it worked because Yvessa was letting him. Ah well, he saw what he needed.

Altar count: One hundred.
Altars generate 50 DE a day.
DE gained per day: 5,000

Perfect. That was exactly what he wanted to check. He didn't care about the points so much, but the beacons being *his* meant they were active in the network. Since his aligned followers could travel to any beacon in said network, that meant they were about to sprawl explosively across Midgard. Just how he'd planned it.

Dismissing the information before he was spotted, he hummed along and followed behind Yvessa. "So they're coming, then? Great! In that case, I have a question I need to send up to Eternium. I'd rather he be aware of this particular stunt that I'm going to pull."

His caretaker plopped on the marble seating available, her fingers lacing as she closed the potion screen after locking him out of it. "I'm listening."

Artorian sat across from her, old-man groaning for effect as he did. "There's one more person I need to add to Dale's party. I have the hunch he originated from it, and I think it might make them happy to have a reunion. Tell me how much DE it costs to permanently summon in Adam, or what other costs might be involved. Given he's currently Cored inside of Cal, or that's where I think stored minds are going? I'm aware that I may need to do some finagling with outside forces, but I need that 'can-kill-demons-permanently' option on my side of the table."

Yvessa wasn't sure what he meant. "I may need to go do some research before I can answer that. I will also need to elevate the original issue up to Eternium. I think it might be better if he sees this directly. Though I will need to pester Oberon for access."

Artorian raised a brow. "Access? Tell me Eternium isn't sitting in some room all by himself. Alone with nothing but screens as company."

Yvessa tilted her head. "Fairly certain that's exactly what's going on. Not that I've ever seen it for myself. Only Oberon can drop down to his active frame of reference. I can't even drop in unless someone takes me with them. Or was it… speed up to his frame of reference? This whole time and dilation business is above my head."

"*Mmm.*" Artorian quieted, his pose pensive. With no further commentary forthcoming, Yvessa made a motion that she would be back, and winked out. This left him alone in his mental workspace as the Forum seat vanished from under his butt. "Whoa!"

Picking himself up from the ground, he sighed and grew concerned about this new information. All alone… in the slowest frame of reference that could be mustered through time dilation? That was nothing less than horrifying. Something needed to be done about that. He tapped his lips to think about it, then smiled as he had another one of his wonderful, can't-possibly-go-wrong ideas. "I have a visitor who plays lovely music. I wonder if she'd like to visit… *others* with said lovely music."

Artorian turned on his heel, speaking to himself as he pranced off to his bonfire space. It was time to meddle. "Oh, *Eterniu~u~um*. Do you like kalimbas?"

CHAPTER TWELVE

One week after Dale and his party entered Eternium, the world of Eternia went dark. Not dark as in the meaning of utter blackness that could not be seen through. Though that was what it felt like those first few moments after the sun went out. Quite directly, as if the lever responsive for the light had been pushed up to turn it off.

Just **fuff**.

The bright ball of happy-to-stab-your-eyes dimmed to no more than an orb of soft celestine luminance, providing a consistent twilight. This new low-light fell over the landscape as the day and night cycle came to a sudden, complete halt, instead bathing the world in a light blue sheen.

Panic crawled across the many realms since the inhabitants could only speculate at the source, but anyone aligned to a certain deity received an illuminating prompt.

Quest Update!
Quest: A Labor of Love.
Notice from your Divine: Through your efforts, my well-being has improved. In appreciation, I have bought you some time. While the sun remains celes-

tine, many functions of the world will sleep. I expect my Suncurse not to assail the wicked until the sun wakes once again. Use this chance to expand, and grow! The demon tide will come. Be cautious, my dears! Unite under the banners of the Solar Gate and Goa'yuld. I am too weak to protect you, but shall keep your boon strong. Do not pray to me. Divert your efforts to the betterment of the many. Make the map! They need you. They all need you.

That notice sent any follower of Sunny into a tizzy. Checking the beacon network let them find that rather than a scant few choices, one hundred options were now available! This began the exploration equivalent of a gold rush, as well over fifty-thousand followers all wanted to see the new places first. With so many people zipping between beacons, the coliseum in Solar Gate had to stop all gladiatorial activity. The traffic became far too frequent as followers ran between budding towns and growing regions.

With Artorian's people beginning a large-scale cartography operation where the enthusiasm of those involved got cranked up to eleven, all sorts of talk circulated. Sunny's people felt like they were filled with glorious purpose as they each began to carry map cases, eagerly speaking of their plight to anyone who asked. This became a rather frequent occurrence since they visually appeared to know what was going on, and none enjoyed living with uncertainty.

As a pleasant boon, this also made a great many people very interested in joining up.

Any new followers Artorian gained received the benefits and the quest immediately on joining. Thus both informing them of the demon problem, and providing a credible source for why the world felt like it had been paused. As usual, his health regeneration boon was received with a stellar reaction. Each new follower felt like they had been added to a secret club, a club with a *real* Divine in it. One that proved itself with missive and might.

Existing faiths fell to their knees at the arrival and rapid spread of this new order, their memberships draining away right under their noses. Existing clerics despised that their beliefs came into question, refusing to buy into this laughable tale of a 'Divine returned.' Clearly their faith was the correct one! The fight the existing clerics desired did not come to pass, as Sunny's followers were far too busy filling their days with action. Rhetoric had to wait.

There was no meeting that could be interrupted. No group prayer they could barge into. No church or shrine being erected that they could interfere with. Existing ones may have been repurposed to cartography and war councils, but nothing new was built. As far as the clerics found, all of Sunny's followers were people possessed. As if their task was too important, and prayer just a waste of time.

That the deity had specifically told them not to was only known to these clerics when they relented, accepting the beacon's offer. Though with that acceptance came a true doubling of their mana pool, access to spells previously denied them, and the kind reaching hand of a Divine that specifically pointed for them to aid others.

Sunny's direct mention to pay no attention to him was taken to heart by many, but some took it to mean that they should pay no attention to themselves. Differences like these caused some internal discord and dissent, but that came second to getting things done.

Celestials above, did they get things *done*.

Katarina's budding new empire received an unexpected influx of support and assistance, which did not come as a surprise to the young Royal herself. Katarina was privy to the quest when it had updated, as she too was a follower. She was grateful for the help, for she knew that she needed much of it. The old Goa'yuld was slowly being abandoned on her orders, and the new location was in full swing of grand-scale construction. When she said they were moving, that order had not been small in scope.

After discovering Solar Gate and visiting with a heavy guard and escort, Katarina realized that walls and gates would do them little good. Anyone aligned would be using the beacons, and few would remain unaligned when taking so much as glance at the benefits. Fast travel between a hundred locations for you and your goods, plus a ticking health regeneration that helped heaps and spades with daily life? Nobody even cared that not having a mana pool made it cost them some experience. They gladly paid the cost for the travel convenience.

There were some unintentional side-effects when being a follower of Sunny, such as the creation of impromptu pillow bands. Coordinated snoring was their music of choice, as followers tended to overwork themselves and collapse in piles. It was an amusing joke that arose from all the aligned bringing their own pillow everywhere, as sudden naptime became a commonality.

This growing trend did create a need for nap spots in the new town, which irritated planners to no end. It was like trying to herd cats! Everyone else loved the little pagodas and gardens. The Queendom took inspiration from this event, which led to the hilarious group-groan within her council when Katarina declared the new Queendom name to be Duvetia. Who didn't love a good, thick duvet when the average temperature hovered around spring-morning cool all day long?

Plant growth slowed down, but did not stop from the change in sunlight. The Everburning Crown had attempted to explain that the flora were still getting light, just not the kind of light Katarina could see. The explanation went over her head, but that's where the crown sat, so she let it slide and forwarded the information to her council. Most of which had grown accustomed to her strange revelations. There would have been more pushback on her words, had her offered revelations not been so effective the majority of the time.

As far as the council was concerned, the Queen just knew things they didn't. A fact they attributed to the semi-sentient crown on her head, which they were currently surmising to be some kind of lost Divine artifact. How else could they explain her Divine Shell ability?

That item had caused both legend and gossip to sprout and race as wildfire. The council was even aware people arrived via beacon just to hear about what Duvetia needed, only to get right to work. Conversations went along the lines of: "Is this the Goa'yuld place? Yes? Oh, it's Duvetia now? Point me in the direction that needs work."

Then off they went while pushing their sleeves up without so much as a consideration to payment. They baffled the council to no end.

The moment these newcomers saw someone else with a pillow on their back and a map case strapped to their belt, they slid into that group like they were extended family, even if they'd never met before. The sight was perplexing. These people that had never met before saw one another and just decided to get along. They made introductions as easily as water flowing down a brook, and, once informed of what the work was, threw themselves into it with a zealous vigor, as if they feared no injury.

The more the council saw of these people, the more that fearlessness became apparent. Even large, painful splinters from woodworking they just pulled out without a second thought, continuing their work without so much as a shred of first aid.

Small fights became a regularity, just to test who had the greater willpower to keep getting up. The person that got up more was declared to be in the right where dead-end arguments were concerned. The events were concerning for the locals who became guards or constables, but the incidents were self-contained, like some minor sociological cue that was developing based on an inherent trait they had.

Until it was nap time. Then the world was one of restful silence, save for the bardic snores.

The council decided to just let the new location run without interference. They would eventually figure out what was causing all of this, even if they suspected their young Queen was playing the giddiest of pranks by keeping it from them.

While progress in Midgard might be going well, it was a

different story inside of Artorian's forum. "What do you mean I need a *wessel*?"

Yvessa drew a sharp breath, her hands forming claws that she forcibly needed to clutch together. "Vessel, old man. I said *vessel*."

She motioned around the Forum space. "Are you going senile? How did you mishear me *in here*?"

Artorian stomped around in response, pushing his way through a sea of screens that parted at his shoulder nudging. "Well, it seems so! I can't do everything perfectly. I'm not Cal! That's terrible news. Why do I need a vessel for Adam? Can't I just magic him in here? What kind of cheatery do I need to employ?"

"There is no cheatery!" Yvessa blew her top, her colorations fuming to red. "I have told you this three times! How distracted are you today? You can't get Adam into Eternium unless he has a vessel. A body that can contain him. Like how your body is currently the vessel for your mind and power. He needs something similar."

Artorian didn't buy it. "Well, Forky can get *forked*, then! That means he out-cheated me by getting demons into Eternium. Unacceptable! Where is my list!"

The old human pushed aside dozens of screens at a time, massively distracted while picking a few up and liberally throwing them over his head. "Where did I put the darn thing? All this abyssal clutter!"

A thought struck him, turning to go the way he came. "Forget the list. Where is the expletives dictionary? I'm adding variations of forked to it. That seems like a much better use of my time."

Yvessa mass-dismissed every screen in the Forum space and appeared in front of him, gripping the old man by the shoulders with easily seven times his strength attribute. "Breathe. Breathe, you daft old man. You're doing what the dungeons did and you're taking it far, far worse than they are. This is not where you belong. Don't lose yourself in this work."

Artorian didn't push her off, but his face did contort into an expression of anger and irritation. "In comparison to what, caretaker? What am I going to do with my time aside from putz around in the deep system access world while I'm a noodle crown? There's nothing to do, save for occasionally chatting with Katarina, and I don't have the DE points to just throw out quest updates like they are spun sugar. They're expensive! Even with no more of the experience being converted. It didn't escape my notice that I have a limitation on how many messages I can give her a day."

"Breathe!" Yvessa wasn't having any of the geezer's flak. "Now."

Grumbling discontentedly, Artorian crossed his arms and closed his eyes, letting the world be black while he focused on his breathing, and breathing deep. That pleased his caretaker, who was used to having such a big brat to deal with. Why were all these high-tier **Law** babies such a handful? Dani had endless stories about Cal, Oberon could go for days about Eternium, and she could break a dozen spoons while recounting this one's tales. Even if there were fewer to go around when the amount was compared, the matter balanced on the same caliber of scope.

When he opened his eyes again, the Forum felt calm. Rather than all the work and clutter, he saw the marble fixture of Dawn present in the middle. It was a good reprieve to see this, rather than the mess he'd made. He squeezed his own shoulders, thumbing them over. "This life isn't for me, 'Vessa. I'm no good at this."

The human form Wisp leaning against a newly created pillow agreed. "You're not a dungeon Core. No matter how much less defined and grayer that area becomes as the years tick by. That's one of the reasons you got me, rather than an already present Wisp. They wouldn't know the difference. You'd likely have also made them permanently swap over colors just so they didn't need to handle you. Cores do not start smart. Lots of leeway for Wisp influence. I'm fairly certain Invictus still has shellshock from what you did to him."

Artorian frowned. "Was it really that bad?"

The caretaker noted Artorian wasn't feeling too stable. "Come have a seat. It wasn't actually so bad, but he will blare up to high heaven that it was. Or at least he did. Dawn ended up fairly upset with him a while ago."

Artorian broke out in weak laughter. "Dawn? Upset? Oh, that poor Wisp! Is there anything left of him?"

Yvessa waggled her hand in a so-so motion. "The pride isn't doing too great and the butt remains singed. He'll be alright. Can I interest you in an activity that won't drive you up the wall like a bored C'towl?"

The old man shrugged and sat down as directed. Might as well. He pulled up the expletives screen and added in his dictionary variations of forked. "Well, if I go down this rabbit hole again, I know the clutter I'll end up in. What's on your mind?"

Her grin shone wide. "Why not spend some time in the tiny body you have stored away instead, rather than the noodle crown?"

Artorian was on his feet within a moment, arms high in the air. "I can *do* that?"

She winked at him, smirking with enjoyment. "You can now. Did you think I've been sitting around doing nothing? I'm responsible to observe you, but let's not pretend I don't care for your well-being. Your attributes will be… what they were. So you won't be able to go far, but it's something."

He clapped his hands together, indescribably elated. "*Something* is everything! When can I go?"

She clapped her hands back, his form no longer that of an old man. "Now!"

CHAPTER THIRTEEN

Merli woke in his room in the Midgard domus that Gomez had put together.

The ceiling was where he'd left it. The smell of earth and wood laid heavy in the air. The young boy moved his hands before his bleary eyes, which needed to blink several times before clarity restored itself. Hands. He had hands. Excellent, tiny, human hands. Momentarily overcome with emotion, he rolled over in the guest bed and took a few minutes to let it happen.

When he used his pillow to wipe away the stains on his cheeks, he sniffled in a breath and sat up. It was slow going with all his physical attributes at no more than a solid five. His mental attributes weren't much higher, but he noticed there was little difference in mental clarity between the intelligence listed here, and in his prior form. He came to the conclusion that he rather liked not being constrained by some number.

Sliding free, he wondered why his foot didn't touch the ground when he dangled his leg off. Right. Tiny stature. A little more and—

Whoop!

Artorian became a pile of limbs laying on the ground, and everything hurt. He was so sore! Auw! One moment. Wasn't this the tester body? Didn't that mean he had…? *Yes*! His form floated from the ground, successfully flying as his Aura wrapped around him like a safety blanket, hugging him tight with all the comforts of an ability he knew very well. How he *missed* such a mundane feeling so.

The rules for tester bodies were different! Fantastic!

His door opened, the noise he'd made not having gone unnoticed. A short, gray-furred rabbit stood in the parting, monocle neatly located over one eye. "Good sir. As my forebears no doubt informed you, it is polite to announce one's visitations!"

"Royce?" Artorian snapped his young eyes to the target, swiftly getting used to flying normally again. The activity circumvented the awful walking he otherwise needed to do. There also seemed to be no change in his mana drain? A quick check later, and he found he didn't even have a health, mana, or stamina bar anymore. "Well, that's odd."

The gray-furred hare hopped forwards, clearing his throat before performing a minor bow. "You will excuse my intrusion, good sir. Royce was a forebear of mine. My name is Jean."

Merli lowered himself while getting a handle on what all was different about this tester body. It worked like a cultivation body… sort of. A Cal Spiritual body in make and model, to be sure. He could funnel his old, original power through it without any fuss. Though the game mechanics seemed to be denying him? Right! This version still worked with the old bracket speak. Now that he thought about it, that was disabled in the current version of Eternia, wasn't it? Everything was spell-this or ability-that.

He recalled the tricks this old body used to have… kind of. He only ever really used one major ability with it. Thanks to Henry being so fond of dying all the time. He had a few other toys, but those tended to be one-offs. Still, he had company.

"Nice to meet you, Jean. I'm… Artorian? Yes. That's still me. Merli's form is throwing me off."

"Very good, sir. This way, please. You require immediate bathing and new attire." Jean hopped away without further retort. Which Artorian followed by supporting his walking gait with flight assistance. He considered shifting to a starlight Aura just to clean himself up, but it never felt the same as a true, proper bath.

The bathtub he was shown to was made and carved from some massive iron tusk. Oh, hey! This was the other tusk from the boar thing he and Decorum had given a good thrashing! Someone here was into recycling.

Jean was no longer the only hare in attendance when Merli's form was being forcibly scrubbed to a level of acceptable cleanliness. They needed multiple large brushes to scrub over his back. How did such a tiny body accumulate so much filth by doing nothing? A full hour of effort later, and Artorian was fresh as a fiddle. Or clean enough for it to count by rabbit-butler norms.

The boy was dressed by fussy squirrels with the tailor profession, but Artorian was used to playing mock up model. As if a few woodland critters could beat out Rosewood, and her ceaseless efforts to hunt him down for measurements and fittings.

He was adjusting his own sleeves while being escorted through the domus, eyes on the changed architecture. They were higher up than he remembered, as several floors had been grown from the bottom up. There was also a brand-new activity afoot! Humans were everywhere! Or they appeared like it, as some of the ears gave the truth away. That the locals were humanized animals didn't bother him. He had either been told directly, or had the hunch that the lack of Cores meant creatures needed to be people.

Perhaps one day, they would somehow have more people than creatures? Then all the Cores could go to adding wildlife, variety, spice, and variation to the world. Ah, well. Not happening without an influx of new souls, and that seemed unlikely.

Merli received a significant personal space allotment when passing through open spaces in the domus. Was it still a domus? This structure was far too big to be a house now. Even a castle felt cramped as a description in comparison. If this place just kept on growing… institution? No, that wasn't a good word. What about complex? Because that was a good visual for how this place felt.

Still, people gratuitously stepping out of his way was starting to become odd. Nobody knew him here. "Jean, why are people being so cordial and stepping back? I know I have an escort, but I was expecting none of this."

The butler bunny hopped along without pause. "It is the badge upon your vest, young master. If one pays attention to the obvious, they will find that each current resident of the Domus Decorae wears them to signify their welcome here. While you have missed much activity over the time you have been dormant, the badge on your vest indicates you are either a founder or an original member of the Domus. The Primarch Decorum left strict instructions for such matters."

Jean continued after turning a corner. "Initially, when the first new people arrived at our door, we had a system where acquiring eight badges would allot one the opportunity to attend a gathering with the elite four. That method has been abandoned since several of the founders have left us. Not all, young master. Do not feel the need to look so frustrated."

If Artorian was frustrated by anything, it was the sassy tone of this gray-fur. Could he punt it? Could he please punt it? He sighed, knowing there was no point. He took the moment to take stock of the people here. Content in appearance, decently nice clothing, nobody in a big rush, definitely all humanized critters. That beaver family in the corner table even had their tails out. "I wonder why they all picked humans. No Elves?"

Some conversations stopped dead, nearby bystanders shooting him dirty looks. Oops! Had he said that out loud? Best to shuffle along a little faster. Jean also had no love for the comment. "Good sir. That was rude."

Artorian placed a hand on the back of his head and mumbled some apologies. "Yes, sorry. Sorry."

Jean shot a quizzical look over his shoulder, seeming to have considered the question and following reaction. "Does the young master really not know?"

Merli weakly shrugged. "Sorry, Jean. No idea. I know it happens, and I have some background idea of why. Though nothing on why always… human."

The youth tapped himself on the chest to make his point, following the butler to a familiar hallway. This one led onwards to double doors where he'd initially met Mahogany and Decorum the last time. Was that their hideout? Would they still be there? He hoped so. It would be great to see a familiar face.

The butler followed the tenant's needs. "I understand, young master. Master Mahogany shall explain it to you. Please allow me to prime him for the topic."

Artorian's heart leapt. Mahogany *was* here, yes! Barely able to contain his excitement, his expression formed a tightly squeezed smile as he barely kept himself in check. He failed for a moment, managed it again, then showed a toothy grin as the doors opened.

The sound of a kick followed as the doors opened. Artorian watched as a mouthy, brown-furred butler bunny was punted from the chamber with dexterous force. "Enough of you and your backhanded compliments! Get out!"

Birch's irritation served as a momentary distraction before he realized the door did not immediately close. Instead, a very excited young child stood in the doorway, holding up a glowing panel made from mana with a very obvious number nine hastily written on it.

"Artorian!" The loud call made several voices in the room sputter, shuffle, and get to their feet. Birch slammed into the youth with a welcoming tackle, all sense of decorum kicked to the curb. "It's been so long!"

It was a graceful tackle, but that didn't mean it wasn't an abyss-blasted tackle! Birch's impact shattered his judge board and removed most of the air from his lungs. **Fhwoo**!

Mahogany got the excited tree off his old friend, helping them both up to their feet. The Sultan's voice was no different from how it had always been. "Birch! Behave! We're the oldest here and you turned into a sapling at the tiniest thing. That said, it's good to see you, Artorian."

They shook wrists, Artorian still sporting a wide smile. "It's good to see my old friends. I'm not going to bother asking how long it's been. Time moves oddly. I am, however, very interested in the commotion. So many people in Decorum's home! Did you get lonely?"

Mahogany eased his hand onto Merli's back, guiding him to a seating spot. "Incredibly so, old friend. We had to adjust for the changing of the times."

For a moment, Mahogany leaned down extra far, whispering a barely audible 'and Cores' as addendum to his changing of the times statement. "We've received some Wisp help lately, or have since back in Eternium, as we are recreating our race. 'Tree people' doesn't sound very elegant, but it's a work in progress. We have lots of information to work with from someone named Chandra, and when we get things to work, the people who reside here will become the first of that new race. Maybe Arboran? How does that sound?"

When mentioning Chandra's name, Mahogany made a show with a rather exaggerated wink. As if pretending not to know who 'Gaia' was.

Artorian played along and waggled his hand, sitting on the wide couch with his grove friends. "A work in progress. It sounds like you're incredibly busy in this ornate complex."

They both nodded, Birch taking over as Mahogany sagged in his seat and appeared to be nursing an old migraine. "When the trio left us, it was very dull and boring for a while. We are content with doing little, but doing nothing was out of the question. So now we take those who are unhappy with their humanization, and are working on offering them an alternative. They also help us with testing. Some results have been gruesome, but still they remain."

Artorian nodded, but conspiratorially leaned closer to Mahogany for a whispered chat. "Are you alright?"

Mahogany opened his eyes, flicking them around to check that nobody was listening in. "Keep this under wraps. I'm struggling just a bit, but there's no help I can be offered that will make my secret goal any easier. Do you remember… the last time we spoke concerning the fate of the Wood Elves who could not make it?"

Artorian made an uncertain waggle with his hand, not exactly crisp on the topic. Mahogany made a motion to Birch, who leaned in to elaborate. "We've been telling people, **cough** Overlords **cough**, that the Wood Elves who didn't make it through the original portal to the Soul Space… didn't make it. We may have been… less than truthful about that event."

Merli's eyebrows shot up so fast they could have injured the ceiling. Birch was pleased to see his friend understood the implications, the hunger for knowledge burning in the young child's eyes. "I'm sure you recall, but Wood Elves share memories in a very direct, visceral, and complete way. Well, in an act of desperation before we abandoned all our cultivation to enter this place, Mahogany and I… linked with the entire Wood Elf populace whose trees were too large for the portal, half each. While we've got no idea how souls work, or really what constitutes a person or personhood, we both have all the memories of just about everyone who didn't come through, experienced as if we lived those lives ourselves."

Artorian had a terrible gut feeling, but if after all this time Birch looked fine, and the worst Mahogany suffered were the occasional bouts of migraine, that wasn't too bad! "You're managing to keep being 'yourself'? I've an old friend called Bob who had something roughly similar happen and that didn't end too well."

Birch looked to Mahogany, who waved off the worry.

"Between us, that little 'Core' mention from earlier? It was a bit more meaningful than I let on. Birch and I have proper Seed Cores in the Silverwood. We were going to wait to tell anyone until Cal had a method together of making easy bodies we could maybe segment and separate these memories into. Unfortunately, after his sudden lapse of consciousness, we ended in a tough spot and made a deal with Occultatum. He's the 'secrets' guy, after all."

Artorian scratched his head. "What are we hoping to get out of this?"

Birch beamed. "The entire old grove, separated in individual bodies, with only their specific set of memories. Then hoping to the celestials above that our daft little plan works, because as it was said earlier, we've got no idea about the souls thing."

Their human friend scratched his head harder. "Why not tell Cal in the first place?"

Mahogany made an unpleasant noise. "Distrust on our part, mostly. Wood Elves have a very good sense of feeling out the 'trustworthiness' in someone. You were always a warm beacon, old friend. Cal felt… colder. More calculating. Like there was something hidden behind his back. We decided to keep it hush and play it by ear. The good news is, the best possible scenario means Rosewood and company are back in action. The possible bad news is that, try as hard as we might to salvage what we loved, this endeavor could fail. Still, we always wanted you to know. Now is simply the most convenient spot to tell you. I already have the feeling you'll be leaving us sooner than we'd like. We know how it goes with you, old friend. Let us speak of pleasantries for a while, I would love to catch up and let my current migraine ebb out."

Not fighting Mahogany on the matter, the trio caught up for a few hours longer before Mahogany's attention was demanded by Jean. Some whispers later, and the elder shot the butler an odd look. "Artorian. I'm told you're unaware of why humanization occurs? Or did I misunderstand, and that you don't know why it defaults to humans?"

Artorian finishing sipping mulberry wine, raising the glass with a noise to denote he'd heard the question. Swallowing and putting the cup down, he waved his hand to the back. "The latter option. I was expecting Elves. Some Dwarves. A Gnome or two."

His two friends gave him an odd look, but deduced that he truly didn't know. Birch motioned for Mahogany to explain it. The Sultan downed some water before getting started. "In short? Humans are *amazing*. Other races are great, but when you need a baseline for true quality, you go human. Some design flaws, yes. Though those are easily overlooked when it comes to the buffet of benefits."

Birch counted some out. "Consider the following. Opposable thumbs. Omnivorous. Extreme thinking capacity. Matchless endurance. Hyper scarring for fast, natural healing. Injuries that would fell most normal creatures are mere inconveniences for a human. Even losing a whole limb isn't a life-ending, or even a life-threatening event."

Mahogany nodded and picked up where Birch left off. "You can run, breathe, and keep your temperature controlled all at the same time. You can eat things that are outright poisonous and call it a spice. A human body adapts, and is masterfully well-suited for Essence cycling. Humans have an energy output to age ratio that is baffling compared to any other species, and my friend, that was the *short* version."

Artorian followed, but reiterated his actual question. "Alright, but why *humans*?"

Birch held up their drinking glasses, filled unevenly with liquid. "Because Dwarves, Elves, and Gnomes are all *biased* in their affinity types. They naturally lean toward certain compositions and combinations, and since we are aiming for utility and maximum compatibility, the only true option is human. Humans are balanced. Entirely unbiased in affinity options. Malleable to a fault. Endlessly flexible. Humans may not be the most specialized race, but they are by far the friendliest option when it comes to having a concept for a 'base' race. There's a reason everything is generally compared to a human. There is just no better standard."

Artorian nodded to show that was sufficient. "I see. Then… why the stink eye from the peanut gallery when I mentioned it?"

Mahogany waved that off. "Creatures come with pre-set affinity combinations more often than not. Generally, not ones they chose. Especially not if they came into being in this world. Some affinity combinations make becoming an Elf or a Dwarf considerably more favorable, but it is also, for a reason we honestly haven't pinned down, straight up more difficult to do. Human form may be the way to go, but it is not the way they all *want* to go. Some are a bit sour about that."

Artorian relented. "*Mmm.* Thank you for that, old friend. Perhaps it's time for something lighter."

Birch and Mahogany heartily agreed. They had much they wanted to show him.

CHAPTER FOURTEEN

After a lengthy explanation on the earlier topic, Mahogany, Birch, and Artorian spent days of their time catching up, caring little for all the large ears pointed in their direction to listen in. It wasn't every day another founder was in the hearth hall, directly conversing with the two most respected individuals in the entire Domus.

The story of Artorian being stuck as a noodle didn't sit well with the Wood Elves, but the backup body was a liberating boon. The news concerning the big reason that he was here was what ate whole additional days of their time.

Mahogany lay back on his private couch, his wooden fingers lacing. "So. Forky is the lynchpin, then? Given the statistics you're up against, and the final location being on the moon, no less… That's a big ask. Especially when you haven't seen exactly what you're up against."

Merli perked up. "Actually… you know what? You're right. I *don't* know what I'm up against, and I should… fix that."

A terrible stream of ideas appeared in Artorian's imagination, and as that became visible on his face, Mahogany and

Birch felt some unease. Birch reached out to his human friend, but the youth just toothily smiled at him before vanishing with a **vwop**.

A shrill screech of panic left Birch at seeing the sudden vacancy where the youth had sat. The younger of the ancient Wood Elves slowly craned his neck to the other, his motions tense. "Please lie to me and tell me he did not teleport to where I think he teleported?"

Mahogany slowly squeezed his eyes closed, his fingers lacing again as he recomposed himself. "Would you expect any less from our old Starlight Spirit? No matter the body, his bloom shines resplendent and strong. We can be fearful about the outcome, or the danger we assume he has yet again thrust himself into. Yet, we will never do anything in this world without courage. Let us plan to welcome our friend, when he returns."

Birch threw his hands up at the Sultan doing his best to appear wise, failing entirely to keep his own cool as his hands began to fidget. "He went to the moon! From the sound of it, that was the demon capital! Who even knows what it's like up there?"

Artorian crossed the arms of his young body, mostly in confused disbelief.

The current sight his eyes were trying to convince him was real… in truth, it was more than just a little difficult to accept. He had been to Ziggurat during the days of necromancer occupation, when said occupation was under the heavy influence of demonic corruption. Or whatever negative, terrible connotation he'd think of to assign to those memories and that style of management.

He'd thought to himself, "I'll pop by the moon! Zip my way through hordes of vile Beasts and clustered monstrosities.

Expecting the kind of revulsion saved only for the most extreme of horrors! Unnatural shapes shall assail me, and sights that would bend the mind and shriek through nightmares shall be plentiful. Most would collapse into a blubbering pile of goopy screams just from arrival where I will be loitering."

Instead he stood on a gray street of packed ash. With gray buildings of just as dull, bland, uninteresting ash bricks. Tall ones, with multiple open windows. These were bordered by gray walking paths, harboring demons in gray clothing, carrying gray briefcases. They stood under gray pole-provided lighting coming from above while a gray wave of ash consistently flowed around the vicinity. The moon was akin to a tiny desert that freely let the winds carry its dunes from one place to the next, except that all of its dunes were the same mottled, uninteresting, life-draining gray.

Artorian saw imps with brooms brushing the flat streets, the light of life gone from their eyes as they tended to their tasks with rote disinterest. He saw dretches and wretches with pull-carts waiting in neat lines for larger demons to come by on a clockwork schedule. So they could board and be carried over to… wherever it was they were going. Looking up, the skyscape appeared no different. Gray ash clouds hung overhead, and even just being here for a few seconds made Artorian sick of the color.

Or lack thereof. Was gray a color? He wasn't sure, but he was very sure that staying here for too long would drain the soul right out of him.

Strangest of all: not a single demon, no matter the size or how threatening it appeared, paid him a lick of attention. Each and every one was downtrodden, defeated, drained, exhausted, and lumbering along to… whatever task they seemed set on.

Artorian took a few steps to get out of the street. Some immense, long demon traipsed by to stop at a designated pole. Its large mouth opened wide, and scores of warriors whose muscles had wasted away to nothing from disuse left via the tongue. Once the beast was empty, the waiting line picked up their things and walked right on in. Again, without paying the youth a hint of attention. The demons looked like their minds were elsewhere, and anything not on their to-do list was just not worth the attention.

Artorian looked around some more, noting that both the building and street layout were symmetrical and identical to every other. Every building was exactly the same. Every street had the same angles and curves. Each lane he could stare down continued until the horizon made it vanish over the bend. There was no variation. No spice. No entertainment. No landmarks. Nothing that stood out. Merely a uniform landscape of apathy-gray.

Taking to the sky for a quick flight, purely in the hopes of finding something non-gray, he found only more of the same. Then more of the same, and more of the same still. Quick conclusion, or perhaps hope, was what he was looking for perhaps did not exist on the surface. Was this moon identical to the Cal one? That one had interiors. He would need to put in the effort to slipspace for such a precise jump, but it beat being here. He didn't want to stay in a place that mentally crushed even abyssal entities.

A considerably smoother transfer later that left Artorian feeling painfully tired, he rubbed at the back of his legs. Rather than residing on the outside of the moon, he was now within. Currently, that was somewhere inside of a long hallway with pale, dead lighting. He knew better than to talk out loud, but this place was a carbon copy of the pathway Minya had walked him down. It even had a ton of black Cores on the wall. One moment. Black?

He touched one, and swiftly pulled his finger away as he heard the wailing screams contained within. Were these demons? All of them? Could he just… get rid of them now in one fell swoop? That would be optimal. Not that he felt like he had a big arsenal in his pocket at the moment.

In system terminology, he was pathetic based on his attributes. Artorian held his shoulder and tapped his chin. Did that truly still matter in his test body? He had access to what felt like most of his cultivation progress. Whether that was from Eternium napping, Cal being unconscious, or some behind the scenes Dev help, he didn't know. Perhaps a combination of the three? He'd never been told of the changes to this young body, but without the cultivation boosts he likely wouldn't even be upright.

Well, if he was going to try to janitor-slide stored demons out of Eternia, he should find the biggest, baddest, meanest Core and go give it straight-up *punt* with Mana! He channeled his **Law** through his fingers just to see if he could, and delighted in gorgeous glowing-pink success. Squeezing his tiny fist shut with a big smirk, he tried to keep quiet while stealthing his way through the inner-moon facility.

He was unable to gauge his Mana reserves. So while he wanted to try to put his S.E.P. field on full blast, perhaps better to save it for moments of uncertainty. That and many of his other toys—save for his Presence; he wore that like a favorite sweater. It provided health, cleanliness, ease of breathing, the works. The real thing this time. Not the chopped and squeezed versions Eternium made him use. He considered extending his Presence to include the Cores, but that would give him away. He wasn't sure how, but he had the gut feeling it would.

Trust the gut.

Four hours of wandering turned into a full day, before Artorian found a more interesting place to be. As if being inside the moon wasn't a feat by itself. On his trek, he'd encountered a few long white coat-wearing demons. Rather than engage them, he decided that sticking to the ceiling to let the unknowing few pass on by was the better decision. The hallways that piqued his interest turned at a sharp angle, delving to the moon's depths rather than continuing along a wall of blackened Cores.

There were… so many of these things. A war of attrition would lead only to failure, because it was now clear that Barry prepared backups. Speaking of the miscreant, a lime green glow emanating from a wide-open chamber near the center of the moon was particularly attention-catching.

Artorian had needed to hide away and nap in an alcove before sneaking his way in. Unlike his proper game body, this one tired swiftly. Or swiftly in comparison, at least. While hidden away in a nook and cranny, he'd overheard plenty of discussions in scree-scree that pertained to progress reports. That and the endless complaints. Connectivity results were poor. Iridium growth rates were too slow, as always. Artorian silently enjoyed the complaints of the long-coated ones. The worse it went for them, all the better for him.

A particular nugget of interest that caught his eye during one such peek was that these demons had, for some reason, chosen ye old High Elf looks. From before the Moonfall out in the real world. They had chosen ears longer than their forearms, and looked incredibly silly.

He wanted to rush forward when their backs were turned, but collected himself with a nugget of wisdom. In handling their affairs, people appeared to often fail shortly before they succeeded. If one remained as careful at the end of the journey as they did in the beginning, then there would be no failure.

Artorian would bide his time, waiting for the sounds to quiet and the longcoats to leave. When they did, he squeezed from his hiding place. Finally, he was properly able to see the source of the lime green glow. Sort of. He crossed his arms, trying to understand what he was looking at

He was in an oversized oval room, with a big domed ceiling and a very flat floor. There were several exits from this room, but only two or three seemed to lead back to the walkway of Cores he'd come in from. That was a bad assumption. The other paths likely led to walkways of Cores that he hadn't been connected to? The moon was a big place. He'd have to check, should he find the time.

In the center of the room was a large pedestal, with a similar-looking box upon it. It was the same kind of box Bob's Core had been kept in. Save that it had far more elaborate seals,

Runes, and spellscript slathered across the entire object—the majority of which looked quite busted.

At the top, part of a fractured green Core was visible. The cracks had been filled in with liquid Iridium, that was easy to deduce. From the container rather than the fractured Core, awkward lines of solid Iridium spiked outwards, connecting to the walls in anything but straight lines.

Initially, Artorian thought they went through the wall, but that was incorrect. Each of the major, solid metal tendrils connected to a large-sized Core that appeared to have been forcibly shoved into place. All but one was swirling with a putrid darkness. He then noticed they were all labeled, and the entry beneath underneath the empty one read 'Pencil.' *Hmmm.* There was a small notice beneath the label. Squinting, he gave it a read.

Location: Midgard.
General Problem: Too many people.
Solution: Extermination or Exploitation.
Overseer: Pencil.
Status: Contact lost, region lost.

Interesting! Artorian shifted over to the notice underneath the next metal tendril over, though he figured they were out of order. That was fine—he would go through a few, since he had the opportunity to.

Location: Alfheim.
General Problem: Too bright.
Solution: Hats.
Overseer: Soni.
Status: Significant losses in might, replenish immediately.

Location: Svartalfheim.
General Problem: Too many valuables.
Solution: Gather it all anyway, extreme taxation.

Overseer: Robar-Baron.
Status: Sheriff of have-nottingham.

Location: Vanaheim.
General Problem: It's empty.
Solution: None? There's nothing here, just grazing space.
Overseer: Mu.
Status: Being a Hel-cow, grazing to conquer the grass.
Note: Secret cow level.

Location: Jotunheim.
General Problem: Too big, too cold, too dinosaur.
Solution: Mercury Ants. Lots and lots of ants.
Overseer: Nivila.
Status: We have giant crabs.

Location: Niflheim.
General Problem: Fungus and Phosgen.
Solution: Burn it all down.
Overseer: Minos.
Status: Do not eat the glowing mushrooms. Or inhale. Anything.

Location: Muspelheim.
General Problem: Too hot, advanced Goblin empire, C'towls and more.
Solution: Full offensive on the natives.
Overseer: Black Hanekawa.
Status: Stalemate, send more troops. Troops that can't get addicted to spice. The spice must not flow. Did these troops learn nothing from Niflheim?

Location: Asgard.
General Problem: Odin.
Solution: Undermine local society. Steal, scam, do not become an obvious target.
Overseer: Guttersnipe Caro.
Status: War of attrition.

Location: Hel.
General Problem: Invisible Dark Elf Bone Geese.
Solution: Pray to Barry we find one.
Overseer: Corvid.
Status: Transparency needed.

Location: Moon.
General Problem: Storage.
Solution: Re-education.
Overseer: Urcan.
Status: Flawless operation.

Artorian read them all, out of sheer curiosity and interest. His attention was wrenched away when the faint lime green light from the Core's sudden activity flickered. Small green lines crawled up the Iridium metal, sinking into other Cores, which then sent their own green lines to… what he guessed were underlings. So did that make these Cores the realm overseers?

Interesting to get such insider information, but now it was time to do something. When it came to slapping someone so hard that their child felt it, there was really only one option. He kicked off into a hover and changed the direction of his personal gravity. The room turned upside down, though to him it felt like he remained in place as the scenery around him made a slow turn.

Artorian pondered a moment how best to smash or destroy the lime green Core, while nobody knew he was here. That would change the moment he did just about anything to make his presence known. He felt a hint of fear on the back of his neck, but assuaged himself with more words of wisdom. 'A man with outward courage dares to die. A man with inner courage dares to live.' Someone famous had said that, he was sure.

A wonderful idea sprung to mind as he observed the green Core. One crafted from childish amusement, and devious old man foxiness. Why didn't people accuse him of fighting dirty? He had such a tendency to. Lunging forwards, he prepared his foot to strike. Testing the movement down towards the Core a few times before he felt like he'd found a good angle. Gathering energy for a sympathy-effect strike, Artorian coated his foot with pink **Love-**tier Mana before snapping his leg forward in an arc.

Kicking an unexpecting Barry right in the orbs!

CHAPTER FIFTEEN

All across the moon, alarms went off. They began with very weak, pathetically warbled klaxons that sounded as if they too had just been punted in the sensitives. Unfortunately, for all the force he'd put into the kick, Artorian's output was limited by his strength attribute. That blasted, worthless five. No amount of cheatery was going to get around that, as all his personal Mana self-invested into interconnectivity. He just didn't hit hard enough with the base strike.

Damaged pride aside, the green Core looked unfazed. Crackers. If only he had something more solid on hand. A Nixie Tube lit up above his head. *Didn't* he, though? He'd neglected it for too long in his opinion, but he should be able to pull it out here. Right?

Concentrating on his Soul Space—and he did mean *his* Soul Space—his hand reached into his own chest as if it were ethereal, pulling a twelve-by-twelve Liminal energy pillow free. It was no Brianna's dagger, but a Soul Item was a Soul Item! Plus, his item was *dense*. Similar to the Ten Ton Tonfas, his Soul Item did not weigh much in his hand. Even if the impact it could bring to bear was far more potent that initial appearance might suggest.

If he had something akin to a superweapon, truly, this must be it.

As he gave the pillow a few swings for practice, he heard the screeching of activity barrel down the multiple hallways. The local demons had recovered from their pride being punted, and given all the green energy being shot through the solid Iridium, Barry felt equally disgruntled. *Good.*

Artorian spun his pillow so fast that it whistled loud from the sheer velocity gained. He had to use Mana to reinforce himself and sustain the speed, but that was fine. As if he had other uses for his Mana lately. Just spend it all and do a tribulation! He decided he should examine his own character after this, as that was a terrible idea. But character was simply habit long continued, and he definitely had a habit of doing things oddly.

The spin of the pillow, which accounted for several tons' worth of weight in density, struck the lime green Core with a soundwave-creating **baf**! A gentle, dull noise considering the kind of oomph-power that followed it.

The klaxon cut out and died with a gasped sputter. Perhaps those noises were live demons, rather than some stationary information system? Similar to the musically aligned one on the throne.

Sounds of creatures falling and moaning in pain occurred directly after an incredibly heavy object had smashed with similarly incredible speed into Barry's Core. An audible longcoat voice pathetically peeped out down the hall, but the words in scree-scree just translated to a very questioning and drawn out, "*Why~y~y?*"

Artorian noted after a moment of close orb-spection that even this strike hadn't done toast. The Core was unharmed, and again only pride damage had been incurred. Even with his Soul Item, victory was out of grasp? Crackers!

He sighed, thinking to try again just one more time as he childishly squeaked out his reply to the whinging being down the hall. Who was just barely close enough to see a small child with a pillow in hand. "Life is a series of natural and spontaneous changes. Don't resist them, that only creates sorrow. Let reality be reality."

In this case, reality was a several-ton-dense smack to the Cores. **Baf**!

Cries of recurring pain erupted from the halls, culminating in whimpered groans that petered out to squeal equivalents. Klaxons that had attempted to start back up sputtered, falling to silent failure for a third time in a row. The longcoat was slapping the ground between cries, tears of agony rolling down his face while gasping for breath.

When it looked like it was just barely able to get up, the longcoat of the inner-moon sector heard something truly unpleasant. The youth yelled it out. In scree-scree no less, but with an awful bracketed accent. "[All-Might Pillow Smash]!"

Alpha-state Pylons flickered and flared to life. Bracket-based spells may have been phased out, but the 'no recycling' rules meant they were steady and present should the need arise for them to flare up again. Such a need arose now as they interlinked with currently active Pylons to see to their ordained tasks, as pink-laced power flung between them. The infused high tier Mana increased both their potency and operating speed, as *finally*, the impact to the green Core did something other than pride damage.

Several of the solid Iridium connections to darkened Cores shattered. The main chamber holding Barry violently shook, large cracks carving deep through the ovoid chamber. The impact's range was immense. From that single smash, the entire planetoid rocked with severe quakes that leveled several moon-city blocks. Turned out that all those similar-looking structures were not so equal in construction after all. Some went down like sandcastles suddenly introduced to some water.

Any demon not already on the floor from indescribable damage to parts they might not even have tumbled to the ground as well. The inescapable moonquake combined with pride damage was just too much.

Artorian **tsk'd** in response as he surveyed the damage done to the Core: None at all, save for some shattered Iridium connections. The system was protecting Barry, meaning he was completely dependent on coming here in his game-body form. Which had the chance to reach statistics that could actually get the job done. What were the S-ranker statistics boosts again, five thousand something?

Ugh. He had his work cut out for him. As soon as he had the stamina, that noodle-crown was going to break from its confines. He had specializations to level. Places to be. Numbers to gain. Then, he would do this again. Preferably with far more *rock-shattering* success.

Artorian wanted to strike more, but the telltale noises of teleportation, gates, and other movement methods audibly popped in nearby. His Soul Item returned from where he'd pulled it since he knew he was out of time. He had company. Company he had no way of handling in his current state. Curse Eternium and his need for **Order**. He could have ended it right here and now if it wasn't for all these infernal rules. Or at least, he thought he could have. He'd never actually shattered a Core before. He only knew how to control one. Wait! What a fool he was! He should just take the Core and—

"Stop right there, criminal scum!"

Crackers! He was caught! Well, that meant it was time to go. Blast.

Artorian glared at the pride-injured green Core, his words spoken in the old-world language he knew only Barry would understand. If the Core could even hear him at all. Artorian wanted to do this with some panache. Who was the one with the biggest grumble toward Barry anyway? Probably Tatum. Ah, but Barry didn't know of any 'Tatum,' did he? This was Mountaindale history, so Tatum's old name would be far more applicable. "*The Master* sends his regards."

Vwop.

Artorian then messily teleported out, lacking the Mana to do a proper slipspace. How costly had that smash attack been? Likely most of his stored pool if he didn't have the juice left for a smooth exit. Still, an exit was made nonetheless, and likely seconds before savants flooded all over that room in search of him.

Artorian was right, even if he didn't see it. The inside of the moon crawled with demonic activity. Their sanctuary that had been considered impossible to breach, assail, or even reach, had been outright invaded. Some *child* had made it in, only to embarrassingly beat them silly with injuries they would tell nobody of. Not ever. Insult could be stemmed from injury, but the attacks they'd suffered had combined those aspects seamlessly. This event would never be spoken of. It would live solely in their memories as the most heinous insult ever received.

Yet, some of the hordes felt painful similarities. A few that had been pulled back out of the abyss had suffered strikes like this before. Vengeance became a swift and hot-button topic when this news spread. An old enemy had made itself known once again, and the demon horde could not wait for that sweet, sweet vendetta to come to pass.

Artorian's test-body received two unpleasant notices, and hoped to the celestial plane these didn't extend to his game body. Though he seriously doubted he was so lucky.

Notice!
Unique reputation event threshold exceeded! The limit of minus five thousand points has been overcome via extreme user action.
Reputation with all Demons: -6,000
New reputation rank: Vendetta
Demons have begun a prolonged bitter quarrel and campaign against you. You will appear on all their minimaps regardless of your position, so long as you reside in the same realm.

Notice!

Unique reputation event threshold exceeded! The limit of minus six thousand points has been overcome via extreme user action.
Reputation with all Demons: -7,000
New reputation rank: Lineage Hunter
Demons have escalated their campaign against you and your kin, allies, and anyone you consider family. You will now appear on all their minimaps, regardless of your position or realm. No effort is too great for this faction to hunt down you and yours.

The small boy pressed his hands to his mouth, unaware that Mahogany and Birch had huddled around him, pelting him with questions. When he became aware of his friends, he made the notices visible so he could share the reason for his shock. That shut them up handily, though he needed to go sit down on the couch to hold his head. "Welp. That… did not work. On the plus side, I have a fantastic idea of what I'm dealing with."

Birch sat next to him, his expression guarded. "Starlight Spirit. If that is the case, then why does your expression indicate that you are sad? To be frank, Mahogany and I are glad you returned at all."

Mahogany laid his heavy hand on his fellow spirit's shoulder, squeezing Birch by the bone while shaking his head. "Because now he cannot stay. According to that notice, all his enemies know where he is now. All the time, if they so much as care to look, and I can't see a reason they would not. Minus seven thousand? I've never seen a reputation rank drop so low. I thought Blood Feud was the limit. I wonder what they're currently thinking."

Birch had a thought, his mouth curling upward on only the left side. He had an idea of how to lift the mood. "About our Starlight Spirit? Easy, they're all holding their valuables and are wheezing: *The audacity*."

Given Artorian had not told his candle-loving friend exactly what he'd done with a several-ton pillow, he bent forwards and broke down laughing. "Ha! Isn't that the truth. Ahh… I only just got this out, and I went and messed it up. Didn't even get anything accomplished save for painting a target on my back. I need somewhere truly safe to store this body now. The Domus won't cut it."

"What luxury you have to just be able to shelve your form. That…" Mahogany was amused at Birch's mention, but his own words appeared to give him some ideas. His fingers slid to his chin, sight unfocusing. "That… that may not be such a bad idea."

When Mahogany looked back to Artorian, his human friend's mouth fell open before forming a giant expression of elation. Artorian's arms shoved in the air with his hand open when he put two and two together. "Mahogany! You genius! Shelve it! I have an archive here! Give me a big hug, you two. I'm fuffing out right away before *they* get their bearings. I dislike that I will not be able to come back to see you conveniently."

Birch and Mahogany kneeled down and embraced him with a tight squeeze. As they did, another spark of brilliance struck Birch, who slipped in a sudden idea. "Unless you have a method of travel or communication that has no cost. Or a cost reduced to zero? That would be the dream."

Artorian gently slapped Birch's back as a gesture of appreciation for his insight and support. "I'll be out on the lookout for it. I think I'm low on Mana, so I'm going to need to use the crudest teleportation method to get out of here. Catch you both when I can, my friends. Stay alive."

With a solid nod from them both, Artorian loudly went **fuff**. A plethora of feathers exploded from the position he'd occupied, and Birch spat one out as his mouth had been open. Coughing as the down very slowly dissipated, it ended with the Wood Elf duo breaking out in weak laughter. "'Crude,' he says! Ah… how far he's come. I can't help but remember the old man who thought Aura was just a storage space. Now look at him."

Mahogany nodded in agreement, helping Birch up to his feet. "The living starlight will be fine. Let us ensure the Domus fares just as brightly. We will properly inform the people here of what has transpired, rather than letting them whisper what their tall ears have sneakily overheard. I'm not going to pretend I didn't notice many of them are playing curious spies."

Birch raised a brow, but then noticed just how many unmoving, hidden figures were present in the room. "Yes. Very wise. I will call for the gathering."

CHAPTER SIXTEEN

Artorian felt drained when he hit the deck. His vision was hazy, insides tingling unpleasantly. He felt smooth wood under his fingers, but chose not to move for a bit when his senses acted like they were swimming. He was safe. He was fine. He'd left on time.

When the world stopped spinning, he found himself in the Eternium version of his archives. His tiny hidey-hole in the sun. Had he been in this version before, or had he solely been to Cal's version?

He grumbled, pushing himself up with incredible effort. Mana wasn't helping him anymore, and it was just those fives in his attributes that he had to work with. Once on his feet, his head swam without warning once more, sending him back down to the floor as he lost track of where he was for a moment. Wasn't being a Core supposed to help with remembering? Oh… he was already feeling the separation difficulties, and needed to sleep to turn that around.

Abyss, that started fast.

Once on his feet again, he stumbled to a bed. Falling face first into it, a tiny groan elicited from his throat as that had taken all of his stamina. It took him a full ten minutes to properly situate himself on the bed, and gosh those covers were heavy. His arms strained to pull them up. They weren't, and he knew that. It was all just so difficult, and he was so, so tired. This body had no endurance to speak of. He needed a nap. He needed a nap badly.

Merli fell unconscious seconds after thinking of it, the body resting while Artorian's mind sank toward the bonfire space. A door to Yvessa's Forum was present, and he reached a hand out to connect the spaces. Their personal mental Forums merged as normal, allowing the old Artorian to run a hand down his long beard for sheer comfort right as he entered. With his physical burdens lifting, his butt sat down on the marble bench. He exhaled long, leaning his side against one of the wide pillars.

Yvessa was present in her humanized form, but she seemed busy with some screens. He didn't feel like talking just yet, the drain from acting as Merli still catching up to him. He thought he was recovering on entry, but no. He was going to get even more tired before he got better. Would it be safe to nap here? He wondered, but laid sideways on the marble bench. It was hard, and unpleasant to stay on. If only he had… oh. Right. What was he doing?

His Soul Item manifested on the marble bench across from him so he could let it fall and flop. Trudging over afterward, he rolled into the oversized beast of a pillow. It didn't matter how he lay on this thing. He was always comfortable. Celestials, this pillow was so soft. He wondered for a moment where he would go if he slept here. Fully, rather than just bodily. Normally he would go to his Seed Core, but in this case that option was locked off.

Dumb gazebo and its dumb rules.

Yvessa looked over from her work in time to see the mental construct of her charge disappear from his pillow. She dropped her panel, though it gently bumped against the ground only to hover back to the place where it had been held prior. She pressed her hands to the person-shaped divot in the pillow, but he wasn't there; his mental presence gone entirely.

Yvessa was about to panic, but… why wasn't the Forum space splitting up like it tended to? The space they shared acted as if he was still present, but Yvessa was entirely unable to tell where he was. This was already a mental-only space, where could he have gone? Her worry turned to grumbles, suddenly thinking that this was another one of his tricks. "You cheeky brat! What did you do this time to steal yourself away from under my nose?"

Artorian had done no such thing. Not this time. He was faintly aware of hovering over an endless lake. His mind was wavering between consciousness and sleep. Stealing only glances of the calm, serene scene. A latent worry blinked on the surface of his thoughts, but it soothed in response to the single chime of a kalimba's plink.

With that small note of sound, Artorian drifted off to proper, serene sleep. A different caretaker watched over him as the kalimba notes began their melody.

In Eternia, the situation was anything but serene. Especially for all those that Artorian had 'insulted.' The disappearance of Artorian's dot from the world map was the most infuriating thing the abyssal forces experienced since their embarrassing recovery.

All the savant overseers operating in the Eternia realms had been summoned with haste, and all of them had been provided their own personal bag of ice. They gathered in one of the unimpressive—but still standing—buildings on the moon. The space was a boardroom by design, but an office space in function. For this emergency meeting, the savants had taken the forms of High Elves, their ears as long as their egos.

At the head of the table, a few imps were installing a contraption of mushed-together Cores. When they finally got power to the fritzing poorly-cobbled object that arced with lightning strong enough to fry one of the imps on the spot, a lime-green outline of Barry appeared.

His military-dressed High Elf form flickered above the Cores as a light projection.

Barry's tone was as amused as could be expected. Cold and obviously offended, his commanding tone lingered with irritation. He wanted answers just as badly as many of the savants who had been on the receiving end of 'the event,' who also did not know what had been going on. "*What* happened?"

A motion was made to the empty seat where Pencil should have been. The clear absence was lost on none present. Given that gaping hole in their ranks, gazes shifted to the next two savants who were lowest in the hierarchy. Nobody with a high rank wanted to stick their head out, not here.

Soni and Robar gritted their teeth and shared a glance, rising from their respective seats. That meant *they* were on the chopping block, as they shared social rank within the group of savants. Soni hopped up on the table first, transforming his form into that of a tiny brown bat.

Cobalt jewelry and other gaudy additions self-embroidered on his full-body black velvet cape by the time his tiny feet struck the table. He held out his wings to balance his landing before folding them back around himself like an additional coat. Jingling as he walked, a brush the size of him manifested to hang freely across his back. After all, it was never a bad time for the brushy-brushy. Soni waddled into position near the middle of the long table, where he was joined shortly after by Robar.

Robar didn't want to be one-upped on flair, flicking his wrist to create a bridge of playing cards. They connected his seat to the table so he could casually walk across it after morphing into a leather-armor-clad squirrel. He'd chosen his attire for its bonuses. It increased his stealth because the material was made out of hide. The robber Baron adjusted his spade and heart cufflinks on the outfit during his saunter, tugging at his sleeves to prevent his fur from sticking out.

He flipped an oversized game chip into the air as he stepped off his card bridge. His cards automatically shrank down in response, shuffling into his back pocket with the skilled choreography of a swim team. When the last card vanished, he tipped his hat at the projection in deferential greeting. The specific tilt allowed the chip to fall right down and stick into the brim of his hat like a feather. He smirked as he looked to Soni.

Robar couldn't resist making the quip, "Let me guess, you are the night?"

Some snickering went around the table until the duo stood together at the imaginary line. They took identical standing positions and performed the appropriate bow of status, regardless of what their personal preferred greetings may have been. It was important to uphold established social rules. Especially here.

The two savants then played a quick game of rock paper scissors to determine who would speak first. Soni got the short end of the stick, hanging his head as he should have known better than to gamble against a professed gambler.

Soni stepped up to the plate, squeaking out a surprisingly smooth speech cadence. A significant portion of his powerset was sonic-based, so a comfortable speaking voice was important to him. "Your gloriousness. As is known, the issues began when Core-breaching to the outside failed. We lost several A-class demons, including our only S-class, Yasura. With the invasion entirely rebuked, it appears the light realmers have copied our initial strategy. At least one light realm creature is now present within Eternia, thwarting our well-laid plans."

Soni rubbed his tiny paws over one another. "Now that more information has been gathered, we have properly determined that Midgard has fallen, and we have lost Pencil entirely. He is no longer present in our moon Cores. Additionally, a majority of my Alfheim forces suffered total defeat when they were lent out. As we know, the entirety of the Midgard forces were… lost. Not even a pyrrhic victory was attained, though the paper-pushers have estimated through arduous calculation that the lack of assault on Alfheim or Svartalfheim indicates our opponents suffered injury."

He swallowed loud, uncomfortable with so many eyes on

him. "Information from Midgard indicates a surge of new activity, but none that appears to lead toward an assault on other realms. The locals are mounting a defense of some kind, likely against our eventual return."

Soni's discomfort didn't get any better. "We must take that realm in order to have gazebo access, so we can commence our second Core-breaching strategy. We sadly lack the needed information on what went wrong outside, as we are unable to summon or call back any of the demons lost on that mission. We do not know why. Eternia seems to simply not be letting us recall or call in any new forces. Which is *not* an eventuality we'd planned for. After so many instances of concurrent success, this recent string of failures has neither reason, nor excuse."

Robar didn't seem like he was going to take over, causing Soni to sigh and continue. "With that stated, due to the issues that have cropped up in the individual Eternia realms, we currently also do not have convenient means to tackle this issue. The Abyss forces will need time to reconfigure so we may reclaim what has been lost. It is expected this will take several months, unless it is the board's desire to gang up on a specific realm first."

Noisy gurgling accompanied dissatisfied sneers and irritated glances from the other members in attendance. These savants had their own issues, and this just added to the pile.

Soni decided this was a great time to change topics. "Which brings us to the news we're gathered for. An outside influence snuck by every last one of our defenses, completely unnoticed. They managed to assault the moon's most unhallowed and blasphemous location directly. We all… *felt* the impacts. It is unknown how a creature that weak could have infiltrated so deep. As while many demons were harmed—particularly where morale is concerned—not a single one perished, or incurred more than minor lingering injuries.

Expectant looks forced Soni to continue. His voice sounded like a touch snippy, but he was clearly trying to keep his tone respectful. "Based on gathered evidence, the infiltrator appears to have been a child holding a pillow. A child that could vanish without a trace when we finally arrived on location, but before we could do anything about it. We have thus convened to speak of what to do about this, and common assent is to no longer allow the moon to remain as unguarded as it is."

The lime green projection snarled. "Where is the child now?"

Soni stumbled over his speech, but the other savant finally tapped him out. The squirrel took over from the bat, his drawl that of a smooth-talking gambler. "Your gloriousness. Several things occurred after the child vanished. For one, as soon as Rhrkltrix, Trix for short, discovered that this enemy in particular showed up on the map, the child was on the move from a location in Midgard we were unable to pin down. Our maps found him in the middle of jungle-y Midgard wilderness, but he left too quickly for us to be able to put a pin down. Currently, the information on the topic is polarizing; as according to any map any demon or anyone with the ability to check… The child appears to be…"

The squirrel's discomfort didn't escape Barry, who remained the textbook example of displeasure. "Spit it out, savant."

"On or *in* the sun, your gloriousness." The gambler Baron nudged an apologetic tip of the hat, as he truly had nothing better to provide. "We all believed the maps were broken, of course, yet the more we looked, and shared our information, the more that same result was listed. The enemy is in the sun. Much like our own base is on the moon. Except I have no idea how anything could survive the temperature there. We can't even get close through traditional means, even with it being celestine. If anything, that harmless-seeming light hurts us *more*."

The projection snarled aloud, its stomach audibly rumbling. That latter sound made each of the savants sweat. Barry drummed his fingers on his Elven upper bicep. "The child whispered to me before leaving. I can confirm it is outside influences coming to put a spoke in our wheels. That little nuisance told me *The Master* sends his regards. Though I cannot believe that workaholic would come up with an attack so… violating.

"Unfortunately for the infiltrator, the language that messenger used indicated it was alone, and working alone. So long as we can find the little nuisance and expunge it, Eternia should fall without problem. Tell Trix it's his job to find the kid. I don't care what deviousness or tricks he has to employ. Tricks are for kids, and this is one. Find it. Catch it. Kill it. It can't stay in the sun forever, if that's even where it really is. I suspect something similar to our illusions and map information obfuscation is at play."

Barry crossed his arms. "Back to your seats. Give me a realm-by-realm report on all problems. We need to change up how we're tackling this."

CHAPTER SEVENTEEN

Up was down. Or was down up? That didn't make a difference when Artorian awoke to the same endless watery blue plain he kind-of-not-really remembered passing out in. Well, not in, but not on either. Hovering as an orb was a sensation best described with, 'it feels funny.' Like his butt had fallen asleep from sitting too long, and getting up was something he *had* to do rather than wanted to do. Except that the awful sensation didn't go away. Plenty of wincing was involved as he decided to put in the effort.

"Where did I land myself this time?" Artorian tried to get his bearings as an orb. The place looked like the zone he'd been in when going up the B-ranks? The water reminded him of the canvas he'd written his experiences in. The one scribed on to crack into A-rank zero. This place was… where his **Law** could check his experiences and actions to tabulate what he knew about the concept. He didn't think he'd be back here, or with so little issues. Still, it wasn't like there was anything to do, so he'd have plenty of poking and prodding time.

Perhaps this mental space was plenty safe now that he was in the A-ranks? Or did it maybe serve a different purpose now?

"Well… hopefully I'm not stuck, but I've rolled around so many different puzzles with limitations of being. What's *another one* in the repertoire? I swear, all this wibbly wobbly, 'what am I' feels like some mad plan to prepare me for something even bigger."

He considered it again, wondering if he'd jinxed himself. "*Nah*, that's ludicrous, that could never happen. I just didn't get lucky this time around and didn't eat enough Wheaties this morning."

Artorian missed food when he thought about it. Snacks of all varieties. Buffets and glorious smorgasbords. He exhaled hard, then was surprised to find the water below him moved as if air broke against the surface. He didn't have a body; how had he just made water move? He wrote it off as something he didn't want to delve into right now.

This one, he was going to let go.

Time to look around properly. Below? That endless plain of water. The sides? Big ol' nothing. Above? *Oh, hello*. Was that *him*? When the orb moved to look up, Artorian saw a visual representation of his mind. Or mental effigy? Stars and lines that outlined the old man version of him, sitting meditation style, with nothing but peace and delicate patience to enjoy the silence. He instinctively knew that mind was him, then wondered why it seemed like there was room for more than *just* him up there.

Was this perhaps a space to move… between minds? Was that why it was so easy to lose oneself here? What was he then, a soul? How abstract and intangible a concept that still remained. On further consideration, he recalled the event of Ember Incarnating. Something had turned inside out, and a new person had come from within. Was this perhaps the place where such a form was created? The thing that was transferred to the outside? He had no true name for this place other than 'the lake space' that he could currently recall, but a word for it was on the tip of his tongue.

It escaped him. How bothersome. He chose to let that go as well. Not everything needed a name. Not everything needed to be quantified and cut into tiny little, easily digestible cubes. For now, this would remain one such place. A concept just barely out of his grasp. Still, might as well assign some values for convenience. Currently, let's say he was in his Soul form. The unformed thing that might one day replace his Mage body. His actual Mage body. Not the simulacrum that Cal or Eternium let him tromp around with.

The stellar form above him was his mind. Or perhaps, the sum of his experiences? The room for other forms so clearly being available made him think this was somewhere he would be returning to if experiences other than his own needed to be perused. Perhaps lived? He didn't know, and was speculating. For now he would go to the visual image of himself, and see where he ended up.

The minor connection between soul and mind connected when he reached for it. Artorian's eyes opened in the Forum space that connected Yvessa and him. He heard something break in the distance, a panel abandoned and tossed to the ground while a lady in the shape of his caretaker sprinted over to him. Why so worried? He was just napping on his pillow. No big deal.

A thought struck him, and he looked up again. This time considering what he'd seen in the prior space, he expected stellar formations. A soft smile graced his face as Merli's shape became visible in the sky, resting in a bed while cocooned with snug blankets. Nearby, the shape of the baby Long form connected star by star as well. The ethereal trapping of a crown formed around the dragon to show where he currently hid.

Now that was far easier to understand! Here, where he was now, was the mind! Up were the bodies. Down was… well, soul must have been fairly accurate of a description since he felt like he came from the 'down' direction. He thought of floors in a house that he needed to ascend before waking up in a body.

It hadn't been like this before. Was he reforming his half of the bonfire space based entirely on his own perception and understanding? That seemed… extremely likely. Yvessa shouted at him before she had him by the front of his robes, frantically checking him up and down. "Old man! Tell me you're not hurt!"

His attempt to be suave failed spectacularly. "Easy! Easy, my dear. I'm swell and fine. Not a crooked hair on my head."

She fussed at him like a hen. "Boy, you are bald! You don't have one hair on your head. How was that supposed to help?"

Artorian knew the drill, and just relaxed as she inspected his arms and legs one at a time. Not finding an issue while his expression remained flat-faced. It was somewhat invasive, but Artorian had long gotten used to worried people being far too zealous in checking on his health. He might as well just let them search to their heart's desire until they were sure, and the worry and curiosity sated. It wasn't like he minded. Checkups were good, and who knew when someone else would find something?

Yvessa leered, but swallowed him up in a big hug. "You brat! I was so worried when you just vanished like that. You're alright from what I can tell, but don't scare me like that!"

Artorian frowned. "I... *vanished*? It didn't feel like I went anywh— *oooooh*. That makes so much sense now. I went to the basement!"

He didn't need to feel her gaze stabbing him with questions to know that giving her some answers was just a good idea. "I... hmm. So, first off, I'm okay. Nothing is wrong. In my flailing, I've found some additional information on places I didn't really understand too well. The topic concerns cultivation, and its peculiar advancements. I may have just found where Incarnates make their bodies before going through the process. I'm not sure? I would have to talk to our resident S-rankers."

He stuck a finger into the sky to point, but Yvessa took it to mean he was about to make a point. She did not look up. "Speaking of, are you Wisping it up forever, or are you going back to being a cultivator at any point?"

Yvessa shrugged, playing along for now. "Both, if possible. I wouldn't mind returning to the cultivator lifestyle, so long as it doesn't come with the extra requirements. I didn't mind my life in the Choir, but that institution has fallen. I honestly hadn't given it any thought. From waking up to now, my life has been a series of hills that I have needed to speedily climb across, without a moment free to look over my shoulder. If it hadn't been for all the explanations and memory gifts, I think I would be shivering in a corner somewhere. This entire way of living is… intimidating. Whatever the method is for getting everyone else out is so they can live in Cal for a while… I hope that this side of the mirror is not one they have to see."

That was a more involved response than Artorian had been expecting. "It… sounds like there might be more to this than I initially thought. My question… Actually, never mind what my question was. This is heavier on you than anticipated. Forgot about me for a while. What about you? How are you?"

They moved to sit next to one another on Artorian's oversized pillow, as if having a girl-to-girl gossip moment. Yvessa held her knees, but then flopped back, allowing the pillow to mold around her back as her human weight indented it. The fluff was so abyss-blasted cozy.

Yvessa spoke slowly. "I'm… I want to say I'm overworked, but I don't get tired like I used to. Not anymore. The whole world is different, every bit of it works differently. I still sleep, but every time I wake up, I need to remind myself that I am not on the planet I grew up on. I am in a dungeon Core. Specifically, in the Soul Space of a dungeon Core. Where the Soul Item of that Core, Cal, happens to be a world. Or an attempt at one."

She kneaded her head, trying to put things in a neat order so explaining wouldn't cause her to flub over her own words. This was such a rough experience to translate into speech. "In Cal's world, there are other Cores who were rescued from the calamity that hit ours. Moonfall. One such Core is Eternium, who also happens to be able to keep a world in their own Soul Space. Eternia, Eternium's world, is a copy of Cal's, undergoing alterations and frequent changes. I am currently in Eternia, with you."

She started keeping a tally on her fingers on how many layers deep she was, because sweet celestials above was this a headache and a half. "In Eternia, the world runs not on natural phenomena. Rather it runs on numbers that try to copy and emulate… reality? Did I use that word right? Those same natural phenomena. Eternia also tried to incorporate cultivation, but that's causing problems. Especially if the numbers for translating them don't exist yet."

She touched her seventh digit as she kept going. "Within Eternia, we currently—that being you and me—are in a purely mental space. Which can be shared between people. Which is where I, my perspective, is sitting right now. Holding a workload that I don't think I could describe to any of my friends if we were to roll the layers back all the way to the real world, where all the people Cal took in came from. I am not going insane due to an incredibly supportive family in the form of Wisps, and having seventeen answers available for any question I think I may have. It's overwhelming. I'm overwhelmed. I'm holding on by the edge of my robes trying to get through each and every day. If the amount of time I experience can even be measured in days."

Yvessa restarted her tally, starting at her pinky. "Eternium and Cal both have additional layers you can use that change how fast you are going. Rather than just where you are. I don't always have control of these changes, and I am aware of layers in Cal that go several hundred times as fast. Y'know, in comparison to something we could call 'normal.' In some, a month worth of time or more can pass while only a second ticks along in the top-most layer. Or… bottom most. I don't actually have a way to tell if I speed up or slow down. I'm referring to the layer where everyone else is. Keeping track of those changes, for me, is impossible. I can't do it. I just ignore time altogether and keep working."

She took a breath, just to even herself out. "What bites the most is that rest, true rest, cannot be attained unless you do it in what I'll just call the top most layer, where everyone is. Resting will lose you the most time out of everything, but not resting just tears me apart. I tried resting in one of the layers where a month of time is a normal second, and it just didn't matter. I rested for that one second."

Yvessa rolled over, her face buried in the pillow. She spoke, but Artorian honestly couldn't hear her. The sound was followed with a muffled scream that she howled into the fluff, followed by bashing her face in because she knew it was harmless. After about a minute of unmoving silence, she nudged her chin up so she could mumble. "Then there's the type of work needed, and I spiral down in a boat of stress. Numbers. Pylons. The fights between the developers and engineers. Wisp politics. Politics then not working as intended because of where I am—"

Her finger shot up along with her eyebrows. "But I have to make sure to remember them anyway! I'm just…"

Her voice petered out. "I want to go back to my Da's. I want my goats. I want to make cheese. I want to sleep in straw and wake to the sun. Just a farm girl happy to work in a field and yell at the boys who thought they could steal my turnips. The days before the Choir. Not be a species-swapping fix-it-all. When I was asked to be a caretaker after initial waking, I didn't have a problem with it. The series of rabbit holes that got me to this point? That's too much. I don't even think I could find the way back out. I'm just so horribly tired."

She flopped against her charge, and Artorian held her just like he did any other lost child. He nodded in understanding, even if he experienced significantly less burden in following it all. "That sounds like a heavy basket, with an easy solution."

Yvessa pulled away, her brow raised in contempt. "Old man, if you have an easy fix, I wanted it yesterday."

He sagely nodded, not finding this all that difficult. "Sleep! Sleep as long as you need, and don't worry about what anyone else says or thinks. In whatever frame of reference it is that gets you there. The world will turn even if you are not present, and everyone else will learn to do without you. They must. To not allow you the liberty of your own well-being dissolves them of any hold they think to have over you. If you are unwell, but demand of you regardless, then it is not you who is at fault. Take your well-deserved rest. Send those who complain to your old man. I'm sure if they have the energy to complain, they have the energy to keep up with me and my shenanigans."

Artorian flashed a scheming, conspiratorial smile. "I might have to lay low for a year and a bit, but if they think I'm not going to be in all of their pies, they've got another thing coming. How about it? I would happily spend some more time in deep system access if it meant you got some naptime. What do you say, shall we give them abyss? You can hear all about it when you wake up. Sip that spiteful tea while they tell you of the fire."

Yvessa considered it, a fake expression masking her features as she indulged in the thoughts of certain bossy Wisps screaming as they speedily floated through wreckage and flame. Her smirk came to match Artorian's. "Oh yes. I do think I'd like that. We shall grant them abyss. I think you're right, Artorian. I'm ragged, and I deserve to rest properly. This is going to be a wonderful nap. They don't deserve my time if they're not going to look at me twice while demanding I do things. Great plan, Sunny. I love it when we're on the same side."

Artorian beamed, his hands rubbing together as a pleased old grandfather does when one of his little ones has something pleasant to look forward to. "Oh, that's our big secret, my dear. We're always on the same side."

CHAPTER EIGHTEEN

Screaming. Yvessa woke to screaming. She'd gone to sleep in realtime, or what counted for it. The location she'd chosen to nap was her designated spot in the Wisp commune. Free of the court nonsense.

She felt fresh. Great. Energized. Yvessa stretched her human arms above her head, popping her bones with minor stretches with the accompanied oohs and aahs of relief. Her human form was chosen specifically to stick it to court rules.

A flurry of activity was afoot, and Yvessa took a deep breath to relish in it. Did that make her a demon? She decided that, for the moment, she didn't care. A little indulging was fine. After all, this outcome had been the one she'd been told about. She settled herself into a cozy terrace, making herself some tea, as was suggested.

When she tried to pull up information screens, she found them significantly improved. There was no longer a delayed stagger when summoning up information, and the color scheme used was no longer one of extremes. It was as if some of the developers had discovered soft colors made for nicer screens.

Yvessa checked the time as a noisy Wisp zipped by, literally on fire as it rolled into the nearby brook to douse itself. A year and a bit had passed. A convenience for her! She could take all the time she wanted to check the logs and major events. Not that it seemed she needed to. She ducked when an incoming Wisp soared overhead in an arc, only to be pulled back by a negligibly visible string of Mana. The string drew taut against what appeared to be a racket.

A well-dressed Gnome was wielding it, and some gears turned inside of the paddle to roll the string up and draw the reel in all by itself. A gout of steam left the top of the device as it whizzed, keeping that string taut. Just so the Gnome could focus on his holler and hoot—somersaulting over both Yvessa and the table—and swat the Wisp further into the distance as he clicked something on the device to let the string unspool.

She didn't need to ask about the commotion. She knew who was responsible. A silver light zipped up to her, shrieking her name. "Yvessa! Thank Cal you're here! Where have you been! There's a war on!"

Yvessa manifested a tiny spoon to stir her tea with. Smoothly moving one leg over the other, she leaned back in her chair to loudly slurp her hot tea, looking at... oh. It was Invictus... through her long eyelashes. "I wouldn't call this a war, Vicki. This is clearly just an airing of grievances. We'll all be friends again soon enough."

Invictus was aghast with disbelief. "Wh... *what*? No! You left your charge unsupervised for an entire year! Do you have any idea what all he's done during that time?"

Yvessa pressed the spoon to her lips, cautiously pondering it. "Mmmm... he made things better?"

Invictus blew his top. "Only by breaking everything else! The Pylons are in shambles! He's re-linked entire networks with the help of the Gnomes! It's awful! Our gorgeous efficiency is down the drain and tubes, and there is rampant information overload everywhere! Worse, we can't get in contact with Cal or Eternium, and Oberon is screaming to get as much sorted out as possible. Dani is furious!"

He ducked as another set of Gnomes blew into some kind of tuba, sending out bubbles of opaque energy which hunted Wisps down all by themselves. Each Wisp a bubble touched got smacked with the kinetic force of a backhand, accompanied by the tuba note it was played with. Enough to bounce them away, but not enough to cause actual harm. Yvessa locked eyes with a few of the enthusiastic Gnomes, and they cheered when they noticed her look. They seemed to recognize her as an ally, and that could only mean the most amusing of things.

Yvessa looked back at Invictus. "Oh, I'm sure it's fine, Vicky. Just let things play out. They'll stabilize soon. Let me guess. You've been demanding the Gnomes work to exacting Wisp specifications, without leeway room. Because… we're in charge?"

Exasperated, he heaved and snapped back at her. That was so obvious. "We *are* in charge! This is rebellion. Mutiny!"

Yvessa understood the problem inherent in the Wisp's perception. "I see. Haven't learned the lesson yet. I guess this will continue a while longer then. Best of luck, Vicky!"

"My name is not V—" Invictus began to complain, but was caught waywardly in the side by a paddle. Which sent him careening off into the distance with an elongated screech that reminded Yvessa of some guy named Wilhelm. A different group of Gnomes jumped from the brush, each holding up mechanical panels that calculated numbers.

Yvessa couldn't hold back her laughter. Those numbers were awfully low, meaning the average expectation was very high. "Oh, I cannot wait to find out what I have missed."

She finished her tea, high-fived a Gnome that jumped up to give her one, and vanish-stepped to Niflheim so she could inspect some Cores. Best to start with the old man. Yvessa was glad she did, because his Core was busy! Fields of Wisps were picketing the Seed Core, shaking angry signs while being rebuked from the site in a fifteen-foot radius by a stationary Incarnate.

Corona turned her head to look at Yvessa when she

appeared, noticing the new addition without a hint of trouble. The S-ranker just smirked, making a 'get going' head motion. She clearly had the local area covered. There would be no direct interference with Sunny's Core. No matter how badly an entire swath of Wisps wanted to stop him from the havoc he was causing in Eternium.

Served them right.

Yvessa nodded in response to the Incarnate's motion, and moved right to Eternium's Seed Core. Oberon and Dani were in the middle of a full-on argument when she appeared. Oberon appeared to be defending Artorian? Dani was, as advertised, not remotely as pleased.

Oberon was continuing on from a long defense, which Yvessa thought she caught the tail end of. "It's internally consistent! So long as the system applies equally and equitably to everyone—which it currently does—then there's no problem! It's alright for Pylons and numbers to get moved around so long as they affect everyone the same. *Nobody* has *any* inherent advantage."

Dani growled at him. "I *want* an inherent advantage, Obi! I don't care about your fairness, or Eternium's. Even though he's slumbering along with Cal right now. Any chance that something might leak out of Eternium and be bad for Cal is a chance too high for me to accept. What happened to your hatred and zeal for the tar-balls?"

"Unchanged!" Oberon swiftly amended. "Yet when it comes to the workings of the game… this is fine! Just a few alterations that are allowing room for improvement when the boys wake back up. Cal and Eternium are going to have so much fun when they pull a chair up to this. They haven't had proper fun in ages, and the old man is just creating a playground for them. How could I *not* see this as a win?"

Dani hissed. "He's messing with Cal's well-made system!"

Oberon disagreed. "He's *not*. Eternium was already just using a backup system. When Cal is back, we can institute his original version, then use Eternium's Soul Space to balance the next round of big, sweeping updates. We have several iterations of time needed to implement all the new, good changes. Of course some of them need tweaking, but it's fine! The demons are just as stifled as the other users! He's landlocked them!"

Dani glared, her tone chittery. "That explains nothing to me, Obi! I don't know how the systems in there work! I didn't even fully understand how Cal's worked. Last I heard, Artorian was advised not to touch Pylons at all. By *you*, I believe. For the reason that they were too complicated."

Oberon defended further. "He didn't mess with the Pylons! Just their connections. Eternium's **Law** focuses on **Order**, and getting things correct and equal. To arrange matters and ideas methodically or suitably. Artorian's **Law** is about connectivity, sympathy, empathy, links between life. Eternium's connections were methodical and structured, but Artorian's connections are *affectionately* efficient. It never even occurred to me to let energy flow freely between Pylons, so they could link up with other Pylons that they *liked*."

Oberon spoke proudly. "We have been thinking of Pylons as tools. Artorian treated them as if they were *alive*, and lonely. His methods are, yes, horribly wasteful and energy inefficient, but I have also never seen a Pylon *happy*. Because it now existed intertwined in a network of other Pylons it could consider friends. I knew some of the Pylons were grown from sentient Cores and Beast Cores, but it just didn't occur that letting them feel as if they weren't alone would matter. Our network output has improved by a factor of *twelve*."

He formed pom poms of glitter and waved them around. "I don't even care that some of the results being spit up aren't correct or don't fit. The speed at which we are getting them is amazing. Cal's system was effective. Eternium's version is methodical and structured to better to allow for… unforeseen additions to actually be turned into numbers. Though Sunny's… Sunny's version makes you happy to be working with the Pylons, rather than feeling like you're in a cold workshop surrounded by hollow-eyed tools."

He dismissed the pom poms in favor of a candle. "The Pylons speak to us. They hum and sing, dance and pulse. He is in that system right now. *Dancing*. For no reason other than to show them how fun it is to… what did he call it?"

Oberon did his best Artorian impression. "I like to move it, move it."

Dani sputtered out an uncharacteristic snort. That did sound foolish enough to be the old man's doing. "That doesn't change my complaint, Obi. The system is obtrusive. There is so much information in there anytime I pull up the smallest thing that I get a headache."

Oberon turned a delighted bright yellow. "Indeed! It's just as awful for our enemies! They pride themselves on information control and management, and now it's all on the fritz! Our mechanics may not work consistently, but now neither do theirs! Artorian has fudged it specifically so that core gameplay features work great, including what he needs to get through the realms. Yet has mucked the world up to the point where you can't expect anything to be real, solid, the level it is, or what it appears to be."

He dismissed the candle and formed some hands to rub them together. "Casualties on their end are staggering, and our end is just laughing. He added a way for anyone aligned to him to have true sight. Seeing the real truth of things, rather than what they appear to be. He has *doves* in there masquerading as roaming bosses! It's fantastic! Meanwhile the roaming bosses are something *innocuous*, like poodle moths and tiny snapping turtles."

Oberon couldn't stifle his giggle. "Except those turtles are brutal and have statistics both unnatural and unexpected. He made his test turtle move at Mach one! Consistently! The demons' screams of panic and terror were *delicious*. Pure catharsis on a cracker, like the finest of cheeses with a touch of exquisite vineyard wine. I *love* it. Then there's the *moths*."

Given the duo was so deep into their argument that they hadn't noticed Yvessa after all this time, the green Wisp strode by in her human form, laying her hand on Eternium's Core to enter. Wisps did not need gazebo-bound points to enter and leave. Instead they were able to do it at leisure.

Perks of being a Wisp.

The sight that met her eyes as she arrived… *huh.* Alright. Oberon had been on the nose with his mention of a party. The grass was turning all colors of the rainbow! It was a slow, gradual change. Though one that was very difficult to miss. The sun remained celestine, letting her know Eternium was still asleep. She'd tried dropping her speed down to that frame of reference, but just couldn't go that deep without the help of someone else. Help that wasn't freely available.

Checking the notice log, she entered some keywords to refine her search to find if this dungeon was okay. It looked like she wasn't the only Wisp with that worry, as Yvessa found a public report by Oberon! Turned out the Core was just fine, but napping to the soft, soothing sounds of a kalimba playing. An instrument whose musical note origins could not be determined. Oberon had added a personal note to just let Eternium nap. His dungeon was overworked and overburdened, and even if it stifled progress… This was fine. They had eternity to work on things, and there was nothing wrong with a break. Not even an extended one.

Yvessa could agree with that, deciding it best to go check on her charge right away. Pulling up her Wisp-access omnimap that could see everything, she nudged some options to filter for anyone with the Administrator title. There was only one result, so easy pickings there. She popped to his location without any effort, but suddenly felt encumbered by an inundating show of rapidly changing lights while music blared loudly.

The rainbow lights were moving all on their own. Lines of them bouncing either off, or originating from, an individual moving on what she was temporarily going to term a dance-floor. Several adjustments were needed to her vision filters before she could see an adult, but not old, Artorian going wild on the floor. What was he doing with his feet? Why was every slight motion making a light arc and bounce from him as if he was some kind of poorly optimized focusing crystal? Where could he have possibly picked up such a foolish idea?

Yvessa called out with a hand up to cover her eyes from the light. "Old man! What is that inane shuffling you're doing with your feet? Put a shirt on! Your muscles are showing and you're flashing the entire world with that washboard set of abs."

Laughter was her first reply. Artorian spun several times in place on the back of his heel, skidding to a halt only to alter the direction of his dancing and make his way over to her. Still fully in motion with a side-to-side shimmy.

He was wearing those sunglasses, though of a design she'd never seen before. Loose-fitting, comfortable pants and matching socks were the only other thing he wore. Artorian's voice was the usual luminously friendly tone that came with him being in a far too good mood. "Shuffling? *Yvesssa~a~a*! Eyyyy! That's a wonderful name for what I came up with. I'll call this dance the washboard shuffle! No Alpacas needed. Great timing. Come dance with me! I've almost got the otters all cheered up. Though they're more into rock."

She blinked at him, certain she would not have believed her ears if she hadn't caught the tail end of Oberon's earlier vent. "…Rock?"

Artorian was close by now, so she could see his nodding. "Yeah! Particularly the ones that roll. They love a good pebble. I made sure to have a whole bunch gathered up so Dev and his friends could circle them around those particular Pylons. Made them so much happier. Brought a smile right to my heart."

Yvessa finally noticed something she'd been overlooking. "You have a body!"

Artorian laughed in response. "I do not! This is a projection. Dev made it for me. Isn't it shiny? It only works in the Pylon holds, but it works! Took a whole five months, but it was so worth it. I'm using reflected light rays and existing energy to make myself visible. I still can't pay any of the costs, but my new friends are compensating for me! Aren't they sweethearts? I bet they just want to keep seeing me be entertaining. It's incredible how good you can get at dancing if you keep practicing! I was Celestial Feces at first. Now I'm smooooooth."

Yvessa considered scolding him to get to work, but she put her hair up on the back of her head instead. "You know what? I'm feeling jolly after a long nap. Teach me how to dance. I could do some good cheer."

Artorian beamed, visibly elated. "Now we're talking! Hey, fellas! Put something good on! I've got a dance partner!"

Gnomes previously hidden cheered him on. Yvessa looked up, noticing several hundred of them having a small party in the balustrades. There was a housing district up there? Wait. There was a *society* up there?

She threw her hands up, putting it out of mind entirely as she hopped down to the dancefloor. One of the Gnomes clicking his drumsticks together to get the beat going. Just because she was awake didn't mean she had to start the day with work. Downtime was important! Also, the not-Ancient Artorian wasn't all that bad looking.

Dawn had taste.

CHAPTER NINETEEN

Yvessa laughed even when she fell on her butt. Dancing was hard! Artorian just hunched down and offered a hand to help her up. It took them a try or two to realize that offer was futile, as currently Artorian was just a light projection. This caused her to fall again, to the great amusement of the oversized-instrument players. Who all lost both their key and beat as laughter blew through large horns, completely breaking the tempo they had going in favor of some raucous laughter.

It spelled the end of the party today—and given the Wisp was here, it likely meant the party was over entirely. The Gnomes had had a great time, but they knew it couldn't last forever. Deverash Neverdash landed nearby, the soles of his boots making a blobbing noise as if some kind of ooze had absorbed the full impact.

Dev called out to them. "Artorian! Great news. The courts caved. We're getting our union! We drove them up the wall well past the point where they could handle it. Bagpipes for everyone!"

Artorian looked elated, repeating what his friend said even though Yvessa was entirely lost on what it meant. "Bagpipes for everyone! That's great news! Are we all set on plans four through eleven?"

Dev wiped grease off his hands with his handkerchief, having rushed over from recent experiments to deliver the news. "Indeed! We're turning it up all the way to eleven. All at once! Your timer on stamina is about expired, and we've got your change back to human form all sorted out. There will be a mana potion waiting for you. Just hurry your change up before that mana burn siphons it all away, because it will. We still haven't found a way to get rid of that effect, and the Queendom you're in is having massive mana issues because of it. You are entirely responsible for keeping all their reserves at nil. Time to move on, my friend, when you're able."

Artorian deeply agreed. "Indeed, my friend, when I've got functional feet that will be one of the first things I'll do. I also have the suspicion that the great majority of my aligned have figured out I'm the crown. Or I'm in the crown. I was worried about leaving Katarina behind without my guidance, but given the sheer volume of help available at her fingertips now, I think she'll be alright. I just need to hurry and get things done before either of the big boys wake up. Well, *hurry*."

They winked at each other with a cheeky celestial grin. Dev slapped Artorian's ankle, but lost his balance when his small hand just went right through the man. "Whoops, I keep forgetting. Alright. Up and at 'em! Are you all ready for the consciousness transfer out of the projector?"

Artorian nodded, turning to his caretaker to explain. "Yvessa, I'm about to stop existing here. I'll be in the noodle-shaped body, in the crown on Katarina's head. I'm about to hit an age threshold, so it's going to burst when my size increases. When it does, I am immediately going to snag up the potion Dev mentioned, down it, and shift into my human form. After that… It's improvising time. I've already sent out a quest update notice that I have enough power to manifest out into the world. I've also told my aligned that I'm going to be very weak, more as a precaution for them not to mob me. That's the news to be in the loop. Are you savvy?"

Yvessa followed that entire string of plans with surprising ease. As if this was the kind of plan she'd been expecting. Also nice to hear that the feud between Wisps and Gnomes might finally be simmering out. "I'm savvy, I'm a clever cookie. Tempered from having to deal with *you* for so long."

Dev looked up to Artorian. "I like her. We're keeping her."

Artorian chucked good naturedly. "You speak as if we could get rid of her if we tried. Yvessa is special, my friend. She has *the spark.* You just wait, she's going to become someone truly amazing. Even now, look at her. A beauty and a genius. Imagine what she'll do when she discovers the rest. I'm looking forward to it."

Yvessa glared at them both. Were they just being cheeky little Celestial Feces to mess with her, or was this serious? She felt her fingers tingle, a spoon already forming between her digits. The manifestation was noticed, and they both clicked their tongues and nervously smiled.

Dev quickly piped up. "Time to go!"

Artorian confirmed that in a hurry. "Yup!"

They both vanished in a flash, making the Pylon hold a spectacularly calm region. The sudden shift in mood allowed her to see that some of the Pylons were in fact humming and pulsing to a beat only they appeared to be able to hear. Other Pylons not necessarily nearby matched their pulse, connected in their own little network. Like a family happy to be together, even if their Pylon functions had nothing to do with one another.

She **tsk'd**, quickly checking her map to see where this troublesome duo had run off to. Surprisingly, to exactly where they'd said. Though the map did mention Dev was invisible. Right, a good reminder for herself as well. Going invisible, she moved right to them, hovering roughly fifty feet above their location to watch the show.

Artorian was present, how was it ever going to be anything else?

She bet that even just greeting her with song and dance had been part of an elaborate ruse to make her not notice something else. Something very obvious that all the splendor was meant to distract her from. Yvessa bit her thumb, wondering what it could have been as she watched the scene unfolding below. Back to an observational role she went.

It was dark in Midgard, as morning had not yet come. Having a general look around, Yvessa saw that Duvetia had grown. Not just in size, but in soul and spirit. She approved.

Duvetia had grown *well.* A true empire in the making, connected by a sprawling web of beacons which allowed its growing needs to be seen to with well-oiled ease. In need of stone? They had a beacon in the mountains. Fresh water? They had a beacon near a spring. Fields of wheat? Beacon. Iron mine? Beacon. Sheep? Beacon. Bacon? Beacon.

That ease of thinking quickly formed a reliable pattern. Mixing the utter forward drive inspired by burning willpower with a clearly defined goal, resulted in a well-mixed broth of success.

The citizens of Duvetia had their own narrative of the events they lived in, while to Artorian and company, this was still a fight to make sure Cal didn't lose out. To the aligned and people in the world, the current goings on had been termed by their historians as 'The First Age.'

To them, as far as they could tell, they were the first civilization. Their history and shared stories pointed to none having come before them. They were the ones who rose from oppression. They were the ones who clawed and bit, reclaiming the land. They were the ones who stood, arm across the neck of a Divine freshly returned. Who held onto them in turn.

When the historians of The First Age had pressed Katarina and her council for matters on what came before, she had consulted the crown. Artorian hadn't thought much of it at the time. He'd been busy, so he'd crafted a swift, fantastical tale of total devastation. All had been lost. All had fallen. None who had come before could stem the tide of black tar, the Ancients of legend from which these demons came.

According to his tale, true success had never been attained. Only incremental victories that left some lasting effect on the world. Large happenings such as the separation of realms; the addition of beacons, the rules that allowed movement between them, and the Voice of the World. All small little additions to one day. One day. Win.

The Divines came from beyond this world. They came to help, but were unable to do much by themselves. Each iteration, the Divines who came weakened, and most fell. Sunny told them that in the beginning, the early days, he had fallen first. Because he fell first, he had the most time to recover. Allowing him to stand up first this time, taking up the mantle to beat back the darkness.

Yet, defeat lay heavy on his shoulders. He told his aligned that in comparison to what he could be, he was weak. So very weak. He relied on them for progress, and that he would empower all those who wanted to help the best he could. To recover, he needed his aligned to just stay healthy and alive. There were levers of power he needed to pull on the other realms in order to open them up, so the aligned could advance. Levers that could not be reached if Midgard was not secured.

The pain and loss could be felt by those who read the screens the Voice of the World provided. The answers they had sought, laid bare along with the litany of failure that had led to their age. It was such knowledge that steeled the aligned. They would not fall like those who had come before. Their victory would not be incremental. They would be the first to rebuke the tide of tar. They would be the first in all the ages to advance rather than recede. They would be The First Age.

The first to rise. The first to win.

From this information, some of it embellished and poorly interpreted to mean far more than what was actually written, developed the society of Duvetia. A place where anyone could nap anywhere, at any time. For when they rose, they would charge into their tasks. The threats of which attempted to sneak in and kill them all. Such incursions were not… appreciated. Sneaky demons were put down with extreme prejudice.

The main event today was the big commotion in a place named the Green Square. A large grassy field which was put aside specifically for large events. Today's event was a little different. Normally the place was packed with activity, small stalls, performances, bric-a-brac nooks and pop-up shops. Instead, the empty square was kept under heavy guard. Not that a guard was necessary as there wasn't a citizen in attendance that wouldn't jump at the slightest hint of a problem.

In the middle of the Green Square stood Katarina. Her Everburning Crown in her hands rather than on her head, laying on a snug, folded robe. The crown no longer looked regal, or finely crafted. Instead it appeared strained; pressured, and bulky, as if filled with another object that could barely be contained. She smiled at the artifact she'd worn for a year regardless; a small smile from a small girl, who wasn't the least bit shy or sad about the loss of an item she'd worn every day for over a year.

Even the knowledge that the water in her lungs might end her on the spot when the crown's effects ended, she stood stalwart. So far, there hadn't been anything in the entire realm that had been able to cure her affliction. The crown was the only thing letting her breathe normally. A fact that her regency council bitterly kept to heart, their majority members gritting their teeth at their failure.

They knew the time was nigh when the light in the square changed. A green luminance overlaid the normal rising celestine lighting which they had all become accustomed to. The only complaint had been that it made their vegetables taste funny. Those hadn't grown any different, save for the diminished flavor. They'd gotten used to that too.

The event they were waiting for was the daily golden glow that suffused the crown at dawn. Which was an occurrence that happened with such exact frequency that the Queendom had tuned their timepieces to the event. The suffusion was the closest approximation they had to the dawn of a new day. That it was correct just happened to be a bonus.

At the start of a new day, energy flowed to Artorian in an amount equal to the followers he seemed to have. When that number increased to a point where his Divine status was classed as a Rank 6, this became rather obvious.

To Katarina's council, figuring out that their Divine either was the crown, or was in the crown, was a matter of child play. Which had caused some hilarious issues in politics, but none that couldn't be handled.

Katarina felt the thrum in the air as the power gathered in her vicinity. She stood alone in the center of the square, the object in her hands shaking as it buckled under the added pressure of power. People waited with silent, bated breath when the brightness began to build.

Onlookers weren't certain what to expect. A shattering? A sound? A flash of blinding light? None of those occurrences came to pass. If anything, the world went silent. Nobody heard a thing when the Everburning Crown visibly shattered into a thousand pieces. Each shard moved tediously lethargic as the explosion happened in slow motion, the tiny chunks harmlessly bouncing from Katarina's being as if they were no more than pieces of foam.

From the shell of the crown, a small one-foot-long noodle pulsed. Though only small at first as the growth happened quick, the noodle bulging in size as the Long dragon went up an age category. This increased its weight and size by a factor of eight. The eight-foot-long dragon hovered a moment as the golden glow clung tightly around its being.

The head dipped forward when a glob of bright blue water appeared before its maw. A few eagle-eyed onlookers spied the truth. Didn't that look oddly much like high-grade mana potion?

Those onlookers didn't have time to question. The Long

drank deep of the liquid, draining the gravity defying water before shining brighter still. The luminance forced people to put their hands in front of their eyes. When they could look again to where moments ago a Long had been, there now stood something else. A man in his late thirties. A fine specimen. One ripped with muscle, yet powerfully contained by flexible grace.

The man, to the eyes of all aligned, had skin that swirled as the deepest milky cosmos. This silence turned from one of surprise, to one of awe. Without speaking, the being turned to face Katarina, their young Queen. With a turn of his wrist, her status sheet became visible for all to see, though he blurred the details with a squeeze. All details, save one.

Reaching into her status sheet, the Sovereign of the Sun plucked out her disease demerit. Crushing the affliction within his grasp to be done with it, a soft smile formed on his face. His luminance ended right as a resplendent orb formed in his opened palm, the attack one of kindness.

Artorian's Resplendent Obliterator removed the vestiges of his mana bar, and his body swiftly regained the ultramarine glow of the affliction he still suffered. But now, that mattered little. The mana potion had given him enough time to become human, and solve a little annoyance that had been nagging at him. His obliterator struck the young Queen with a casual toss, cleansing from her body the water still trapped in her lungs. She staggered and shot her hands to her chest, but felt considerably better than she had. Katarina was speechless, and could only gawk and gaze at him.

When Artorian glanced to the sky, Yvessa knew the look was meant for her. While invisible, she nodded. Understanding the inherent meaning as she turned off his deity title, altering its effects slightly so people would no longer see him as a swirling cosmos even when it was inactive.

When the man in the square lost his splendor, his otherworldliness, and what seemed to be the majority of his power, sound picked back up. He eased his arms behind his back and performed a slight bow toward Katarina. Artorian wore the pants and socks Yvessa had seen him in earlier, though he lacked the sunglasses.

A deep breath later, he spoke with a mixture of relief and freedom. As if that had been his first, proper breath in a whole year. "Hello, my dear. I believe you know of me already, but please let me say that it is my very good honor to meet you, and that you may call me Sunny. I am very glad to make your acquaintance."

His smile made Katarina's whole world light up. She didn't even hear the burst of cheering that exploded around her, merely choosing to extend a shaky hand as the status above her head vanished. Her breath also felt fresh, and new. It had been a very long time since her lungs had felt so free.

She replied in kind. "Katarina, Regent under the Regency Council of Duvetia. I am honored to meet you, and you may call me Kat. We have all been very eager for this day. My council tells me they believe it would be your preference to be treated as an equal by all, rather than some great being to be bowed to. Is this the way of things?"

Artorian had missed feeling proud, setting her at ease with his words, as he was in no way a trickster god. At least, he preferred it that way. "This is the way of things. I cannot wait to tell all my aligned just how proud of them I am. Do you mind if I address them?"

Katarina released the welcomed grip, and stepped out of the way. Artorian smiled, and nodded in appreciation before turning to face the crowd. Even if the crowd was all around them. Uncertain if he could be loud enough, he decided to do something kind: Provide them a quest update, and sink his considerable DE points into something useful.

Quest Update!
Quest: A Labor of Love.

First stage success! You have supported your Divine to the point of awakening properly. With a body restored, the second stage of this quest can now commence. Rejoice! None have ever progressed this quest this far! Your Divine has expended the grand majority of his power to grant all participants a major gift.

Gift: All aligned have been raised to level 10! As the majority of aligned spent their not inconsiderable efforts on tasks other than gaining experience, this has affected over ninety percent of all aligned involved. Your hard work and dedication have paid off! Specializations are unlocked! All aligned who were already above level 10 have their minor boon upgraded! Health regeneration is twice as effective. Due to your own actions, this boon will upgrade for all aligned who reach level 11.

Note from your Divine: I am so, so proud of you all. Now let's go kick some keister!

CHAPTER TWENTY

Artorian donned the robe the crown had rested upon before he began to meet… almost everyone. There wasn't an aligned in Midgard that didn't want to personally shake hands with their Divine in the flesh. They mobbed him on the Green Square, but Artorian took it in stride.

Picking up Katarina with a palm to hold her up and away so she wouldn't get bowled over, he handed her over to a group of highly concerned counselors, who whisked her to freedom above their heads. Katarina made a bit of a dramatic show of it, which had Artorian guffaw in amusement. "Of course, *that* rubbed off. Of course."

Artorian didn't mind, meeting the crowd to discover that height wise he was easily a head taller than Ladder, the tallest male. Ladder was roughly five-ish feet tall in comparison to Artorian, coming up to about his chest. Ladder's ears were not included in that count, though his humanization was fairly stellar given the regional average.

People were so diverse! The type and manner of different personalities he met was staggering. Some were reverent. Others obsessive. Some he just knew could have become good friends, if only he had the time.

Every group had some bad eggs, and this group was no exception. He was lucky that there were only a handful of… he was going to call them 'the obsessed.' People so lost and out of touch with his message that a well-applied Suncurse went with them before being dragged away.

Honestly, who thought it was a good idea to *stab him* to show how much they adored him? That was just… not okay. Being adored at all was silly. He was here to help, and had to repeat that fact several times when a few more zealous individuals attempted to install him as some figure to worship. That was still a big no-no for him, and a few mentions that he was against it shut such attempts down. Just as certain… advances had to be shut down. It wasn't for him.

He did have some fun interactions! Any scholar that he met gushed with questions. Their thirst for knowledge was extreme, and they flubbed many sentences. Some questions were so on the nose that he asked for their removal to be halted when people attempted to drag them away. He understood why they were mistaken for zealots. The people dragging retorted with sass. "Their questions stabbed my brain and it hurt, and we established stabbing was bad."

That had made Artorian laugh. So just to have fun and to give his self-appointed protectors some social grace, he gave these scholars a combination of cryptic and painfully plain answers. Mixing them thoroughly just to incite some gossip and speculation. One interesting question pertained to what his true race was; a query that silenced much hollering.

Artorian had just smiled at the scholar, not seeing the problem. "Well, my boy, if you meant what is my Beast shape? That would be a Long. Which is a type of dragon, though I'm not certain if that makes any sense. If you meant what you currently see, I'm a High Human. Which is a state that a normal human can obtain after a journey of self-discovery and self-reflection. Attaining it has nothing to do with any power you might have. So if you are wondering if anyone can do this, the simple answer is yes."

That news had the expected outcome, with the small misunderstanding that 'high' meant 'tall.' A fire in the hearts of all aligned lit when that nugget of information spread around. A human form was already an attained one, and with much effort. That there was a higher level of human that could also be attained—and didn't account or care for any power one had—set spirits ablaze.

Artorian adored the light in their eyes, and it wasn't much of a secret that he was rather adored in turn. Boons and gifts aside, people felt their Divine had given them concessions he hadn't needed to. One such example was that his non-galactic appearance and shape went rather appreciated. As far as they saw it, Sunny put effort into looking as much like them as he could.

Even if he now looked as mortal as the rest of them, it delighted people to discover his clear and obvious love of naps and food. Because, Celestial Feces, Sunny could eat! The feast of meals intermixed with haphazard sleep took a week by itself. Time Artorian had purposefully set aside to recover from being a limp noodle, just so he could get on his feet.

Being on his feet at all was… refreshing!

All he had system-wise was stamina, but that was a world of options for him. With his attributes capped at an eighty-percent demerit across the board, he'd determined that just running off wouldn't work well after all. Plus, he'd just really missed being around people. Regardless of what they thought of him.

During the days where he got used to having a body again, Artorian was more than happy to answer questions, and happier still that people let him sleep when he leaned to the side for a sudden nap. Napping was a highly accepted social custom, and none really wanted to wake him when he slipped away. It was too pleasant to have Sunny around.

The man was jovial, bright at their presence, and ever happy to meet them. Like he thrived from their well-being. For some, it was a prophecy fulfilled. For others, it was a defeating feeling seeing the person they thought so glorious and immortal appear so very fragile and vulnerable. As if he hadn't told them he was weak—and they just had to see it to believe it—but didn't dare complain since he'd pulled them all up to level ten. All of them. Easily over half a million people.

Most Midgard residents had been around level two, the lucky having unlocked professions at five. Just going through daily life didn't grant any experience, and learning new information didn't necessarily reflect in one's intelligence or wisdom scores.

When Artorian woke the following day to the light of his own suffusing glow, he stretched. Starting up his daily warmup motions that others had begun to copy in droves. When he went on his morning run, he did so with the company of a small city. If their Divine did morning stretches and workouts, then they would too. That the reason Artorian did it was to get used to his body again either didn't matter, or was lost on them.

The ground trembled with the footfalls of so many, particularly when they synchronized. Which became a satisfying, glorious feeling in unity. Regardless of the pounding the landmass took. That was an Eternium problem, for when he woke up. His **Law** was doing a fantastic job of keeping that big baby swaddled and napping. Go, **Love,** go!

At the end of the run, he was provided a towel, and wiped the sweat from his forehead as he caught his breath. Not having those beefy seven hundreds in all statistics meant he actually got tired. What a twist.

As of his 'today' count, he'd been meeting his followers for several weeks. The amount of people who wanted to meet him for the first time didn't seem to have an end. Though, he did catch a familiar face that he was mighty pleased to see. "I say, Oswan! Is that you?"

The strong sheep herder, who had left his village leadership to his oldest son, waved back with a huge gleaming smile as he hovered closer. Sitting stationary on the back platform of Artorian's old racer. Artorian felt mighty happy when he noticed. "Oh hey, my racer! Is that a Red Panda in the control seat? Hello there! How is Woffo doing these days? Those goggles look spiffing on you."

Oswan also appeared to have a red ferret on his shoulder, then noted Oswan himself had donned a red shawl. Red must be their team color.

The crowd parted for his banged-up-looking racer that sputtered along. From the sound of the thrusters, it wasn't getting enough mana to the focusing crystals. Each time it hovered closer, he could hear it go **chitty-chitty bang-bang**. Did they shove cats in the interior or something? What was making that terrible sound?

Artorian gasped when he started to really see the damage as his racer pulled up. She was doing worse by the second, as the mana reserves of those operating her were no longer replenishing. With a defeated **piif**! she stopped hovering and thunked into the grass. Artorian was at his racer's side immediately, his tone distraught. "What did you do to her? She's a wreck!"

While True, Oswan, and Ruffle wanted to reply, they were unable. The mix of guilt combined with the sudden sick feeling from the mana drain did not do them well. The sudden cessation of all mana recovery felt like a sour pit that roiled in their stomachs, unable to replenish with needed nutrients.

Their silence gave Artorian plenty of time to snuffle all over the banged-up craft. Had they rammed this platform through a few mountains with sheer brute force and then used it as a sled down spiky gravel? Had he not been covered in ultramarine flames, he would have just poured more mana into his racer than it knew what to do with. Or so he wanted to do in the hopes of patching her up. As was, she was a stationary landmark unless he left. Nobody was going to have the mana to properly move her with him around.

This made him consider the effects of his presence, and knead his brows. "*Ay-aaah.* Crackers and toast."

Artorian was holding his chin when Oswan managed to

stagger up with a handshake. Artorian gripped him nice and firm by the wrist, which caused a notification to pop up with a **ding*!

Quest Completion: Language Grant.
Oswan of the sheep-shearing village has completed a language quest. Sunny, Sovereign of the Sun has gained their local language.

Artorian smiled, happy at both the reunion and quest completion. "Hello again, old friend. Thank you kindly for the language. Would you mind naming it?"

Oswan felt his spirit strengthen at the greeting, staggering for words. "Well met once more. It… uh… it's just called *Baa.* My base creature is a sheep, if that wasn't obvious, sir."

Artorian waved that last part away. "Sunny. Call me Sunny. Anyone that talks to me like I'm better than them is getting an odd look from me. Baa it is, then. I'm sure that entry will fix itself in my sheet now that I heard it."

He glanced meaningfully at the source of a stationary green light above him, knowing Yvessa had gotten the hint. Now he knew Baa! How Baautiful!

After giving the racer a gentle pat, he then remembered he could probably store it when he saw the spatial ring still on his hand. Would that still work? He'd not given it any thought since he'd not noticed the ring was there, but the mechanics of how it stored matter was odd. Could he? Would it take multiple slots? He directed his will once the trio had exited the vehicle, making it warble out of existence with a bubbly **pop**.

The empty space where the racer had been made the crowd gasp, and Ruffle shriek. He'd gotten so good at piloting the platform! Now it was… gone. Artorian nodded approvingly at the successful attempt. One slot. The racer had only taken one slot in the spatial ring. So object size wasn't particularly important. Good to know.

He put the racer back with another bubbly **pop** so Ruffle could gasp in relief and stop turning blue. His shriek had gone on, and on, and on. The poor panda collapsed in the grass, faint from sudden exhaustion and shock. Artorian went through taking and placing the racer several more times to test ring limitations, until he'd satisfied his fancy. "That works as intended. Good to know."

True was freaking out. "You can make objects appear and disappear at will?"

Artorian made a face of uncertainty, waggling his hand from left to right. "Kind of sort of. It's a little more complex than it looks on the surface. I'm still getting used to things. I'm trying to place where I know you fro—the dream! That's right. The golden ferret and the darkness. Did that get sorted properly?"

True gasped, eyes wide, his tiny paws pressed over his heart. "So that *was* you!"

Nodding sagely in response, Artorian took a moment to look at the distance and squeeze his chin. "It was. That… brings up an excellent thought. Birch, you bellflower. I am a fool! You gave me such an obvious hint for getting around, and here it went right over my head. Dreams are the answer! Hah! You bodacious bloomer! A thousand candles to your good fortune."

That outburst was odd for the Divine, as none nearby knew what he was on about. Still. Very interesting to watch. So their Divine had… friends? Their Divine had friends! More Divines! That was fantastic news, and many leapt to their feet to go spread the word that Sunny was just the first to return. Though he was far from the only one!

Artorian said nothing and watched them go, realizing that he had perhaps lingered too long. His spatial inventory held but a bow he couldn't draw, and racer that he didn't have mana to fuel. Problematic. He could go back to the old battlefield now and pick up the tonfas… but they may have to remain a local landmark since he no longer met the strength requirement to lift them. Artorian had the feeling that tonfas were the wrong weapon type direction of where he needed to be, and they didn't actually increase his progress with the goal.

That goal was acquiring his second specialization.

He bit his thumb while thinking it over, face squeezed in thought and consternation. His aligned remained quiet while he did so, whispering among themselves to guess at his musings. When he finally did speak, they all sported a wide smile. "I need bows and arrows. The more the better. The bigger the better. It's time. I have things to do and meetings will have to happen as time becomes available."

Action was what his aligned were used to, and this spurred the feeling of a return to normalcy. A goat raised his hoof, though he shook his arm to fix his humanization, properly turning it into a hand with fingers after putting in some effort. "We have a baaaa-lista. Does that count?"

Artorian shared their merriment, enthusiastically rubbing his hands together. "A ballista you say? Now that sounds like a bow that can hold up to my handling. Lead me to it! I would also like to meet the creator. War machines are something I could do a lot with."

Someone else stuck their bow into the air, a bundle of arrows following. "You can have my bow!"

The sentiment followed through and repeated. "And mine, plus my sword!"

"Mine as well!" several more replies came. Each holding up their own bow and arrow bundle in desire to help.

"And my axe!" The sound of a deeper, gruff voice caught Artorian's attention. His body turned to face the direction, spotting a Dwarf proudly holding up his axe. An honest-to-celestial Dwarf! The lad was young, with already a short tuft where a glorious beard would eventually be.

The Divine nearly bowled a few people over in his speedy stride toward the man, whose courage wavered as Sunny approached with such directness. When the Divine stopped before him, the Dwarven youth didn't know what to say.

Artorian had him covered. "Well, hello there, my stout friend. Where might you be from?"

"Svartalfheim," the youth stammered out in a hurry, not

really thinking before speaking. "I'm from Svartalfheim. Grew up there, crossed the bridge to escape the turmoil. Found this merry lot. Joined up. Loved the perks. Stuck around. Didn't expect to meet the feller that I… uh. Well, y'know. I thought you weren't real."

That got some glares, but Sunny clearly couldn't care less, offering a welcoming hand that was swiftly accepted by the Dwarf. "Sunny. Good to meet you, lineage-son of one of my extended family. What is your name, and what is *hers*?"

Artorian moved his eyes to the Dwarven axe, which brought a massive smile to the youth's face. The Divine knew! Though the extended family mention caused some murmurs. "I be called Yorn. This lady here be Throat Coat. I apply her, and people be gettin' rid of their nasty coughs! Course they got 'em cuz I kicked 'em in the teeth, but ya know…"

The Dwarven drawl! Oh, how Artorian had missed hearing it. It made him terribly homesick for the Modsognir and Fellhammer families. His fist clenched without him realizing it, expression so pained that Yorn put a hand on the Divine. "You…uh. Y'alright?"

Artorian nodded, taking a deep breath. "I miss my friends… my boy. I miss my family. I miss their laughter, their joy, and their squabbles."

The Divine stood slowly, though with a composure that clearly indicated he was controlling himself. "It's not your fault. Don't feel pity for me, my boy. I'll see them again. I will. Though now my feet demand I move. My arms demand they swing. My heart demands it rages. I need a bow. I need many bows."

Artorian's eyes were red from the tears he held back when he addressed Yorn again. The Dwarf had taken a step back from the pressure the ultramarine-fire being exuded, even if the barely-present flames themselves were known to be entirely harmless. The blue flicker was down to the occasional ember lingering on Sunny's skin.

Sunny collected himself, and spoke with purpose. "Can you show me the bridge you crossed?"

Yorn's nod was sharp and stern, his arm moving to point the direction. Artorian moved, hand outstretched to accept the offered bow and arrows as his feet took him forward. Any who had their weapon taken considered it an honor. Just like that, the aligned found a new purpose. It was hunting time, with their Divine intending to lead. Artorian popped his neck and rolled his shoulders. The war machines would wait. His heart demanded action.

So action, it would have.

CHAPTER TWENTY-ONE

Artorian stood at the edge of the rainbow-colored Bifrost bridge. It would have been a marvel if the grass wasn't showing it up like a slighted performer. Maybe he'd plunked a few too many Pylon chords down in the holds? Nah! Based on his position, he could plainly see that the realm it connected to was rather close to the orbit of their own today. It was a very short bridge in his estimation, particularly if measured against the theoretical leagues upon leagues they were meant to bend and stretch when the two connecting realms weren't as close as Midgard and Svartalfheim currently were.

"*Ow*!" He had nudged at the bridge with his foot, and just the attempt felt like he'd stubbed his toe against something solid before ever making contact. Holding his foot with a groan, Artorian hopped around on one leg while holding slightly crushed toes; fussing at the rainbow machination that wasn't going to let him cross without that second specialization. "Couldn't set the gravity trigger to occur at the *end* of the bridge? Who designed this!"

Yvessa made some swift notations overhead. That did sound like a better way to do things. More chances people would get squished from their own hubris that way. Though, what if someone ended up on or in a realm they weren't supposed to be? In a spark of insight, she also noted to implement a two-minute timer before the crushing gravity effect kicked in. The rules said one had to take the Bifrost, and circumventing that should be frowned upon.

Stifled laughter around Sunny died out slow as the small army at his back looked away, cheeks pink from embarrassment at having found that so blasted funny.

He waved them off to say it was fine. "Laugh! That was dumbfoolery on my part. Yorn! What's the rule here? Remind me how this works. If it even works the same as I remember. It's been a while for me. Also, as a personal curiosity, could I know your base race? Your name carries a staggering resemblance to an old wyrm friend of mine."

Yorn strode forth and stepped on the bridge without issue. Apparently coming from a higher realm and going to a lower one didn't have any issues. A quick glance at the young Dwarf's attributes also told Artorian they were currently higher than his own. Most of them hovered around a cozy two hundred. Odd that Yorn didn't have a mana bar. That seemed unusual not to have that feature even with such stats. A mystery for later! Yorn was talking.

"Bridge crossin' is a sacred tradition. I'm not sure how it got called a tradition since part of it is 'don't do it,' but that's what it's called. To cross this one, you need to have either come from the realm it connects to—like a staircase that ya were on a higher floor of—or if you're starting on the bottom, ya need something called a specialization. Specifically, the second one in a series. As I didn't even have the first of my own until I suddenly got bumped up to level ten, I can't help you there. Goin' down is easy. Goin' up takes work. As for my base race… I'm… I'm a hedgehog."

Artorian understood with ease, notching one of the arrows on the borrowed bow. He empowered himself to the limit, and momentarily felt very strange. Like the Pylons didn't know if they were supposed to pull from his base numbers, or his diminished numbers.

Yorn hadn't sounded particularly confident about his base race, so Artorian gave him a supportive mention. "A respectable creature! I suppose I'll be here until further notice then. Say, that tower on the other end of the Bifrost with those dark shapes in it. Friendlies?"

He gruffly grumbled, his grip tightening on Throat Coat. "Not in the slightest. They be the reason I had to run. I now know that lot be called demons, and they're the reason it's all going to the depths in Svartalfheim. Nothing but thievin' our mining labor. Some nut named Robur or sommat is in charge of the realm. Taxin' us half to death. Since it's death *or* taxes, we don't got much of a choice."

Artorian calmed himself, noting the distance was too far for a normal arrow to reach. Normal was anything but out of his reach, finally having a use for Zen Arrows. It had taken much time to prepare, but when the arrow flew, it flew true. The dark creature in the tower shrieked, audible even from the other side of the bridge.

Artorian went **tsk**. "Got 'em in the eye, but that didn't kill it. Arrows just don't do a lot of damage. Looks like I'll need a steady supply."

The onlookers gawked in disbelief. Repeatedly throwing their arms between Sunny and what had been an impossible, yet successful, shot. They had seen it firsthand, and still didn't buy it. "You *made* that? *How*?"

Artorian looked over his status sheet, pulling it up just to confirm some things. Currently, his only mana bar modifier was the Resplendence field. Cost of twenty-eight percent. With Empowerment off, his attributes suffered an eighty-percent malus. Leaving his average attributes around one hundred and forty-six-ish each.

Shoving the remaining seventy-two percent of his mana bar into Empowerment calculated the end result poorly, for some reason. He thought it would have used that one hundred and forty-six as a base number and propped those numbers back up, but that just wasn't what was happening. Pylon limitations? With Empowerment active, his attributes evened out around six hundred seventy three-ish. That was... probably not how it was supposed to work.

Given that it meant he had numbers to work with on the other hand, he didn't complain. Better to expend his mana bar to pull himself back up to a niveau of functionality, and keep deliciously quiet about it until that error needed addressing. Artorian would have considered himself a dirty cheater, if being one hadn't meant he could actually *do the thing*. Besides, it was fine so long as it worked like this for everyone. Yeah. That was the excuse he would live with for now.

"On second consideration... what am I thinking?" Abyss that! No regrets! Embrace the cheatery! He would be one with the shenanigans! He called out loud, a look of determination filling his eyes. "More arrows!"

His second shot struck true. As did his third. Fourth. Twelfth. Demons on the opposite end of the bridge scrambled for safety, but it mattered little as the arrows punctured defensive structures. Shattering through the wood and managing to—even if barely—nick and cut them. They wanted to escape, but they couldn't just abandon their posts! The paperwork they'd have to do for that would be maddening! One of the imps snapped at another, his voice pitched. "Send word for an attack requisition! We can't keep getting stabbed like this from across the gap!"

The imp who ran for it made it seven feet out of cover before a critical strike to the head took him out. A normal, innocent, boring old wooden arrow had brained it.

Artorian loved critical hits! They did actual damage. Or what felt like accounted for actual damage. Abyss these numbers. His specialization experience ticked up, and that made him smirk. He had a method of gain, and a target rich environment. "Come at you me, you caliginous tar-bags! I see you for what you are. I didn't fear the very Blight itself, and you will fare no better! Come at me!"

Artorian didn't care if his enemies didn't hear him. He yelled at them anyway, unleashing a storm of Zen Arrows. He was firing them as soon as the skill came off cooldown, eating through quiver after quiver of ammunition.

The aligned understood their role and kept up a healthy supply line. Their Divine was the bait, trying to lure out the enemy which their own arrows would take down if their enemies ventured too close on the bridge. That was what had their Divine so interested in war machines! Well abyss.

Yorn yelled out when he saw the recognition appear in the faces of those around him. "Forget taking the Divine to the machines. Bring the machines to the Divine!"

Many of the aligned felt like this had been obvious in retrospect. Why hadn't they ever considered reinforcing this bridge-point before? It was the only way into their realm. Clearly this location should have been a stronghold. Had something prevented them from considering the idea? It felt... hazy. The thoughts were difficult to grasp and keep a hold of. They shook themselves out of it and scrambled. There was a fortress to build!

When Artorian began to feel tired, he momentarily flickered his Sustenance field, trading some Empowerment oomph for feeling refreshed. It unfortunately didn't stop his newfound need for sleep, which he definitely did not like. When had they fixed that feature? How dare they. He blamed Wisps. When in doubt, blame Wisps. That, or use a fireball. He sighed, considering that latter idea. He wished he had a basic fireball, or the ability to use it. "*Ugh.* Mana. That toy would need mana."

No matter. He would remain stationed here and rain whistling death down upon the other side!

"Sunny!" The use of his name made him pause a shot. One of the beaver clan had come in under escort of a group of ferrets.

Artorian wasn't certain what was going on, so he addressed the voice. "Yes?"

The beaver stepped forward, introducing himself. "Snagtooth Cloptail, machine expert and master carpenter. I hear someone was in need of my work?"

Artorian pointed at himself, trying to puzzle out why the beaver was a beaver, rather than in a human shape. Was he becoming a speciesist? Best not. Beaver was fine. "Indeed! I need a ballista that can function as a bow. I want to manually pull the cord back and release the bolt without a pulley or lever mechanism."

The beaver gave the ferrets a look. "Do you have any idea how strong someone needs to be to get that done? There isn't a person in all of Midgard with that kind of oomph."

The response from the ferrets was to point at Sunny. The beaver was taken aback at their blasé retort, scrutinizing the taller than average human up and down. "*Humph*! I'll believe it when I see it. Fine! Don't come complaining to me when you can't do it."

Stomping off, the beaver did not appear to know quite who he'd been talking to. That didn't matter to the person in question; Artorian's grin spread from ear to ear. "Challenge accepted!"

Just for that, Snagtooth was going to make the ballista draw extra impossible. His stomping intensified as the horde of ferrets bounded alongside him. Artorian had a thought, calling out a name. "Yorn! Go with him! Give that ballista some Dwarven flair."

A curt nod and a quick hustle became Sunny's reply as the young Dwarf got to it without complaint. A little extra animosity between the Dwarf and beaver was sure to build, which would result in a spitefully completed project. Preferably one with fantastical draw-strength requirements. Just how he wanted it.

Speaking of crafting. He should… put some things together himself. Specifically, Artifacts! It was getting to the point where he was going to need tools and toys that simply didn't exist in Eternium. Unfortunately, he couldn't use his DE points for anything that didn't get automated in the store. He'd either need to wake Eternium up or find another way. Preference to the latter.

Still... how? In Cal, he'd fashioned Decorum a weapon. He could likely do the same here, if only he had the means and the materials. A thought struck him. "Are any of you mages or casters by chance?"

A llama's foot went up. That person swiftly humanized, then ran up to introduce himself. "Cuzco. I run Cuzco's Poisons, and Poisons for Cuzco. I'm a Malchemist. Magical alchemist. How can I help?"

Artorian shook the eager man's hand, who didn't let go and kept shaking for a solid ten seconds. "I... yes. Good to meet you as well. Please let go. I need to know if mana can be stored in exterior means. Such as an object it can be taken back out of later. I'm in need of a massive quantity, but I'm still afflicted by... well. Your mana isn't regenerating either right now, I bet."

Cuzco grimaced painfully. "It never does when close by. We've... become aware of the problem. It happens near the beacons as well. There is a way, but it requires a very powerful Core. Those just aren't easy to find. We would need a quality of Beastly or better."

A Nixie Tube flashed over Artorian's head. "Oh, really? Anything else?"

Cuzco motioned that there was not. "Just a good enough Core. Something above Beastly being preferred. Cores have a maximum capacity of mana they can hold. They just need some preparation before you can invest *your* mana into them. It's a skill. An easily attained one, but a skill nonetheless."

Artorian understood, his bow lowering so he could think. "Then I just need materials, a crafter that knows their trade, and enough basic knowledge myself to get started. Yes... Yes, that will do!"

He looked toward the other side of the Bifrost, Noting the

defenders had all but fled or been shot down. He let fly his last arrow, and put down the last imp. The opposing side was now undefended. "That should buy me some time. Cuzco! Make those preparations and install them nearby here when they're done. I know where I can get a good Core. I know the crafter I need, and I know where to get basic training."

Walking away from his firing position now that his heart was satisfied—and with his aligned engaged in a new building project—he could move on with this next idea. He handed the bow and empty quiver to a waiting hand in the crowd, Artorian plenty sure that the weapon would find itself back in the hands of the person who'd handed it out.

Cuzco saw the strength with which the Divine moved, and hurried along after him. "Of… of course! That's not too hard. Where can I find you if I'm done early?"

Artorian nodded, his walk aimed directly for the closest beacon. "I need to go to Solar Gate. You'll find me at Cra's. If Yorn and Snaggle are done before I'm back, tell them to keep refining their product. I may… have an improvement of my own to add afterwards."

Cuzco nodded, but could no longer keep up. His stamina emptied out while Sunny trucked on without a pause in gait. *Note to self,* he thought. *Do not get in front of that man. Do not.*

CHAPTER TWENTY-TWO

Cra's Crafts had gotten big!

"A whole building? You go, girl! With flags!" He loved a good flag. That pretty blue base and silver detail combination really meshed. Cra must be raking in the profit. Artorian nodded in approval, fist-bumping the few aligned that had come with him, who had been more than happy to cover his teleportation beacon fee. They'd found it hilarious when he'd gotten to his own beacon only to get stuck.

"Caretaker?" Cra's voice traveled across the air, bouncing into his shoulder in the clear tone of a question. When Artorian turned to look at the door, he saw the bowyer. She was just as he remembered! He, on the other hand… was not. "No… Are you the son of the caretaker by chance? You look so similar. Is he well? He hasn't been by my shop in far too long."

Sunny eased his hands behind his back and wiggled between the passing people to be in easy conversation's reach. "No, it's me. You've got a good eye. I'm actually wondering why nobody has stopped me to comment about the fire."

Cra was taken aback. Fire? What f— "You're on fi—!"

Sunny stopped her with a quick hand on the shoulder.

"Harmless. Just strange how nobody is pointing it out. Stranger still that you didn't notice right away."

He tapped the side of his nose. "I've the feeling some perception meddling is afoot. Can we speak inside? I was hoping you had a moment concerning bowyer-y. Before you cut me off, I'm not here to buy. I'm here to learn."

Cra leered at him, noticing the flames only when she searched for them. How… odd. "Affliction?"

Artorian moved his hand to form a thumbs up. "Affliction. That's right."

Cra understood and snapped her head toward the door. "I have several errands to run, but I can spare the time. Even with a dozen assistants, I'm still doing things myself. Some tasks you just can't entrust to others."

She waved off several assistants who ran up to her. As, no, she didn't have the unique materials yet. Nor did stepping out of the workshop only to step back into it magically make them appear in her arms. The dejected helpers sulked, slinking back off to their prior tasks. "Things have been odd ever since the sun turned celestine. Old caretakers turning younger is a new one, but not out of the ordinary so long as you're not a vampire."

Artorian blinked. "A what?"

Cra was surprised he didn't know. "Vampire? Some of the Nobles that lived in the castles were cursed by some kind of affliction that caused them harm when they went out in the sun. That effect has… diminished since the change. Now they roam freely, and have taken that moniker onto themselves since they found a way to retain their youth, energy, and vigor by consuming the blood of others. It's caused a very nasty socio-political climate in the Solar Gate. They're very active and have broken into several clans while they vie for power."

She sighed and dismissed the topic. "You said you needed to talk?"

Artorian scratched the tip of his nose. Now that he thought about what he needed to ask, he recalled how staunchly he would have declined himself. "I need to learn how to craft bows. Properly. The little I know isn't cutting it for what I need to do."

Cra sputtered, slapping the table before taking a breath to laugh. "Skies above, no! I don't have the time for a direct apprentice. Not even for the Caretaker. I have far too much to do, and the fee alone is something that even the Nobles can't pay. There's nothing you can offer me th—"

Her words stopped cold when Sunny turned his palm upwards. The palm itself was unimportant. The item that appeared out of *thin air* was a different matter. Her eyes sparkled, pulling up the properties on the bow immediately so she could consume the delicious details. "Is... is that actually *Wispwood*?"

"I thought that might get your attention." Artorian smirked, silently pleased to see the thread of conversation had snapped in favor of the prize in hand. "A year and a bit ago, you told me that unique materials made for better bows. I'm sad to say I haven't had the opportunity to collect any, but I ran into good fortune. Even if the curse on the bow will forever prevent me from having a fortune. Do read that carefully before you touch it. I forgot the exact wording."

Cra's hands shot back to her chest when she read the poverty affliction that using the bow caused. "That is... a nasty side effect. Though I could count my fingers worth in Nobles who I'd love to use this on. I'll rescind my earlier mention. If you're intending to barter with this for lessons, I'll accept. Though I thought you said you knew how to make bows already. I don't see why you need my help."

Notice! You have been offered a profession.
Profession: Bowyer.
A bowyer is a craftsman who makes bows, which can be used for hunting and archery. More than just tying sticks together and adding some string, the bowyer profession will allow the crafter to make all types of bows. This includes their closely related variations until a more specific profession is created for them.

Do you wish to accept this profession?

Artorian leaned back in his seat and accepted the prompt. His mind then moved along with his words. "I know nothing. A person cannot learn a topic which he believes to already know everything about. Or in my case, thinking that what I know is sufficient. I find it insufficient."

Cra scoffed. "Look at you talking like you're the smartest person in the room."

Artorian closed his eyes and shook his head 'no' while holding his own hands, before the bow was handed over. "If you are the smartest person in the room, then you are in the wrong room."

He smiled pleasantly, eyes opening to regard her. "I'm not in the wrong room."

Cra felt her cheeks flush, her hand fanning herself as it had suddenly gotten rather warm. "Well, don't you have a way with words? Alright, you charmer, stuff your charisma back into your bag. Sweet-talking me with respect for my craft isn't going to win you bonus points; I already agreed. If you're going to be my apprentice, you may as well come with me and meet my unique material supplier. She's a gem."

Cra considered something when she got up. "Since you're so good at talking, maybe you should handle negotiations for prices. My strength lies in being a professed bowyer. If I didn't know better, Caretaker who has lost years rather than gained them, I'd have pegged you for a politician. You've got that way with words."

Artorian played grievously injured, his hand egregiously pressed to his chest in mock insult. "A poli—me? Oh no. No, no, no. Never. I'd start a fight that had nothing to do with words. I'm a crude, crass old man on the inside. No tact whatsoever. None."

He winked mischievously, causing Cra to snort and giggle as she made the come along motion. "You joker, let's go meet our supplier. Tell me what it is you want to start learning after I tell you the basics on the way. Also, I can't keep calling you Caretaker."

"Sunny," he helpfully amended, noticing Cra had vanished the bow in a similar method to the way he'd made it appear. Oh, she also had one of the spatial ring doohickeys! Neat. "Please, do lecture all you'd like! I'm quite famished for a good lecture."

Cra did not hold back at the invitation. Much like her preferred use of her own crafts, she pulled back on the string all the way; overdrawing before releasing. It was fascinating to see how she could breathe and talk at the same time. Artorian was dying to know what her base creature was, because that was a marvel to behold.

He didn't even notice the rows and streams of people they passed, each going about their lives while he caught up with the striding and speaking bowyer. He was enraptured by her depth of knowledge as she just jumped into the pond of the topic and fully expected an apprentice to jump in right behind her. Then keep up!

Artorian thanked his lucky stars for having a good mind. It was necessary! Cra's oral method of teaching was one of plenty. He'd have filled two full chalkboards by the time they made it to a strange little shop called 'Odds and Ends.'

"Administrator?" The man in question snapped from his academic pursuits. Facing the very familiar voice even if the face that had spoken didn't quite look like he remembered. A touch of age? On a Mage? "Oh my *Cal*! Artorian!"

"Minya!" As was his norm, his arms shot into the air, his dumb smile plastered wide on his face as they quickly and explosively hugged with force. The ground beneath their feet visibly and audibly cracked apart since they stood firm during the event. Attributes over five hundred would do that in a place capped at one-fifty. "It's so good to see you! I was hoping I would run into you one of these years! I was told Dale and company had accepted, but I didn't think I'd be blessed with a meeting so soon!"

"Oh. If you were looking for your old disciple, I kicked him out and sent him off with his friends to stock my store. He's as capricious and self-interested in getting stronger as ever." She sighed, holding her head. "At least he is enthusiastic. Now let's hope he learns to be capable, rather than blowing himself up like he used to."

Artorian slapped his knee. "I didn't realize we were so alike in that regard! Still, it's fantastic to see you. I've just signed up with Cra the Bowyer here to learn her craft. I'm in need of specialization advances and they rely on that specific tool. I figure it would be easier if I learn how to make the weapons I keep breaking on every use."

Minya's eyes sparkled, her eyes going wide. "*You* are why Cra is ordering special materials from me?"

Cra shook her head no, but didn't have an opportunity to get a word in. Apparently, her supplier and her good-with-words new apprentice knew one another. On second thought, this could only lead to discounts! She'd keep her nose out. She loved discounts!

Artorian tapped his chin, other hand on his hip as he looked at the static scenery of the sky. "I don't think so. I also don't think it's safe for me to be using them without the skill."

Minya smirked, getting a knowing look from Cra on a piece of information Artorian didn't have yet. Minya then mused out a question. "What skill? Skill and ability acquisition halted and stopped dead when the sun turned celestine. You can hear the Voice of the World snoring. Nobody is getting anything not automated by the system. All crafting is manual, based entirely on skill. You're going to have to practice!"

Cra had not intended to give that piece of her information. She'd been trying to hint at the discounts! She had no idea what this 'system' or 'snoring' mention was about. Maybe it was some joke between the two of them. Yes… that was likely. Get back to talking about discounts!

Artorian appeared dumbstruck, then slapped his own face. "I'm a fool! I didn't think about that at all!"

Minya bellowed out laughter. "Ha! On the plus side, the lack of consistent day and night cycles broke the wildlife. They have no idea when to wake or sleep, and they are very discordant and disorganized as a result. So gathering special materials has been a whole heap easier than anticipated. The system may not be keeping proper track of most advancements, but that doesn't mean people haven't been improving."

Minya nudged her nose at the greenery in the distance. "Your disciple and his party are even trying to complete tasks without triggering experience gain. Our base attributes are all too high for Midgard. We've been holding off on realm hopping until the tip of our spear was ready to lead the charge. Then again, we essentially needed the whole year just to get used to things. So don't feel too bad or discouraged."

Artorian nodded in understanding, Minya turning when he looked back up. She motioned for them to follow. "Let's catch up inside and talk business. Your crafting instructor is nearly salivating."

CHAPTER TWENTY-THREE

Artorian and Cra left Odds and Ends several hours later with both their spatial rings full, and enough extra raw materials piled on Artorian's shoulders to make him look like a pack mule. Cra didn't know how he was seeing underneath all those goods. When she'd yelled at him just to get her voice to carry through the piled matter, the muffled response had been 'Electrosense.' Whatever that was.

By the time they arrived back at her workshop, Cra had changed her stance on the matter. She *wanted* whatever Electrosense was. Her apprentice hadn't so much as bumped a flower pot on the way back. That notion felt strange to think about. 'Apprentice.' Sunny, or Artorian to his closer friends, appeared to be a person that had been around for a while.

Cra suspected that the ability to turn younger may have been in play for longer than the time she'd known the Caretaker. Or Administrator. Or whatever he really was under that pile of wood. Maybe it had something to do with his base creature? She wasn't certain.

Cra became ever less certain as the weeks passed. Sunny received some *strange* visitors. Some were downright reverent, and he hushed them with whispers as if there was some big secret to keep. Giggling, winking, and dragging someone off for aggressively whispered conversations became the norm.

Sunny was at least a diligent learner, and threw himself into her lessons with fervor. Unless the unique material provider and her friends showed up. Then he dropped what he was doing and hustled off with a big dumb smile on his face. Cra didn't mind as much as she should have, as it gave her ample opportunity to inspect her apprentice's work.

Her apprentice… did some strange work.

In the beginning, he'd followed her instructions to the letter, as if he really didn't know anything about bowyery and the delicate intricacies of the nuances involved. That guise had slipped after two months in her shop. Sunny may not have noticed, but Cra certainly picked up on the little details and wood-shaving methods that trickled into the construction process. Techniques she'd never taught him were laid bare on the raw wood. Techniques even she didn't know, but her 'apprentice' clearly did.

Was Sunny toying with her, or did he actually not know what he was doing? Based on the model she was currently inspecting, which Sunny had made while significantly distracted, she found few of her lessons and methods in this bow. Well, that wasn't fair to say. Her lessons were present, but given the curvature of the weapon in her hands, they had been integrated with other methods.

The oddity that she didn't understand was *how* the grain of the wood had been altered. This was Ashplex, a very flexible wood, normally found in the dark gray set of hues. It was very pliable and bendy, thus the name. Yet the specimen in her hands was the definition of stubborn rigidity. The grain twisted, spiraling within in the shape of a fractal-looking pattern. Which didn't make sense. What also didn't make sense was the abyssal *weight.*

Cra was a sturdy, strong woman. Yet she needed both her hands just to lift this thing. Setting it down, she pulled up its properties. Foul play was at hand here. This was no Ashplex. Ashplex didn't…

"What the flabby bowstring is this?" Cra blinked at the information in front of her. This couldn't be right. Ashplex was of rare quality, so… why did this unfinished thing have the *Artifact* rank? Maybe she would find further details if she dug deeper. "Apprentice… what are you up to?"

Name: Fractal Groove Spirals, Version Four
Material: Ashplex
Rarity: Artifact
Damage: 1–20 Kinetic.
Special Quality: None.
Special Ability: None.

Cra scrutinized the information, her fingers tracing the odd patterns in the wood grain. Her eyebrow arched as a tiny glint caught her attention. Aha! Something hidden! It took some careful fiddling, but Cra successfully made the notes section appear. She'd see what Sunny was up to!

Notes: Version four shows the success that version three lacked. Four didn't twist itself to pieces during grain fractalization. I discovered that spinning the direction like a spiral solved my tension issue. Version three shredded itself to pieces from internal pressure, but four is reinforced from within and supports itself due to the directional pull away from the handle.

The new main problem: The handle is brittle and will snap if squeezed too hard. Additional weight was an unforeseen side-effect, cause currently uncertain. I've no idea what I'm doing wrong with the damage output. It stays at 1–20 regardless of what I seem to do, even when successfully managing alterations to the rarity ranking. Does rarity have nothing to do with the effects on the tool in question? Or is it like classes, where the rarity solely reflects the amount of them that exist in the world? Perhaps version five will hold the answer. Version four is another failure. It will destroy itself on being strung; the internal tension can't handle the external force.

Cra needed to wave the information away. Then she needed to sit and knead her brows with her hardened thumbs. Her head hurt. Not because of the bow information, but due to the attempt at understanding how rarities worked. She had no clue herself. Her face was buried in her hands when she tried to disprove it. Surely, she had made a bow with a higher rarity when copies of it already existed? Rarity couldn't just be how many of them existed. That would be heartbreaking.

She drew a deep breath, squeezing her hands to her knees. No. No, there had to be more to it. Material mixes caused special effects to be applied to the bow. Cra glanced at the bow, and noted it wasn't even strung. The notes had said it couldn't be strung… What if that assumption was wrong? If she could disprove that, she'd feel much better. She had far more skill than Sunny in her craft, even if he was doing strange things.

Standing, Cra pushed up the sleeves of her leather apron. Her eyes were both hard and aflame with purpose. "Can't be strung? *Phah.* Challenge accepted. You're going to be a musical instrument when I'm done with you, little number four."

She wrapped a string loop around one end of the bow, and the resulting **puff** confused her. The item had turned to dust in her hands. What the abyss? That was new. New and unpleasant. Now she stood there, dumbfounded and holding a string while she stared at a pile of dust on the floor. "*Huh*?"

Inspecting the dust for information, she pulled up the properties on it, which told Cra a very plain piece of information. "Skill rank too low to affect Artifact rarity items. Artifact item below stability threshold. Item destroyed?"

She scratched her head, not noticing Sunny had returned and was standing right behind her until he spoke. "Well, so much for that one. I knew it was fragile."

"*Eeee*!" Cra jumped, turning with a shuffle to raise her hands as fists. Her breathing was labored and swift, eyes wide until she realized it was just her apprentice. "Don't scare me like that!"

Sunny inspected the dust, and shrugged. He'd try again

with the next one. "Take a breath, teacher. You have a person here regarding sales. Her name is Rose, and she's looking to buy a new bow. Hers got destroyed in a recent fight. I can clean up here if you could spare the minute to go see her? She's with the party over there."

The apprentice motioned to a group of intimidating people. The group consisted of a monk-like warrior with his hands wrapped in bandages, a rogue who was balancing three daggers atop one another, a mountain of a man with a hammer the size of *him*, and a very upset-looking lady glaring enough daggers at the rogue to make him put his weapons away. She was holding a snapped bow. "Yes. Yes, that sounds good. We will speak about this later."

Sunny nodded when his teacher left, moving his hand over the dust to store it in his spatial ring. Artifact-quality dust could still be useful somewhere. Everyone loved pocket sand! He chose not to pay attention to Rose buying her new bow. Minya's team was a marvel, and he'd told Dale they would catch up again when they could.

His schedule was surprisingly full; he still needed to check in with Chaos, Discord, and Entropy. Though he was certain they already knew he was here. He'd put it off due to the bad news he needed to relay. He was going to have to take the Core out of the broken solar ring, which meant many features about Solar Gate were going to permanently turn off.

It seemed like a terrible idea to just rip the Core out on the day he got here. He wanted to understand just what aspects of local life he was mucking up before doing so. Otherwise he couldn't plan replacements or contingencies for them. Wrecking the social functions of a whole city was not his idea of being loving.

Barging into action and kicking doors down was fine and all, but if it involved other people, that didn't sit right. This meant doing things took time. He'd chosen to throw himself into one task at a time for now, even though he had several he wanted to get to.

Currently, that was covering up his attempts at making Artifacts. A task that would have been impossible if he wasn't able to cheat with Yvessa's help, who let him use his Administrator and Deity titles to occasionally peek under the hood.

He needed to be especially careful with those. People couldn't be allowed to see him when he used those titles. He physically looked and felt different in their vicinity. Not being noticed was useful right now. Especially around a group of people that weren't aligned. He'd wondered why Cra and the beaver had treated him normally. Turned out they had no interest in aligning. That was fine. People should make the choices they want to make, and that included not making the choices they don't want to make. Artorian approved wholeheartedly.

He'd gotten a few updates so far from the visiting aligned, who slipped him bits and pieces of information concerning the progress on war machines and the realm war-front. The gate being erected at the Bifrost progressed smoothly, though they had not managed to replicate his ability to shoot arrows at ridiculous distances. Not even the ballista prototypes they tested there were up to snuff.

Katarina and her council were busy spreading the empire and reinforcing the local land around each beacon. Some of the beacons were having shrines or temples built on or around them. Not for Artorian's benefit, but for the people. It was good to have somewhere to immediately rest. Not everyone had big mana pools at tenth level, and more than a few arrived sick and exhausted after a beacon trip.

Having a safe place to rest right away helped with that. Artorian approved again, thinking of his disciple as he prepared the materials for Artifact attempt number five. He'd offered Dale and company the aligned option, but they'd declined. Some in the party for differing reasons, as they were also going to test deity functions when Eternium was back. Still, they saw the use of it. Artorian hoped it would help inspire their own boon creations when the time came.

When he did get time alone, he worked on his tasks while narrating a haphazard how-to guide. Yvessa noted down what he said, and it would go to Dev for formatting. Then Yvessa would smuggle it out of Eternium and sneak it into Dawn's possession for mass-distribution. He was on how-to document three by this point. He figured he'd have a whole guidebook soon enough. Based on what news he was getting from Cal's Soul Space, it was mostly politics and Vanaheim repair on that end. With Tatum working on some super-secret special project on the moon.

There was also something going on with Dawn, but everyone he'd asked was being tight lipped about it. It was a surprise, they'd said. He grumbled thinking of it. He wanted to know! Gazebo hunting was currently low on the darn list, but his curiosity was still biting him and he wanted to go see her.

Then there were all the new discoveries he also wished he could go check out himself. Though the race adaptation one was a topic he'd be running into regardless. He wanted to know why it was the human race as the default for Midgard, yet the Dwarven race as default for Svartalfheim. Rumor was that Elven models were the default in Alfheim, and tall blue people in Jotunheim. So…Jotun. That bit at least made sense.

Vanaheim had been the oddball. There was nothing interesting on the whole landmass. Just endless fields of grass with cows grazing, and the occasional tree. Except that the cows took exception to any company and all carried giant bardiches and axes, going bipedal when on the attack. He'd heard something from Minya on that model of creature originally being for Hel, though it hadn't met the standard and was moved to another realm. Thus, Hel-cows. Lots of 'Moo.'

Hopefully, model V would bear fruit. If this one came out as a success, he'd finally have a bow that didn't snap on heavy use. It needed to be good for rapid multi-firing, and slow heavy draws for Zen Arrows. Hard to do both for some reason, the bow needed different resistances against the pressures he applied. He'd figure it out. Both could be done!

Artorian cackled like a mad villain, opening up windows for information when he was alone enough to start the true crafting process. Making Artifacts was involved, but he had years of broken item repair experience, and he could cheat! Adding information in the required fields directly to inform the automated Pylon system what he needed, rather than go the trial-and-error route a normal crafter had to go through in order to figure out how to add values.

Turning Barry into a fork was no longer limited to the realm of amusing side commentary. He was getting closer to a solution! Although there were some hurdles he'd need to jump through and problems to divide up beforehand. Who could have known that changing people into doors would turn out to be so useful! He loved some well-kept documentation. More giggling ensued as a result, his smile wide under his darkened goggles as sparks flew from the metal bench.

Yvessa thought Artorian's antics to be hilarious, so she wrote that down in the guide as well. Underlined once. "If you are having a good time, cackle madly."

CHAPTER TWENTY-FOUR

Corona cackled with raw enjoyment when she perused the latest guide document. Yvessa had heavily embellished it with her personal thoughts, and Dev had seen fit to remove none of them. Instead, he'd added his own commentary from a mechanic's perspective, leaving Dawn with a document that read like Artorian lectured—complaints included—with the sassy student in the class adding notes, and the class lead pushing glasses up his nose to pitch in his own two coppers.

The documents were hot items in Cal's Soul Space, spread and read by all the supervisors, who took time out of their busy days to go through them. They were both funny and informative, and any break in monotonous work was a good thing. Cal's Soul Space just needed time and effort, as there was no actual threat at play with the Core in question asleep and healing.

The only danger source was Eternium, and that Core had been sent to la-la land. When the supervisors finished what tasks they had, it was time to push up the sleeves and go in to help with the war effort. Odin, Brianna, Artorian, Minya, and a smattering of other assorted 'help' had already been applied. Now it was time for Henry and Marie to go as well.

They still didn't want to, but it was that or get in the Incarnates' way. They didn't want to go to sleep in their Cores like some of the others had, so it was time to actually go practice being better rulers. Or given the political situation in Eternia, just people.

Henry squeezed Marie's hand. He didn't mind just being people for a while. The squeeze back let him know she didn't mind so much either.

After they were each assigned a Wisp, they vanished from Cal, entering Eternia while Corona waved at them with a smile. One more task crossed off the list. Eventually they were all going to end up there, but there didn't need to be a rush. She and Tatum needed to finish Vanaheim, and that wasn't a job that would go quickly. At least the picketing had stopped. Wisps were too busy running off to do the work Eternium couldn't.

Corona stretched, handing the guide to one of the Gnomes working nearby. They were measuring the land, wanting to get the reconstruction exactly right. Thank Deverash for that **Law** of his. It made the reconstruction much easier. Looking over her current portion of the work, she got back to it, wondering what Sunny was up to now.

Over in Eternia, Artorian was in a great mood! He'd done a terrible thing! He'd blown up his private workroom! Not on purpose, mind you, but the singed and still partially on fire apprentice ran through the rest of the building. Cheering while holding something above his head. It looked roughly bow-shaped, but there was no bow in existence with a strange shape like that.

He was loudly going on about needing a string, but none of the strings he found seemed to cut it. The apprentice didn't appear to notice parts of him were on fire, entirely dedicated to rushing through the workshop in order to locate his prize.

Nothing the apprentice found seemed to do the job, until suddenly he stopped mid-pose, freezing in place while a realization twinkled in his eyes. His voice was a whisper, but everyone heard it before he turned on his heel.

"I need to go see Minya." Throwing his arms in front of himself before zipping off with a quick step, Sunny yelled out an obvious: "I'll be baaaack!"

"Was he on *fire*?" one of the aides casually quipped, his eyes tightly squeezed as if not accepting what they had just seen. "I think he was on fire. Oh hey, my mana is regenerating again. About time!"

Minya jumped from her chair when a singed Artorian burst through her front door, his moustache clearly glowing with orange embers while pieces of his robe smoked. **Slam**!

"Minya! I need a string!"

"A string?" The ledger in her hand snapped shut, not as easily kept off guard as the majority of people here. Her gaze was all business when seeing the item in his hand. "Put it on the desk so I can see it. Put yourself out. I don't want those live embers on you to turn my shop into a bonfire."

Artorian put the bow down and noticed the state he was in, working to patch himself and his clothing up while Minya checked the bow. The wood wasn't one she recognized. "Djinniper? That's an odd material name. I sold you this?"

Sunny decided his robe was wrecked, and just tossed it into the bin before answering. "I don't believe so. I got that batch of wood from Discord, I think. Some experiment he and the boys were growing in the backyard. They sent it in with a letter after hearing what I was up to, saying to try it. I haven't had the opportunity to go ask directly."

Minya nodded, and tossed the bow into his hands. "Consider the opportunity to be at hand. I've got nothing that matches this. I don't even need to look. You'd need Artifact-quality string just as a suitable match, and I've got nothing like that. Stop putting off seeing your friends, and get out of my shop."

With a quick salute, the Administrator ran off. He knew better than to linger when told to book it. Minya considered asking Artorian how the abyss he'd gotten his hands on an Artifact, but given the information about a certain backyard where unique materials were being grown, her curiosity leaned elsewhere. She had a new place where Dale and his friends needed to go out on an adventure: the gardens of Discord!

Said gardens were where Artorian ran into the owner. It took an hour to get there since the correct gardens were in the mountain castle, and barriers and doors were more of a suggestion than an actual hindrance. Just like walls. Who needed walls?

Discord was in his Djinn form, sporting a flower-patterned apron while holding a powder blue watering can. He was humming some songs only he seemed to hear, doing minor bounces while wiggling a thick digit on his other hand high in the air. He performed a shoulder flounce while scooting from left to right, then got back to watering his weeds.

He didn't notice Artorian until the man was right in front of him, Discord turning only to shriek with a high pitch. The startle made him fumble his watering can and spill the contents. Artorian smirked and cheesily began the conversation. "Hello, old friend. What-aaah, whatcha doin'?"

"Nothing! Nothing to see here!" Discord was flustered, seeming awfully defensive about nothing. "Wh… where'd you come from? I didn't hear the gate."

Artorian just pointed to the wall, reminding his friend that some people had no need for things like doors. He'd just scaled it and hopped right over. Easy! "About yonder. Say, do you have any string? I made a bow out of that wood you sent my way, though I've got nothing to string it with."

Discord looked around his garden in a hurry. Looking for a scapegoat. "Uh, I do not. Where's Chaos? This was his blasted idea. Ah! There he is!"

The Djinn pointed over to a different garden, where Chaos was sunbathing in his Wood Elf form, a large reed sticking from his mouth. Artorian nodded, and left Discord to whatever embarrassing secret little project he was trying to hide. "We might have a catch up get together later, buddy, just to let you know."

"Sure thing!" Discord smiled wide, tactically blocking his plants with his body so Artorian couldn't inspect them. Discord was in luck! Sunny was in a hurry, and not all too interested in what was going on with discordant plants.

When Chaos waved at Artorian and they got to talking, Discord heaved a deep sigh of relief. Turning and bending low, he ran a soft hand over the wide leaves of his project. "Safe another day, my sweet little Spriggan. Safe another day."

Chaos was all smiles when Sunny jogged close. "Buddy! There you are. I was wondering how long it was going to take you. My own fault really, you never know with my ideas. There's no order to them. Did it succeed?"

Sunny was glad that his friend seemed to have an awareness of the issue. "Indeed! One Artifact, stable and functional. Lacks string though. Got any?"

Chaos blinked, gears clicking into place behind his eyes. "Is *that* why I thought I needed a string this morning? Well, that makes sense now! Yes, I have a string. Couldn't for the life of me figure out why I went out of my way to get it, but here you go. Sorry about that, old friend. It can be difficult sometimes to have the answer, yet not know the question."

The Wood Elf handed over a simple wooden box with a basic copper hinge. Artorian flipped it open right away, and thought he was looking at a lock of hair. "Chaos. Are you sure this is a string?"

Leaning over to look at it, Chaos understood his friend's confusion. That item was indeed not a string. "Ah. I suppose string components are the right term. Now that you mention it, that is, in fact, hair. Will that work?"

Artorian grumbled and sat down next to his friend, licking his finger and starting to weave the hair together into a string that could do the job he needed it for. "It'll work once I finish it. This is going to take a bit. How have you been? I haven't been able to check in."

Chaos lay back down, resuming his sunbathing. "We're all well. A little birdie also came to tell us about what you are planning to do with the Solar Gate's area effect. We already talked it over. The Immaculate Core is safe to be removed anytime. Entropy was sour about his regional effect ending, but he's had his fun, and gob-tons of stolen experience. So not *too* sour."

Artorian paused his string-making to weigh his gaze on the sunbathing Elf in a towel. "What *kind* of bird?"

Chaos pointed at the invisible source of blue light in the area. Artorian understood right away that Chaos had his own Wisp. "Nooo. Not you too?"

The Wood Elf calmly nodded. "Sorry, Love, we're all stuck with one now. They can't afford not to keep tabs on us. The loss of a title slot doesn't bother me so much, and my Wisp comes with perks. He loves to talk! Might just be my influence. Funny you came for a string really. We've all got strings on us now. They watch everything we do. If you've been wondering why we haven't been causing the kinds of problems our **Laws** lean to."

Artorian looked around, discovering that Discord was also under surveillance. **Hmmm**. He didn't like that. Something about the idea sat poorly in his stomach. He bit the thought away, focusing on finishing the string. When it was done, he carefully put it down and rolled his shoulders. He threw open a myriad of menus and started slamming information into the empty fields.

Artorian was getting used to it now. He had a decent idea of which fields needed what for an Artifact to be made. Mostly it came down to making sure no other object of this type and design existed, so he'd needed to get creative with weaving. Filling in the last field, he closed the menus after nudging an option in one of the screens that made it check for current values. He didn't have another way to make anything update, not with his mana on lockdown.

The string hummed with energy. On swift inspection, Artorian felt giddy. Artifact quality! Perfect! Exactly what he needed. Now came the dangerous part. Finishing the product. "Chaos, this might explode when I combine it."

Chaos just lifted his coconut, taking a long drink from it. "Please do. Can't wait."

Artorian almost scoffed at the nonchalance, but that was Chaos for you. Standing with the items in hand, he set about the task of carefully connecting the string and adding tension to the bow. "Easy now. *Ea~a~sy*."

Nothing happened when the loops connected and the bow was strung. He was expecting some sputtering, maybe even fireworks. A whole lot of nothing happened, but Chaos didn't seem to be perturbed. That was just how things went around him. Random chance for everything. Artorian scratched his cheek. "Huh. I guess… it's finished. Well, that was anticlimactic."

He gave it a playful **twang**, mighty pleased when the world didn't go up in flames. "Alright then, time to inspect it and see what we've got!"

A prompt came up with a warning, and some options.

Notice! This Artifact is compiling. Please name this Artifact so weapon effects can be determined. Options for finalization are visible below. Only one can be selected. Selection is final. No information is available before selection.
Option 1: Three Wishes
Option 2: The Sound of Silence
Option 3: Bunker Buster
Option 4: Barragan
Option 5: Two Fangs

Artorian put his hands together, easing the fingertips against his lips. "*Hmmm.* No information available before selection. That's not helpful. The specialization options gave me something to work with. This is chaotic guesswork."

Chaos greeted him with his coconut drink, pretending not to be responsible. "You're welcome."

"*Mhm.*" The Wood Elf got a soft glare in response. "Cheeky brat… I don't know what any of them do so I'll just pick one."

Selecting option three, he waited for some kind of change.

The exact same notice popped back up again. Was that supposed to happen? Artorian shrugged, and selected option two instead. Maybe option three just didn't work as a real option for some reason. Though he felt suspicious that Chaos was once again involved.

Notice! Selection confirmed.
Compiling.
Name: Bunker Buster, the Sound of Silence.
Material: Djinniper
Rarity: Artifact
Damage: 1–20 Kinetic.
Special Quality: Sturdy.
Special Abilities: Barrier Breaking, Silent, Hypersonic.

Sturdy: Doubles the maximum strain this bow can handle. Strain is calculated by a value of 10 points per rarity rank. Maximum bow strain: 140. Straining a bow decreases its firing rate by half a second per rank applied.

Barrier Breaking: Arrows shot from this weapon pierce any material less than 1 inch thick. Ignore armor values and effects if all armor is pierced. If the arrow shot strikes a wall, barrier, fortification, or protection other than something with the armor tag, it is destroyed outright.

Silent: Arrows shot from this weapon do not create sound. This includes the release, flight, and impact. In addition, arrows will cause a silence effect on any creature struck, preventing the activation or continuation of any ability or spell requiring a verbal component. This effect ends when the arrow is removed.

Hypersonic: Arrows shot from this weapon will accelerate to exceed the speed of sound, dealing 100 raw bonus damage to unarmored targets. Hypersonic arrows increase the maximum bow range by one order of magnitude, or the currently applied range value times ten, whichever is higher. If a Hypersonic arrow strikes an armored target, the bonus damage does not occur. Instead, the bonus damage becomes charge damage and will be funneled into the Martial Arts Maneuver: Sky Breaker, activating it without needing to pay the maneuver cost.

Notice: The name of this Artifact is too long, please shorten it.

Artorian scrutinized the item. His earlier query had been answered. This was definitely unintentional, and the options were not meant to stack. They had been plastered atop one another, and now the Pylon responsible likely couldn't handle it. The notice at the end wasn't asking anything complicated, so that was nice. If that was the only problem, this was a pretty fantastic bow!

"Let's see. BBSS? If I just mush all the letters together. Though that's just repeating letters twice. Why not just BS? That works fine. Sure. The BS-Bow." He added the information after deciding on the name without thinking about it twice, finalizing the Artifact crafting.

Artorian lifted it in his hand to test the weight, determining a normal person would be unable to pick this thing up. Now he just needed ammo. It was time to get that second specialization! "Chaos, my friend. I love hanging out with you. This bow is better than I could have dreamt of. Though I'm afraid I'm going to need to head out with the Solar Gate Core in my pocket. Are you three able to hold down the fort?"

Chaos snickered, clopping two halves of a coconut together. "We will be fine! Chiffon will be screaming, but that's part of the fun. The politics are going to collapse. I am going to have a great time. My **Law** is going to have a great time. Paradise in Eternia. Coconuts for everyone. Speaking of Chiffon, why don't you go see him to get rid of that awful curse? Unless you like being poor. Chin-chin!"

CHAPTER TWENTY-FIVE

On his way to see Chiffon—as Chaos had brought up the very good point to do so—Artorian just about tripped over himself when his nose tingled. A detail in the crowd he passed stood out to him like the sorest of thumbs. His grandfather sensors beeped at him in morse code, forcing him to stop on a dime and adopt a stance as if the ground were moving, and he needed to stabilize. Stop!

Grandpa time.

His head snapped from point to point in his surroundings, trying to regain the captured tingle of attention he'd so briefly passed. The flurry and flutter of clothing as people passed? No. The tic-tac-tic of a cartwheel over cobble? No. The tiny half-plucked flower in an oversized, hairy hand? Yes!

Said tiny offering was held by a dejected, nervous-looking giant mole. Was it a mole? Hairy all over, a bit burly, big ol' snout, claws for days. Indeed! Now why did this detail stick out? The mole man was exhaling deep sighs, those claws of his plucking yet another petal from the stem.

Artorian slunk against a wall like a cheap thief, sticking to the shadows while observing the scene for a bit longer. His eyes twinkled as his nose informed him he'd found the target of the tingle. "Trust the tingle. The nose knows!"

The large mole looked up at a second-floor balcony, currently unoccupied, though holding potted flowers of the same make and design as the kind hairy-sighs over there was holding. The plot thickens! A lovely lady passed by the open window, a gorgeous smile on her face. What a beauty she was! "Oho. What have we here?"

Artorian steepled his fingers. He already knew what he had here. One of life's greatest little pleasures! The opportunity to meddle, and indulge in a tiny distraction. Those were the best parts of life, the tiny distractions that made you smile. So, a meddling he went!

"Why the long face, my boy?" The old man inside of Artorian seamlessly slid free, even if his body was the strapping example of a thirty-plus prime adventurer. The depth of his eyes betrayed the opposite, for he looked at the mole with a mixture of concern and resolved drive. He'd slung himself onto the bench next to the creature just about his size, if a hair taller. Because of the hair. "You look like you carried a bag of bricks and forgot to tell your mind to put the bag down. Look at that hunch."

The mole chucked, glancing to the open window. The lady within was gone, and his eyes fell, face downcast. "It's nothing. Don't... No need to pay attention to me."

Artorian quirked a brow, his own gaze following before settling on the man. "Fancy the beauty? I've seen works of art with less depth to them than the way she wields that smile."

A dumb smile appeared on the mole's face, his cheeks flushing just a bit. His paw moved weakly to push the bench compatriot away, but he may as well have been trying to juggle a pair of cargo ships with all the success he had. "A little. She's... She's beautiful. I don't mean on the outside. She was nice to me, and now I'm... I don't know. It's all sparks and tingles in my stomach. Yet I'm afraid to talk to her. I mean... look at me."

Artorian eased back, sternly studying the details of the mole. "I have looked at you. I don't see a problem. You said you saw her for more than the depth of skin. Wouldn't it be unkind to extend the same? Tell me about her."

The mole flushed harder. "Oh. I… I don't… Maybe I shouldn't be talking about this with a strange—"

"Artorian." He already had his hand extended, having expected some weak rebuttal. So interrupting the mole came about both easily and swiftly. "Though, please, call me Love. It's a nickname for friends."

The mole enjoyed a laugh, though he shook the human's offered palm. "You have a strange sense of humor. I'm Gazette. The lovely lady I don't know what to do about is Sillaine. She spared me some of her time while I was just sitting around. I wasn't expecting it… honestly. Nobody looks at me twice. I can't humanize. I keep messing up. Nobody wants someone who keeps messing up. I think she felt sorry for me."

Artorian's nose tingled, his face refusing to move while his eyes flicked to the balcony. *Well, well. What's this?* Someone was spying. Sillaine was trying to do a good job staying hidden within the drapery of her curtains, but you couldn't hide such details from a devious old man with a plan. So, consensual and mutual interest then? Conditions met!

He was originally going to offer the lad some sturdy advice to get him on his feet and help with life in general, but it seemed there was someone else interested in the position. Someone who didn't seem to care much about the shape or design of the skin. "Are you sure? Did she give you that flower?"

Gazette tried not to smile. "It… fell from above when I wasn't looking. I don't know how. I've just been sitting here trying to figure out what to do, but now I think I've been here too long. I must look like such a creep. I… I should go. I'm being a bother."

The strength with which the human next to him pressed down on his leg made that difficult. When Gazette looked to speak, he saw the warm eyes of a person who looked like he'd been through the same. "No, my boy. Take it from a person who isn't the least bit proud of all the broken hearts he's made in his lifetime. Some things aren't coincidences."

Artorian winked. "Besides. My day just cleared up; I have lost my schedule. Why don't you get that heavy weight off your chest? Tell me about Sil. Where you met. How. What you felt when you saw her. What she did that made your heartbeat briefly increase with each mention of her name."

Gazette blushed fiercely at the last comment. He was thumbing the stem, and Artorian noted that Sil had dared lean in closer after overhearing the prompt Gazette had been offered. Gazette didn't notice her, and Artorian was intent on keeping it that way. His genuine feelings would be spilled, and that was worth its weight in gold. Gazette was entirely responsible for his own path in life, but that path was best followed when guided by the strings of the heart. Even if the mind enjoyed disagreeing.

The mole man didn't disappoint. With the sudden chance to talk about the burden on his heart, words gushed free like a wild stream. A stream that turned into a raging river as he didn't know what to say, only that he needed to say it. While most people in the vicinity gave the gushing man a wide berth, those interested glued themselves to the conversation.

Gazette remembered he needed to breathe, but rolled right on. "So then I went home from my work in the mines, and she was sitting there with that little umbrella. She smiled at me when I passed like it was the easiest thing in the world, and all the weight and drain from my long day just... fluttered off. I smiled back, but my words became a grunt. I was so embarrassed that I just walked on. Then I went to the place she likes to sing in the evening. I just... sat in the back. I don't know what to do."

Artorian nodded, grandfatherly. "Sounds like you do, though you're unsettled and unwilling to accept it. It isn't difficult, my boy. Don't worry about the if, or if not. The do, or do not. Spend time in her vicinity. Be considerate in your actions.

Enjoy the time around what your heart craves, but let your mind tell you when too much is too much. If you enjoy time around her, be nearby and provide kindness. Though stay out of her way."

He let go of the mole's leg. "The sky has gifted you a small flower. You know what she likes. Bring one when you go to listen. Leave it behind when you exit. If she does not think of it, or appreciate it, then you will know. If she appreciates it, or likes it, then she will *let you* know. Love and romance are not a struggle with a victor, or a battle to be won. It is a sharing of experiences, and sometimes that leads to blooming. If it does not, accept that it does not. Take the lesson to teach your heart, and let it go. If you were wrong, the other will let you know."

Artorian smiled and gave the man a nudge. "Above all, my new friend: Be considerate. Think of her life and situation, and how to best assist without trampling over her garden. If this is what your heart yearns, then let it speak freely. Let your heart be your drive, and your mind the guide. Think not where to advance, but where to step back. You will find advancing comes naturally. Don't think about it. If you worry, act. Specifically, act with consideration."

Artorian made a small gesture down the street. "Go see her. If you're worried about how you are perceived, then see to your hygiene. Be clean. Smell nice. Then forget yourself and think of her. You will find that how you look matters little, when you lead your actions with thought and care."

Gazette's mouth gaped in wonder. "I… huh. I still don't think I'm courageous enough to even get started."

Love supportively slapped his back. "What is there to fear? You'll never know unless you try—and so long as you keep the right intentions in mind, Sil will see through that shape and skin you're so worried about. It is up to you to be your best self if she does. Only you can show that. You have nothing to lose, and can only gain lessons of the heart. Life is the little things."

The mole looked at the mostly plucked flower in his claw. "You think?"

Artorian squeeze-rubbed Gazette's back better, having possibly slapped a little too hard. "I know. Don't let your appearance hold you back. It's not something you can't work on if it truly bothers you. It may take years, but perseverance can see you through. Your humanization is an eventuality, just keep working on it. You'll see progress, little by little. Don't look at everyone else, or how far they've gotten. Or what it is they cannot do. That doesn't matter. Measure yourself only against yourself. If you are better next year than what you were today, you have grown. Hold on to that. Think of that."

Gazette rolled the flower around on his paw. "When will I know—"

"Now." Artorian slapped the answer in right away. "You know right now. Does your heart pull? Do your feet move you to her? Does your mind flicker to thoughts she is in? Do you hear her voice without prompting, or see her smile without reason? You already know, my friend. You've always known. You just needed to let yourself speak the truth, so your ears would hear it. That you happen to have done so to a person who has gotten his cheek slapped so much that the lesson of being considerate really got whacked in there… That's just a nice bonus for you. As for your humanization… Do you want to know a secret?"

Gazette nodded, leaning close as the experienced human whispered. "It's all about believing in yourself. It never happens overnight. It needs practice. Recurring practice. The little sinister voice in the back of your head says you cannot do it, but it lies. The little voice says you're not good enough, but it lies. The little voice tells you that you should be listening to reason, grab it by the throat and squeeze the life out of it. You stab your claw at it and say: 'You're not reason. You're a little piece of abyss.' Got it?"

Artorian patted the big mole's back when he nodded to say he understood, eyes full of ideas.

"Believe in the me that believes in the you." Giving him a wink as he got up, Artorian smirked, his next words whisper soft: "Hygiene, my boy. You never know when the person you like might be watching. Remember; not acting when you are certain is sometimes more important than rushing to act when you are uncertain. Think first, then do, and do with all your heart."

Gazette was lost in his thoughts, but now had ideas where vacancies once lived. Artorian liked that, glancing at the lady leaning on her window frame. That artistic smile of hers beamed while her cheeks were flushed with deep pink. She noticed Artorian's look, the deep pink turning red as she looked away. That sly fox had winked at her, in on the devious truth which he'd helped set into motion.

Sillaine had also listened with rapt attention. She hadn't been fully certain if that speech was meant for Gaz, or for her. That scheming traveler! She narrowed her eyes at him when he waved without looking behind him. As if he *knew* she was glaring. Her attention was torn when Gaz whisked himself away. *Aw*… well, it was fine.

She'd see Gazette again. That big, shy sweetie who had stolen her heart. He said the sweet words, was honest, and put his heart into his work. Plus, he apparently liked her just as much! Her day couldn't be any rosier, and she scampered off with the biggest smile on her face to go tell her friends.

There was gossip to share and more well-placed flowers to plan for!

CHAPTER TWENTY-SIX

Chiffon did not recognize the expert-looking adventurer that showed up in his court, only that his bones felt like they rattled at speed. A terrible memory. He did know that the man's smile was magnanimous, proud of himself for some scheming nonsense he had just pulled. Aha! Another Noble ready for a Suncurse. Even if they didn't do much right now.

Life had become difficult with so many self-proclaimed members of the Nobility running around. How did they keep increasing in number? He was cursing them as fast as he could find them! Kneading his human brows, Chiffon did a quick check to remind himself which sleeve he was in today. Sleeve being his name for the guise ability his profession provided. It allowed him to look like anyone, but he had preferences. His current sleeve was one of his favorites.

Human, male, late twenties, pinnacle of attractiveness, donning the best threads a tailor could make, and loaded down with just enough wealth and jewelry so he could still move. His every movement was a jingle of metals and jewelry, and Chiffon enjoyed moving often. Each little shift could cause sounds to drown out the person he was speaking to, or was trying to speak to him at any rate. Usually about title this, importance that, I've accomplished… *blah blah blah.*

Chiffon did not care. He lounged about the obese idol of ostentatious wealth, which to others must have looked like some kind of throne. The idol was a metal-cast statue with its hands cupped together. A statue as attractive as him, because it was a statue *of* him. The hands were filled with enough pillows and soft finery for Chiffon to lie down in.

The statue stood at the end of a grand rectangular hall, the ceiling of which was twice as high as it needed to be. He'd embedded the upper walls with panels of colored glass in the supposed imagery of great deeds that Chiffon had performed. All lies, of course. Not that anyone could disprove him. It was much more entertaining to try to assassinate him. An activity that had become somewhat of a game among the Nobility clans. Those bloodsucking sycophants.

Vast spiral staircases doubling as pillars kept the roof up. Easily twenty-two of them stood in the long rectangular hall. They each led to some small balcony, or alcove, or hidey-hole that Nobles liked so much. Or to places offering a view from up high that simply could not be found anywhere else. Well… sort of. Two other places allowed it, as Chiffon had this ostentatious cough-show of a room in each castle. So three of these displays of wealth in total.

They all had the staircases, but in the others, they led to things like different floors and meeting rooms. Chiffon would say he didn't know them very well, but he knew each of them by heart, as he'd specifically had them built there so he could escape from any crowd. It meant another assassin could have their chance, but it wasn't listening to droning manifests of crud—otherwise known as hearing Nobles talk.

Chiffon's opinion of them was just that wonderful. As a plus, he didn't need to descend from his throne. People would come up to him and make themselves easy to ignore, standing on a carpet so thick it obscured their feet. The floor finery matched the color of the flags and drapes that were hanging around, ever more gaudy and awful, as his attendants were on standing orders to enrich everything and anything they saw.

Even his water cup was a gem-encrusted object with custom Inscriptions and who knew whatever else went into making objects this expensive. There were days Chiffon was convinced he was the reason half the economy kept rolling. Art piece? He likely commissioned it. Furniture? He had several thousand pieces on backorder.

His train of thought broke when the new visitor jogged up to his throne and leapt, landing on the edge of his throne's hands so he could hunker down and rest his arms on his knees with a big smile. "Hello there. Splendid performance! Might you fancy a short chat? I would love to hear of your exploits!"

Chiffon's dramatic flair response fell flat, betrayed by the sound of a high-pitched inhale. His voice dropped to a whisper, Chiffon's mind screamed the truth at him even as his eyes tried their best to disbelieve. "Caretaker?"

Artorian winked at the false King. "In the meat popsicle! It's been a year and a bit. How are things? Ready to pack it in? Your performance has come to a close, my young friend. Are you still wanting to end it with flair?"

A thousand responses lived and died in Chiffon's mouth before the exhale of sudden relief overtook him. He slunk back into his pillows, suddenly deflated and torn. A weight of responsibility had both simultaneously been relieved from his shoulders, while the weight of being tired had replaced it.

His ring-covered hand rose to stop the guards that approached in a hurry, informing them to go away with a wave. It was fine. This was fine. "I… I have wondered if this day would come. I had such responses. Such quips. Now I am just tired. This performance has drained me. Is it… is it truly over? Am I free?"

Artorian had not expected Chiffon to appear so spent. Had this not been the role of a lifetime? "Indeed, my friend. You look worn, and weathered. Tell me of your burdens."

Chiffon pushed himself up a little, scooting over as he

started to take off pieces of his ostentatious garb. Which weighed more than he did. "I'm so done with this. This ridiculous Bravi hat for starters!"

Artorian flopped down next to the King, or who everyone else took as one. The Nobles present were looking between one another while holding their fine glasses of their favored beverages. Artorian didn't like how the contents looked like blood and smelled of iron. To each their own, he supposed. That thought didn't sit well, so he shot a quick inspection at a glass while Chiffon was creating more breathing room for himself by slowly disrobing the unnecessary layers. Artorian frowned, displeased. "Crackers… that's *real* blood."

Chiffon sighed hard, getting his arms free from his third robe. "This role hasn't been a good time. I don't mean due to a year of goading and insulting people. That was fun. What's going on lately is… ugh. The vampiric Nobles tried to turn me, but I'm still undead on the inside. I'm immune to whatever madness they prescribe. Things were going as planned until the clans moved in during the sun problem and essentially took over. I'm barely looked at by some of the major players, as people who have been here a while have puzzled out I'm a fraud. Just a fraud that's hard to kill. That bit brings me endless joy."

Artorian tugged at Chiffon's heavy sleeve. "What is this thing made of? Solid silver?"

Helping to get it free so Chiffon could keep talking, which he gladly did without one ounce of care to whoever might be listening. "In short, these bloodsuckers around me have been draining more than just the smelly red juice. They've been skimming from the economy too, and I can't turn that around. Honestly, another month and I would have been either a puppet ruler, or gone ignored altogether. The clans have most non-aligned in their pocket. Rulership all comes down to money."

When the third robe was finally fully off from the performer's shoulders, it was tossed down, where some aides absconded with it like a pack of hungry rats. The Caretaker observed the phenomena. "I see. I don't believe you don't have any solution conjured up after all this time. That would be odd."

Chiffon purred when he got his boots off. "Oh, I do! The effort took me months, but I can make platforms like you now, and jump through the air. That was my big escape plan. I was going to drop curse bombs from above. A pox upon all their houses! Then laugh and vanish into the distance. Sadly, I don't have the juice to both make the jumps and make the bombs."

Artorian's internal clock ticked with an idea. He extended a hand toward the performer. "Well, I might have just one thing for you. Interested in a new curse? I think you will see what I have in mind as soon as you take it."

He ignored the curse theft prompts when Chiffon grabbed his hand. Far more interested in the growing grin that was spreading across the performer's face. "Oh. *Oh.* Well, thank you. This does give me an excellent idea."

The Caretaker scrunched his face, cheekily saying 'I know' without the use of words. "I'd love to hear it."

Chiffon wormed his way out of his second coat, throwing that away as well. The expensive cloth was just dead weight now. "These vampire clans love their money. This curse is… free to use? I currently don't have any coin on me, but I do have this handy dandy spatial ring with significant storage."

An idea flashed behind Chiffon's eyes. "You are correct, Caretaker. I do want to go out with flair. Do you want to go rob a bank?"

Artorian checked his status, noting that the curse had been removed from his sheet. Good. One less worry. Though Chiffon quickly replaced that empty worry space with a new one. "Do I want to rob a bank? What are we doing with the contents?"

Chiffon rubbed his hands together, now that they were free of rings and gloves, save one. All the rest were discarded to the greed-hungry crowd gathered below, who were making it very difficult for the Nobles to overhear the conversation Chiffon was having. "Why, Caretaker, I want to sing while prancing through the sky. Money falling from my pockets while I perform a dance most sly. To steal from the lechers and give to the needy, so would my vengeance be sated against all those who are greedy."

Artorian joined Chiffon in villainous hand-rubbing. "We're going to bleed them dry and toss their money into the sky? Oh, Chiffon. That is the best idea I've ever heard of from you. I have things to do, but I'm in! Let's be quick about it. Why don't you get on my back rather than in my arms like the first time? I think I'll be needing my hands. Do you know the way?"

Chiffon discarded everything but his underclothes, kicking it all from the statue while feeling liberated by the lightness he experienced. He wasted no time and jumped over to sit on the back of the Caretaker's neck like a child being given a ride. His arm swung wildly to the windows above. "The swift route to freedom! To glory! To being a complete and total *aby~y~yss*!"

The Caretaker leapt to the window, then crashed through said window. Colored glass shards rained down from above as the duo improvised their sudden stroke of genius by running straight toward the goal. Or the regional equivalent. Artorian may not have had mana for platforms, but he had the attributes to scale walls and jump hills. He was also deliciously fast, making a chase difficult!

The Nobles had overheard some of the plan, and scrambled in a panic. Which would be to no avail. They were never going to reach the bank before Artorian and Chiffon did. Nor were their guards, assassins, or servants. While high in the air after Artorian leapt up from another building, Chiffon pointed at a large structure that was most easily described as a brick. "That one! The large, square, box-looking one with the duck symbol on the front. That's the proprietor. He likes swimming in the mountain of coins he's hoarded. What a scrooge."

Artorian nodded and bounded that direction the next time he came down for a landing, breaking the land under his feet and crumbling the ground as if a spike had been driven in. Anywhere Artorian landed, a new spot for a well opened up.

Given he wasn't being subtle in the slightest, his antics called for quite the clamor and crowd. It wasn't every day you saw a grasshopper in human form having the time of his life. Which was the base creature that most people were confusing him for. He could hear them from below. "His lady is going to bite his head off when he goes home. Making a fuss like that!"

Artorian was quickly descending on the money-filled brick, his question asked in a hurry. "What's the quickest way to get into the treasury?"

Chiffon had him covered, having this all planned out for months now. "Through the roof! Vault is in the back of the building; the only way in is through the vault door. Quickest way to the door is through the roof. The entrance is high up so the duck can dive into his money. I don't like this duck. I prefer the other one. He is a real cinnamon quack!"

The roof of the money brick did not hold up to an Artorian-shaped piledriver. Chiffon's Divine Shield protected him from the residual damage, but not from the dust the broken roof created. Had nobody been up there to ever clean it? Such copper-pinching! He coughed and waved a hand while Artorian walked; not breaking his stride in the slightest as he bore down on a large, round, iron door with strange tubes sticking from it.

When Chiffon had finished waving the dust away from his face. He tried to be helpful. "I've been here before. The lock opens depending on where the rods are, and how they turn. You need a very careful, precise combination to—"

KCHUNK.

Chiffon shut up when the Caretaker decided to skip precision, choosing instead to rip the door right out of the wall. Hinges and all. With nothing more than his hands! The man threw the door behind him like it was a piece of slag, where it crashed through the floor from sheer weight. "Alley-oop!"

Clapping his hands together to wipe them off, Artorian proceeded into an illuminated vault chamber that held a veritable sea of money. He sputtered when his eyes took it in. This was even more than he'd stolen from Chasuble, and had loaded on the carts. That was a children's heist in comparison to this!

"Crackers and toast! I thought you said they were *skimming* from the economy. This is not skimming. This *is* the economy. Get in there!"

Hoisting Chiffon from his neck, he hurled the entertainer right into the money mountain. The entertainer cackled, not caring about the damage since his shield took it. He was back-stroking through the coins until he lay still, relaxing with a happy sigh and a smile on his face. "Time for the Midas show!"

Artorian adored the sight of money vanishing into Chiffon wherever it touched him. The man himself sank to the bottom of the vault, while all the money around him piled into the new hole. Burying him alive. Not that he was either alive, nor being buried as any coins that touched him went right into his spatial ring. Chiffon was giggling as he rolled through the space, opening his mouth as it fell to pretend he was eating it. Even if Artorian knew it just vanished, he didn't say anything. This was just desserts.

When the last coin was all gobbled up a scant few minutes later. Chiffon climbed the ladder back up to where they had started, with Artorian waiting for him. "All set? They're coming up to bother us. I'd like to be gone before they knew it was us. That vault door seems to have broken the main stairwell, so we bought accidental time."

Chiffon opened his arms, pointing at the ceiling. "Beam me up, baby!"

"Ha!" Artorian laughed, and threw Chiffon up through the broken ceiling before following with a jump. "What a saying."

He caught Chiffon on his way down before landing on the roof himself, walking to the edge of the poverty brick while pressing his hands to his hips and looking to the distance. "*Ahhh…* That was a fun, swift jaunt. I suppose this is it, then. So you know, old friend, your shield won't last much longer. I'm removing the Core shortly."

Chiffon looked too liberated to care as he stood upon the building's edge. His arms were stretched wide as he soaked in the celestine light. "This opportunity has been glorious, Caretaker, to have been your acquaintance. I yearn for the life of a street performer. The freedom of travel. The practice of my desired arts. Where none will know my face, but many will come to learn my new name. I consider the lack of shielding to be little more than an additional freedom from this task. This performance has gone on for too long. Let them sort themselves out. How I wish I could be greeted by the true sun as I ventured forth, into life anew. How fitting of an exit that would have been."

His arms fell to his sides, the entertainer's eyes hollow, but full of hope. "I'm going to turn the curse on as soon as I take my first jump. Caretaker. Before I go… did I ever learn your name? I do not recall it, and remember you solely as Caretaker."

Artorian walked to the man, extending his hand. "I have many names, my old friend. You, you can call me Love."

Chiffon chuckled at the irony. "That's… yes, that's what you said a year ago. Your offer was madness. Yet you called it… a labor of love?"

He extended his own, shaking Love's hand as if it was the first time ever. The light of someone new behind his no-longer-hollow eyes. "Chance. My name is Chance. It is nice to meet you, Love. May tales of my exploits reach your ears for years to come, and if there is some cosmic law of luck in the world, then I hope she finds me welcome. For I am a performer in her theater, and speaker in her court."

Artorian squeezed Chance's wrist with mirth. "I shall hope to. May you never hear of mine, my new friend. Have a lovely trip, though perhaps, take it with my final gift. Even if it puts me in a spot of trouble."

With a wink, Chance was released and given a small push, forcing him to jump right away as Artorian nudged him along in his new life. One of impossible tricks and tasks, of performances sublime, and of tales beyond wonder. So it was that Chance survived his fall, money raining from his being as he pranced along pieces of solid sky. Laughing as he went off toward the horizon without a care. Ready to start a life of true flair.

The vampiric crowds below were unaware of Chance's current use of the poverty curse, their interests far too distracted by the literal rain of money that currently pelted them from above! Just like how glass shards from a broken glass could end up all across one's household, golden coins flung themselves across the city reaches of Solar Gate. Any attention to the commotion at the bank was thoroughly quashed as people all over the city dove both for cover, and the pursuit of wealth.

Out of all the rains the citizens of Solar Gate had endured, this one was by far their favorite! As a bonus for Artorian, the performance also completely used up everyone's attention span. That critical aspect to his upcoming plans now had a big, convenient, mental green checkmark next to it. With an effort of will—and some quick and mischievous whispers—Artorian then pulled one more stunt.

As Chance went, the celestine sun shuddered and then burned bright orange. The clock of the universe ticked once more as the sun changed and became too bright to observe. The time of the great pause had ended, purely to give heart to a performer most soulful.

When Chance looked to the world below, he laughed louder, dancing with glee while his enemies burned! He cried with joy as the vampire Lords ran rampant through the streets, beautifully combusting. "A most fitting exit! A most fitting beginning. Onwards, to reunions most auspicious!"

CHAPTER TWENTY-SEVEN

Artorian booked it out of the Solar Gate region immediately after he'd retrieved the Immaculate Core. Best to coincide one big event with another; rather than link it to an adventurer that ran up to the broken solar ring, moved his hands strangely, and then ran off with a shiny rock in his grip before the gem was stored into a spatial ring.

He supposed that was reason *one* for running. Reason two for running was that in order to give Chiffon his well-deserved exit, he'd needed to wake Eternium up. Or rather, ask his **Law** via feelings to halt the kalimba magic for a bit, to which **Love** pleasantly obliged!

As a downside, he was quite certain that the glowing storm of **wooping** flashing light behind him was a small army of Wisps. Eternium was piiiiiiissed. If the numbers ticking down on his Karmic Luck weren't proof enough, the noisy litany of notices that all yelled at him in bold text, combined with several flashing red and blue Wisps chasing him and loudly demanding he 'pull over,' was.

Artorian did not 'pull over'! Whatever that was supposed to

be. He had places to be! Though currently that boiled down to there being running to do, in the direction of not-civilization. As swiftly as his Karmic Luck ticked into the negatives, Eternium was clearly cashing in those penalties to make constant small disasters erupt in his wake.

If he had been running any slower, those would have occurred with him smack in the middle of them. Earthquakes tore the land open. Rivers mysteriously blindsided him from around a hill. Underground volcanoes decided to say hello from below. Boss monsters congregated and gave chase for some unknown grievance. A rock he nearly tripped over was turned into an angry earth elemental, whose only ability seemed to be an instant-kill spell called 'Rocks Fall.'

Which they did! In droves! Artorian's only saving grace was his speed, and the bonuses to it. He kept altering how fast he was going to try to throw his pursuers off his trail, but given the world was turning apocalyptic everywhere he ran, that was easier said than done. "Toast, toast, toast! Go, speed-racer, go!"

That Speedrunner title was saving his bacon, though Artorian was entirely responsible for keeping it at the right temperature. Or his ass was grass.

Yvessa popped next to his head in her Wisp form, easily visible as Artorian drew in deep breaths to keep up the less than jaunty run. "Morning, sunshine. Nice to see you outside of places where people are so I could check in. I see you woke up the big guy. Surely you knew that was a bad idea?"

She was entirely too nonchalant for this! He nearly fell into a tumble during a particularly sharp turn to avoid a hill that looked like it was getting up, growing arms to swat him! Like the hill was some sort of vengeful mudman. Artorian called out the first thing that came to mind: "How are you here? All the other Wisps can't seem to catch me!"

Yvessa shrugged, making the sound of smacking her mouth as if chewing on a reed. "Oberon and I have tethering capabilities. We can rubber-band people. He's a little busy handling

Eternium's tantrum, who is quite upset. More so since he figured out who was responsible for his little nappy-time. Since I'm your designated Observer Wisp anyway, I popped over to watch. I can't say I'm even a little surprised this is the kind of mess you got into."

Artorian leapt over the sudden formation of a wide chasm, heralded by the crunching noises erupting from beneath and the visible tear that occurred before the landmass split. "Help me!"

The sound of a nail file cleaning up fingers rasped from Yvessa's orb. "Mmm… Nah. You got yourself into this mess. You get yourself out. Besides, you've pulled more impressive feats out of your keister. Figure it out."

Artorian's mind was racing. Faster than his feet! Though not as fast as the racer, if only he had access to it. Sadly, it wouldn't have helped. The racer's speed was constant, which Eternium could calculate with ease. His movement was spastic and sporadic, breaking the ground under his feet when he made sudden stops and turns to throw the dungeon off. He had plenty of practice against the Hel goose in Cal's Soul Space. "Thank you, Wagner!"

The situation was dire. He hastily pulled up his character sheet and skills mid-bolt, scrolling through when he had a second, and glancing when he had another. Something on this list needed to be helpful. Bloody *something*! All these mana boosters were useless!

A glowing portal opened nearby, gargoyle-shaped things pouring out to give chase. Hold on. *Demons*? On top of everything else. Demons were portaling in on his location? The audacity! Artorian didn't have time to deal with them. As a minor bonus, the apocalypse trail took care of them handily! He could evade that mess. The interlopers could not.

Artorian confirmed this when he watched an active volcano spout burst open underneath the glowing portal. A cylinder of magma disappeared right through the gate as the spell was engulfed, covering whoever was on the other side with surprise lava! That was even better than pocket sand. "Surprise lava! Hah!"

He was suddenly very concerned why this demon incursion hadn't happened in Solar Gate, then remembered the crab Core had been powering the area protection effect. That melted them as well! Albeit via a different function.

A Nixie Tube appeared above his head. Why was he still paying the field costs when the Core was in his pocket? He rescinded those costs, feeling twenty-eight percent of his mana bar appear. Success!

In short, no demonic annoyances in Solar Gate. Now that he was out and about on the other hand, they were both fully capable of tracking him, *and* attacking without consequence. Artorian was being assailed by demonic forces that were being gated in, and those forces didn't know the abyss he'd raised. The karma storm was currently hot on his tail, and those portals looked awfully *stationary*. "*Hehehehe.*"

An idea struck him when the entire landmass beneath his feet began to tilt upwards. "I have martial arts skills! Artorian, use them you fool!"

Flow Like Water, Breathe the Air, and Impeccable Focus all sprang into action, sharpening his senses as the world turned to turmoil around him. "How does one fight the land itself? *Uh…* not well!"

That was when several things on his sheet caught his eye all at once. Skills were something he'd overlooked. They were just a nice bonus, such as Mobile Archery! Zen Arrow did not require him to stand still while using it. Then there was the line 'ignores all environmental factors.' "Aww yiss. A plan is coming together!"

The entry also said nothing about the skill being unable to be combined with Multishot. Unlike last time, this bow could handle overdraw! He was going to need to wait for a minute cooldown between Zen Arrows anyway. That gave him all the time in the world to line up an empowered shot.

He needed to get away, but so long as he could avoid the apocalypse… Technically he had demons portaling in to play with him. He needed that second specialization, and that meant using Zen Archer skills.

A solution of pure madness flickered before his eyes as the spider web of thoughts led him to several crazy ideas. Each as bat-guano insane as the rest. "Yvessa! Which direction is the Bifrost to the next realm?"

Grinning, she turned her orb into an arrow. The system couldn't fault her if she happened to play with her shape. She, after all, didn't say anything that the log would record as an answer. "Who knows? It's a very pointed question."

Artorian's eyes glimmered with joy. The teamwork was back! She'd just been waiting on him to get all of his abyss together, put it in a bag, and throw it over his shoulder! He altered his speeding direction right away and flickered his abilities. Sustenance was given long enough active time to make him well-fed and well-hydrated. He didn't leave it on much longer after that, having had a wonderfully foolish set of ideas.

He checked the general feeling of his spatial ring, finding that his supplies from Cra's Crafts were all still in there. Including all the arrows he'd been making during practice! A bundle of fifty per location slot. He supposed fifty arrows counted for one item, or however that worked. It wasn't terribly important right now as he retrieved the BS-Bow from his ring. He called forth five arrows right after, which were all swiftly nocked in one go. He wasn't going to question how that worked so easily.

He really needed to name this bow design! It reminded him of Yuki in some way. Artorian just couldn't put his finger on it. What if he just changed a letter? Yumi? Yes. This was a Yumi bow.

That meant it was time for the breakdown. He focused on Zen Arrows to make them a constant. A timer appeared in the corner of his vision, reminding him of the cooldown that would occur after he released a shot. Except that it would be five shots all at once thanks to Multishot. Five shots that would all be overdrawn to the maximum value, since this bow very helpfully told him exactly what that number was. Thank you, *Sturdy*!

Mobile Archery was going to take some of the penalties off, and he was roughly convinced five arrows with Multishot wouldn't hurt him extra right now. If he was wrong, he would cool off attacking for a while. He didn't have the focus to look at the exact number. There was a dungeon's wrath to evade, which took precedence over setup.

Hard to focus on a target to shoot when a brand-new thunderstorm tracked him from above, all too happy to throw bolts of lightning down while volcanic activity seemed to occur wherever he stepped. Creation of a new mountain range? Landscaping? Landscaping! He liked that word! Now what to do with that twenty-eight percent mana bar?

Body Mastery didn't seem like it would help right now. Oh, that took stamina! Never mind. Soul of Zen? No, same problem. Took stamina. Unlike the prior option, that would probably actually help right now. More time to process and react was an incredibly valuable commodity. Yes, he'd definitely use that in a bit. First, this mana bar. No point using Electrosense in this mess. It would just confuse him with all the maddening activity between hot and cold temperatures. That was the exact trick he'd used to off one of Cataphron's disciples back in the day. He knew better.

Sustenance was a pro option. Except that it was better when flickered, since the buffs stayed for a while. He wasn't having significant trouble breathing, so no Omnibreath. What about reclaiming the use of his own Resplendence field? He currently wasn't hurt; being dirty wasn't a big deal since he needed to dash for it anyway, and he was honestly happy to have it off for now. It felt sore.

That left Empowerment.

Had he ever thrown all one hundred percent of his mana bar into Empowerment? He had not! Why did that feel like a terrible idea? Like it would come with dangerous consequences? "*Eh*. Dale it!"

The threat was only demons who hated his guts, and the dungeon he was in liberally trying to slap him down like some roach that wouldn't stay dead. What was one more terrible life choice into the mix? Easy! It was entertainment. A choice that, even if bad, was one he would not regret.

No matter the heck-scape one found themselves in, it was important to keep the spirit up. Y'know, live a little. "Empowerment, one hundred percent investment. Here we *go*!"

The field of energy around Artorian thickened and tightened. Vibrantly humming with the sound of some large energy condenser charging around a Pylon. The noise built as if something big was about to pop off. Artorian felt excited, but didn't receive the satisfaction of some big malfunction to kick Eternium in the chin. "Dangit!"

Instead he inhaled deep, preparing for what was likely going to be pain. The experience was a carbon copy of becoming an A-ranker. Being squeezed and squished under the pressure of forces that comprised his own being. Had he not gone through this before, he would have stopped attempting pouring his whole bar into the ability right away. This felt like being murdered via gravity, or worse.

No sane person would willingly go through this pressure. Did that mean he'd lost it? "No! Needs must! Do not yield in the face of adversity. Push on. Push through. Strive on and break through. The only acceptable outcomes are survival, victory, and success!"

The mana bar maximum emptied to zero percent as he kept running at top speed, then winked out entirely with a sudden blip.

Keening loudly, the pressure glowed sharp and aggressive around Artorian as the compressed power reached its peak. Words came to mind before his power exploded, his dark brown hair turning bright gold while energy spirals swirled around him. He yelled without thought as his eyes became celestine, screaming the newfound words that left his lips. "*Ad Astra*!"

Artorian suddenly went a whole lot faster, and this time, *he* was the reason the landscape exploded.

CHAPTER TWENTY-EIGHT

A Pylon malfunction may not have kicked Eternium in the chin, but this latest stunt from Artorian certainly had. Eternium's attacks were temporarily halted as the dungeon staggered, coming to terms with its own system momentarily rebelling against his control. A threshold had been met, and it required addressing before further commands could be applied to the world. Eternium cursed his own humanity for setting important events to come to the forefront and block out other functions.

Fine!

Eternium addressed Oberon, even though the dungeon was without a body. The human version of his bonded Wisp sat nearby, seeming out of breath from all the yelling the bright orange man had done. Yelling that had fallen on deaf ears.

Eternium spoke Rhys, his favorite language. He did so with a voice that was calm and collected, though it carried an aged, almost Dwarven cadence and depth. "What happened?"

Now that Oberon finally had Eternium's attention, the Wisp took a deep breath and berated him for being an impetuous child. Throwing a tantrum because he woke up from a nap? What kind of a baby was he? "You're making a mess, that's what! You're supposed to be a third-step S-ranker! This display is embarrassing! Get a hold of yourself! You've been letting your emotions get to you non-stop, and ever since you started playing with Karmic Luck, you have been an unmanageable teenager out doing his own thing. I know being in Cal weakens the personality boundaries, but celestials above! What even!"

When Oberon pressed hands to his knees to heave in another breath, he felt hoarse. He summoned some water just to drink it and throw the cup on the floor, where it vanished into particles rather than make the satisfying thwack he'd been hoping for.

The dungeon fell silent, a thousand flashing windows going ignored. "Did not…"

"Did too!" Oberon found his breath right away, his long finger levered right to Eternium's current perspective. "You can't hide it from me! You can hide it from everyone else, but not *me*! You have been letting yourself go and indulging in being a cheeky child. Because you knew you could. Because you knew there would be no repercussions to 'slip' for a bit. It is my skill as a Wisp to sweet-talk and slither through clever words to guide you back onto the right path. This needs none of these skills! Your current predicant needs an old lady to smack you with a broom. In fact… You know what? I saw something in Artorian's memories that I think would be perfect here."

Oberon vanished, the orange light of his distorting as he abandoned his current human form for something more… impactful. The slipper that struck a tiny, rough, calloused open hand was nothing like Oberon's prior form. This lady had both experience and voice in spades, as the form of Ephira Mayev Stonequeen impatiently stabbed her gaze toward Eternium's perspective.

Oberon's vocal tone changed to match her voice. "This requires the touch of *Grandmama*. You want to be a little child? Fine."

The slipper struck Mayev's hand again, handing over the reins of control to the personality he was importing from the memories of everyone stored that knew her. This was not a feature they were going to advertise the use of, much less the existence. That didn't mean it wasn't something they couldn't do. When Mayev spoke again, it was all her. Glaring Eternium down like a baby Modsognir. "Grandmama's house, Grandmama's rules!"

When Eternium finally yielded after getting his perspective beaten around by a slipper containing the **Law of Explosions**, Mayev sat him down and thoroughly lectured the boy. That was all the respect he got right now. 'The boy.' A little, rambunctious, trouble-making snoot. No better than the other problem children running around in Eternia.

Ephira pointed at the screens. "Now explain!"

Much like Cal who didn't have much of a chance against Dani when she was truly on fire, Eternium had little defense against Oberon when the pot finally boiled over. He mumbled out a weak response before getting to work. "Yes, Grandmama..."

With a return to focus, Eternium extended himself and his senses once again. To assist in his focus, a dark organ rumbled to life in the background. The sounds of mechanical depths combined with electric thrumming. The tone was slow, and methodical. Orderly, and contemplative. Powerful, and deep.

Thousands of screens shifted in parallel. Moving one moved them all, their pattern holding in a complicated three-dimensional star design. Each screen was unlike those that the Wisps had access to, as each one was a compressed flat surface containing several thousand screens. Combined into one flat panel like a massive tome made thin.

When a screen opened before Eternium, it was the entire vast tome of knowledge that did so. Unfurling secrets, the truth of things, and the mechanics of the world involved with that function.

A hologram of the Pylons responsible for the pause in his workflow connected to the network involving the key functions was pulled close. Once selected, the information bloomed into being around them as if they were standing in the Pylon holds. There would be **Order**, and with but a movement of the mind, Eternium summoned close the pertinent, immediate needs that had to be addressed.

His screens and windows had no interesting, lively colors to them. They were all a rusty brown, save those that needed attention. Eternium preferred color use for denoting the kind of attention something required.

It was thus to his great displeasure to once again be looking at a colorful landscape pulsating in the star pattern of his creation. So much broken. So much disconnected. So much new was not properly added to the needed functions. The automated Pylons had done their best to keep up in his absence, with the entire society of Wisps hard at work trying to keep on top of things. It was a kindness of an effort, but they would never work Eternia with the mastery he could muster.

Oberon had been right. He'd been slipping. It was so easy to do in Cal's Soul Space. He may have started as an almighty, ancient, triple S-ranker, yet time here had given way to his rigid ways and views. For all his superior might, the balance of **Law** tiers was undeniable. Cal had one-upped him, and that tiny difference shone through in spades.

One day, Cal would also reach the triple S-ranks. On that day, he knew that no matter his might, Cal would walk past him. Then one step further. **Acme** was undeniable. Of that grand source, **Order** was but a fragment. Even if it would take Cal much longer to achieve his goal.

Eternium had been playing around in the newfound freedom of no longer needing to be in charge of everything. Of needing to balance the world. Of conjuring up endless solutions to the maddening pain in the Core that was Xenocide.

The **Law** of **Madness** could shove it.

The **Law** of **Love** could too. Even if Artorian wasn't an iota as malicious as Xenocide. Very much the opposite. He'd needed that nap, and would never have admitted it. As Oberon said, he'd been a petulant child: denying the need for naptime, but immediately snoring on a pillow if he was so much as tucked in, or guided to slumber by the plink of a kalimba.

How Artorian convinced a Heavenly rank to pay attention was lost on him. Eternium had rarely been able to make **Order** so much as look over the shoulder at him. He'd needed to put in eons of effort for a wink of affirmation. He understood how the role that Heavenly played required constant attention to their task, yet it didn't make Eternium any less jealous of Artorian.

A fact which had made him lash out ever harder.

He needed to get a hold of himself. This was getting out of hand. Best to start there then, as he took himself and Oberon—even if currently in Grandmama form—all the way to the time-frame of 'mundane.' The slowest available speed. Or fastest? Depended on how you looked at it.

Eternium opened the knowledge tome that was flashing a stream of precious metal colors at him. The issue he needed to address before his ordered system would bend to him. It seemed someone had dinged an ability to the Sage ranks. That was odd. That didn't just happen out of the blue. The evolution warning was flashing gold, informing him that the ability needed to be updated depending on the Sage's use of it so far.

Eternium pulled up the ability notice a new Sage initially received. He tended to put personal touches on ability gains, since Cal undoubtedly would as well.

Ability gained: Empowerment. Not strong enough at the moment? Trade one power for another! By investing a percentage of your chi bar, you can increase your base physical attributes. This ability belongs to the Monk class. Notice! You have mana, not chi. The Generalist class will allow mechanics of the existing math to be kept the same.

Notice! As a cultivator importing this knowledge, know this. Permanent increases to power other than those established by the system will not be allowed or tolerated. Attempting to breach the Mage ranks will be circumvented. A temporary power boost via an X to Y trade will be unlocked instead.

He would have slapped his forehead, had he one. A glance at the name of the person in question revealed the culprit to be none other than **Love's** A-ranker. "Of course. It's Artorian again. Why would it have been anyone else?"

Oberon snickered even if his dungeon was just talking to himself. Eternium opened up the use over time log, reading all the entries of how this had come to pass. "He kept it active for *how long*? Why *that high*? Constant strain from Empowerment like that should have ripped him to pieces… Why isn't that listed in the description? Where is the rank scaling for this? … Why isn't it here?"

Eternium groaned when he saw the import mention. "We didn't have the Pylons. **Hnnnggg*. Fine. I'll just need to update the whole thing and add it. There should be limits to this ability's maximum Empowerment cap based on rank and level."

Ability Updated: Empowerment. Not strong enough at the moment? Trade one power for another! By investing a percentage of your chi bar, you can increase your base physical attributes. This ability belongs to the Monk class. This ability can affect 10% of your chi bar and attributes per rank.

Eternium pressed 'finished,' but the automated Pylons complained. The organ blared an error sound in the background. The dungeon frowned, digging deeper into the problem.

"Ah! Sage was the ninth rank in the system, so this current calculation would only allow an investment of up to ninety percent. Artorian has gone the full one-hundred already." Eternium fiddled with a swift alteration behind the scenes. Something that would not be visible to anyone without deep system access. He added a tenth rank labeled 'Deity' to the system, temporarily linked to the title as a prerequisite.

This made the organ cease its complaining melody, opening up the evolution option on Eternium's prompt. Good. "Looks like he invested fully, which caused the Pylons to think he reached the maximum rank threshold since one wasn't listed, triggering the warning."

Oberon nodded in understanding, watching Eternium work easily a hundred screens at once with information alteration. Eternium had no issues talking while working. "There was an oddity during the trigger. I don't actually know what 'Ad Astra' means, but I will open a slot in case we can ask or figure it out in the future. The pressure he survived… right. A-ranker. He's gone through this already. The excess power from the Pylon imparted some physical changes on his additional nature form. That's fine. Now for the Sage effect."

Eternium's perspective popped as if he cracked his fingers. "He seems to be focusing on speed rather than power. Though I think watching a live recording would be more helpful than the logs. Obi, can you give me a view of the last minute of activity?"

Grandmama whacked the air with her slipper and a screen appeared. The images on it flickered before moving, adjusting to the local time-frame before they watched Artorian blur through a landscape which exploded and broke around him. Lightning crashed from above while volcanic activity chased him and erupted from below. Demon gates opened without warning within that entire mess, letting gargoyles burst forth only to be incinerated by the environment. Or be blown to chunks by a few Zen Arrows at a time.

Artorian was a golden yellow blur of movement, never staying in the same location for long or revisiting it twice. He seemed too fast. His operational acuity was far too high for the baseline reactions speeds he should have, even with the A-ranker statistical boosts.

Eternium checked his active abilities. "Ah, that explains how he's keeping such high combat clarity. Soul of Zen is active. It's hurting his stamina regeneration some, but maximized Empowerment gave him a bonus when his attributes altered. Odd how they are only twenty percent higher than baseline."

A few more screens read, and Eternium had that figured out

as well. "It's interacting with the age penalty of his other form? I didn't realize those would overlap like that. I was certain Humanization and Additional Nature had individual Pylons. That does not appear to be the case and will be remedied."

Slating it for Wisp attention since it was a Pylon that needed to be grown, he moved on and watched the one-minute time lapse of the fight again. Oberon noted the pause, letting the Grandmama guise go for the moment. "Something wrong?"

"No," Eternium said. "Just more jealousy. Before you got on my case, I was angrily setting up recurring patterns to chase Artorian around, using the Karmic Luck mechanic as fuel. They aren't guided attacks, and he seems to have figured that out. He's avoiding all the environmental damage before it has a chance to get to him. He's even moving in some odd triangle formation in order to *guide* the pattern onto an open demon gate. Smart of him not to jump through. The gravity on the other side would squish him."

Oberon understood. "So what's this evolution thing? That's news to me."

Eternium made the screen in question larger so it was easier to see. "Evolution is a mechanic that occurs the first time a skill or ability reaches the Sage ranks. My Pylons work on a feedback loop in order to send in improvements. When a skill reaches maximum potential, that loop cannot continue. So it's up to me to review activity and use of the skill, and create a capstone. An evolution of how that toy has been used thus far. Something special."

Eternium pondered, then thought of an idea. "Ad Astra…"

Oberon looked over to his dungeon's perspective, rather than reading the screen. "Come again? That was the odd duo of words Artorian used. You said they had no meaning."

"They had no meaning *yet*," Eternium corrected him. "Interference is at play. I'm using that as the name for the capstone. I'm going to make it come with a title. I think reaching a Sage skill should allot a title. Effects pending. When it comes to the ability evolution, my idea of Empowerment was as a method of short-term attribute increase. Artorian has not used it like that, and the evolution needs to reflect that. He's used it because even with his ludicrous speed, he still needed to go faster. So I'm thinking of dropping the strain entirely and adding ease of actions. Once you reach maximum Empowerment, you should unlock the 'stable' form of it."

"The Ad Astra form? Strange to say. What about the Astra form? It just sounds like a super-form derived from the existing ability." Oberon mentioned his thoughts after tasting the words, then smiled. "Super-Artorian doesn't sound too bad either!"

His reply was Eternium silently updating the ability once more.

Ability Evolution: Empowerment. You have reached the Sage rank utilizing this ability, prompting an evolution to its base functions in accordance with your use. While using 100% of Empowerment, you will enter the 'Astra' form. A stable form of Empowerment that reduces strain caused, and increases ease of actions.

Evolution effect: The Astra form causes a minor change in appearance, and provides the Novice rank in Soul of Zen, providing this ability if the user did not have it before, and automatically activating it for free so long as the Astra form is in effect. If the user already has Soul of Zen, then the costs for using the Novice rank are considered free if it, or higher ranks are used.

Evolution downside: New timing mechanic. Astra form is not something that should be active all the time. For every twenty seconds it is in use, stamina regeneration will decrease by one point until deactivation. The strain for normal Empowerment has been set to one point of stamina regeneration lost every ten seconds.

Eternium was pleased. A good balance that was going to get plenty of testing. If things went well, there would be another update! "*Now*. Onto the rest. My world is broken. **Order** must be mended."

CHAPTER TWENTY-NINE

Life became easier for Artorian when the Soul of Zen costs suddenly disappeared. He felt the change rather than see it, though now that he paid attention, the angry notices had stopped as well. They were even cleaning themselves up from the blasted, destroyed parts of the battlefield. He hadn't given his log the time of day with how busy this battle dance kept him.

Now that he had the hang of sidestepping Armageddon, that became an option. Especially with how much less draining the activities he was going through felt. No further apocalypse patterns had been added to the dance. Which was a good thing, too! He wouldn't have been able to keep up with another one.

Artorian saw his attack cooldown flash—making him swivel and turn—then release his held shots at the next closest demon in view. He had plenty of targets, and his specialization experience bar got hammered with gains. If his shots didn't off his enemy, the environment would. Nice thing being that he still got the experience in full when it did! Looked like getting killed by the environment was a 'your own fault' kind of thing, currently resulting in no experience being divided. He was on a roll! Any arrow shot now, he expected to get the second specialization slot. Any shot now!

Ding!

Artorian smiled wide and paused his assaults, taking the moment to run off in the direction of the Bifrost. He was burning with anticipation to read notifications and check to see if he'd gotten what he wanted. Yes, he pulled the trails of doom along with him, but he could stay ahead of it so long as he stuck to the established zigzag pattern. This was just like dodging arrows. Zigzag!

Notice! Due to the abundance of notifications in your inbox, cleaning operations have begun. Only pertinent information will be shown, some of it combined into one.

User: Artorian, has lost an incalculable amount of Karmic Luck. Negative Karmic Luck is constantly being expended to sustain currently unnamed effects. Effects will end when Karmic Luck reaches 0.

Titles Gained! Notice: You are currently at 10 titles. A title must be removed in order for a new one to be slotted.
Title gained: Sage of Empowerment.
You have reached the end of a particular skill or ability, and are the first to do so. The ability 'Empowerment' has evolved based on your actions and uses in the world. As there is no current Sage in any of the chi arts, this title has automatically been upgraded to Sage of Chi. A separate title has been created for the specific ability.
Sage of Chi reduces the cost of all Monk class skills and abilities by 20%.

Title gained: Starlight Warrior.
You are the first to unlock the Astra form of the Empowerment ability. This title doubles the strain allotment of how long one can remain in Astra form before a point of stamina regeneration is removed.

Artorian figured he'd missed something important and took this opportunity to read the original Empowerment ability. "Wow! What an update!"

He veered off toward a flat grassy plain so he could run without needing to pay too much attention to where he was going, so he could read all the changed text. Something Yvessa had mentioned bothered him. Wasn't it impossible to change abilities like this on the fly? Or was this Eternium's way of cheating? Didn't matter. The ability update was fabulous. He'd even skipped past all the limitations!

"Hehehe." Artorian wasn't going to complain even a little bit about that.

That explained the titles, and their effects were solid. He threw out the Legend and Trailblazer titles without thinking about it. He was then momentarily confused about why his mapping ability had vanished, along with his entire minimap. He fussed at himself. "Artorian, you fool."

Trailblazer was what gave him the mapping ability, and he'd just thrown it away, too distracted by being in a hurry. One should never make important decisions in a hurry.

"Still. Two new titles!" They made his abilities feel lighter right away, and that felt great.

Artorian was about to read the next notification, but he smacked right into a big tree, disorienting him for a brief moment before his skills removed the debuff by force. Who put a tree in the middle of a field! That was like putting a single cactus in the middle of a desert! On second thought… someone would find a way to run into it. Just like he had, by not paying attention.

Rubbing his forehead, he had to ignore that he'd left a him-shaped indent in the tree trunk. If someone else ever saw this, he hoped they got a laugh out of it, because he needed to run. He still had negative Karmic Luck to burn off and those environmental effects were still tailing him.

No reason to dally.

Zipping back off, he checked his notifications to see many of them were removing themselves, making it very hard to read the contents. Of the few he saw, the notices being removed were mostly angry messages from Eternium. Each with a hefty karma penalty. Once those were all gone, none remained.

"None? What about my specialization?" Had he really not crossed the threshold? There was no way. He should have by now. Checking his status sheet, he grumbled to himself. The second specialization box was all chained up. "Crackers!"

An odd feeling struck him, making him dismiss the notifications altogether, log included. It felt like he'd just lost a point of something. Stamina regeneration? Right! Empowerment had functional strain now. His title didn't remove the penalty outright, but it diminished the drain he was now stacking up. Was his stamina regeneration going to keep ticking down until he turned it off? That would be terrible with his attributes penalized.

"Time for a safety check." If he dropped out of Empowerment, he needed to make sure he was actually somewhere safe. In Midgard, that may be anywhere. Since he was planning to realm hop as soon as possible, that became less of a certainty so long as his Karmic Luck remained on the fritz. "Yvessa. Can I get an expected time for how long that storm is going to keep chasing me? Will my karma hit zero before I get to the bridge?"

The green orb returned to visibility now that there were no demons to see her. "It will. I don't think you'll be able to keep Empowerment up the entire trip, but the answer is still yes. What are you going to do when Empowerment deactivates, and the demons are still portaling in?"

Artorian bit his lip with a frown, his feet booking it as the landscape zipped by. "Improvise! I'm going to start by running until I just can't anymore and need to let Astra form go. Nudge me a minute beforehand. My focus is going to be on getting a move on!"

Yvessa understood, and went invisible as Artorian did what he said, and ran for the hills. Deactivating all abilities that drained stamina save for his Astra form, just to run longer.

With a stamina regeneration of four hundred forty-three, losing one point every forty seconds, and moving at a speed of one thousand seven hundred and fifty-eight feet per second. So long as conditions were perfect and the ground remained flat, doubled by the Novice rank in Soul of Zen, he was going to make quite the distance.

Artorian didn't currently feel like doing the math on that, choosing to trust Yvessa instead. It would have been easier had he still been able to see where the beacons were. Granted, that only helped if he could use them, which he currently could not. The minimap would have allowed him to see how far away the Bifrost was, but he'd bitten that arrowhead already and had to let it go.

Luckily, the trip was uneventful, save for a few branches to the face, and the accidental punting of some random wildlife into the atmosphere. He'd apologized, though it dawned on him a little late that the critter likely hadn't heard him.

Yvessa appeared when he was starting to feel his regeneration statistic seriously dwindle. "Old man. One minute. The running strain costs are about to overtake your regeneration number."

Artorian was keeping his breathing steady, having passed through enough landscapes to put his trip with Ember through the season-changing grove to shame. Still, he was coated in sweat, and definitely felt the strain. "You got it! Looking for a place to hunker. How're the demon gates?"

His Wisp was on the ball with information. "They stopped hours ago. I'm guessing the mana costs to open and close them isn't gentle, and the environmental surprises weren't a bonus. As a heads up, you can only remove stacked strain with a full rest. So expect to need to be out a full eight hours. Sustenance isn't going to help you any here, but you're going to want to flicker it, at minimum. You are taking the severe malus versions. That cut down your running time."

Artorian sure felt those. "They don't feel great, that's for sure. I ache and hurt all over. I see a hollow. I'm going to slow down, dive in, and call it a day. I'm going to try to sleep, but I'm slapping on Electrosense. I don't want to get snuck up on if the portal-boys change their mind."

Yvessa's temporary light dimmed to invisibility again, though she stuck to his shoulder when Astra form deactivated. The ability deactivating immediately removed his special colorations and energy pressure before he dove face first into the large hole. Something likely lived inside of said large hole in the side of the cliff face, but that was a problem for future Artorian.

He tumbled hard.

The exhaustion caught up with him right away as he slammed into the back wall hard enough to add a few more feet of 'back wall.' The tree roots and packed dirt stopped him, but it shook the hill hard enough to scare all the local birds off their trees. He groaned and held his head, noticing the minor concussion malus populating in his character panel. Great.

With a motion, Electrosense, Resplendence field, and Sustenance all returned to say hello. Allowing the old man to breathe a sigh of relief as he crumpled up in a corner, his legs feeling like logs on perpetual fire.

"Ha! Speaking of perpetual fire, the Mana Burn flames dimmed. Were they gone?" Checking the maluses, he sighed as Endless Mana Burn was still there. It just didn't have anything to burn. Did that have anything to do with how bright the ultramarine was? Who cared? Not him. Not right now. He pulled his Soul Item from his sternum without thinking about it twice, let it flop on the ground, and rolled himself on top of it since his legs aptly refused to listen to him.

He didn't even have the time to be surprised he'd managed to pull his pillow free before passing out. He was totally overtaxed from who knew how many leagues of running. When Yvessa asked him a question, the only reply was a vast snore that rocked the cavern which the hollow led to.

While there was indeed an animal living in the connected underground section, the aware-bear did not feel like exploring.

Not when a snore belonging to something much larger rumbled from the entrance. The order of the day was hiding. The bear would go out to hunt and eat when the noisy *thing* left. The aware-bear wasn't risking a thing. Waking something like that up could only have terrible consequences. It knew. It was aware.

Terrible consequences that the demons who portaled in discovered for themselves, when Soni managed to get a portal to connect. The Resplendence field turned summoned troops and convenient non-demon fodder into gooey butter when they stepped foot outside of the safe zone. Which inconveniently comprised the entire other side of their gate.

The demons could see their target prone on a pillow in the back of the hollow, but they could not reach him. They did note that the target in question did not look like a child, and matched the description which some gargoyles had provided. Based on the ledgers by Pencil's personal gargoyles. Who had survived the kerfuffle at Triplicate by running away early. Soni found that interesting, but had to remain focused on just keeping the portal stable.

A few of the more intelligent among them had the bright idea to rope-tie several spears together at both the tip and aft. So they could reach the long stick out and poke their enemy to death. Their attempts broke apart when the seventh one was tacked on, which by the look of it was still several spears too short.

Not good enough, but alternatives were coming up dry. A few more impatient demons jumped through with sword in hand, but that caused the expected side-effects. Soni slapped his tiny hand over his face and grunted out the name that had been coined for the effect. "The poofening."

After some fumbling and several more unlucky test subjects that proved the field was near-instantly fatal to low-level moss like them, the portal in the hollow closed back up. They'd had their fill of seeing demons turn into celestine *poof*, and Soni wasn't about to risk his own hide.

The Resplendence field ability had been active for over a

year straight in Solar Gate, which had done wonders for its rank. Now that it was back with the owner, the Pylons were able to update it properly, dinging Artorian with his second Sage quality ability, and grinding Eternium to a screeching halt in his workspace once again.

Yvessa just smiled, closing her eyes as she could swear that she heard the tirade all the way to where she lounged. Only for the irate commentary in Rhys to be brought to swift silence by the **fhwap** of an explosive slipper.

CHAPTER THIRTY

Artorian woke feeling straight up wonderful. He lounged on his pillow, stretching and kneading it like some fat spoiled cat. Yvessa interrupted his pleasant waking. "All set to get going?"

He grumbled and pressed his face into the pillow, pretending he had neither heard her, nor was present.

"Get up, you sly old man! I know you heard me."

Artorian yowled and scowled when a spoon of mana smacked him on the keister. Forcing him to curl up and hold it. "*Ow~w~w.*"

After rolling around a bit and rubbing to make the pain go away, he shot his Wisp a glare, knowing full well she was in the right. Easing off from the most convenient Soul Item ever, he stowed it without difficulty and hopped in place after. "Everything feels good. Thought I was going to burn to cinders before falling asleep with how much it all ached. Status sheet shows the usual, and it's always nice to see the well-fed buff. I'm surprised nothing woke me up."

Yvessa took her human form, just so he could see her grin. "Oh, they tried! Check your notifications."

Artorian did as his caretaker told him, laughing heartily

when he received the Sage skill notice. "Another one! Poor Eternium. Ahhh… speaking of… How's my karma?"

Yvessa shot him a thumbs up. "Even zero. All sorted. You outran the effects yesterday. I'm not sure what that's going to do to the landscape, but if all goes well, the land will be reset next iteration anyway. Unless it's a good alteration we want to keep. Some Wisps will investigate. Did you see the evolution update for the field?"

Artorian hadn't given that a proper look, so he pulled it up. He recalled the initial explanation on Resplendence field had been a big one.

Ability: Presence.
Utilization: Resplendence field.
Zones affected: Inner, Body, Outer.

This is an imported function. Explanation: The Resplendence field is a derivative of the original cultivator ability known as Starlight Aura. This field performs multiple functions in a lesser capacity, and requires a constant flat percentage of a mana bar's maximum to be invested in order to sustain its upkeep.

Flat cost: twenty-eight percent of total mana. Equal to four percent per active effect. This field heals, cleanses, cleans, revitalizes, restores, regenerates, and invigorates via the formula n%x. Where n represents the rank of this ability, and x represents the rank of each other individual ability listed.

As this is a field-based ability, this effect is indiscriminate, affecting any valid target present within the radius. The radius is determined by 30r, where r represents the rank of this ability. Individual levels are not taken into account to calculate the radius.

Notice: Due to the individual abilities not being unlocked, their values will remain static. If the listed abilities are unlocked, their individual leveling track will increase the potency of their effect in this field accordingly.

Notice: This ability is light-aligned. Light-based creatures and their adjacents will be immune, or gain additional benefit. Dark-based creatures and their adjacents will take additional damage, or gain additional demerits.

He'd done something wrong. That was the original notice he'd gotten when he gained the ability. How did he check for the update? "Yvessa. What do I do to see the changes? This is the one I knew."

Glancing over from her own screens—which seemed to be parts of his character panel—she saw the issue. "Just swipe right on that explanation. That changes the panels to show your last updates manually, if they don't fix themselves automatically."

Artorian swiped, and the information changed like Yvessa said it would.

Entry: Resplendence field
Rank: Sage

Ability Evolution: Since imported functions cannot be made cheaper, they will be made more effective. All skills or abilities that Resplendence field required have been permanently unlocked for the user, even if they had not been acquired yet, as the 'n' value of this ability can no longer increase.

Evolution effect: The user gains the following cleric class abilities: Heal, Cleanse, Clean, Revitalize, Restore, Regenerate, and Invigorate. In addition, the radius of this field effect has been doubled. This ability is now calculated at a radius determined by 60r, where r represents the rank of this ability.

This field effect now ignores all physical barriers.

Yvessa spoke to him before he finished reading. "You also have another title waiting. Looks like you get one if you're the first Sage ranked in something. I wonder how those spots open back up."

Artorian finished reading and replied without a fuss. "Likely when they die or move on. I'm not feeling very attached here. If I leave this game permanently, I would want those titles to be available for others. I'm sure it might have more importance to people who put real time and effort into getting there. Rather than my blatant cheatery. Not fair otherwise."

He tapped the notification.

Title gained!: Sage of Resplendence.

You have reached the end of a particular skill or ability, and are the first to do so. The ability Resplendence field has been evolved based on your actions and uses in the world. As imported abilities cannot be made cheaper, this bonus has been modified. Note that a user may only have one Sage title active at any given time. Activating this title will permanently replace Sage of Chi.

Sage of Resplendence applies a special bonus to all skills and abilities with 'Resplendence' as part of the name. These abilities may now be shaped just as a normal spell. Skills or abilities that can modify shaping costs will affect this. In addition, the total output of any effects by skills or abilities with the 'Resplendent' tag are doubled after the formula has been calculated. If an ability with that tag previously did 10 damage, healing, or other related effect, it would instead do 20 with this title active.

Artorian didn't hesitate and slotted the title. "Goodbye, Sage of Chi! Someone else can have you! I didn't expect the replacement method to be built in. This works just as well. I'm taking this Sage title over the other one. It likely helped to have that reduction cost, but this is my shtick."

Yvessa didn't need a long explanation. She just agreed, given the tools he had available in his repertoire. "Shame that the fireball derivative is still so expensive. At least it will do more now. You really should try to get your hands on the fireball spell somehow. It's holding back the output of that ability by a large margin."

Artorian performed his morning stretches, wanting that

flexibility booster now that he cared about his attributes a little more. "I'll try. What direction is the bridge once I'm out of the hollow?"

His caretaker pointed at the wall, but that was enough direction. Artorian nodded, finished his routine, and stepped in something gooey on his way outside. "What the…"

He frowned as he lifted his foot, trying to shake his leg to get the gunk off from his mostly destroyed footwear. He did give it abyss from all that running yesterday, may as well just give up on shoes. Tossing the discarded, destroyed pair back into the cave after stepping back to be out of the goo.

Artorian had a quick shake. He hopped in place before acrobatically climbing up along the wall and clambering his way out of the hollow without needing to touch the goo field that both floor-coated a large chunk of cavern, and waited right outside. "I don't want to know. Don't tell me."

Yvessa snickered, amused. Though she said nothing since he requested it. Demons didn't leave much behind after heavy exposure to the resplendence field, and the gates had stopped entirely when higher echelon demons looked through the opening to see the horrible melting effects play out. There was no reason to throw troops away to that fate, and higher echelon members didn't want to be reduced to test bunnies. So much for Soni's night-attack plan.

Artorian took a heavy breath, the air around him condensing before shimmering to billow outwards as he took on his Astra form. As before, his hair turned a bright, healthy golden color. Artorian's eyes shone celestine as he took his launcher pose before taking off, causing the concordant sonic booms shortly after as he smashed through the sound barrier.

Once he was long gone, the aware-bear poked its nose from the hollow. It explored around for a few minutes to make sure the coast was clear, then began a smellpedition. Turned out, demon goop tasted surprisingly much like honey. The bear felt mighty pleased, and the cycle of life went on.

The new defenses erected at the Midgard-end of the Bifrost

were nothing to scoff at, even if they were in mid-construction. One major tactical decision was they had made the left side tall, allowing for a few lookouts to keep tabs on the other end of the bridge. Or bridges, since the impending use of the Bifrost had prompted some Wisps to trigger the conjoining effect early.

Normally Midgard needed to finish the tutorial before the Alfheim and Svartalfheim bridges merged. Normal was not the rule currently applied after a year of Artorian's meddling. The Wisps didn't have much time to complain. Artorian was a hair away from his second specialization, and the connections needed to be ready. They all knew he would cross as soon as he was able.

The Duvetian lookouts saw Artorian coming, though it was difficult to distinguish between him and the blur of glowing movement coming their way at ludicrous speed. Artorian's bolting run had increased his level of that skill up to the Master ranks. Meaning his multiplier improved! On a flat plain, he was now going two-thousand, six hundred, and thirty-seven feet per second before Soul of Zen's Novice rank doubled it. Artorian's current speed was a couple hundred feet per second shy of Mach 5. A speed he *could* attain if he really wanted to.

Dirt kicked up when he skidded to a stop, reaching so high that it formed a hill barely a mile out from the Bifrost gate's position, with a massive ditch carved in leading up to the new landscape bump. Several onlookers immediately thought that the new hill was a great place for another lookout tower. Or something similar. The top of the hill burst open when Artorian freed himself from the empire of dirt, brushing himself off as the glowing effects subsided.

He strolled down toward the gate as if he hadn't just made enough space for a new river, his smile wide as he walked toward the stunned crowd. "Hello there! Sorry for dropping in unannounced. Is Cuzco, Yorn, or Snagtooth Cloptail around? I have a mighty need."

The dirt seemed to clean itself from the man, and it took a while for people to put two and two together and realize this was the Divine of the aligned without the bells and whistles active. The ultramarine flame unfortunately flared back up since he was in an area abundant with mana. So much for walking around incognito… It would diminish when the available mana did. He needed to get rid of that somehow. Chiffon hadn't automatically taken it. Though it also wasn't listed as a curse.

He talked while he walked. "Yvessa, can you discreetly look into Endless Mana burn? Specifically how I get rid of it. This is getting silly."

The light around him flashed green, but was unable to reply with so many eyes and ears pointed in Artorian's direction. He took it as a yes, and started shaking hands with the aligned that ran up to greet him. It was going to be Katarina's Green Square all over again for a few days before he could get work done. That was fine. He was where he needed to be, and the people he asked for would find their way to him. Especially with so many noses sniffing around for them now that he had very loudly asked.

Hearing an accent he liked call out from the distance tore away his attention.

"Sunny! Am I glad ta see ya," Yorn bellowed over the general murmur of the crowd. Unlike the crowd, he seemed concerned about a time sensitive matter. "Ah need ya! Snag's gonna blow up the whole darn workshop! With yer contraption in it!"

CHAPTER THIRTY-ONE

A tent city had been erected not too far from the Bifrost gate. Some of the inhabitants were currently busy wiping dirt from the flaps. Artorian overheard some local bickering while he followed Yorn. The blame for the sudden dirt rain tossed around between the people who didn't know Sunny was back yet. He decided to keep his head down for the moment regardless, as he headed toward the angry sound of actual complaints. Those seemed to be backed up by a ballista that tracked people as they moved.

When the puffed-up beaver saw the culprit, his wide tail bristled. "You! Don't think I don't see you! Your boys have been haranguing me every day for *weeks*. Asking if it's done. I blame you for these bothersome interruptions! Do you know how annoying it is for others to come pester you about work you're trying to get done? When there's hundreds of them who all think they're being sneaky and helpful? What do you have to say for yourself?"

Artorian straightened up slowly as the pointing and accusing went on. His arms crossed at a similar speed, the furrow on his brow deepening. "Did they really? I can't say I approve of that. I'm certain that means you can point them all out so they can apologize and make it up to you. Yes?"

Snag had not expected that response. Since he was still feeling heated, the kindness of the gesture went over his head. "Of course I can point them all out! They're bothersome louts! Fleas in my fur! They are the reason the hand-ballista isn't done. Even if there is still no way you can wield or pull it."

Artorian looked up, watching the ballistae tracking him since the beaver's accusatory finger was pointed squarely in his direction. "I see. Yorn? Could you please get an account of every aligned that decided to be a bother? I don't approve of the actions and would like them to apologize and do something nice for the war-machine crafter. The pestering has to stop."

His attention turned to the heated beaver. "As for you, my tiny friend, I accept your challenge. Point me at a ballista. A finished one. I'll pull it right in front of you."

Snag chittered with discontent, his pointed rage faltering as he stamped into his oversized tent only for some loud crashing sounds to follow.

"Fine! You can touch Silpheed. She's the unfinished chassis against the far pole. I'm putting this nonsense to rest so I can return to crafting meaningful projects. Like more trackeristas. Even if they take a Core."

Something about that sentence caught Artorian's attention, though he hid the scheme in his mind by keeping his face flat and expressionless. The beaver was upset enough without being given additional reason to be. When directed to the unfinished machine, Artorian ran his hands over the craft. "Smooth wood. Sanded edges. Not a splinter in sight. For an unfinished ballista, this is already quite the beauty."

He tugged on the thick string, but it didn't budge. Not with his current attributes anyway. Snag scoffed, his tiny beaver arms crossed with an 'I knew it' scowl. Artorian winked in his direction. "Let's pick her up and take her outside, shall we?"

"Silpheed is bolted to her—" Snag shushed at the display of Sunny just shimmering with energy that took its time building up on his skin. A rush of air passed through the machining tent, fluttering the tent flaps as Artorian picked Silpheed up. Base and all. Snag's jaw fell, hanging open as Sunny just carted the unfinished ballista outside. The pulley system wasn't ready yet! "H… hey! Where are you taking her? Don't kidnap my princess off to another castle!"

Snag hurried after the large human who put the entire war-machine on his shoulder, walking it over to the unfinished towers near the Bifrost gate. The beaver was starting to panic, but had a moment to catch up when a llama hurried up to the human. The being was squealing about some finished ritual circle or something. Snag didn't care. That was wuju-nonsense. One of his tender contraptions was being hauled like cheap cargo! That was far more important. "Be careful with her!"

Artorian smiled at Snag, since the weight wasn't an issue. Silpheed was light as a feather. "Cuzco! Good to see you. How's my favorite Malchemist?"

The llama adopted his humanized form, making a thin, tall man with a smile wider than his hips, and equal amounts in flair. "Sunny! So glad you're back. We've been done for days and have been tweaking the containment circle to charge a Core. We're mostly all set. We've all been dancing on our toe tips, giddy about seeing whatever Core you might have brought. Did… did you bring it?"

Artorian pretended to reach into his inner pocket, even if he retrieved the Immaculate Core from his spatial ring. He tossed the Core over to Cuzco like it was a common rock, whose eyes turned to stars at the very sight of it. Followed by shrieking panic as he dove forwards to catch it. Just so such a thing didn't touch the dirt. "An Immaculate! How? Are you sure you can just trust people with this? This isn't some standard fare Core."

Artorian paused his stride, not certain what Cuzco meant. "Really? Would you mind giving me a breakdown of the full list, from weakest to strongest? To answer: Yes. I can trust you all just fine. I can give you that Core and fully expect it to be charged with mana when I come to pick it up. Ready and unsullied."

Cuzco didn't quite share the Divine's sense of trust, then took note that said person was also hoisting a ballista on his shoulder like it was a small child. "I… uhn. Yes. Of course! In order of weakest to strongest that we know of, Cores follow the following rankings: Memory, Flawed, Weak, Standard, Strong, Beastly, Immaculate, Luminous, and Radiant. Books we have discovered explained that those Cores correlate to the general power of the realm you're on. Midgard is abundant in Memory quality Cores, but poor in Flawed Cores. You'll almost never see a Weak-quality one. It all depends on the level of the monster you got it from. I've been told by Yorn that Svartalfheim has Flawed-quality Cores in abundance, with Weak Cores in poor stock, and an occasional Standard Core. Our guess is that it goes up by one quality level per realm."

Cuzco waggled his hand awkwardly. "Though Yorn has never seen a Memory-quality Core before, and that was a little odd to find out. Memory Cores just don't exist where he's from."

Artorian pointed at the Core in the llama-man's hand. "So how did you know that was an Immaculate Core, if it doesn't sound like it's possible you've seen one before?"

Cuzco beamed. "Mana-charge maximum! I can see the statistics when I inspect this item, which I did the moment I laid eyes on it. Then confirmed when I touched it. Each Core has a maximum numerical value it can use to store mana. A Memory Core can hold one. A Flawed ten. A Weak one hundred, and so on. This beauty has *seven* number slots. That makes it an Immaculate Core. We will be extra careful during charging so it doesn't blow up on us. Core instability causes pure devastation! One point of damage per point of charge may not sound too dangerous, but one point of charge also accounts for one extra meter of radius worth in mushroom cloud explosion. I'm surprised this beauty is not named. Usually they have some kind of designation."

Artorian understood, and considered adding one. "Oh. Well, alright then. It's a fancy rock… so how about… Ragna. Yes, Ragna the Rock. That will do. I suppose it may take you much longer to get it charged then. Do feel free to take your time. Just come nudge me when it's done. Of course, it will help if I'm nowhere near when you do. I still have the negative effect on me that your mana—"

"Doesn't regenerate," Cuzco finished for him. "We know. Well aware. I'll take this to the circle and we will start tinkering away. I'll come find you personally when all is said and done. Though charging it up all the way may take… a long time."

Artorian wasn't in a rush. "I have several uses for it, which change depending on when and where that Core becomes available. You take your time. Turns out I didn't need it to make my bow like I thought I might. So that has opened the options up. Best of luck with it. Don't explode!"

Cuzco held the Core above his head, running off like a Goblin who had found a shiny trinket. Artorian couldn't help but laugh at how ecstatic the man looked. Cuzco's eyes were full of life and his expression burned with unbridled excitement.

Snag was still walking circles around him, eyes affixed on Silpheed as she precariously leaned back and forth on Artorian's shoulder. Even if she was plenty stable. Seeing the beaver's apprehension and worry, Artorian marched on to the unfinished tower and picked Snag up before leaping up to the top of it in a single bound.

Snag's noisy protests went ignored. Artorian favored putting him down before setting Silpheed onto the scaffolding. "Time to give her a pull."

Pulling the ballista was more difficult than initially assumed. Not because he lacked strength, but because the thing was so large and unwieldy. In the end, Artorian had to use some clever acrobatics to make the idea work. Even if it had involved removing the ballista from its base. Pulling the string like it was nothing alone made Snag clutch his chest and gasp. Though less dramatically than he might have done so before he'd been brought topside in a single bound.

Keeping his right foot planted, he put his left foot where his hand should have been on a bow grip, just so he could lean and stretch the string back all the way until he was in a rather simple T pose. His torso went sideways so he could get the maximum draw possible from the ballista. "Ha! I call this success. Hand me that bolt."

Snag needed help just to lift the bolt, but Sunny had no issues being patient, waiting for some muscled Red Pandas to help out and give his free hand the shaved and sharpened tree trunk meant as a projectile. Nocking it took some doing, but he got there.

It was an awkward display. With one hand keeping the string drawn, and the other getting the bolt into place, he finally looked at the other end of the bridge in the distance. He noted that the fortifications there had been pumped up as well. Given his cooldowns were all ready to go, Artorian tried to funnel several skills into this awkward shot.

When the bolt was released, it didn't do so with the whistle of an arrow, but with a satisfying **k'thunk**. Artorian had plenty of time to ease out of the T pose and stand normally, his hand covering his brows to block out some sun as he followed the slow-moving shot. In comparison to an arrow anyway. "Looks like it's going to hit the gate."

The pandas and beaver around him nodded, having copied his sun-blocking hand trick to watch the bolt fly. Snag squinted, curious. "What all did you put into it? Bolts never fly that far by themselves. I haven't made a single machine that can even span the distance of the bridge."

Artorian rattled them off. "Nothing much. Longshot, Overdraw, and Zen Arrow. The strain allotment on Silpheed far exceeds even the last bow I made. Puts it right to shame, even though my bow has a Sturdy quality."

Snag didn't know what those were, but then again he wasn't an archer. He'd asked for curiosity's sake. "War machines like my ballistae get fifty points of strain per quality rank. Doubled due to my mastery in making them. Silpheed is Uncommon quality, so her base strain allotment was two hundred before my bonus. That's *without* her being done."

The bolt reached the other end of the bridge, saying 'Hello! Good day!' to the Svartalfheim darkened front gate which didn't withstand the tender knock-knock joke that was about to follow. Instead the front gate of Svartalfheim's Bifrost barrier just caved in like wet paper, crumpling the surrounding walls as the portcullis behind that main gate didn't fare any better.

The pandas all cheered in unison. Their paws went for the sky as they bounced around to clamor out their win. Snag wasn't remotely as amused as he surveyed the damage using some extending tube with glass in it. It let him see the enemy gate as if he was right in front of it. "Hmmm. Well, you win. You can pull the string, and use ballistae in a way I never thought possible. That also means Silpheed is not the right girl for the job. She's meant as a stationary installation. Now that I know you are actually going to be doing acrobatics, and firing them in that… awkward fashion… I need to return to the drawing board."

Artorian placed the ballista back onto its base, using his fingers to reconnect and tighten the bolts. "I understand. I'm aware my request was sudden and somewhat impossible."

The beaver squeezed his tiny hand into a fist. "Pfffft! Impossible? Such words do not exist to engineers! You proved it can be done, with an unfinished model. It is the gift of the engineer to figure out how to make things work, and I am a Master crafter. My dams back home are legendary constructions! No sir! I will not let such a small detail deter me from my work. A fire has been lit in my stomach, and I will make this ballista."

Artorian laughed, easing down to a knee to shake the beaver's paw. "In that case, it is my good pleasure to meet you anew. Shall I stick around to learn how to maintain your creation? That way if I am ever out in the field and something goes awry, I know what to do."

Snag slapped his hand in and squeezed with all his might. Not enough to dent Artorian's grip, but still notable. "You want to be a Machinist? I warn you, that requires the dedication of a professional slot. Don't go making that offer lightly. If you want to be my apprentice, your life is not going to be easy. I make the best, but I demand the best too."

Artorian opened his profession tab after letting the tiny hand go, having used two or three fingers for the handshake. His first listed profession was Dreamweaver, something he hadn't done much with since the ferret days. He was certain that one day it would be a saving grace. His second profession was one gained from Cra: Bowyer, slotted into the profession slot of level fifteen. Given he was currently level twenty, that gave him access to his third profession slot, which currently sat empty.

The decision was easy. "Snag, consider yourself to have a new apprentice."

The beaver's smile showed off his big teeth, his mirth finally on par with the partying pandas. "No more getting harassed! I mean… Wonderful! Bring Silpheed back to the tent. We have much to discuss about building. I accept!"

Notice! You have been offered a profession.
Profession: Machinist.
Machinists of the current age refer to this word when they mean to discuss war machines. Such as ballista, onagers, trebuchets, and other siege engines and weaponry. This profession is difficult, requiring significant practice, learning, and crafting in order to see any kind of success.
Do you wish to accept this profession?

Artorian accepted without worry, causing the beaver to squee in delight.

"An apprentice! An honest to Eternia apprentice!" He'd scared off his last few due to the demands of his rigorous quality requirements. Yet if anyone could learn what he had to teach, surely it would be the Divine all these aligned couldn't shut up about.

That last fact hit him late, and rather hard. Snag didn't know how to feel about that. He was going to teach a Divine. The fire in Snag's stomach burned hotter. Did that mean he was going to ease up? *No*. The opposite! It was detail time!

CHAPTER THIRTY-TWO

Sparks flew when hammer hit anvil. Yorn had joined Artorian in the crafting arts, but was clearly far better than the human. Yorn's aptitudes yearned for nitty gritty details that machines required. Artorian struggled with most things not rooted in the esoteric. The human did his best to copy the Dwarf, since Yorn took much better to Snag instructions. It took Artorian significantly longer, a time sometimes counted in days, to catch up to something Yorn had picked up on the fly.

Clearly the intelligence and wisdom attributes did not reflect one's ability to learn in Eternia. Artorian shook his head at the thought. No reason to be salty. This just happened to be something he wasn't good at. Snag and Yorn got along well, rather than mixing like oil and water. In this workshop, it was Artorian that felt like the oil.

He had the attributes to see to all the complexities of the task, but lacked the aptitude to grasp the mechanical explanations unless he was shown them. Several times. Even then, his first ballista fell apart even though Artorian couldn't figure out what he'd done differently from Yorn's, whose ballista was a flawless piece of deadly machinery.

This led to many days of Sunny stamping off with a grumble, bow in hand, to shoot some demons on the other side of the bridge, just to relax and feel like he was making progress somewhere. A nice calm arrow always helped. Especially when it killed something he didn't like in the process.

Small bonuses.

One of his silent arrows picked off another imp when Yorn got up on the scaffolding with him. "Oi! What's got ya up here this time? Ya still sour from yer ballista not turning out well?"

Artorian reached for the next arrow, but didn't put it on the string once it was in his hand. "I… Yes. Yes, I suppose I am, my young friend. I've gotten used to picking things up quickly, you see. It's frustrating to actually fail at things over and over. I know I tell people to persevere, but sweet *crackers* is it irritating to work on something that just *falls apart* on you."

His vision squinted at the distance, looking for a target. "I think I'm doing it right, then you walk in holding up a bolt that was supposed to go in the middle somewhere. I have no idea why this is flustering me so. This is not an issue I had when I was making bows. Yet when it comes to this new profession, I'm a fish out of water. Just flopping and flailing. How long have we been doing this?"

Yorn sat down on a finished crenulation, though held on to a piece of scaffolding regardless. "Two months an' a tick. Though I suppose I have some pleasant words for ye?"

Artorian sighed and stuffed the arrow back in his quiver, stowing all the items, bow included, into the spatial ring. "I wouldn't mind some pleasant words right now."

Yorn nodded, shoving his thumb over their shoulder. "Well, let's start with something you're good at. What do you see?"

Having a gander, Artorian saw the remains of the tent city, which had evolved into insulae and communal homes. Square in design with an opening in the middle. Meant for a small gathering or gathering area. "Society on the rise."

Yorn nodded again, as that was the easy one. "Now for the bit that's harder to see. Listen. I'm aligned to yer particular network, if I can borrow words from how the beacons work. Ye've been tellin' us not to treat you differently, but that's been tough. Really tough, Sunny. Ye've got people sneaking glances wherever you go. I try not tah mention it, but everyone sees the gawkers. It's rough seeing the source of where you get a chunk of yer power from just walking around. For me, it was easier when I thought you weren't real. Yet here y'are."

Artorian wasn't sure he followed. "I don't understand. Where are you going with this?"

Yorn smirked. "Failure be mortal. Ya haven't been paying attention to the change in the way people have been looking at ya. They watch ya struggle. They watch ya fail. In a way that's been more humanizing than taking the form. See, we see ya shooting arrows and hitting targets we never could. We see ya jump whole buildings in a single bound. We see ya pick up and carry stuff that would take twelve of me to accomplish the same."

The Dwarf softly punched Artorian in the shoulder, and the old man fully believed Yorn had no idea how much that gesture helped. "Ye've got a reputation that's building of yer exploits. Yer more than just some name listed on the panel that the Voice of the World gives me. You're the proof."

Artorian quirked a brow. "Proof of what?"

The Dwarf pulled out a flask, offering it. "Proof that even Divines aren't flawless. That no matter how mighty ya may be, yer stuck learning things like the rest of us. I don't think you grasp just how much that boon o' yours does for us. It's life changing. An entire culture has grown and developed to adapt around rapid healing. People aren't scared of little injuries anymore. Those tended to be life-ending events at times. We can do more, and for longer. Yet then when we come and look at ya, y'know, to *gawk*… Yer pounding away at an anvil, cursing to the skies above about how yer siege engine ain't working. It's… I don't know. I call it a relief. To see there's something ya can't do well."

Artorian cocked his head. He sort of understood. He

scratched the back of his head, then leaned back to look at the other side of the Bifrost. His pause in shots had given the demons some willpower to continue their work. Granted, it was little more than repairs and damage control with all the dents he put into their gate. "I suppose… so long as it comforts others. I can't be too upset."

The Dwarf slapped the back of Sunny's shoulder, watching the human take his flask and enjoy a swig. Yorn was expecting a deadly cough, but Artorian made a face as if to say, 'Yeah, not bad.' Yorn looked at the flask when it was in his hand, wondering if the drink had been diluted somehow. Taking a drink himself, he coughed hard, his eyes turning red and watering while he knocked himself on the chest. "Oh sweet anvils… there she be. Oh, she hits hard, she does. *Fwhooo*. Oh, I take it back ya tall bastard. Yer a monster. Ya took that withou—**cough*.*"

It was Artorian's turn to pat Yorn on the back, amused at seeing a Dwarf have such a rough time with his own homemade brew. "Hehehe. You know, that does sound better. I've been called worse things."

"Ah pyrite… she burns. Ah'm fine. Ah'm fine!" Yorn caught his breath after a bit, needing to grip the haft of his axe to steady himself. He wiped his face with the back of his hand, but Artorian flickered his field to help clean the Dwarf up. He hiccupped out a distracting question. "Worse? **hic** Like what?"

Artorian shrugged. "I was called a tyrant for a while."

"Ha!" Yorn did not believe him. "A softie like ye? A tyrant? Musta been another life. Yer as sweet as some of the caramel candy apples they be sellin' down there. I ain't seen ya lift a finger to harm a critter once, save for lendin' a helpin' hand or a kind ear."

The human sighed softly. "We were all someone else once. I didn't like being that person, so I'm glad I'm not anymore. Yet, in some way I will always be that person. Simply one that no longer desires to use those traits. I didn't just learn to take

Dwarven gut-punchers like that brew of yours out of nowhere. I had practice! The Fellhammers had a…"

Artorian stopped, and trailed off as his words died on his tongue. "A… never mind. Not a good time to talk about it. Anytime that comes up, the nostalgia and guilt start to eat at me. I have other Dwarven friends, Yorn. Ones that didn't start as critters. I hope you can meet them one day. It's a lot of effort on my part to get that done."

Yorn punched Sunny in the shoulder again, but much harder this time. "Don't let the past get ya down. I ain't sour I began as a hedgehog. Life as a Dwarf is where it's at for me. Of course I'll meet these friends of yours. Be hard not to with the kind of charge you can lead. What's the current holdup?"

Artorian pointed to the other side of the bridge. "I need my second specialization, and it's just. Not. Triggering. I've got the level. I've got the tools. I thought a few months ago that any arrow was going to do it. Any arrow now! Now here I sit like a fool, with his one specialization."

Yorn didn't judge, and Artorian recognized the cogs moving behind his eyes. The Dwarf had an idea, or perhaps a plan. "You mind if I try somethin'? I had a thought. May not help. Though it's still a thought."

Artorian didn't see the harm. He even thought it was kind. His young friend was trying to help. "I would be delighted. What's on your mind?"

Yorn pointed at the new crafting structure their workshop was in. "It's something I heard my Da say. It ain't enough for a specialization to see what you've been doing. It's also important for what ya want to do. Can't rightly say I know what that meant, but after seeing ya shoot that ballista a while back… I gotta ask. You ever made a shot with a finished one? I don't mean the ballista. Y'know. Showing your actual intent? Could matter."

Artorian wasn't aware of this requirement, but after swift consideration of his day one entry testing with Yvessa and how gaining skills worked, thought it worth testing. "Do you have a ballista we can use?"

Yorn became all smiles. "No… but Ah know someone that does. We just have to nick it for a bit. From under his beavery nose."

Artorian smirked, his hands coming together in a steeple. "I do love a touch of cheekery. Lead on!"

A mere ten minutes later, and the dastardly duo had found and smuggled Snag's ballista project out of the workshop. Artorian was playing with it when they were back at the tower. "It's so convenient! Look. I can look where I shoot and pull at the same time because of the open design. I wonder what this thing is called."

They both jumped when Snag slammed his wide tail on the ground, having caught the duo red-handed on his return from the market. A caramel apple was still held in one hand. "Her name's Ikaruga, and I was gonna tell ya she was ready tomorrow. After I'd rested. But *noooo.* Just had to go pick her up and cause me trouble."

Yorn and Artorian attempted to flash innocent smiles, but the human got an apple to the face, while the Dwarf received a curt kick to the chin. "Bad apprentices! *Bad*! Now get on that tower and show me if she works!"

Artorian was busy trying to peel the sugar from his face while slowly whining. "*Ew. Ew.* Oh, it's so sticky. Ew. Why does this theme keep coming back? *Ugh.*"

He needed to carefully shape his field so that his face cleaned up without destroying the confection. At the same time, he wrapped Yorn in a bubble connected to the field to heal up that minor chin-grievance. They both felt better soon after, Yorn finding his composure first. "Did ye say get on the tower? I figured you'd be wanting Ika back in the workshop."

Snag huffed. "I do, but we're here now so we might as well. Sunny can't make a war-machine worth its scrap in value, but maybe he can use one. Up with both of you!"

Shooed up to the top of the tower, Yorn held to the scaffolding while Artorian set up. He adopted the same T pose as last time, but found the strange design of the ballista to be one of far greater convenience. He could easily plant his foot in the inner workings of the siege engine while keeping the other planted. It had been made with oddities in mind.

Artorian spoke to himself, slowly getting lost in the art. "Similar to learning skills maybe? Like jumping. Intend your growth… Intend your growth."

Yorn handed over a bolt, which Sunny seamlessly nocked. Again, thanks to the odd design. The fluid motion of pull and release was a stark comparison to the last time they'd seen Artorian hand-fire a ballista. Where the original attempt was crude, sloppy, and rough, this shot was acrobatics and bowmanship combined. The bolt smashed into a Svartalfheim tower, crumbling the base before it tilted, leaned, and fell over to crash and crush some not-so-innocent imps.

It wasn't the spectacle that made Artorian happy. It was the prompt!

Notice!

You have reached the tenth level in your first Specialization, and have unlocked all requirements and crossed all thresholds for your second one. Second Specialization unlocked! Your performance has been reviewed, and a follow up Specialization has been created based on your unique, individual path.

As there were no Zen Archer paths that existed prior to your adventuring, save for routes which you did not take…

A path has been created for you!

Specialization: Ballistic Bowyer

Congratulations! You are responsible for the creation of a Legendary Specialization! Why use bows when you can tout ballistae? All will know the tales of renown of the person who walked into battle with a siege engine, only to use it as a shortbow. Only a mad lad would have come up with something like this, and we doubt we will ever see anything of its like again. Even giants still go for the bow, but not you! Every two levels of this Specialization, you will gain a +2 to every attribute except for Karmic Luck.

Notice!

Abilities for this Specialization are being compiled.

Artorian gently put Ikaruga down so he could bounce on his tiptoes and **squee** like a tiny child. He read the prompt over a few times with a bright smile, his hands clapping together while the other two looked at him like he was crazy. They didn't see the prompt, and Yorn motioned at the enemy. "I mean the tower crash was a nice touch, but that was too giddy a reaction for me."

Artorian stopped and waved it away. "It worked! It worked, you beautiful, mad Dwarf! I have my second specialization! I can cross the bridge!"

His attention returned to the prompt and accepted it while Snag and Yorn came to terms with what had actually just happened. Neither of them had a second specialization, and they would not be able to follow. Now that they thought about it… did anyone in Midgard? Their stomachs felt full of rocks as Artorian accepted the upgrade.

He quirked a brow at them, seeing their dour looks. "What are you two looking so down about? I'm not leaving right away. Ikaruga needs ammo. Enough to fill up my spatial ring. We'll have a big party before I head off. How about that?"

That set Yorn at ease, the weight in stomach easing. "Yeh… Yeh, that sounds good. I appreciate that Sunny. Felt awful thinking of you just runnin' off. I guess I didn't think about what it meant if you succeeded. Let me go talk to some folks before you pop off. Ah'ma head out. Looks like Snag's got something to tell ya."

Snag kept quiet until the Dwarf left, his tiny face looking up at Artorian. Who was massive even when he leaned down and took a knee to make it easier on the Master crafter. "What's on your mind?"

Snag scratched his neck, his tone somewhat morose. "Wasn't expecting it to work. Wasn't thinking you'd leave so soon after I got myself an apprentice. Guess I scared off another one."

Artorian extended a finger for the beaver to shake. "You have a far better apprentice in Yorn. It was clear a week in that I was never going to have the aptitude for siege engines that he does. He's your true apprentice. I was just the door. I learned enough to know what makes an engine broken, and when I will need to return for repairs. That counts for something, even if I did not accomplish the crafting goal I set out for. You just get a workshop up and running. A true, proper one for when Ikaruga needs maintenance. Besides, you'll need proper tools when an Artifact comes to lie on your bench."

Snag shook the offered finger, but frowned hard. "Artifact? What are you talking about? Ikaruga is of Uncommon quality. That's *with* being finished."

Artorian winked at him, laying a hand on the oversized weapon. "My deeply appreciated teacher, allow your student to show you something wonderful while it's just the two of us up here."

The beaver-made ballista hummed under Artorian's touch, his hand looking significantly more Divine and cosmic as Yvessa helped with the titles. "What do you say? Want to see what she can *really* do?"

CHAPTER THIRTY-THREE

Yvessa sighed as she watched her charge work, the beaver getting ever giddier as Snag watched an Artifact being made with wide glittering eyes. Artorian wanted some more information on his new specialization, and those books that were mentioned earlier, but first came making this goodie. This part he could do! Even if making the siege engine itself was something he'd proven to be downright terrible at. When the process finished, they were both dying with curiosity to see what the result was.

Name: Ikaruga
Material: Onyx Sunglass
Rarity: Artifact
Damage: 100–200 Kinetic.
Special Quality: Master Crafted, Onyx Sunglass.
Special Ability: Twin-Linked, Explosive.

Master Crafted: Doubles the maximum strain this weapon can handle. Strain is calculated by a value of 50 points per rarity rank on siege engines.

Maximum strain: 800. Straining a siege engine decreases its firing rate by a full second per rank applied.

Twin-Linked: Each bolt fired from this siege engine duplicates itself once, resulting in two bolts being fired side by side that each apply their damage individually. Any effects or skills applied to the first bolt will be present on the duplicated bolt.

Explosive: On impact with either the designated enemy or a solid enough surface, bolts fired from this engine will explode, dealing damage in an area and destroying the bolts in the process. The total damage of a bolt will be used as measurement for the area's diameter. The total damage of the explosion alters depending on where an enemy is within it. Reduced by 10% damage for every 10% distance one is away from the center-most point of impact.

Artorian drummed his fingers together, eyes dancing over the listed details. "*Oooh.* Onyx Sunglass? That was unexpected. I wonder what that is."

Snag repeatedly tugged on his sleeve. "Forget the material, look at the specials! Mine's still listed! Also unless my eyes deceive me, that says explosion."

The human nodded. "They do deceive you. It says Explosive. Not that I think there would be much of a difference, given that description. Oh, this is so neat! Wh… Why did I just lose a whole bunch of DE points?"

Snag looked from the panel back at Sunny, who was frowning heavily and hurrying to pull up some other screens the beaver could not see. He could, however, see the horrified expression on the Divine's face. "That backstabbing brat! He docked me DE points! Plus retroactive costs for the bow, and… What is this 'other shenanigans' tab?"

Snag watched the human's face carefully. The details upon it were a painting of emotion and reaction as Artorian gasped. His expression changed to affronted, relieved, then affronted again as his body pulled away from the screens Snag could not see. The Divine's hand pressed to his chest like some besieged Noble. "Even Katarina's sickness? But I patched that by… What's this notice?"

Artorian touched the notice option, a long letter unfurling for him to read that narrated its message in Eternium's voice.

Notice!
Personal message from: Eternium.

Artorian. This needs to stop. I don't just mean your antics, but my behavior in response to them as well. We have been escalating and building retaliations off one another, and I for one am not versed in the ways of spite.

Testing fields and functions is one thing. Being put to sleep because I went too far is another. Our playful back and forth has crossed the hostility line, and I for one do not want to leave it there.

Effective immediately, I am ending my retributive acts against you. I cannot afford to be put to sleep via the interference of your Heavenly. To facilitate this ceasefire, I have done several things.

Listed below:

All actions performed via the Administrator function that could have happened per the Divine function have been altered to have been done so. Actions without cost cannot be allowed unless the act of being an Administrator could not be otherwise avoided. Given your frankly immense DE pool that you have accumulated from your follower amount, the resource was used to balance that out.

*I have personally reviewed your full activity with a clear, well-napped mind, and have come to the proper understanding that you are not actually here to play the game. You are here to uphold your deal with Cal. If the demons I saved per the requirements of my **Law** were to breach, then I am lost and*

Cal is in jeopardy. I am ashamed to admit it required a forced nap for me to come to terms with that reality.

I have been so obsessed with making Eternia function methodically that I did not account for the free will of intervening agents. Too long have I been taking control as the norm. With so little, to outright nothing, able to challenge my authority. It pains me to write that I feel this no longer to be true, and that truth is upsetting. I do not know what to do.

I have always been superior. More powerful. More capable. Then the world came to an end, and rather than my expected end with it, there was Cal.

My ***Order*** *did not account for Cal.*

My methods did not account for Cal.

My ***Law*** *did not account for Cal.*

I did not account for Cal.

I mistakenly wrote him off as a temporary measure. A vessel for my safety before I could resurge into the open once again. After having done a great amount of math, and having recounted how many million years we have already been here… my hubris hurts horribly, and I feel properly kicked. Cal will outstrip me both in power and ability. It is only a matter of time.

So no more negative Karmic Luck events. Not unless you truly did something to garner those points by yourself, rather than my interference in adding them.

In recompense for my clear failings, I have conferred with Oberon and a council of Wisps. Yvessa included. It's possible you likely didn't even notice she was gone. The result of which comes down to the following actions:

Artorian received a small prompt that interrupted the

narrated message. Since the narration refused to continue even when he tapped the larger message that still had plenty to say, he read this new one.

Notice! You have gained the special character trait: Absolute Unit. This character will receive maximum system assistance against the unique entity: 'Barry the Devourer.'

When the new trait cleared, the narration picked up again.

We decided that would be a good start. Your Wisp was very clear on your intentions to 'finish him,' as she so delicately explained. It is my personal addition to inform you that entities cannot be destroyed in Eternia. They can only be repurposed. If you desire to end Barry with finality, you must remove him from my Core. This information has been provided to Occultatum, who will disseminate it in the other Soul Space.

For my part, I am required to keep Eternia running as a game, dependent on my functions of ***Order****. I promised both Cal and my* ***Law*** *this. So I cannot simply hand him over, as much as I understand how convenient that would be. You will have to physically make it through all the realm barriers, and reach the moon from Hel in order to properly reach Barry.*

That is a part of the process I cannot influence. What I can influence is the ease of your journey. Effective immediately, your attribute maximum limitations have been removed. A notice prompt has been separately provided for when you wish to apply all the attributes you are so far due.

I unfortunately cannot undo the age penalty limitation on your Long form. That will still require time. Due to your contribution to the system's efficiency, and proposed additions, I am adding a skill that allows you to use your specialization equipment while in your dragon form. I have also modified the growth pattern of the Long so the limbs aren't so incredibly awkward.

The system for growth and flat bonuses depending on attribute thresholds was… very nice. I liked it. It will take time to implement that system, and for the moment we will still be using the inferior method, as those Pylons are stable and complete in full.

I have also added the skills you are due for Artifact crafting, and siege engine operations. Your specialization will allow you to use siege engines in… unconventional methods. Such as using them in ways identical to bows, regardless of being in your human or dragon form.

I have read the logged complaint that I was taking Bob's work in vain. I agree, and you will find that your Long form now has evolution options when you increase an age category with it. One of which is pending. I unfortunately have not been able to untangle the mess keeping your form's attributes connected to one another. There's a certain pink energy preventing me from properly repairing those Pylons.

Considering the same energy is somehow making Pylons 'happy' by keeping similar core species together in a family network… I will not put effort into undoing it. When it fades naturally, the Pylons will be mended then.

For your information. Making Artifacts will always cost DE points. If anyone should be making them with ease, it should be the Divines. I am working on an easier method of data entry, and will otherwise randomize factors inherent to their creation, per the fields you were unable to affect, such as making the materials an Artifact is made of more… interesting. I hope you like Ikaruga. I took the liberty of ever so slightly improving the design so your dragon form wouldn't get *fwapped* *in the tail with each string release.*

Back to the topic. Due to some of your meddling that I am currently mending, the realm progression path has altered slightly. The swiftest way to reach Barry is to acquire your second specialization; then go from Midgard straight to Vanaheim, unlock your third specialization, bounce over to Jotunheim, Muspelheim, or Niflheim to gain your fourth, then shoulder-bash into Asgard when you have it. In Asgard, you will have to defeat Odin in order to pass through to Hel, unless you can discover some clever way to get by him.

He is stubborn in the same fashion that you are wily. He will refuse to let you pass without a clear defeat. I strongly suggest you have a method to pull all your attributes up into the three-thousand range before you do. He comes here to play around, and is quite adept at the things he enjoys.

Terrible for testing, but I digress.

Once past that obstacle, you must find the correct gazebo in Hel in order to transfer to the moon. Per your new trait, the exact gazebo will be outlined in light, rather than needing to guess which of the many thousands it might be. Hel has a secret puzzle component to it; this will allow you to skip that. Once on the moon, all demons which you have so far not dealt with will congregate to protect Barry, as he is their primary summoner.

Removing Barry's Core is as difficult as picking it up, so long as he has not managed to create a body for himself. If he manages a body, he will receive the attributes he is due. At which point, you will need methods for handling a being with attributes in the five- to six-thousand range. He has already acquired titles that will improve his prowess due to actions taken in the world. Those titles are simply not active without a body.

To answer some lingering questions: Crafting results are dependent based on the realm you are in. Anything made or finished on Midgard will only be Midgard-quality at maximum. This is why your bow damage remains in a range of one to twenty. Making a weapon into an Artifact will never alter the base statistics. Only the special effects.

This and many other aspects of Eternia may change in the future, as we roll over into the next iteration. I have gained much knowledge on how things should improve from this point. Unfortunately, I require Cal to be conscious to implement many of the changes. You will have to use the current system to see to your goals.

Lastly, Endless Mana Burn can only continue to plague you so long as you have a mana *bar. If you have further questions, please direct them to your Observer Wisp. Please review your new skills, specialization ability descriptions, and other notices to unlock your attributes.*

Kind regards,
Eternium.

CHAPTER THIRTY-FOUR

"Huh…" Artorian wasn't sure what to say after that long letter. He sat cross-legged on the tower, feeling somewhat defeated and relieved at the same time. "Looks like we made up."

"Are you alright?" Snag nudged him in the hip for what must have been the sixth time. It was just the first time Artorian noticed it, though, and his mouth finally closed. "You were very out of it, and those expressions you made didn't all look entirely pleasant. Is something wrong with the engine?"

Sunny appreciated the beaver's sudden kindness. He'd grown fond of the dam builder over the last two months. He gave instruction well, and was diligent, even if Artorian's own crafting results were a hot mess. "I will be alright. I received my own message from the Voice of the World. I mucked some things up and just got news of the result. I need some time by myself to sort it out. How about we put Ikaruga back in the workshop for a bit to show her off? On a nice pedestal, so people can see what you're responsible for."

Snag rubbed his tiny beaver paws together. "I would like that very much!"

They did just that. Artorian took Snag down, installed the

siege engine on a nice pedestal in the workshop, and slunk away to a nice quiet place so he could think about what he'd just read. Not to mention check the rest of his notices. He had a few, and this time they couldn't wait for long.

Eternium realizing his petulance was… nice. Unfortunately, that meant he'd have to reel his own back in as well.

It took a few repetitions to people that came to nudge him for attention, for the message to get across that he needed a spot of alone time. His aligned chalked it up to Divine work that needed to be done, even as they peeked regardless. They wanted to see what such a task would come down to, but sadly couldn't see any of the screens he didn't want them to see.

After changing locations for the fourth time, Artorian pulled his Soul pillow out while in the attic of the rowdiest tavern that had been built. He was surrounded by stout drink, but cared for none of it in favor of some peace and quiet, even though the cheering howls from down below pressured the 'quiet' portion. "Yvessa, you around?"

The human form of the green Wisp slid into being, Yvessa seating herself on a wooden casque. "Present and accounted for. How are you handling Eternium's big letter?"

Artorian sat back, his hands folding. "Heartfelt. It was heartfelt, and I'm trying to consider how to respond in kind. I poke when I'm poked, but this was akin to a self-discovery. An awakening, other than the one from his nap. I must respond to that in kind as well, and I can think of no better way than to simply be kind. Would you mind sticking around while I open these notices up?"

"A request to stay? First time for everything. Usually you're running for it *so* fast." Yvessa nudged him playfully. "Of course I'll stay. It's more than just my job, you old codger. The notices are likely not in a sensible order, so don't be surprised if you get an explanation for what you read after you needed it."

Artorian threw his hands to the air for a moment in defeat. He'd had that one coming. "Yes, yes. Let's begin then. I'll just address them as I get them. Let's open these up, because I'm eager to get to Vanaheim."

The first notice was the prompt to remove his attribute limiter. Yes, please! Artorian smashed the 'accept' option, feeling pleasantly tingly. "*Hohoh*, that tickles."

Yvessa pulled up his statistics and made them visible for both of them. "Let me adjust so the Long age penalty doesn't show. So we know what the new base averages are. You just received all your system bonuses from achievements, titles if they gave any, twenty levels worth of attributes, and ten levels worth of specialization. You have thirty points of attributes to spend, and twenty points of skills, which in the current system means two ranks."

Artorian squeezed his chin, one of his legs easing over the other. "Fifteen in strength and fifteen in constitution. I need that stamina regeneration. What can I put the ranks into?"

Yvessa had a quick check, adding the requested points. "Points can be invested up to the Master rank of a skill or ability, but nothing above or over it. That has to be gained the hard way, since Cal expected people to figure out their own twists to the toys from that point on. So he could see new things. Crowdsourcing, I think he called it?"

Artorian nodded, going over his own lists. "*Any* skill or ability? Soul of Zen. All of it. I need to be faster."

Yvessa dumped two ranks into the Soul of Zen ability, pumping it from the Beginner to the Student ranks. "Done. What's next?"

"How many DE points do I have to convert? This seems like a great time to test the level up capacity." Artorian motioned for her panel. "Also show me my current attributes without the age penalty please. Mine only shows it with the penalty."

His Wisp pulled up his Deity information, whistling loudly at it. "No wonder you managed to pull so many people up to level ten. That's impressive. You should start sinking these DE points into things daily. Although your current count is… uh. Sorry, Artorian. Your slate got cleaned shelling out for all those taxes and fees on converted payments. I think it may have been easier to set it to zero on the Wisp's end. I know it's what I would have done. I love me some hand waving, but it shouldn't have cost you everything. I'll send out a message to Deverash concerning a tax refund. Here's your Deity numbers while I send this out."

Deity: Rank 6
Follower count: Six hundred twelve thousand, nine hundred and forty-two.
Followers generate up to 25 DE a day.
DE gained per day: 15,323,550
Altar count: One hundred.
Altars generate 50 DE a day.
DE gained per day: 5,000
Shrine count: Twenty.
Shrines generate 100 DE a day.
DE gained per day: 2,000
Temple size 1 count: Five.
Temple size 2 count: Two.
Temple size 3 count: Zero.
Temples generate 250, 500, and 1,000 DE daily in order of rank.
DE gained per day: 2,250
Total DE Gained per day: 15,332,800
Conversion experience gained instead if active: 153,328

Artorian joined Yvessa in the impressed whistling department. "See, *now* it makes more sense why it cost millions of DE to do anything. I didn't realize it would scale this high. This is somewhat insane. Have I gained this amount every day since I leveled everyone up? I know Eternium just tore heaping chunks out of my reserves…? Speaking of, why can I not see my reserves?"

Yvessa frowned, tapping her screen. Then chuckled and broke down into a laugh as she got a response from Dev along with the sound clip of a mirror shattering. "Because the number broke the Pylon! Ha! It couldn't count that high when the refund hit. Well, that needs to be mended, but the Gnomes aren't operating on our time frame so that could happen either any second, or sometime next year. I have a notice from Deverash on my end, he says the number will be manually calculated every time you want to do something with your DE points. They will do their best to keep a running tally. Should I send in a query of how many levels you can gain?"

Artorian gave her a thumbs up while scrolling through his own numbers. "Please do."

Yvessa gave him a thumbs up back. "I've sent in the request. I'll let you know when I hear back. For the DE conversion thing, you won't gain the convertible number you saw since that fluctuates daily. I turned off that glowing effect, by the way. You're welcome, in case you didn't notice. It was getting rather bright."

"Thank you. I will admit I did not notice no longer being the shiny clock everyone kept their morning-time by effect going away. Appreciated." Artorian motioned for the next notice after he took a long look at his current attributes. The ones Yvessa was helping with since they did not list his dragon penalty.

Name: Artorian
Character Level: 20
Class: Generalist
Specialization: Zen Archer
Profession: Dream Weaver
Hit Points: 7,560 / 7,560
Mana: 0 / 44,460
Mana regen: 0 / second
Stamina: 7,545 / 7,545
Stamina regen: 384 / second
Characteristics:
Strength: 758
Dexterity: 742
Constitution: 761
Intelligence: 741

Wisdom: 764
Charisma: 741
Perception: 763
Luck: 734
Karmic Luck: 0

He hummed a question while busy. "Is there any reason this says Zen Archer and Dream Weaver instead of Ballistic Bowyer and Machinist? Also, while I currently have no mana, that pool seems high."

Yvessa replied without looking. "You can change what's shown manually, otherwise they reflect the fields in which you have the most experience. I'll send in a request about changing that to the last entry gained, but we likely won't see that change occur this iteration. Just change it manually by tapping it and selecting the one you want from the list. You can also turn on your title view, and make that screen show what level each entry is."

She glanced over with a small lean. "As to the mana pool. It's doubled once from secretly having the cleric tag, and doubled again from your Mana Consciousness skill. We still haven't been able to fix the former. Divines are new territory."

Artorian didn't want to change his sheet just yet. "Thank you, dear. It's fine as is. I'm still not that invested, even if I care a bit more about the numbers now. I have to raise those puppies up into hounds with a value of around three thousand each to face Odin? That's going to take some ingenuity. If I didn't have an age penalty, my Astra form would double these numbers. Right?"

His Wisp made a few segments on the calculations table glow. "It would, but that only gets you halfway. A few more levels would help, and with the limiter removed your options have increased. Statistic training is possible now, though it may be an unfeasible task, given how long you'd have to train before seeing an increase. Leveling up your new specialization will get you some points, and the information should be in the relevant prompt. Gear can boost your numbers, and you currently don't have any. Lastly, you can get some attribute points out of your profession but, much like training, it's easier said than done. The easy way would be to rack up system bonuses or get achievements."

"None of that sounds easy. I'll dabble and see what works," Artorian mused gently, moving the attribute screen away to pull up the next notice. "I did notice Eternium's mention of Mana Burn. Only works so long as I have a mana bar. Sounds like a Skyspear-quality solution needs to be used."

Yvessa paused. "I don't know what that means."

She saw her charge nod with a cheeky little grin. "Few do. In short, I think I grasped where Eternium was trying to lead me without saying it directly. When I received my class, it mentioned it would adapt things to make them fit. When I got one of my Monk skills, it mentioned my mana bar effectively functioned as a chi energy bar as well, but *didn't* replace it. Just made it work like it did. I think I need to… switch those around somehow. Anything you can do on that end?"

His caretaker took a moment to stop what she was doing, squint her eyes, and turn to look at him. "That's abyss clever. That might just get around the Endless Mana Burn. I'll write it up and send it to Deverash. I can't help it, but he might be able to tinker with some mechanics down in the hold."

Artorian loved teamwork. "Fantastic. Time for the next prompt."

Notice!

A new evolution mechanic has been added. This mechanic normally has an extremely minor chance to trigger when a creature changes age categories. To test this feature, each age category your 'Long' dragon form gains is guaranteed to trigger this option.

Please select one of the evolution options below. New options will be added each time evolution options appear. Note, due to your particular race, your age categories have been renamed. As an example: Baby has become hatchling. Your new age categories are: Hatchling, Wyrmling, Youngling, Juvenile, Budding Adult, Adult, Matured, Old, Venerable, and Ancient.

Evolution options:
Breath attack: Rainbow Blast.
Sensory advancement: Echolocation.
Innate sense: Bone Spellscript.
Muscle: Improved Physical Attributes.

Raising a brow, Artorian reached over and selected the spellscript entry, allowing a new prompt with an explanation to appear.

Notice!

Your dragon form was born or created with advanced spellscript covering its bone structure. This spellscript has several functions, and will grow in power and potency with each age category. Choosing this evolution option provides you an innate sense of what that spellscript does, and how to use it. Note that this will not grant you actual knowledge. Merely a feeling of what is right.

Would you like to evolve this innate sense?

Artorian elbow-dropped onto the screen with dramatic flair rather than accept it in any sort of mundane way, twisting in the air to come down upon the prompt with a deep certainty, and cackling loudly as he did so! "Abyss *yes*, I accept! That solves many of my problems. Gimme!"

CHAPTER THIRTY-FIVE

After picking himself up from the floor and brushing himself off, he tried his best to ignore his caretaker's look that elbow-dropping a prompt had been a terrible idea. He mumbled out a weak rebuttal. "I was in the moment. It seemed like a good idea at the time…"

"*Mhm.*" Yvessa's noise was one of rote dismissal. "Well, sit back down on your pillow. I was looking over the dragon growth pattern and found something neat. As a human, your base statistics aren't modified, unless you came from another creature. Humanization gives others bonuses, regardless of the end result being a human, Elf, or Dwarf. I thought it might be the same for you, and I was right. Your Long form has an individual table, and I just dug it up. Have a look."

Dragon Attribute Alterations by Age Category:
Hatchling: -90%
Wyrmling: -80%
Youngling: -60%
Juvenile: -20%
Budding Adult: 0%

Adult: +20%
Matured: +40%
Old: +60%
Venerable: +80%
Ancient: +90%

Artorian pressed his hands to his mouth in a steeple. "Now that is handy knowledge. So eventually my overall attributes will increase. Just because I've been around for a while? I cannot say that's not appealing. Especially considering the plight. Any idea how long it might take per age category to tick? I wouldn't mind knowing when Youngling happens, considering I'm currently in the second bracket."

Yvessa already had her hands on it, moving the screen over for the next one. "I did. I also found out you're going to double in physical size every category from now on. The times eight as a wyrmling was a one-time deal."

Dragon growth needed per category, versus total age:
Hatchling: Born, 0.
Wyrmling: 1 year, Age 1 total.
Youngling: 2 Years, Age 3 total.
Juvenile: 4 Years, Age 7 total.
Budding Adult: 8 Years, Age 15 total.
Adult: 16 Years, Age 31 total.
Matured: 32 Years, Age 63 total.
Old: 64 Years, Age 127 total.
Venerable: 128 Years, Age 255 total.
Ancient: 256 Years, Age 511 total.

Artorian needed to rub the back of his head, glad Yvessa had told him to sit down. He would have fallen if not already on his butt. "That… that is a very long time. Far longer than I want to be here. I'm suddenly rethinking the age category as an option. I'll just be happy if I can get the penalties reduced. Still… *years*? Real time years or sped-up years?"

Yvessa shook her head, as she didn't have good news. "Real time years. Timeframe cheatery won't..."

Her sentence faltered, eyes narrowing. Artorian hoped she'd just had a genius idea. "Question. When you have the Soul of Zen ability active... and you're doing things. Does it feel like time is passing normally for you?"

Artorian crossed his arms and looked at the ceiling. "It's... Yes. Pretty much. With the whole jumble active, I am moving at what feels to me like real time while everything else is particularly slow. I think if someone else had a similar effect active on at the Novice rank... then we would both be going the same speed while everything else was slow."

He pressed a hand to his chest. "My heart beats the same as it would normally. It's how I'm acting in comparison to everything else that changes. Just like Mage speed from the old days. I am really starting to miss the old days. This trick actually used to be one of my favorites for handling problems. I just didn't quite have the same mastery. If I ever get out, what I've been doing in Eternium is going to sharply increase my potency."

Yvessa sat down next to him on the pillow, her hand on his shoulder. "You'll get out. We all will. In the meanwhile, Vanaheim in Cal's Soul Space will become a pleasant, temporary copy for the old-worlders to live in until it's exit time. Vanaheim in Eternium has a bovine problem. They're big, angry, and axe lots of questions. Not too clever, but vast in number. I'm personally excited to see Ikaruga take them out to pasture. Those rude things..."

Artorian figured there was more to that story, but didn't pry. "Yes. We will. I just have to keep reminding myself of that. Eternium mentioned it has already been quite some time. I hope we have a world to go back to. Until then, work with what you have, not with what you don't. Thank you for the age information. I'll see if I can't use Soul for some cheatery in the future. Next prompt?"

Yvessa patted his back, agreeing. "Next prompt."

Skill gained! Artifacting.

Why make the mundane when you can make the magnificent! Turn any normal item into one of Artifact quality or better! Courtesy of being a Divine. Each attempt at Artifact creation will cost several million DE points. The end cost is variable depending on the power of the special ability granted. Certain abilities may be more potent on certain creations, resulting in a cost increase. These costs will be deducted from your DE total afterward. It is possible for your DE point total to hit negative numbers while doing this, and you will have to regain DE points over zero to be able to access any DE menus again.

Creating Artifacts does not have a guaranteed success rate. For each rank gained in this skill, the success ratio improves by 10%, starting at 50% success chance at the Novice rank. You also have a 1% chance per rank to create a Legendary quality item instead of an Artifact quality one, culminating at a maximum of 9% at the Sage rank.

Note that if you create a Legendary item, it will be considered restricted immediately, as items of that quality have effects too powerful for the current balance of the game. It is requested these items are given up to the system, to lock behind special events and requirements that allow them to be attained. Positive Karmic Luck will be awarded for this.

Artorian looked to Yvessa, but ended up turning his palms up in a 'not bad' motion when her expression asked for his opinion on the skill. "I'm getting lots of points. Now I have ways to spend lots of points. Not to mention the original options in the Divine shop that need a second look now. That's for later. Next prompt."

Skill gained! Siege Engine Mastery.

This skill gives a small boost to the use of all siege engines in combat, or other weapons that qualify. Accuracy, damage dealt, and armor ignored when using siege engines increases by a bonus of +10n%, where n equals your rank level. Siege Engine Mastery also determines how many projectiles you can fire over the course of a minute, equal to one projectile per rank. Time between shots will increase due to setup and pull penalties.

Firing one projectile has a flat cost of 1,000 stamina.

Skill gained! Ballistic Bowyer Mastery.

This skill relies on Siege Engine Mastery and Bow Mastery. The ranks of both will be averaged to determine the rank of this skill. Ballistic Bowyer Mastery allows you to take a ballista-class weapon, and use it as a bow! While a projectile will still cost 1,000 stamina to fire, you may now do so at the calculation provided by Bow Mastery, meaning the determination of how many projectiles you can fire is counted based on a round, rather than a minute. This skill also allows your bow skills and abilities to apply to siege engines that qualify under Ballistic Bowyer Mastery to be used without a penalty.

Ability gained! Siege Engine Sizing.

Some siege engines will simply be too large for you, or perhaps in your case, too small! This ability allows you to upscale the siege engine you are holding equal to your current size. This will provide a variable bonus to damage due to the increase in projectile size as they alter to scale with you as well. Any special effects the projectiles might have will not scale up with their size. This ability costs 100 mana per second to sustain, regardless of scaling. This ability has no levels or ranks due to Pylon limitations.

Artorian was not able to hide his smile. "It accounted for me getting bigger as a Long! Oh, this is going to be so neat. So my bow can't increase in size, but the ballista can? A good enough compromise. I was planning to swap between them depending on my needs, but this adds options. I like options."

Yvessa was holding a screen of her own. "I've got another spot of good news. Was that your last prompt?"

"It was," Artorian confirmed. "What do you have there?"

She cackled just for fun, reminding herself to underline the action in her notes a second time. "I overheard you talking with Snag. I found what Onyx Sunglass does. It's *spectacular*."

She showed him, and Artorian joined her cackling. Oh, they were having a good time now! Best make that three underlines. Her charge bounced on his toes, giddy. "I have to go try it. I have to go try it right now. I think some ammunition was stored in the workshop. I'm going to hustle over, fill my ring up with what they have, and then…"

"Then?" Yvessa queried.

Artorian's smile tilted just a little bit towards the evil side. "Surprises!"

Yvessa became invisible as normal when Sunny left the attic. He high-fived a few of the bar patrons on his way out, mentioning he had a show planned in a little while. He'd be on the tower with a contraption. They'd know when it was time.

For now, he jogged at a decent, careful pace over to the workshop, finding Yorn in the process of stacking the ammunition he needed outside of the main doors. "Yorn! You clever man. Did Snag tell you I needed them?"

The Dwarf wiped the sweat from his brow with the back of his hand. "He did. Hard ta miss that crystal spectacle of a ballista. What with it being on a pedestal an' all. Here to take it off? I'm tired o' hearin' that beaver gloat. It ain't even been that long. Already sick of it. The longtooth won't shut the abyss up. Am hopin' he punctures a lung from talkin'."

Artorian sputtered from trying not to laugh, his hand over his mouth as he moved to touch the stacks. He stored bolt after bolt into his spatial ring until it simply didn't let him add any more. Bolts took up far more space than arrows, and didn't pack into as big of a bundle. "I have that affliction from time to time. I can't say anything."

"Ha! I bet when yer gabbin, at least folk want ta' hear it," Yorn replied toothily. "Now come on. Get this engine out of my face."

Artorian had to take some arrows out of his ring to have the room to store the engine, but that was a minor loss he was willing to take. Actually, did it need to be a loss? He could just wear the quiver normally. Ah, never mind. Not at the speeds he ran. Best to leave it for later. "Such is the hope. I'm all set to knock down a gate and head to Vanaheim."

Yorn looked like his heart fell, the matching expression clear on his face. "Oh… yer… not gonna go to Svart? I was hoping that… never mind. I didn't even realize other bridges were…"

That had slipped Artorian's mind. He hadn't told anyone he'd messed with bridge positions, and their respective amounts, during his year of downtime. The human held his chin to think. He recalled what Eternium had said. At the end, when he got to Barry, every demon he hadn't 'taken care of' would come to his defense. Those were not good odds, given the trouble Pencil had given him. He did actually want to go see Svart and clear it out, but he was on a schedule and didn't particularly want to go alone. "Do you have your second specialization? I would need a guide."

Yorn perked up. The response hadn't been a no! "Ah do not. Not yet at least. If I get it… will ya go with me to free mah clan from the Baron?"

Artorian winked in response. "Indeed. Let us do that. Get some practice with Throat Coat and acquire that improvement. I will come check in periodically, or have a messenger do it for me. When you're all set, I will be back and we will go to Svart together. That way you can point out the right problems. In fact…"

He had noticed people were listening in. "If others have their second specialization, it would be prudent of them to go adventuring with us. A big break out from Midgard to save the other realms. Now that would be a tale worth telling for the generation of The First Age."

Yorn nodded in stern agreement. "Aye! That it would be! Alright then. I be gettin' my keister in gear, and I'll go out and do some swinging. It's gonna take a while, but with a quest like that on my conscience, I ain't gonna tread lightly. I'll be here when I'm ready. You just see to making it back. We got us a realm to free!"

Yorn looked like he would have said more, but his axe now pointed at something in the distance. "What the pyrite is that?"

Artorian turned. He was struck by a flash of inspiration when he saw the demon portal opening. His field wasn't on, but that was fine. He extended his hand and made Ikaruga appear. Taking pose and position right away, he made one of the freshly acquired bolts appear and slotted it before pulling back on the siege engine. "Uninvited guests. Say, Yorn, do you happen to know what Onyx Sunglass does?"

At the mention of incoming hostiles, the surrounding aligned called out the alarm, swords and spears finding their way into friendly hands. Yorn flanked to Artorian's left, his axe at the ready. "Can't say I do."

Sunny smirked. "It does *this* to any projectile fired."

Before he released it, the loaded wooden bolt changed. It crackled and popped from within, turning into something much different than a wooden bolt. Catching fire from the inside out, the bolt incinerated itself while keeping the general shape contained in a field of the same rough outline as the original projectile. Where the wood had been, dark plasma now roiled in place, contained by the bolt-shaped field as Onyx Sunglass applied its properties to the ammunition.

Onyx Sunglass was neither wood nor metal. It was crystalline. It focused energy, but twisted it around to an unstable form. At least until that form was also crystallized, as the black plasma hardened and stabilized… for the moment… into a long, sharp, jagged crystal spike.

The previously ordinary and uninteresting wooden bolt had become crystallized black plasma. It looked onyx in hue, using sunstone—per the mineral—for the striation pattern. When it was released, the listed effects of the ballista came out to play. The jagged crystal spike twinned itself, duplicating the effects of Zen Arrow invested in the first. Even if that wouldn't do much here.

Unlike the bow arrows, which were silent as death, the spikes accelerated with all the force a siege weapon afforded them. The duo careened through the freshly opened portal to skewer and strike the forces readied to exit. The storm of shards resulting from the imminent explosion after they did so scattered far and wide. Some shards even returned through the portal to cut and slice deeply carved pathways in the ground and surrounding buildings.

A few aligned were in need of immediate medical help as they were struck, but their boon would see them through. To speed their recovery up, Artorian flared his Resplendence field, restoring all those nearby to optimal capacity. Even a lost limb wasn't a setback as they would quickly regrow in his presence.

The demons on the other side of the portal were not so lucky. The spikes had skewered not just the frontal guard, but their shields and armor as well. Like it was wet paper a sword just stabbed through. When the explosive effect triggered, the damage became widespread, though that didn't account for unstable crystal plasma suddenly combusting, sending slowly dissolving dark crystal shards in every direction.

Artorian had a thought as he watched the carnage on the other side of the portal. He shaped his Resplendence field and sent it charging through the opened gate. Once through, he let it billow out like a luminous death cloud on the other end, finishing several badly wounded demons and poofing them in a celestine flash.

A golden light suffused Artorian, gently lifting him into the air before letting him drop to his feet. He had just dinged to level 21. Just how many things had he murdered with a single shot on the other side of that portal?

No aligned remained seriously hurt, and shrugged the rest of the accidental wounds off like they were nothing. The silence on the other end of the demon gate, though, was deafening. All that ended up coming through the gate was a tiny shape, torn and bleeding. A tiny shape that looked very defeated.

Artorian was intrigued, so he stowed his weaponry and let

his field drop for the moment. The tiny bat he saw was in pain. That pain eased when the field went away. He could thus deduce it was a demon without checking. The amusing part was that the black-leather-clad brown bat, draped in gaudy jewelry and an obscene amount of cobalt, had his hands in the air.

Its tiny, peeping voice was equally entertaining. "Alright. I give up. I quit. I surrender. That was my *entire* Alfheim army you just fragmented. I am sick and tired of being sent to the forefront when I don't belong there. Any time I open one of these gates, it's my winged ass getting beat. I'm done."

The bat shook his head, squeezing a bit of flame on his ear to put it out. "Lightning, lava, mud elementals, resplendent death, arrows that go faster than sound, and now—if my ears heard things correctly—celestial-cursed siege weaponry. Our intel is that you are a Mage of some kind, but I haven't even seen *that* repertoire. So you know what? I'm on the wrong burned side."

He sighed, saluting. "My name is Soni. The Alfheim demon overseer. I'm done. I'm out. *I defect.*"

CHAPTER THIRTY-SIX

Artorian wasn't sure how to take this. His bow manifested into his hand, expecting to just shoot the demon and be done with it. "I should care about your defection… why? A change of heart doesn't suddenly make you not a demon. Regardless of the form you hide in. You're not *good*."

Soni stuck his tiny finger into the air. "One does not need to be good to realize they are playing on the wrong side of the board! It makes no difference if I'm treated poorly by this side, or your side. I'll be treated poorly all the same. The value of a savant is dirt in Eternia."

An arrow appeared in front of his foot. Soni had neither heard nor seen it, it was just there all of a sudden. A good sign to get on with the better reasons, both his clawed hands reached for the air in surrender. "I can be of use! I make the portals! You don't need to *trust* me to *work* with me!"

"I'm pretty sure I do, and I don't!" Artorian loosed another arrow, causing Soni to hit the deck with his hands on his head as Artorian snapped out the ultimatum. "Not falling for it! You've got one sentence left to convince me not to skewer you. I really want to skewer you."

Soni fumbled out an answer. "I know where all the demon troops and overseers are stationed! I know how to gate to all of them! I know Barry's weakness!"

A third arrow did not get loosed, even if it sternly aimed at Soni's face. Artorian's voice rumbled, both angry and pensive. "…Go on."

A reprieve! Soni didn't want to waste this chance. "I'll tell you everything you want to know! What do you want me to go on about?"

Artorian had a different idea in mind. An idea called tactical superiority. "A bit of truth is a nice start. You say you're the portal demon? Close the one behind you, then. If you're really defecting, you knew this was a one-way road."

Soni felt a knot in his stomach. Of course the Mage was smart.

"As… as you wish." The portal closed without a fuss. Closing was easy! Opening was difficult. That required all sorts of fine tuning. Fine tuning nobody *appreciated*. "How is that?"

Artorian was good at snap decisions. Or he thought he was, because today this had him stumped. A demon that surrendered? Lies and chicanery. This could only be some well-planned ruse to get behind friendly lines and cause havoc. Demons only ever belonged in one corner of the morality chart. The one you shot on sight.

He was feeling apprehension, and it showed in his voice. "Not a bad start. Though, you understand why believing you is a matter of great difficulty."

Soni sighed, his hands back in the air. "Alright. What else do you want? This is a surrender. I'm burned either way."

The arrow pointing at the small bat didn't go away. Several had even been added from other directions, though he had the distinct feeling those would all be toothpicks in comparison. Overseers were the strongest members in the opposition, regardless of the form they took. Given all the failures in checking the bat's status, that told the aligned enough. They could guess just how much higher Soni's attributes were. The bat wasn't even trying to block them.

Artorian picked up on the clue, and pressed into it. "Why would you be burned either way? You have a pleasantly high position in your faction, while you're seen as purely hostile in ours."

Soni scowled, though his tone was meek. "Not as pleasant as one may think. There is a hierarchy that doesn't bend well, and when the others find out about the total loss of my Alfheim troops, my status is going to drop below that of Robar. Barry isn't known for being kind or generous, and he's been aching for someone to *eat* to make an example out of. My failure just now… puts me on the platter."

Soni swallowed loud. "I do so much as report in, and I'm a chew toy. A very short-lived chew toy. As my direct summoner, I cannot disobey his commands very easily. No matter how much savants enjoy playing up the fact that ordering them around isn't possible."

The bat visibly discolored, uncomfortable beyond words. "So like I said. One doesn't need to trust me to work with me. As of that fragmentation from a little bit ago, I'm an outcast. I don't enjoy the thought of being eaten, and I don't enjoy being on the losing side. If I'm going to die anyway, I may as well take my chances with the enemy. At least if I die here, I save face, and my Core doesn't get cracked."

Artorian's gaze bored through the bat. He desired very badly not to believe him while weighing the tactical advantages. "So, if you return to camp, it's over for you. If you come to us, you have a sliver."

A moment of silence hung between them before Artorian spoke again, Soni shrinking back an inch. "Then I suppose you have a sliver. Though you may not like the cost it comes at."

Soni shook his head. "Anything is better than Barry. Anything. I accept your terms. Whatever they are."

The tall man's eyebrow moved up, but the edge of his lips curled up with it. "Oh really? Well then, demon-lad, you're about to learn something very interesting. Follow me. It of course goes without saying that any suspicious events will cut your opportunity rather short."

Soni kept his tiny bat hands in the air for everyone to see, not even daring a word at the moment as a few hundred toothpicks were tracking him. What bothered Soni wasn't that he knew they wouldn't actually do anything, it was the cohesion with which the arrowheads moved, and the zeal that burned behind the eyes of those who held them.

These were the forces waiting for them in Midgard? Robar was hosed if the order to assault was given. Though, that was the Baron's problem now. Artorian stowed his weapons and made a motion to some of the warriors near a large building. "Seal the windows and close the doors. I want everyone out while I have a chat with our defector in private."

He paused to lay a hand on the meerkat near the door, his voice whispering. "I don't want anyone to see what I'm about to do. Ensure it, my boy."

The guarding meerkat snapped to attention with his tiny halberd tightly gripped in his paw. It took a minute and a half for the building to be vacated and secured. After which the Divine and the demon entered, the meerkat guarded the door once it closed, his tiny frame barely blocking even a single slat of the door. It was the effort that counted. The structure may have been given space, but easily several hundred aligned watched it like hungry hawks, their weapons remaining at the ready.

Artorian cleared his throat, but Soni noted the man did not appear to be speaking to him. "Yvessa. I need a link to the outside. I have a pertinent question: Do vows work in Eternia, and can we transfer this entity to another Core?"

Soni silently watched as the man was given a prompt that the bat could not see. Based on the hand movements, though, Artorian was clearly interfacing with it. That was difficult to hide. The Divine nodded at nothing shortly after. "I see. No vows then? That's unfortunate. In that case, please escalate this to Oberon and up for the latter query."

Soni raised an eyebrow, not following the conversation. He didn't know any of the names being mentioned, but also didn't need to. It appeared they had company. Very pressured and heavy company as the tiny bat suddenly experienced several times normal gravity. Pressed to the ground with a **fwap** as breathing became difficult, Soni realized something else was here. Something without shape, but with colossal pressure. Like the world itself was cramming him into a box.

Artorian kept his hands behind his back and watched as the strange opaque egg-shaped field surrounded the bat. "He can't hear us now?"

Oberon winked into being in the shape of a glowing orange ball. His usual. "He cannot. Nor see us. I would apologize that it took so long for me to get here, but I remembered that for you it hasn't even been a few seconds. Eternium was intrigued by your strange willingness to spare a demon. I take it you had conditions."

Artorian nodded as Yvessa popped into being as well, the green glow of her orb adding to the room. He spoke with finality. "A vow of fealty to Cal and his well-being. Just like we all had to take in the beginning. That will prevent even a demon from acting against our or Cal's interests. Which somewhat makes me wonder why Barry is able to get around this. I want some answers on that when possible. Until then, Core transferring is something that goes way above my head."

Oberon slowly bobbed around the room. "There's no precedent for this yet, but we needed a guinea pig. You need a gazebo link to come and go. Wisps do not. A creature with a Core in Eternia, but not in Cal? I know we have places where we've stored defeated demon souls. Nothing yet on a live one. I think it's doable. I think this would be a great opportunity for Invictus to repair his reputation, so I'm going to fetch him to have the demon make the vow. I'm sure they're both plenty motivated.

Yvessa will notify you of the exact point where this demon will be returning, when imported back into Eternia."

Artorian nodded, and both the Wisps vanished along with the demon. The opaque field trailed out of existence like a smoke haze given fresh air, leaving Artorian to wonder if he'd just made a grave mistake. He wasn't a man for pity. A demon was not something he should care for. So it was a terrible twist in his stomach… that he did.

He stood there and held his arm, biting his thumb as thoughts rocked around in his head. The situation didn't make sense. Demons defecting? Sure, any circumstance poor enough was one a mind wanted to escape. Though that had to be one abyss of a bar for a demon. Then there was the Barry misery. Now that he thought about it, there was just no way Barry would be here at all without a direct vow. The man was an S-ranker, and Cal hadn't been when the escape from Mountaindale occurred.

So why wasn't Barry getting beat down by the contract Heavenly? Weren't his actions against Cal— A Nixie Tube lit above his head. "Those are… our assumptions. We have been thinking Barry is coming to control Eternium and eat Cal. What if he's not?"

Artorian shook it off. He couldn't work with that information. It didn't matter, because the original crime was clear. Barry summoned demons which escaped Eternium, and posed a threat to his Core stored family. An unacceptable line which had already been crossed. Fork-boy would get forked. End of story. The rest was minutiae.

Yvessa popped back in, though in her human form. "We're all set. That went surprisingly smoothly."

Even Artorian was surprised, his back straightening as his shoulders pulled back. "That was too fast. What happened?"

Yvessa pulled up a prompt and handed it over to her charge's eager hands. "Soni took the vow in a middle-space where Eternium made a direct connection to Cal. Don't worry. Heavy security. Invictus had Soni make the vow even if the savant didn't fully understand what was going on. Soni experienced the vow-binding effect, and Occultatum was more than eager to see if the transfer worked. The man was just about salivating at the chance for lush hidden knowledge."

Artorian snorted, but didn't hide his smile. "I'm glad Tatum had something fun to do. What's the end result?"

Yvessa twirled in place in her heel. "Great success. Soni's soul experienced a full handover to a Core of similar quality. He has vanished from Eternia, so if someone was keeping tabs on his original Core… That one is now empty, as if he were dead. Since we pull dead demons, and they know that. That whole can't-leave-Cal difficulty requires some clever solutions. Soni can be imported back into Eternia, but… it doesn't have to be immediately."

Artorian closed his eyes and handed the panel back. "He's the most useful now, while his information is fresh. I understand the draw to just keep him Cored, but no. This crackpot idea was a success, may as well take it all the way. It would be handy to have a portal Mage on our team. Especially one that is stuck between dusk and dawn."

Yvessa rolled her eyes. "I swear… you two are in such sync. She said the same thing when Tatum Cored Soni."

That tiny mention made Artorian feel like a small, giggly child. How pleasant. "Any chance you can import him to the Midgard Bifrost connection? Here?"

Yvessa pointed at her feet with confidence. "I can make him appear in the spot he left. We have so much more control now. So it's not a surprise later, Soni actually made two vows. The second was to Eternium. Same deal, same result. That demon is either on our side, or a piece of suddenly scorched toast. Want me to pull him in?"

"Please do." Her charge nodded, taking a step back to allow for the room. Soni appeared in a flash, not a hair different on his head. Save that his eyes were wide and his expression screamed horror. Artorian amusedly eased out his words. "Welcome back."

"I have made a terrible mistake," Soni mumbled out, his form wobbling until he fell on his tiny butt. "I thought Barry was powerful. The two… out there… abyss on a stick. I should have defected sooner. We were never going to win."

Artorian figured Soni met Dawn and Tatum, with Tatum in a very enthusiastic, experimentation-loving mood. That must have been an expression far more frightening than any level of destruction Dawn could cause. The thought made him smile.

CHAPTER THIRTY-SEVEN

When Artorian walked with Soni back out of the building, they had made some alterations. DE points were fantastic! He'd had no idea cosmetic items had been an option. No mechanical bonuses, but that was fine. Rather than his prior attire, Soni now wore a white velvet coat instead of a dark one.

The image of a celestine sun was clear and obvious on the back; and Soni had been allowed to keep all his precious cobalt, and his brushy-brush. An item which had seemed to make the Divine rather happy.

Soni noticed the man smile. Smiles were good, right?

Artorian's enthusiastic expression remained once out in the open. He clapped his hands together, speaking like an old professor addressing a crowd. "Good news, everyone! We have ourselves a new ally. He will not be aligning, because that would make him go up like a torch. He will be assisting with information warfare on the enemy, and creating portals to their strongholds once enough people have the right specializations."

He clapped his hands again, waiting for the crowd to erupt in a great cheer that did not come. He awkwardly stood there, forcibly holding a now uncomfortable smile as most of the onlookers glared at the bat. "What? Not convincing enough?"

As Artorian pressed his fingers together, Soni just quietly looked at him, since it was very obvious nobody believed he was 'one of them' now. Didn't take a sharp rock to figure that out. Artorian sighed and made a 'come along' motion. "Let's try this. Walk with me and tell me about Vanaheim. I want to do some cow-tipping."

Soni nodded, following along the walk in a gentle jog since Artorian's strides were so much larger. His tiny feet moved very quickly as he kept up, following the Divine in the direction of the Svartalfheim Bifrost. "Vanaheim goes mostly overlooked by the savants. There's nothing there. Aside from some hills and the occasional tree, its fields of green grass. Overseer Mu is in charge, though behind his back he's called the Kingly Cow. Although the demons there look like the animal in question, they are actually creatures we managed to smuggle out of the realm of Hel."

Speaking hurriedly, Soni spared a glance over his shoulder to see he was being stalked by a few hundred humans. "Initially, we thought adding large, aggressive bovines with oversized axes to the realm-point anyone would *have* to cross to go back and forth was a good idea. At least, before the bridges began to behave erratically all of this last year. We did not expect the Hel-cows to… not be that clever? They speak a language called 'Moo,' travel in packs by the thousands, and care only about grazing."

For a moment, Soni's tone turned irritable, like he'd been subject to their ire. "Interrupt their grazing, or come close enough, and they will get up and start trying to scare you off with their voice. *When* they get close enough, they will swing those axes, which are far more dangerous than their silly 'intimidation' sounds. Their call does nothing except catch prey off guard. We have lost many imps who didn't see the danger and laughed at the oncoming moo'ing."

Soni shook his head in disappointment. "Any demon that

inhabits a Hel-cow is known as a wrangler. Unfortunately, the forced penalties for being that race imposes a serious intelligence demerit. I don't think they even realize they're demons anymore. Not that it matters. Any Hel-cow has a minimum health pool of about five thousand, and a strength rating that hovers around four-fifty. Their axes are unique to them, and they will always cleave on any strike. Cover is meaningless. They will slash right through it. Hiding behind the bodies of the fallen is not a viable tactic. We tried."

On a roll, Soni temporarily forgot about the stalkers behind him. "Wranglers have the same strength, but double the health. Mu himself has about twenty thousand health, and A-ranked attribute bonuses. Why he's not that clever even with those numbers… I don't know. We all chalked it up to some mad cow affliction they all share."

The bat became animated, his cobalt making clicking noises as he vented. "If you get the attention of one Hel-cow, you get the attention of the entire herd, easily a thousand strong. They move faster than you expect they should, and look strangely harmless *until* the axe comes down. It may actually be their Moos? Perhaps they do have an effect. I never stuck around for the results, and Mu isn't talkative unless Barry forces him to be. Vanaheim is often jokingly referred to as the secret cow level. Savants tend not to go there."

Artorian had gotten the gist by the time they reached the Svartalfheim Bifrost. He carefully stopped at the edge, and just barely edged his toe over the line. "No squish? No squish! *Aha*! Fantastic."

Confident about the test, he strode fully onto the solid rainbow, a bright smile on his face as he pressed his hands into his hips as he replied to Soni. "Well alright then! Sounds like a good Vanaheim primer. I think I'm going to, just for safety's sake, step a toe onto the other landmasses, in case it's important for something else."

He pressed his hand over his eyes, peering into the distance at a strange rainbow protrusion jutting out from the side of the

Bifrost. "I see a new connection has been added to the path. The bridge seems shorter than I remember it as well. Strange. I thought I'd seen the shortest distance."

Artorian glanced over his shoulder, calling out for a general response. "Anyone know why the bridge looks shorter?"

The majority of the crowd near the gate kept silent. Many walked over to have a look at the bridge now that the addition was pointed out. The general murmur of 'I don't know' passed over the crowd. The question spread around, and eventually someone appeared to have some information.

A hamster stuck his leaf shield in the air, then hurried over after the High Human prompted him with a 'come closer' handwave. Artorian hunched down at the end of the bridge to hear the hamster out, whose voice didn't at all match the tiny critter's stature. When the hamster spoke, his voice resounded. Richly saturated and full of depth, but buttery smooth when spoken. "The distance between the realms changes constantly. The Bifrost bends, and alters to do the same. It has been so long that we have not been able to see the end. Today, the realm distances happen to be short. That additional protrusion is another Bifrost intersecting to this one. It leads to Alfheim. I took it in order to escape to Midgard. Please don't ask me to go back. I'm… I'm not ready."

Artorian adored this, and replied with a respectful nod. "Thank you kindly. Now that I think about it, aren't I supposed to have the ability to go to Vanaheim from here as well?"

The hamster waggled his hand in a so-so motion. "The bridges have been odd this last year, and have been flickering in and out of existence the last few weeks. They look to be… I don't know. Reconfiguring? I'm not going to be holding onto my existing bridge knowledge much longer. The world is changing and I can't say I'll know where the new connections lead when their flickering ends."

Soni on the other hand stuck his paw into the air. "I can get you there. I don't know the reason behind why the Bifrost isn't behaving, but a portal is a portal. I know most all of the old bridge locations; abyss knows I've had to ferry savants to and fro plenty of times when they felt too lazy to walk."

Artorian approved of the notion. "Very well then. Prepare a gate to… honestly, whichever continent currently connects to Vanaheim. I don't feel like getting squished on arrival because I didn't meet some mystery threshold."

He then paused and looked back to the bridge, gently kicking it with the tip of his foot. "Hmmm. I wonder how sturdy this thing is. Time for a stress test?"

Soni didn't need further prompting to begin preparations, already in the middle of forming the somatic components while the human did something strange. Artorian took position on the bridge as if he were on a starter block, then looked over his shoulder to give them a warning. "Everyone hold on to something. I think if this works, there's going to be a lot of backdraft!"

The air around Artorian sounded pained as he activated some skills. Without him moving an inch, a wave of heat erupted from his position; one that slowly focused to form a cone that flared behind him, the visible force slowly concentrating into a tube. The heat battered against the Midgard gate and made critters of all kinds dive, roll, and scurry out of the way of the sudden orange-red flare. One of the guards called out in panic. "The gate is melting!"

Artorian figured that he'd charged up enough if effects like that were occurring behind him. Best to just pop the cork. "Soul of Zen, Power Launch."

Air thrummed, then burst, erupting with a loud **boom** as the sound barrier broke instantaneously upon his launch. To the Bifrost's credit, it didn't so much as ripple underneath the tension Artorian's feet forced down upon it. Instead, that blur of a being remained centered on the path regardless of how it bent and flexed, blitzing straight for the Svartalfheim gate. Artorian had a plan in mind, speaking his thoughts as if the skills wouldn't otherwise work. "Phalanx Breaker. Land Breaker."

Artorian felt hot as he charged forwards. His surroundings

seemed as if they were on fire, even if that wasn't the case. He chalked the heat up as a side effect of going faster than his mind could keep up with, but that was fine. He didn't need to be precise. He just needed the right timing.

The imps manning the Svartalfheim gate knew it was a day for bad news bears when the glowing projectile sped towards them. Particularly when the glowing projectile was using the bridge as a guided ramp. Throwing weapons aside, they cast themselves away shortly after. Some imps chose to outright leap from the three-story structure. That may have seemed like a terrible choice at first, until the glowing blur hip-checked into the triple-reinforced front gate. That new gate was so sturdy it was essentially part of the wall, and many builder imps took some pride in it.

Some imps near the ground level heard something they recognized as words, though it wasn't scree-scree. It sounded more like 'Sky Breaker!'

The imps who had chosen to remain stationed on the defensive structures experienced a new form of transportation. Rather than crash through the gate as they expected the blur might have, it smashed into the gate, then did nothing. A man stood where the blur had been, while the entirety of the gate, towers, adjoined structures, and all, took to the skies like trebuchet projectiles.

The imps on the walls saw the land below them get small, then tiny as they traversed several hundred feet up into the air, before realizing what went up also had a tendency to come down.

The gatehouse and towers crashed down into Svartalfheim soil with a noisy rumble and painful crumble. At least for the imps still in it, when the building changed its tag from 'structure' to 'pile of rubble.' The gate was slag.

Imps near the bridge dropped their weapons to gawk at the distance where the crushed pile of rubble now lay. That strange blur had just yeeted an entire defensive position over a small hill, by hip-checking it. When they turned to look to see what the blur had become, an arrow through the noggin was as far as they got. Though they knew of no arrows that whistled jolly tunes while they were fired.

Artorian hadn't expected that stunt to work! What a great day. So Sky Breaker worked in part like his rail palm. All his momentum went from him into the other thing. He was essentially almost standing still already after landing the Sky Breaker maneuver. Good to know. "I'm satisfied. That's my feet confirmed down on Svart soil. Now to do the same to Alf, and then see how trustworthy our portal bat is. Onward-ho!"

When it came to the Alfheim gate—which Artorian reached by taking that offshoot in the Bifrost—the second verse was sung much the same as the first. Though it had no guards, and no maintenance love like the Svartalfheim one benefited from. It allowed for confirmation in proof of concept. Sky Breaker could hurl buildings into the sky, so long as the system considered them 'all one thing,' and he kept that specific target in mind during the attack. Just like with higher **Law** functions, being specific had its benefits!

Soni was done crafting the Vanaheim portal when a pleased as punch Artorian hopped and skipped his way back onto Midgard's soil, having tapped the other two with a foot. "That was a hoot! Time for the event. Soni! Got that gate up and running?"

Rather than state the obvious, he motioned to the large round gap in space. Nothing but green pastures surrounded by sun-blocking hills were visible on the other side, which connected to a Bifrost bridge where the hills split. "Opened a gate to a spot in a forgotten corner of Alfheim. There is a stable Bifrost connection to Vanaheim nearby that was found maybe a week or so ago. The bridge is a bit long considering realm spacing, but that's the only downside. There are so few demons that know about this bridge that I'm fairly confident we won't run into any. I don't exactly want to go around announcing my continued existence to so much as an imp. So when possible, I will be picky with my in and out destinations."

Artorian approved! "Excellent! Alright everyone. Start dumping ballista ammunition through. I'm going to need every last piece we have to make a dent in the local demon populace. Soni, I hope you don't have bags, because you're coming with me!"

The bat blinked. "I… I am?"

Artorian smirked cheekily. "Of course! You're my only way in. So you're also my only way out, unless you'd rather stay here under all these friendly gazes?"

Soni changed his mind at the drop of a hat, which reminded him he'd lost his. "You are completely right. I am going through with you. Yes. Great plan."

Artorian rubbed his hands together to jump through, but paused when he saw Cuzco speed up to him. "Malchemist! How goes?"

Cuzco wobbled when in speaking range, so out of breath that Artorian activated his Resplendence field to help, molding it to exclude Soni. That made the llama feel worlds better. "Oh my potions. That's such a nice effect. I came to bring the good news. We have charged Ragna by one percent!"

"*One* p—" Artorian wondered if the llama was joking. "Was that the expected number after all this time?"

Cuzco beamed. "We're ahead of schedule! The Core started with seven percent charge. We're now at eight! Magnificent progress."

Artorian just smiled and patted the llama's shoulder, suddenly having serious doubts. "Excellent work, my boy. Good luck with the rest of it. Don't overtax yourself."

Not wanting to be caught in a conversation about the intricacies of Core charging, Artorian turned and leapt through the open portal. He landed in some very pleasant soil, the grass under his feet crunching with a satisfying squish. Soni had no desire to stay behind, flapping his wings to follow though.

Artorian was inspecting the ground when Soni landed and re-folded his wings, the first batches of siege ammunition making their way through the portal shortly after. The savant looked around to see nothing but Alfheim green in every direction. "What do you plan to do now?"

Cleaning his hands by wiping them off on his pants, Artorian let his field do the rest. "Now? Now I cross the bridge and hunt. It's time for me to use my second specialization, and start building up my third. I'm excited!"

CHAPTER THIRTY-EIGHT

After crossing the bridge with surprising ease, and after locating a small herd of the Moo-monsters in question, Artorian decided to nap out of sight. He wanted to feel tip-top before the big adventure, since it had taken half a day with a major case of the zoom zooms to find this Hel-cow crowd. Not seeing the need for a tent, he lay on the grass out in the middle of the wide, open clearing, getting some shut-eye while Soni clung to the sole tree they'd found in wide-eyed terror.

Putzing around at the speed Artorian enjoyed was an experience that left the savant frazzled. Sure, he *supposed* someone with A-rank attributes could go that fast, but what madman would actually do that? There were no numbers that could save Soni from screaming while hurtling through the sky at a breezy Mach four. Or however 'slow' Artorian had gone when the man told Soni he'd been taking it easy, wanting to make sure he spotted the questioners. Y'know, with their axes?

Soni did not appreciate his attempted repetition of the joke. Nor did he delve into what nonsense the man was up to when napping didn't come easy. It took Soni a good hour before he felt steady enough to speak. "Do I even want to know what you are doing to that grass?"

Artorian lay sideways on the ground, his face half-pressed to the dirt cheek first. He was holding a blade of grass by the very tip, keeping it straight for measuring before suddenly plucking and eating it. His chews were pensive, slow, and studious before swallowing. "*Hmmm*. Interesting."

He perked up when he'd realized the bat had spoken, taking the grass he'd nicked from the other three realms so far from his pocket to compare. "What am I doing? Just some Administrator stuff. Interested?"

Soni wasn't certain how to respond. He certainly didn't want to eat grass. So he decided on a clever bit of wordplay. "My ears are very good for listening."

Artorian didn't appear to catch the reference, busy inspecting and comparing blades of grass. "Curious. Well, it goes a little something like this… But first, is my light green?"

He looked around, and noted the pleasant glow was indeed nearby, even if it confused Soni entirely as the bat didn't see it. "It is. Excellent. So I was wondering if there were any inherent differences between these realms. You know, you can hear all the jabber but you never know for sure until you check yourself. I figured grass seems reasonable. Not like I can bite into some dirt for Cal everywhere I go. Found that first flavor profile by accident."

Soni decided to sit and hold his head. On second thought, he wished his ears were very bad at hearing right now. What nonsense. Who ate dirt and grass? Save Mu, of course.

Artorian was unperturbed and cracked on. "Unfortunately, flavor-wise they're all bland. Couldn't even use this as a spice. However…"

Rather than speak the next part out loud, he pulled up the individual inspection information on each. He was delighted to see his assumption matched the numbers provided, a pleasant twinkle playing behind his eyes.

Inspection:
Object: Midgard grass, one blade.
Rarity: Trash
Deep System Information
Energy if converted with complete efficiency: 0.001.
Nutrient Value for inspecting species: 0.

Inspection:
Object: Svartalfheim grass, one blade.
Rarity: Trash
Deep System Information
Energy if converted with complete efficiency: 0.01.
Nutrient Value for inspecting species: 1.

Inspection:
Object: Alfheim grass, one blade.
Rarity: Trash
Deep System Information
Energy if converted with complete efficiency: 0.01.
Nutrient Value for inspecting species: 1.

Inspection:
Object: Vanaheim grass, one blade.
Rarity: Trash
Deep System Information
Energy if converted with complete efficiency: 0.1.
Nutrient Value for inspecting species: 10.

Out of curiosity, Artorian tapped the word energy. He hadn't expected a functional prompt to appear, especially not one with information in it. Still, what a delight!

Deep System Access Information: Energy of a consumable item.

Energy refers to the capacity or availability of power. In reference to conversion, it refers to how much pure essence is required to create one of these objects from nothing. Mana and Spirit calculations not shown due to difference in scale.

In reference to consumable objects, nutrient value refers to how much energy a creature can gain per the requirement of their operations, or how much stamina this object restores over time if consumed when at full satiety.

Wisp translation: If hungry, food will feed you. If not hungry, food will recover stamina.

The average daily intake requirement is equal to one thousand nutrient value for a grown, adult body, with an additional one hundred value needed per level the user has above zero.

Wisp translation: More powerful people need to eat more food to feel full. Everything consumable has a number that increases how full a person feels. This is reflected on the status sheet as the 'fed' and 'well-fed' statuses until we have better terms.

Gnome note: A single unit of 'nutrient value' is also called a Calorie, using a capital c, as the lowercase word for calorie is likely going to have to do with heat measurements of some kind. Something concerning raising the temperature of water. I told you we shouldn't have let the Wisps edit these entries, look at the mess they're leaving!

Wisp note: Speak for yourself, you undersized racket. There is no need or reason for that Calorie notice to even be in this segment. Get that out of here!

Gnome note: Make me!

Wisp note: I am having the word 'Calorie' inscribed on a chunky piece of wood just to whack you with, tiny! Pick a time and place and we'll be there to knock you out of the Pylon hold!

Gnome note: Bridge Pylons. Today. Midgard high noon. My paddle racket needs another notch. Come alone, if you dare. Bring all your friends if you don't. You'll still draw first during the standoff like the newlight you are.

Wisp note: I'll see you at high noon, cracked sprocket.

Notice!

This feature is currently not implemented. All creatures will operate at full satiety, which will be provided by the system. Users will still feel a driving need to eat, but all gains will go to their stamina. Some objects will have a nutrient value that does not affect satiety, such as old-world health and recovery potions, and poultices.

Notice. Satiety system Pylons are complete. Engage?

Artorian kept quiet while reading the flame war in the comment section.

A fact which Soni considered blissful as the tiny bat massaged his own ears. He'd trailed off after that 'However,' but Soni just sighed in relief when nothing further was forthcoming. The scheming expression on Artorian's face was significantly less relief inducing. Soni repeated a new mantra in his head, having discovered one on the spot. "Don't ask. Don't ask. Don't ask."

Artorian didn't notice the bat give himself a headache, wondering if he should push the button or not. He was contemplating what he had just learned. Yvessa had mentioned before that Midgard-quality was a thing. Or was that Oberon? He also roughly recalled something from an old meeting back in Cal that different realms would have different levels of sturdiness.

The Vanaheim grass hadn't been flavored any different, but there was a notable difference in how difficult it was to chew and eat. It also gave him more energy, should he have needed it. Which brought him to his current dilemma: If the game imposed a hunger system, just like reality did, then everything would need to eat. More, if they were powerful.

This was starting to sound like needing to keep a certain amount of Essence in you just to keep kicking as a cultivator. That part he didn't dislike. The people he'd met in Midgard had food production covered. Now that he thought about it, those demons on the moon… *did not.*

The variants here would likely be fine, given eating was their way of life, and his people would remain a-okay since farming practices were up and running. Higher up, on the other hand… perhaps not so much. Were demons used to eating? He had one to ask! "Say, savant. Do demons eat? At all? I have some grass I can interest you in."

Soni felt appalled, looking at the human in disgust. "Grass? *Me*? I would never. Of course I eat. I just happen to prefer fresh meat of all varieties. Most demons prefer it that way, and some are pure carnivores. Bonus if the creature being eaten is still alive when it occurs."

He lifted a batty digit to the air. "That's the rule. If it cannot scream out, do not bite in. Not only will it not taste good, but you'll end as hungry as you started. Even Mu is just pretending. He swallows another cow whole when hunger strikes. I've seen it. He just unhinges that jaw and makes one vanish. The herd doesn't notice."

Artorian's expression fell flat. There was discomfort, and his eye twitched a moment. He chose to quietly push the engage button, activating the hunger and satiety system since it was ready. Also because he could. Mostly to turn everyone on the moon hungry. Chaos would be proud. "No grass for you then."

Soni agreed with that statement while climbing up a tree to hang upside down from a branch. He'd successfully shut the human up, and considered that a fine accomplishment since the man rolled over to attempt another nap. It didn't take very long for Artorian to gently wheeze during sleep.

The demon bat felt conflicted.

If there was ever a moment to strike and betray, this was it. Right? The human was cut off from any support or backup, alone in a big empty nothingness. Soni had made vows to Cal and Eternium, yet when he'd asked if one was needed to the human as well... The Wisp had smiled and waved him off, calling it 'unnecessary' and saying he 'doesn't want it that way.'

That latter one bothered the bat. Was the human just waiting for a chance to see if he would? Or was there an eye in the sky that kept tabs on what he would do when in close proximity to an undefended foe? If he took this one out, surely the demons would win. Right? Soni shook it off. That was the old survival method talking. That would get him slain under the current circumstances. Plus... he couldn't forget the meeting with the people that had apparently taken down Yasura.

Taking a second to really inspect the human, Soni heard something odd. Was that the sound of grass growing? The greenery was doing so much faster than it should. Especially if he could hear it. The bat glanced around, but the sound definitely appeared to be originating from or around the napping one.

Squinting to focus his not insignificant vision, Soni watched the grass grow. In a break to expected boredom, it turned out to be a fascinating occurrence. In a bubble around Artorian, the grass flourished. Like there was some tiny, invisible field around him that was invigorating the ground and plant life. The tree he was hanging from also gained this mystery benefit, as the branches slowly sprouted healthy flowers.

Plucking a single strand of fur from his pelt, Soni let it fall to the ground only to watch it dissolve into nothing where he suspected the edge of the bubble to be. On second consideration, unprotected was not something the human was. His location was a demon trap. Approaching too close would poof him like he'd seen happen to so many of his old soldiers.

Soni rethought his strategy. There was no winning here, and it had been smart to change sides. Folding his wings around himself, he tried to squeeze out the awkward feelings. Soni may have been a demon, but he was no fool. He would need to learn in order to survive. He made a brush appear in his hands, then moved it around to scratch his own back. Some brushy-brushy always made him feel better.

Artorian continued his pretend sleep until he heard the bat make sleeping wheezes of his own, after some scrubbing sounds had passed. A peek with Electrosense told him the bat used a backscratcher before tucking himself in. Was that a Soul Item? It appeared to be. How interesting!

He noted that the uncertain bat decided not to engage him here. A shame. It would have been a great opportunity to prove he was correct about demons, and would have felt no qualms with blanket-wrapping the bat in his active Resplendence field. He'd kept it pulled tight for the moment, discovering that turning the satiety system on made the old growth effects of his Aura work again as well.

It made him think of that old chestnut tree in Chasuble. What a good tree that had been. Perhaps he could find some chestnuts when this was all over. Get a new chestnut grove going? How pleasant a thought.

When he didn't think he was going to successfully ensnare Soni, he decided to let the field do its thing, giving himself over to sleep while planning out his tactics before dozing. As usual, why play fair? If the enemy had no ranged weaponry, kite them, and remain out of their range while keeping them in yours.

There was plenty of room in Vanaheim to run and remain mobile, and he had ammunition for days. For both his weapons! Still, growth on the new specialization likely required exclusive use of the siege engine. There was also the new convenience of having a good gut feeling about that spellscript in the Long. He should definitely attempt to combine those.

He should… **Snore**.

CHAPTER THIRTY-NINE

Artorian woke to a mental nudge from a Forum space. He groggily accepted, not awake yet as his personal Forum merged together with the ticking interior of a large clock. That was new. Not Yvessa? "There you are! Sprockets and Pylon parties. I love the taste of success!"

"Deverash!" Artorian felt far more awake in a flash, swiftly sitting up. "My favorite clever Gnome! How are you, my ancient friend?"

"Ancient?" Deverash walked into the scene as the most dapperly dressed Gnome in all of history. "Venerable, good sir! Venerable! I'm well-liked and respected in my personal circle, and despised by the developer community as a whole. It's glorious! No Wisp shall go unpunished for their saccharine Celestial Feces. They can't fool me."

Artorian smiled while raising his eyebrows. "Sounds like it's still eventful in the Pylon holds! What brings you for this sudden visit?"

Deverash motioned around himself. "To see if this worked properly, for starters. I didn't like how the Forums were all white marble in empty space, so I found a way to customize and personalize them! When they now merge together, bits of your personal Forum will come with it."

Artorian spent a few moments to look around the partially finished inside of the great clock. All those gears, smoothly turning. He considered it art in motion. "I like it. Just the Forum?"

Deverash sat himself down on a mechanical chair that altered in shape to conveniently fit him. "*Ahhh*... ergonomics. Love it to bits. Of course not just the Forum, I am here for..."

He scrunched his face, trying to remember as if the thought had just escaped him, even though he'd just had it. Moving his hands up to compose himself, he picked up a thread he had in mind. "I finished a big project and had a spot of rare free time; I'm checking in on my people. You're my people. The logs don't tell me everything, and it's good to check in personally. That's what friends do. I can't just throw boat blueprints at you with a mad cackle like the old days. How are you holding up in there?"

Artorian waggled his hand in a so-so motion, sitting down on his white marble bench. He was plenty happy with it for the moment, even if he was strongly eyeing Dev's chair. "I need to remind myself why I'm doing this fairly often, but it goes well. I was rather sour because I couldn't get out of Eternia at will, but I've resigned myself to it with a big sigh. I'll just see it through. What project did you finish?"

Dev beamed. "Weather systems! Right, expect it to rain soon. We're testing rain everywhere, and proper wind now that we have it. Next on the chopping block is functional seasons. The temporary measures we've been using for emulation are breaking down, ever since someone paused the celestial motions."

Artorian looked away when the Gnome shot him well-meaning side-eye. "Yes, yes. It all turned out fine. Eternium is better off for it. While you're here, is there any way to... remove strings?"

He wasn't specific about what he meant in the verbal sense. Instead, he pulled up a character sheet and turned it while pointing at his first title. The one in red that said 'Observer Wisp.'

Dev leaned on his fist, thinking it over. Any work that made life more difficult for Fae of all kinds was work well worth doing. "Interesting request… Why the sudden interest?"

Artorian dismissed his screen. "Something I overheard that I didn't like from other people with high-tier **Laws**. Something smells fishy. I'm all for kicking the chair out from under a crooked administration, but I don't know enough to go on here. I thought this was a good baton to pass."

"Consider it passed." Deverash was furiously motioning to a screen Artorian could not see, adding new information with an ever-growing grin. It was good to have friends. "I'll let you know what I find. I don't want to interrupt too much of your time. Doing anything interesting? Saw you were in Vanaheim. Congratulations, by the way."

Artorian half-shrugged. "I need to hunt down this Mu guy, the demon overseer in charge of the place. I have a lot of ammo, but not infinite ammo. The Wispwood bow was great while I had mana, but the burn on me made that thing a snappy piece of wood. I've got some hints on how to get around Endless Mana Burn, but it's too soon for proper solutions. I'm making do until then."

Deverash stuck his finger into the air. "I have something for that! You need to get to Asgard for it though. I *might* be able to sneak it to Jotunheim, but no promises. Best to bet on Asgard. I figure that might take you a while."

Artorian snorted half-heartedly. "A while, you say. My friend, if I was counting these adventures via the length of books, Asgard would definitely be the next book. That's not happening in this one. I need a third specialization to enter the next set of realms and I just managed the second. Thank you for the mention. No, today it is playing with my new toys and hunting for the overseer. Then figure out what I'm doing when I run out of bolts and arrows. Perhaps my new tag-along will allow for replenishment. I had some thoughts to make new abilities, but I've got no chance to do that without mana in the tank. Speaking of, do you know any way I can get my hands on the Fireball spell?"

Dev winked and jumped from his chair. "*Ohoho.* You just leave that to Neverdash the Venerable. Get to Asgard, that'll solve a lot of your problems. It's not like you're the only one working to make progress against Barry. You're just the farthest ahead. Best of luck, buddy. I'm going to head out. Oh! I updated the description on your siege engine. I noticed the sunglass effect wasn't listed. It does what you know it does. No changes."

They shared a swift handshake before Deverash unmerged his Forum, leaving Artorian to wake up in a forest of tall grass he did not recall going to sleep in. This fortress of green blotted out the sun. He wasn't fond of this one bit. "Bloody inconvenient!"

Soni called loudly from above, his tone distressed. "Human, is that you? Abyss, end that growth effect of yours! I have been beating this grass off from the top branch, but am losing ground!"

Artorian didn't need to look around. There was grass in every direction. Like a field of oversized wheat or something. "What a day to not have a scythe. Actually, hold on a moment. I have one better!"

Focusing stamina to his fingertips, he slashed his hand around in a wide arc. "Reap!"

He spent about two hundred stamina, but the cutting effect went no further than a hundred feet. The grass went down without a fuss, and the tree bark suffered no more than an enthusiastic dent. He'd only done ten percent of the total possible damage, and only because Reap's Novice rank gave him that freebie. The field of green cleared, giving way to fresh sunshine. Artorian pressed his hands to his hips, watching the dark clouds gather overhead. Looked like it would rain today, just like Dev said it would. "Better up there?"

The tree was no longer just some sapling, now a hefty

purple wisteria with one gloriously colorful canopy of the matching violets that name would expect. At the very tip, Soni kept beating back blades of grass which had gotten stuck with his Soul brush. Dueling with the defeated greenery. "I give 'em a *Ha*! And a *Hiiyah*! And a *Woo-ah*!"

Then he kicked it off the branch and posed victoriously. Artorian scratched the top of his head at the display. That was not the demon behavior he expected. Was being in Eternia or Cal somehow allowing or forcing them to adopt differing traits?

**Ding*!*
You have received a notice from: Deverash.

Distracted from his thoughts by the message, he tapped it to read the missive.

Buddy! I remember what I needed to tell you. I just wanted you to know without Wisp interference. A month of current conversion DE points racks up around four and a half million general experience. You're currently level 21. If you apply that conversion, you will jump to level 97 or 98. If you use your entire stored pool, give or take some leftover numbers we don't want to get into, you will hit level 185 exactly. Conversion experience is mad! How did you think of this? Even I think this is blatant cheatery. Quickly use it before anyone catches on; I've added an option to do so at the bottom of this message. This notice will self-delete from the logs in 5… 4…

Artorian slammed the accept prompt, and closed the notice so it wouldn't blow up on him. That was one Gnomish stereotype he didn't want to deal with or chance. He was nervous until the mental count in his mind hit zero. He felt the tightening pressure as a golden glow pulled him into the sky, but this was no gentle lifting.

Artorian hurtled into the sky as if an angry Friar had tossed him into space out of spite. He howled the entire way up before being nailed to the stars while bright golden light infused and suffused him with a violence. On completion, and having made himself one heck of a target to that Hel-cow herd he'd been hoping to sneak up on, Artorian was hurtled back to the ground. His fall was broken by the large pile of cut down grass. Not that it helped the pain, or the indentation he made of himself in the dirt.

He hoped there wouldn't be landmarks in the future. The iterations would wipe this... right? Yeah. Sure. He groaned and rolled over on his back, his field patching his lost health back up. Soni yelled at him from above. "Hey, *uh*... human? You've got incoming! You got the attention of more than just one herd with whatever stunt you just pulled. We're going to get swarmed!"

Artorian rubbed his nose, just happy he could get up without anything broken. Cataphron hurling him through a wall had hurt less. His response was swift, needing to see the problem. "Portal me up there!"

Soni moved his arm in a quick circle for a quick-cast, short-lived portal. Artorian fell through the portal as it opened under his feet, disorienting him as he landed on the top branch next to Soni before the portal closed with an audible **bwop**.

Artorian brushed himself off as he balanced himself. In a hurry to get up, he didn't think to look at his character sheet. There was a bit of a problem heading his way. Oh, plus rain. It was starting to rain as the first crack of real thunder broke overhead with a flash of cloud-lightning. He winced at the numbers of Hel-cow swarming towards them. "Aw... *Abyss*. That's so many of them. Welp... best get Ikaruga out. Savant, anything you can do to keep this tree stable would be helpful."

The bat demon grumbled. "The name is Soni! Also, yes. I can do that. I think... By just holding it. My portal juju doesn't lend itself to tree stabilization."

A better idea struck the old man. "Are you able to make portals that would allow my bolts to hit center mass on those incoming herds?"

Soni liked that idea much, much more than being in the

thick of it, since these brayers weren't going to cut him any slack. "I'll start on them right away!"

**Ding*!*
You have received a notice from: Yvessa.

Artorian slapped at the notification to open it up, far too busy manifesting the siege engine to glance at it right away. When he got it set up, he fired up his Astra form right away, though then felt an odd pulling pit in his stomach.

Something was wrong, so his eyes went to the notice.

Old man! What did you just do? Your level jumped to 185 and your attributes unbalanced in the process! Generalist doesn't give you Luck growth! Your Luck is now a category lower than all your other attribute thresholds. You're going to be taking a slew of bad events if you just let that sit there!

A prompt that Artorian could not stop opened by itself, smack in front of his view range to block the first shot he wanted to make.

**Ding*!*
Warning! Your Luck is a category below all other thresholds. Mass debuffs applied!

Strength is a threshold higher than Luck!
Debuff: Power Overwhelming—Being too strong has downsides, including doing nothing when you could have done something. 1% chance to do abyss-nothing instead of the intended action.

Dexterity is a threshold higher than Luck!
Debuff: Overcompensated Accident—Trip. Stumble. Stubbed Toe. Hit the rock you meant to avoid. Turn too fast and you'll lose balance. 1% chance to fail any dexterity action.

Constitution is a threshold higher than Luck!

Debuff: Loved-by-Arrows—That spot that would be really inconvenient to get hit in—right now—? Yeah. There. 1% chance to receive a minor but incredibly inconvenient injury one is otherwise immune to.

Intelligence is a threshold higher than Luck!
Debuff: I Know Better!—Spoken in the background by Lemony Cal: Little did Artorian know that he did not, in fact, know better. 1% chance to make a terrible decision.

Wisdom is a threshold higher than Luck!
Debuff: Foolish Mortal!—Long ago in a distant land, I, Calu, the shapeshifting master of darkness, unleashed an unspeakable evil. 1% chance to make foolish decisions.

Charisma is a threshold higher than Luck!
Debuff: My, what a guy that Calson!—Style over anything. Minus stats to everything else in favor of swagger. -5% stats in all attribute fields.

Perception is a threshold higher than Luck!
Debuff: Yes. I know that dragon was polymorphed and trying to hide, and didn't want to be seen, but I saw it anyway, and that's why we're running. 1% to notice truth that nobody will believe, or want to.

Note: Dani, one threshold may be too tight of a squeeze. Add in a note for me as a reminder to consider making it two? Also, five percent jumps may be too high? Let's get some metrics on this and get back to it. Thanks, dear!

Artorian made a sound equal to the gasped squeal one makes when suddenly realizing that instead of taking a bite out of a sandwich, they had taken a bite out of something that might one day be called a ghost pepper. He gasped and wheezed from the debuffs swimming in front of his eyes.

This couldn't… No. Just *no*. "Yvessa! All my points into luck. All of them. *All of them*!"

**Ding*!*

Debuffs cleared!

He sputtered out another cough as all those debuffs vanished from his status screen, which gained a sudden increase in his attention given the abyss it experienced. Mass level ups were a terrible idea! Or he thought it was, until he saw his luck score jump from seven hundred thirty-four to one-thousand and nine. A new unstoppable prompt replaced that hellscape litany of debuffs from before.

**Ding*!*
Warning! Your Luck is one or two categories above all other thresholds.
Mass debuffs applied!

Cal's voice spoke through the screen that appeared like an old recording, recounting part of a conversation while this feature was being made. "I have no idea how high luck could be bad. It's luck for you. More is better. Dani, please set luck thresholds to give a one percent stats increase bonus in all attribute fields that luck is higher than. Per threshold, I mean. Thanks, hun. I don't think anyone will ever invest in this attribute since it has no direct major benefits."

Artorian blinked at his statistics. "Oh, Cal… you beautiful soul. Dani did not hear you right. This is so much *more* than a one percent increase."

Sadly, based on the flicker of green, Yvessa noticed that as well. Artorian knew that a fix was already in the pipelines, so if he wanted to use this system error, he'd need to be swift. Realizing he was on a timer for this temporary bonus, Artorian let a bolt appear between his fingers as he drew back on the engine's string. Smiling as he let go, the shot launched into the distant death herd.

He watched the first projectile conflagrate into black plasma, crystallize, duplicate, then zip off into the distance to explode on impact. Violently fragmenting into the sunglass equivalent of deadly, cutting obsidian chunks that easily went four to five times the distance his initial explosions caused.

Interestingly, the bolts did not match their explosion diameters. The left one showed a tiny boom zone while the right one experienced an average one.

The worst thing… was that it didn't kill a single Hel-cow. Though it did tip some over! When they got back up, their axes were out. Hungry with queries. Artorian grumbled. "Vanaheim critters are so much tougher than I thought! Soni! I'm going to be flurrying non-stop, as fast as my stamina can keep up. Hold fast against the waves of questions. I am preparing my lecture!"

Artorian drew back on his ballista again, getting in the zone as he rolled his shoulders, letting bolts fly as fast as he could fire them. He had a pleasant thought. One day, his arrows would blot out the sun!

CHAPTER FORTY

Unfortunately, today was not that day. Artorian was in no way able to fire off ballista rounds fast enough to make significant dents in the approaching blob. Was it right to call it a blob? A great big splotchy blob of brown, black, and white that constantly went 'Moo.'

Yes, the Moo-blob! He needed to un-moo it. He released another crystallizing shard that shot off into the distance, but didn't have time to watch the splendiferous cacophony that followed on impact. The initial explosion was a gorgeous symphony of a thousand varieties on the color black while the shard-storm that followed as result moved in an umbrella pattern. That which went up, also came down.

He was surprised he wasn't leveling up from the constant waves he was putting down, but didn't have time to think about it, much less do the math to figure out what the difference in amount was to reach level one hundred eighty-six. For all he knew, it was one hundred eighty-six thousand. "No time for numbers, only time for shooting! Only more shooting! No take, only throw!"

It didn't take more than a minute of firing before Artorian

could clearly see this was a losing battle. They were surrounded on all sides, and no amount of shard explosions were effective as a deterrent. The darn things were too stupid! Walking over their own dead without a care. "Soni! Change of plans! Your portal needs to take us behind their lines. We need to hoof it, and fast! We've got another half a minute before they're at the tree, and I do not want to aim this thing down!"

Soni worked in a frenzy, adding Rune after Rune to fine-tune his portal needs. This wasn't something you could rush if the end-portal was out of visual range! "I'm working on it! Can't you just run through them all?"

Artorian wished that was a solution. "Every small bump slows me down. Eventually I'd stop, and likely still while in the thick of the herd. I've got nothing good for melee, and even if I had, I do not want to get stuck in a blob that thick. I can't even see grass where the cows are. Ten seconds!"

Soni was not going to make that happen. "Can't do it! I need at least a minute and a half from this point, uninterrupted!"

Artorian didn't like that news, and tried Multishot, then discovered Ikaruga couldn't fire them. Ikaruga hadn't been designed with multiple shots in mind. Artorian hurriedly made a bolt vanish and fired off his fortieth or fiftieth shot before making the weapon vanish into his spatial ring. He made the bow appear instead before he realized it was also not meant for up close and personal business.

His Yumi was a sniping tool. These cows had no armor, sound was of no consequence, and speedy arrows would pierce maybe a few before it didn't matter. Abyss! He put the Yumi back into his ring and figured he would need to lean into more… daring maneuvers. "Finish the portal and yell when it's done. I'm going… I'm going to go buy you that time."

Soni glanced over worriedly, seeing the human concentrate and take a breath before turning into a blur. Artorian mumbled something under his breath, but Soni's hearing was legend. He heard the human's ability activation anyway. "Soul of Zen... Student rank!"

With his Astra form active, his current stamina regeneration came out to exactly five-hundred. He loved a smooth, convenient number. He wasn't sure if his luck error affected it, but now was not the time! "Gift horse. Mouth! That thing!"

Since the Astra form covered the cost for the Novice level, that meant three ranks of Soul that still required payment. Payment of a hundred stamina per second each. Should he quickly tell Yvessa to buy two more ranks with points gained from levels, or did he need the higher attributes more right now? He just didn't know, and didn't have time to think. Now was the time for doing as he leapt off the branch and gathered his wits. "Flow Like Water. Breathe the Air. Impeccable Focus. Martial Arts Style... *Pantheon*!"

The tightly pressured Aura around Artorian turned red. An aggressive, burning, heated red that flickered and flared as he slammed into the skull of a Hel-cow, crushing it underfoot while hoping he'd killed it.

The hope was pointless. **Moo**!

The axes of those around it came hacking down, slashing that bovine beast to pieces after the red blur had long passed. For every round the cows could act, Artorian received four. Even going that much faster made Sunny think this might be a losing battle, so he started by running circles in a wide diameter around the tree, kicking or pushing off one of the standing bovines to quickly alter his direction, while sending that opponent away. The cows flew off from the charge damage applied to them as they clamored with more distressed mooing.

Everywhere they saw the red blur, their axes struck! Regardless of that location currently being occupied by what should have been friendly herd forces. The Hel-cows did not appear to be able to tell the difference, or differentiate friend from foe in a meaningful manner. They see blur? They swing axes. Artorian very loudly stated his dissatisfaction. "This cow level sucks!"

Soni only heard the blur's speech due to his hearing, parsing the four or five times as fast words together as he worked on the portal. He tried not to watch the show of periodical cow-punting that went on below. The red blur had taken to running on the heads and shoulders of the standing cows, as they were so numerous that the ground wasn't an option. The blur was visibly trying to play keep-away from the tree by making the herd hack themselves to pieces.

What Artorian was actually trying to do was keep going in circles until the cows had carved out a hill that they couldn't climb over and cross. A task far more difficult than anticipated as the Beasts had zero issues muscling their way onto the ever-growing pile of their own dead. "Crackers and toast! They just keep coming!"

Artorian thought he was going mad from the **moo-shink-moo** that played in slow motion. The sounds were grueling, pulled out to lengthen and last.

A problem Artorian discovered was that his stamina did not scale with his speed. He recovered two hundred stamina per second, which was awfully slow when he was spending it four to five times as fast. Power Launch was fantastic for keeping his speed up, but it wasn't helping dish out the hurt. He just didn't do enough damage without a weapon in hand, and while Reap had been effective against grass, it was not as useful with actual enemies!

A slow-motion Nixie Tube dinged above his head. He just needed to get a weapon, and axes were littering the area! With a hop, skip, and a jump, Artorian yoinked one of the axes right out of a Hel-cow's grip and pulled it along to the speed he was going.

"Alright! Harvesting time." Reap was full damage out to ten feet, or five? Always short-range reaping then, to test if it mattered. In a blur of aerial acrobatics, Artorian spun head over heel and let his first strike fly. He wished he knew how much damage it did, because he felt like a butcher, cleaving the death-bovine in twain while significantly damaging those behind his target. The arc even had a red tint to it from his pantheon style being active.

Well, no time like the present to carve one's way through life's problems. He just needed to keep tabs on all the other falling axes and he'd be aces. An attempt to swing a second time found negative success, as the axe turned to brittle chalk in his hands. It cracked to dust from the stress of just that initial swing, in a timeframe it wasn't meant for.

Artorian didn't have the freedom right now to check what happened to the axe. He just took it as part of the pattern and moved on. Axes were good for one swing, and then they were spent. That meant more yoinking!

Given how fast he was in comparison to the slow-moving blob of mooing death, and that the axes were as difficult to avoid as a slow-moving door, he had another weapon in hand in no time. He swung it once, slashing after planting his foot in a bovine's face and coiling on his hip axis to get the swing going. The strike, like last time, carved through the immediate victim, and deeply cut foes in the attack's vicinity as Reap reached out to extend the harm.

It wasn't enough. Artorian became a blur of red cuts, but he was no Brianna. His attacks expended every axe he got his hands on after a single strike. Ten cuts. Thirty. Sixty. It didn't matter. The blob just kept blobbing, and the strain was catching up to him faster than he expected. Acting in several times your frame of reference took a hidden toll beyond the obvious cost in stamina.

He was starting to slow, having trouble keeping up after nearly a minute straight of time-dilated activity. To the blob it had been a minute, but to him it had been four or five. A gruesome amount of time for endless high-octane activity and stamina expenses. He had also forgotten to account for the drain costs his martial arts maneuvers caused, and it messed up his calculations.

Artorian turned them off, realizing a second after he shouldn't have done that. Even if it relieved pressure from the burden, the sudden lack of situational awareness bonuses made him take a slow-moving door in the shape of an axe to the back. The axe blade had been in the path of the direction he chose to dodge. Two thousand four hundred health relieved itself from his health pool, dropping it considerably from the nine-thousand eight-hundred cap he had. "Ouch!"

He missed the next yoink, which made him falter and bounce around on the blob for a while before finding his stride again. This couldn't continue. He couldn't keep this up like he thought he'd be able to, and the blob seemed endless. It was cow heads, moos, and axes from where he stood all the way to the horizon.

"Time to bail." He zipped his way up across the crowd, letting their own axes crash down like before until he reached the tree. Vertically running right up the trunk and bouncing the rest of the way to the top before finally letting his Soul of Zen go. He gasped a deep breath when the weight and drain dropped from his shoulders, though all his muscles ached from that level of activity without forewarning or preparation. "Tell me you're—"

"I'm done! Grab me and jump through. It's not stable and I need to hold my hand in this p-ooo-oo-os..." Soni's hurried yelp turned into a wail as his last word stretched. Trying to say the word 'position' was difficult when a speedy mass snagged you and hurled its way through the gate. The opening of which snapped shut moments after they passed through, since Soni's spell stability snapped and broke.

They both fell butt-first into a small lake when they came out the other end, thinking they were drowning for a moment before Artorian realized he could just... stand up. The water was not even passing his knees. Not a lake then. Well... he felt silly. At the same time. No cows! "Yes! We're out!"

Soni crawled up Artorian's leg with a miserable expression, spitting out a line of water from his mouth. He despised feeling soaked and soggy, more than happy when the human walked onto dry land so he could let go and clean himself up.

While Soni twisted and squeezed his cloak while he looked like a wet rag, his eyes squinted against the terrible luminance. A fact that didn't go unnoticed by the human, who also desired the use of a hat. "Where are we? It's so dang bright here."

Soni shook himself, still trying to get the water out of his ears. "Alfheim, this time not conveniently in an area that blots out some of the sunlight. I couldn't get a portal up that fast to a place I didn't know. So I had to go to a place I *did* know. We are so *not ready* to tackle Vanaheim."

Artorian checked his inventory and winced. A measly forty-eight ballista bolts remained. Not good. Not that artillery felt like it helped against endless blobs. Not when they were actually endless. That something as strong as a Vanaheim axe broke on every swing wasn't good news either. "I need weapons... tons and tons of w—"

A light lit in Artorian's mind. A memory of a time long ago resurging. "Soni... how well do you know Alfheim? Landmarks and such?"

Soni bapped the side of his head, keeping an eye closed as the last of the water was removed from his left ear. "Fluently. I know everything about Alfheim. It was my corner. There's no structure in this realm I don't know the location of."

Artorian steepled his fingers, his Astra form released so he could bundle himself in his Resplendence field to clean up. "Good. Do you happen to know of a statue or marker of someone named Yiba-Su-Wong? It appears I have an old appointment to keep."

Soni leaned his head back, not liking that tone of voice. Still, best to answer in that most awful, painful of ways: *Honestly*. His own answer sounded strained, full of cautious concern. "Yes?"

The human's smile bent wide, its presence intimidating. "*Take me.*"

CHAPTER FORTY-ONE

Artorian crossed his arms when he looked up at the modest statue of Elder Yiba the Generous. His eyes remained squinted from the light, and he wondered if this eye-stabbing awfulness was what he did to others. It was cookie-cracking effective! "Note to self: acquire more shiny."

He wanted at least one opponent to clasp their face and yell out 'my eyes!' in dramatic fashion. Perhaps some recurring villain? No, he didn't have any of those, not if he could help it. Far more important to make sure they didn't get back up, and his chances of finding an incompetent one to keep around for giggles was nil.

Soni, not having found a hat, opted for the blindfold option. It saved his eyes from the usual Alfheim misery, letting him echolocate without a fuss. Preferably, he wanted to pay as little attention to what was going on as possible. Random schemes, regardless of source, were not something he wanted to deeply involve himself with. Not anymore.

While Artorian got all up in the statue's business, searching nooks and crannies for some kind of secret lever or mechanism, the bat decided to huddle under the protective shade of some trees and bust out the brush. Everything was better with some brushy-brushy time. An event that gained value and enjoyment as the days went on.

Artorian noticed none of this. His sizable attention was entirely spent crawling around the statue, pressing his ear against it to listen; testing his luck with a lick... but finding it tasted like boring old calcite. He'd been hoping for something *special*, since the entire statue was pearly white, like all the paint and color had been stripped from it over time. It wasn't until he flicked Electrosense on that he felt like a fool.

Slapping his forehead loud enough to make the bat jump three feet into the air and scare off a flock of birds, Artorian momentarily traded his senses out to activate Astra form. He walked to the front of the statue, put his hands on the base, and just pushed.

Electrosense showed him there was a descending staircase beneath Yiba's effigy, which seemed an obvious thing to check for in retrospect. The grinding rock of the statue crunched like gravel, but moved easily enough when Artorian applied enough oomph to solve the problem. He'd been expecting some clever little thing, but no. Straight up strength check. He supposed nobody other than what Yiba used to call a Grand Elder was capable of the feat, so this was fairly clever to keep everyone else out.

When enough of the staircase was exposed for Artorian to head on down, he looked over his shoulder to address the demon. "Soni. Please do wait here and keep an ear out. I don't want anything coming in behind me. Though, no killing. No attacking."

Soni shrugged, then sighed as his brush waggled in the human's direction. "Sure, sure. No killing. No attacking. No letting anything in. As if there'd be a threat that could make such a thing matter."

The bat didn't recognize the nuance in the old-man-smile

he received in return. He returned to grooming activities while Artorian walked down.

The stairs themselves weren't very impressive, nor did they go very deep. Enough to bring him to the equivalent of what should have been a sewer system that was never used as one. It was too clean, with little but moss and the occasional mushroom on the floor and walls.

He made some light just by being in his Astra form, but traded it out for the light from his Resplendence field. It also allowed him the use of Omnibreath and Electrosense, in case some less than gentle traps were down here. Instead Artorian just found a dead end to this tunnel, and a flat wall just covered in more moss. He scratched the back of his head, a little confused. Crossing his arms, he held his chin to observe this wall for a while as the moss grew. An eyebrow rose when excess moss grew out from the split between the floor and the wall. "One moment. A split?"

Easing to a knee to lower his head, he pressured his Electrosense, successfully getting it through the tiny gap under the wall enough to notice the tunnel actually went on quite a bit further. Well, that had an easy solution. "Dale it!"

Brick and mortar turned to brittle chunks when a powerful shoulder rammed through the little blockade. Artorian apologized to it, even if it was just an object. "Sorry, wall. I've got places to be."

Brushing himself off, he remembered he could just use the field to— "*Yup*. There we go."

Performing a twirl on the back of his heel, he posed upon stopping. Glitteringly clean, just the way he liked it. Artorian enjoyed a deep, firm breath, savoring the fresh vigor as he cycled his Sustenance effect. "Best not to field that one. Wouldn't want this moss to go wild."

Oh no, he was talking to himself again. Perhaps he should have taken Soni along? No. This was temporary. He tried not to pay attention to it and marched further down the tunnel until he noticed the floor changed its angle. It was minor. An insignificant event. Artorian cocked his head to the left when he noticed it, and kept it in mind now that he was clearly descending.

A few minutes, and another angle change occurred. Now the path was going downwards in a noticeable manner. Was this important in some way? What an odd design. He ignored it again until he reached the end of the tunnel. Somewhere midway through, the moss stopped. When he reached another impasse, it was another plain wall, with another slit at the bottom. Easy to notice, since it was the same problem as the first time.

This wall he didn't want to break. It had inscriptions on it! Artorian rubbed his hands together. A find! A find in… his language? Excitement turned to concern, so he held his chin and mumbled the words under his breath as he read them out loud.

Here lies Yiba-Su-Wong. Su Patriarch of the Yi-Ying Era. Of all Su Patriarchs, it was Yiba who turned his attention to the common folk. He cared for their farms. Their crops. Their plants. The Bluebell Patriarch will remain known through all ages for his kindness. Even as he lost his loved ones to plague flame, his children to war, and his people to drought.

Over his reign, this Patriarch was responsible for many great works. He built the waterways, planted the blue fields, gathered all great family weapons, and knew the thousand techniques of transformation and stasis.

The text ended. Artorian didn't have a clever quip, feeling rather cold. "Yvessa… are you here?"

The green light illuminated the tunnel far better than his field did. Yvessa took her human form as she slid from one space into another. "I'm here. I thought you wanted a moment alone."

Artorian waggled his hand in such a so-so manner that

made Yvessa change her mind. She eased up against his side and took a hold of his arm with both of hers, prodding him with a correction. "You're slouching. What's wrong?"

He grumbled to himself. "I've got a bad feeling. I didn't want to be alone. This wall says nice things, but it's a wall with more tunnels on the other side. This description was written here by someone who knew Yiba, yet it was clearly intended I be the one to read it. The mention appears glowing on the surface, but the keywords didn't sneak by me. Yiba did not have a good life, and I cannot help but feel that I am responsible for influencing him. Even if our time together was brief… all I did was give him a bluebell."

Yvessa looked through the wall, her own posture straightening. "Oh, that makes more sense now."

"What does?" Artorian matched her stance, quirking a brow. She squeezed her mouth shut in the patented Tibbins expression, informing him that she couldn't actually say. Artorian just nodded at her. "*Ah-huh.*"

The wall went down with a simple palm strike. Artorian elected to ignore the rubble and get a move on to find the nugget of information. It was a short journey to the next wall, though this one was not some generic note. This one was personal.

Dear Grand Elder from the Trial of the Mountain. Su Patriarch Yiba-Su-Wong is ever at your service, as he was when but a mere inner court disciple. As I carve this message, my last days are visible before me. It is the way of the house of Su, to not run from challenges. So as I carve these words, it is my deepest wish to convey that my greatest challenge has concluded.

It was a source of great confusion to me, for many years, why you were kind to me, that day on the mountain. Even now, as I sit here wasting away, your words ring as falling water upon my mind. "Please raise your head, my boy. Why don't you take this, and spare me a moment of your time?"

It was the first time an Elder had ever asked me to raise my head. It was the first time an Elder asked for my voice. It was the first time I experienced such wanton, unbrooked kindness. You gave me the prize of the mountain without a thought. Asking only for answers to questions I had difficulties with. Yet you did not punish me when I faltered.

In my youth, I thought my end of days had come when you asked me: "Would you say those who live here are good people, Yiba?"

For I knew the answer was poor, and realized upon hearing that very question: That the answer was no. I was certain that was the end of me. Then you patted my shoulder, and told me: 'All's well.'

Yiba-Su-Wong has fought in many an arena, yet never have I felt the defeat that my preconceptions experienced that day. I was dumbfounded. Then you confused me, as your attention wandered to weapons scattered across the lands. It was my understanding you had come to retrieve them, after I was given leave, and returned to the household. I arrived at the news you had already been there, having defeated every Elder and Grand Elder without so much as raising a finger.

Yet, whispers spread as fire. It was said the Grand Elder cursed our household, in reference to the sword of the Su Patriarch. I was told the visiting Grand Elder said: "This item is more likely to bring your family incredible ruin than some kind of saving grace. I'm with Cal on this. Keep it."

We do not know who this 'Cal' was, but assume it to be some great, powerful entity for such a mighty Grand Elder to reference him. One cruel in his ways, as this 'Cal' is implied to have suggested a pox of ruin remain with us.

In my rise over the years of my adulthood, I have seen fit to gather all these weapons from all of Alfheim in atonement. So one day, when the Grand Elder returns, he will find Su Patriarch Yiba-Su-Wong on his knees. Ever at his service. Ever thankful for his lessons. Ever apologetic for what my forebears have done.

I am Yiba-Su-Wong, and behind this wall lies the armory of atonement. May the sins of Su be cleansed. May they be cleansed. May they be cleansed.

Yvessa squeezed Artorian's arm tighter. The man was biting his hand with a deep frown, wet lines cutting down his cheeks as he attempted to retain control of himself. "Yiba... you young fool. You clever, beautiful fool. You shouldn't have wasted your life in pursuit of an activity like that."

Artorian hunched and leaned forwards with his eyes closed. His forehead came to rest against the wall as it was him who felt defeated. "Not for me. Never for *me*."

He softly bashed his fist against the wall, despising feeling the pain inherent in the concept that someone gave up that much of their life for him. He hated it. "Normal people should get to live their lives in ways they want. Not in a way that forces them to pick up the mistakes of a fussy, sad old man."

Another hammerfist crashed against the wall as he tried to stand properly. He got a hold of himself as Electrosense picked up new waves coming from the other side of the wall, now that there was a big enough hole in it for the sense to properly penetrate. Even bricks, when thick enough, seemed to get in the way of his abilities. A shame it didn't get terrain-ignoring bonuses like his Resplendence did.

He steadied himself with a breath, then opened his eyes to the sight of soft white-blue light coming through the gap. His hands reached for the opening, pulling the meager stone split apart with enough force to rend it asunder. Artorian's heart felt squeezed at the sight.

It wasn't the carefully catalogued weapon displays on the wall that stole his attention. It was the perfectly preserved glowing bluebell in the middle of the armory chamber. Sitting untouched by time under an overturned glass jar. With little twinkles floating about in its confines.

Stepping forwards, Artorian saw the plaque below the bluebell. It had a simple description, which he read out loud when close enough. "For all time. I bow in apology."

Artorian wasn't having the best time with his emotions. His face was held by his hands as squeezing cold clamped around the insides of his ribs. Weakly, he addressed Yvessa. "I… I see now. You could always see this bluebell. It just didn't make sense why it was a bluebell. It looks so similar to what I remember giving him on that mountain. Ah… Yiba. How I wish I could apologize."

He stood there as the cogs in his mind slowly began to turn. Nothing in Cal was wasted. All things went recycled. Even souls. His words were bated, apprehensive and uncertain. "Yvessa? What happened to Yiba after that old iteration? Who did he become? Did he have good lives as the iterations went?"

His Wisp checked, but frowned right after pulling his name up. "That's not right."

Artorian didn't like those words, his face snapping towards her. "What happened?"

"Well…" Yvessa turned her screen, making it visible and pointing at it. "Yiba-Su-Wong does not have new iteration logs. Not a one. He has old iteration logs, but he doesn't even properly show up for anything after the one you met him in. His last action is logged as 'Transform and Stasis.' Though I'm not sure what he affected."

The soft chuckle from Artorian turned to weak laughter. "Oh… I am such a fool. It was in front of my nose this whole time. It seems I'll manage that apology after all."

Yvessa didn't understand until he slowly turned, making a tender hand motion to the bluebell. "I would like to introduce you to Yiba-Su-Wong. A gentle soul who finds lessons where none were intended."

His caretaker mouthed an 'Oh,' but wasn't sure if Artorian meant more than that. "Well… you have no mana. So it's not like you can change him back."

Artorian did not dry the wet lines on his cheeks. He merely

smiled at her as pink energy in the vicinity built and crackled with a charged **vrummm*. "My dear, *dear* Fringe caretaker. For labors of **Love**, I *always* have Mana. Tell Eternium this is going to tickle."

CHAPTER FORTY-TWO

Yvessa gasped when she realized what he was doing. Pink lightning sparks began to flake off from his skin from the *real Mana* he accumulated. He was about to *cheat*! She needed to move, right now! Artorian watched his caretaker stumble and vanish with a pop. Likely straight to Oberon.

One sharp motion to the bluebell was all it took for the **Love**-tier Mana to work its magic. The stasis and transformation were both undone with a crack of pink thunder, leaving behind an ancient-looking man in an Emperor's garb, his head bowed to his hands.

Yiba drew a sudden, needed breath. He was awake, and felt surprisingly good as a soothing effect tingled across his skin. He felt fed; his thirst, too, vanished swiftly. He felt good, and clean, and uninjured. The wasting he experienced had stopped, seeming to reverse itself as caustically burned flesh fell from him only to reveal a healthy new variant.

Artorian drew a deep breath, his Omnibreath field spread wide as the pink lightning continued to build. "I accept your penance, Yiba-Su-Wong. No more shall curses befall the household of Su, nor shall you be held responsible for the negligent actions of a foolish, flaky old man. It is my great pleasure to welcome you back to Alfheim, Yiba. I have but one question."

Yiba looked up to see a younger version of the Grand Elder, yet it was still undoubtedly him. His head smashed to his hands right away, Yiba speaking his words without any thought. Though rather than the weight Artorian expected them to carry, he heard only freedom, and relief. "Disciple Yiba-Su-Wong. Ever at your service."

Artorian walked close, laying a hand on Yiba's shoulder to help him back up so they could look one another in the eyes. "Would you permit a foolish old man a chance at an apology? Would you like a second life?"

Yiba's lower jaw trembled. His eyes watering as he felt his entire life had just been vindicated. "I… I would like that very much, Grand Elder, though I am old, and—"

Yiba silenced himself when Artorian's shoulder grip turned from a hold to a squeeze. The pink lightning stopped being so aggressive and uncontrolled. The rolling waves of pink light softened. As they coalesced and flowed over Artorian's arms, they changed direction like a raging tide, crashing into Yiba with the ferocity of an ocean.

Yiba gasped, but felt invigorated. His age melted away inch by inch, until the shoulder Artorian held once again belonged to a visual copy of the inner disciple he had met so long ago. "You are young, full of ancient lessons and incredible wisdom. I thank you, Yiba, for accepting my apology. Though, please, call me Sunny."

The young-again Yiba was helped off the pedestal. His stance and feet were wobbly as he did his best to get his bearings in a body that he wasn't used to. Artorian was a master at that song and dance, plenty patient with Yiba. "My thanks, Gran… Sunny."

Artorian wiped his face when the boy didn't see him, and calmly nodded. "You'll get your balance back in no time. Are you well enough to stand?"

Yiba wanted to say yes, but both his hands snapped to the

pedestal to prevent him from falling. When it seemed Yiba intended to stand solely via his own power, Artorian let him be as he walked to the wall and touched one of the jians stored there. The pink waves flowed from his hand, crossing over the weapon to infuse it.

The sword trembled against the hook on the wall before spinning free with a metallic snap to hover in a small circle around Artorian. The **Love** Mage was pleased, reaching out to grasp the sword. "Iridium. As I know it. That means this should work as well?"

Holding out the sword towards the others, he desired the same effect as when he held that initial Li coin. Similarly, the metal in his vicinity thrummed as his Mana infused it via the call that rang out from the one he held. Liquifying from their posts, the swords, halberds, spears, armors and more turned into metallic water.

Each of the morphed weapons surged to fulfill their requested task. The Iridium moved in a rush, bending to the highest will as a river of metal rushed into the object Artorian held. He didn't care that it got heavier and heavier. When the lost drop had merged into the Li-shaped coin he was holding, he felt some kind of ancient task completed. Even if that task was no longer one of his burdens.

He tossed the coin into the air, catching it before thinking of something. The coin instantly morphed into a longspear of Phoenix Kingdom design, complete with the oddities and glaive modifications he'd applied over the years. This wasn't just a glaive. This was *his* glaive. One honed and sharpened by whetstone over many an empty night under the stars, where that steady scraping had been his sole companion.

It resonated with his memories. The wholeness of it filled Artorian with a nostalgic happiness, as the weapon in his hand finally made him feel that the body he inhabited fit. Not just as a form he could operate, but as something natural.

His pink glow winked out the same moment a green glow returned to the area, informing Artorian that Eternium had altered the reality he stood in. He could also feel the weapon in his hand being altered to fit the system. It was akin to holding a metal rod that had a charge running through it. "Odd, but interesting."

Taking a breath, he gave the glaive a few swings. A few swings turned into elaborate flourishes. Elaborate flourishes turned into an eyes-closed weapon dance that made Artorian feel as if he were gliding over an icy cloud. His weapon whipped and zipped around with careful, controlled actions. The blade cut precise slashes into the air as Artorian felt like Tzu once more, going through those endless morning drills under the eye and stick of a fussy drill instructor.

Artorian was about to lose himself in the motions, had Yiba not been gawking at him. The stare prompted him to salute, which made Artorian falter from his maneuvers. He stopped awkwardly, ending in the middle of a set of incomplete motions. The others didn't appear to notice that he had failed the twelfth movement of Mauling Phoenix.

He looked to the weapon with an expression bordering adoration. While in his grip, the glaive changed to a longsword, then a jian, then a warspade, then a heavy pick, and lastly half of a giant scissor. Artorian stored the weapon in his spatial ring, pleased that it responded to his desires as quickly as it did. "A thousand weapons made one. An old friend brought home. An old lesson learned late."

Yiba bowed when Artorian approached him. His ability to stand had much improved. "No need for grace like that, my boy. Consider me a friend, rather than a superior. That would make me happy. Much has happened, and the world as you knew it no longer exists. Instead, ready yourself to adapt, and learn life anew. Have you hidden anything else in this armory, or was this it?"

Yiba shook his head no, his hands still together in a half-bow. "The weapons and myself were all. I am ready. I shall ready myself to see a world anew. Though I am ashamed to admit I do not know my place in it."

Artorian placed his arm around Yiba's shoulders, nodding as they walked along to leave this place. "You are in Alfheim, though not the one you knew. I don't know if it is easier to explain that it is a separate Alfheim altogether. Or if it is the same, merely after much time has passed. The short of it is this, Yiba: There are people in this land, but they are fractured and broken. They need a uniter, and I am not able to keep my attention bent to this realm. I read you might have some experience in these things?"

Yiba puffed his chest out, seeing where he might fit. Like a puzzle piece in a divine plan. "I have understood what you need of me, Master Sunny. I shall do this. May I know more?"

Artorian wasn't sure how to feel about the Master title, but he could tell Yiba was trying his best. "Of course, my young friend. Alfheim is one realm, in a starry sea of many. This Alfheim must one day connect to a realm named Svartalfheim, where the rules of the land will dictate that the inhabitants vie for supremacy. While I don't like that this is the case, it is. Alfheim must be prepared for this event, and I will not be able to lend my aid. For in this contest, I must remain impartial. As a judge who watches from afar."

Yiba's heart fell, his face betraying his thoughts. This was a man who wore his thoughts on his face and his feelings on his sleeve. "I… understand."

Artorian gave the boy a strong pat on his back, nudging him back into step as he extended his free hand. His Yumi bow formed, making Yiba's eyes bulge at the sight. "It's dangerous to go alone, where you will be going. Take this."

When Yiba accepted the BS-Bow, several quivers appeared and dangled from Artorian's fingers. "Take these as well. They're all the ammunition I have left for her. I'm sad to say I technically still need her, but she will not help me where I fear I must go. I instead leave her in capable hands. Please do give her a good name? The one I came up with doesn't do her justice."

Yiba squeezed the Yumi, his eyes lighting with ideas. "Lady Justice is an excellent name for her, Master Sunny. For she is the instrument of penance, and uniter of that which is right. In my hand, she will point the way to all that is righteous, and good. Her arrows will be as impartial as her judgements, and my words will whisper on each shot."

Artorian kept his arm close around Yiba when they ascended the sharp pathway; the youth still wasn't a perfect walker. Yet Artorian had the strength to carry both of them. "A noble pursuit, Yiba. I'm afraid I likely must leave you when we exit your statue. Please do keep an open mind on who you meet."

He tapped the side of his nose. "Many are animals made into Elf or man. They are not inherently bad. They just lack proper examples. Give them guidance. Give them heart. That bow will serve you well when eventually you meet the Dwarves from Svart. I expect the traits on that bow will give you an excellent leg-up. I merely hope that there is a chance for peaceful resolution, in the end."

Yiba blocked the sun with his hand when the duo came up from the staircase. Finding the environment blinding in comparison to the vaguely illuminated tunnel underground, he staggered when Artorian let him go, leaning to the base of his own statue for a moment of rest.

The Grand Elder walked toward some out of breath bat creature, who appeared both disgruntled and satisfied at the same time. Artorian cleared his throat before getting too close. "What's all this then?"

Soni wiped his forehead, motioning at the unconscious wolf pack around him as if they were the topic of the question. "This? Just some uninvited guests. Don't worry! None are dead. None were attacked. Though I did… defend myself. They didn't take well to words."

"I'm proud of you," Artorian said simply. "Well done."

Soni felt unsettled, some kind of unpleasant feeling rolling through his fur. Was he sick? Had he just been attacked? What a strange, awful sensation. Why did he want it to happen again?

Almost like it had been good. Ew. *Good.* "Yes… well. I'm just… following the rules. Are you done?"

Artorian noticed Soni motioning over to Yiba, and he nodded in response to the bat. "All settled. I've the things I needed, and picked up a bonus friend on the way. I did have a thought while I was walking back. Are you able to open a portal directly above Mu's position? That would save time instead of looking for him."

Soni felt dumb. That was… such a good idea. Why had he not thought of it earlier? "Yes. Yes, I can. It will take me a few hours, but that isn't even difficult. It will merely take time."

"Outstanding!" Artorian posed and punched the sky, doing a little victorious shimmy right after. "That is going to save so much time. I feel silly for not thinking of that earlier."

Soni smirked. "Don't be so hard on yourself. It takes a while for people to think with portals. Even as a user of them, I'm not exactly an expert." The bat cringed hard after he'd said that, feeling another nauseous wave of discomfort. What the abyss was going on?

Artorian, on the other hand, was trying his absolute best not to smile, mentally checking a box on a rather lengthy list. "Doing alright there? Tell you what. Come talk to Yiba for a while. I want you to tell him everything there is to know about Alfheim. When you're done… wake me up. I am in dire need of another nap to make that mystery strain go away. I swear, the systems in Eternia are just… *ugh.* I'm going to have an entire document to send out just on this."

Soni tried not to snicker, covering his mouth before doing as requested. He said nothing as he eyed the weapon in Yiba's hands, wondering who this kid was that would make Sunny just hand over an Artifact-quality goodie. The kid likely didn't even know what he was holding. "Hello. I am Soni. Please sit, I have much to say and little time to say it. Let us begin."

CHAPTER FORTY-THREE

Artorian choked on his own snore when kicked on the bottom of his foot. He groggily ground his fists against his eyes, blinking as he squinted against the bright light. It wasn't even evening yet, surely it would have been dark by the time the portal was up?

Soni barked at the sleeping form, "Wake up, oh great monster of snores! I've been trying to get your attention since yesterday. Do you not wake up when the sun isn't out or something? You slept for ages!"

That sounded odd, so Artorian rolled over on the grass and began morning stretches. Intent on going through the entire routine. "I'm up. I'm up. I'm guessing I missed the portal window? How did your chat with Yiba go? I don't feel him in the vicinity."

Soni pointed off to some mountain in the distance. "Left as soon as he woke up. We ended up talking for much longer than I anticipated. I've armed him with all the important Alfheim knowledge, plus some tidbits I thought were pertinent after he figured out what he needed. Respectful boy for his age. Very considerate, patient, and willing to learn. Reminds me of you in some strange way that I have trouble describing."

The small creature motioned with a wing. "I sent him off to the largest collection of impris… that is, *poorly-handled* Elves. He's off to free them and set up a new society. Not that it will be difficult without any demons in his path. Those Elves remain trapped by their own fear, and little else. All he has to do to help their spirits is just show up. Everything he's armed with just guarantees his success."

The bat joined in on the stretches as he watched Artorian do them, though without realizing he was copying. "Much like my portals, all Yiba needs to make something out of Alfheim is time. Speaking of. I'm going to set back up now that you're awake. The portal will be up and running in two hours and fifteen minutes. Where do you want it?"

Artorian figured the demon did not mean physical location in the vicinity. "Top down. I want to launch bolts through the portal, and hammer Mu in his center mass from above as many times as I can before he realizes he needs to move. Then I'm going through myself and engaging in the boss fight. Of course, if I can cheese the entire affair, I will abyss-blasted do so. I ain't looking for a fair fight. Only victory."

Soni walked a few paces away. "Well, Mu isn't *bright.* You might get more shots in than you think. I was hoping surrender might be on the table, but this overseer wouldn't listen to you anyway. Robar might… but it's unlikely. *Uh.* Nivila, no. Minos, no. Urcan, definitely no. That flappy bear-bird is all juiced up on his own superiority."

With a grin at the thought, Soni continued, "Hanekawa has been a livewire of stress dealing with C'towl and their catty abyss, so he's as likely to eye-twitch at you and charge in screaming, as he is to just throw his weapon down and bury his head in the ground to quit. Caro would rather ensnare you in one of her schemes or scams than engage in anything that remotely resembles a straight up fight. However, if you get her to talk and have something worthwhile to trade that will allow her to make life more difficult for Odin, that's a probable yes. She's got a mighty hatred against Odin."

Having found a good spot, the savant put some lesser Cores down in a ritual circle to help stabilize his portal craft. "Corvid… you may have a really good chance of getting Corvid to up and quit the faction if you can break her tether to Barry somehow. She's been stationed on Hel and that's been taking a toll. Savant-class demons do not enjoy being forced into fearful hiding because of suddenly existing at the bottom of the food chain. Hel is no joke. She told me in the last meeting we had that she's made a safety spot under one of the pagodas, because you can't see the bone-monsters until right before they take a bite out of you. Otherwise they're invisible and deathly silent. All you see is their footprints."

Soni experienced an unpleasant shudder. "There are no hunters on Hel that aren't native. Only the hunted. No amount of power you have will prevent that place from putting an entirely new fear in you, because the invisible bone monsters are just *one* of the things roaming about. Sure, the geese variants are even worse, but don't make the mistake that the enemies you can see are less of a worry than the ones you can't. The only reason we even got demons on that realm was because back then we had Yasura, and even he got stumped when it came to the pagoda puzzle. I just… I'm going to work on this portal now."

Artorian kept the names for the definite 'no's in mind, deciding to check his character sheet while Soni got busy with portal craft. He decided to walk a good distance away before saying anything. "Yvessa? How are things on your end?"

While she didn't materialize since Soni was around, he did receive a green prompt. He tapped it and got to reading.

Soni's hearing is too good for me to speak. It's a mess. You made a mess. I needed a lot of explanation to understand what you did, but the short of it is that every time you use your ***Law****, Eternium's system goes on the fritz. I also heard you're one of the few people able to do this. How… wonderful.*

Please read that last bit in the most sarcastic voice you're able to imagine from me. Make it ooze with joy.

Artorian giggled under his breath, figuring this to be the case. "Well, it's over for now. What's going on with the Iridium weapon and my stats? Is that luck thing okay? Do I have anything open that needs to be addressed?"

He tapped the next green prompt that came up.

The weapon is currently under mass review by several Wisp committees. It's too good for a Legendary rarity, but for some reason nobody is able to wrest control of it away from you for it to be edited properly. Personally, I think that ***Law*** *thing of yours is interfering. The pink lightning frying skeevy hands trying to influence things is you, yes?*

Currently we have the rarity set to one level above Legendary, known as Mythical. Another one of those Deity-ranked slots we had to cobble together. We may need to directly escalate this to Dani because of the problems we're having. If she fixes it, the rarity will be set to: Dani. Trust me that there will never be anything higher. Even Cal will get a rarity lower than her if he personally meddles. You know the drill.

Your luck attribute being higher than everything else isn't detrimental. If anything, it sets you up to be well-balanced in the future, and at the moment you're getting a properly accounted 1% bonus per threshold. Though... actually, one moment. That isn't reflected in your statistics. Blacklights! Alright. Never mind... we... we'll fix it.

You've spent all your attribute points from that insane level up of yours. All that's left is the skill points. You got one per level, so... quite a few. I would suggest going through your skills right now and telling me which ones you want boosted.

Artorian nodded, and dismissed the conversation screens before pulling his status sheet in front of him. He really needed to order these better. Eh, another time. For now let's just see what was where. "Jogging, Journeyman. Fine. Running, Master. Excellent. Jumping, Apprentice. Fine. Calm Mind, Beginner. *Mmmmm.* Not so good. That's the Psychomancer protection one. Yvessa, maximize this one please. All the way to Master rank."

He watched as fifty skill points vanished from his pool of one hundred sixty-five, and the rank of Calm Mind dinged to Master, granting him a sixty percent bonus to mind altering effects. He wasn't sure how much that was or how exactly the formula worked, but bigger numbers were better. He got on with it. "Meditation, Beginner. Fine. Mental Manip—oh, crackers! I read it wrong!"

He slapped his face with his hand, feeling dumb. "This one is the one that needed to be pushed to the Master ranks. Toast! Yvessa… I… maximize this one please. I don't think I can get those other points back, but… my fault for jumping to conclusions. Abyss, I hope Cal doesn't make a skill out of that. I'm so glad he's asleep."

Sixty points vanished from his skill point pool, bringing Mental Manipulation Resistance up to the Master rank. This provided him a new total of eighty percent mental resistance. That left him fifty-five skill points to work with, or five ranks in… anything. *Eesh,* he burned through these fast! He went ahead and skipped over all the mana skills, and mulled over Flexibility. "I'll… put that one aside as a consideration. I've been frivolous by being dumb."

Martial Arts seemed like a good option. So did Bow Mastery, given how much he needed it. Still, because he used it so much, wouldn't that level well by itself? Another for the consideration pile. All the bow tricks were nice too, which only made him feel all the dumber for dumping points into Calm Mind. "Too late now, old man!"

He read over Monk Weapon Mastery when he got down to it, and realized he hadn't received a prompt for Polearm Weapon Mastery. Was there just not one? "Yvessa. I didn't get a ding for my little dance with the glaive earlier. Any news?"

He snickered when he read the prompt in Yvessa's voice.

Uhhhh… So, we don't know if what you were holding was a polearm or not, given it can be just about anything. No updates will happen until the classifications are sorted. I did tell you whole committees were on this, right?

Artorian let it go, reading over the tonfa and Pantheon goodies. He snickered again when he read the sparse entry for the First Kiss maneuver. Description: Null. Ha! Then Artifacting, Siege Engine Mastery, Ballistic Bowyer Mastery, and it was on to abilities.

He had all those cleric abilities now, even if he couldn't use them without mana. So they were solidly stuck at the Novice rank. There was no reason to look at the Sage skills, which I—Mapping? Why did he gain a Novice rank in mapping? He hadn't gotten a notification for this. He didn't even know how he'd gotten it, but there it was in the sheet. Huh. Oh well, he'd leave it.

"Echolocation!" He'd forgotten he had this! Was the description still busted? Oh, it was. Still no cost listed! "*Hehehe.*"

He'd keep that one in his back pocket for an opportune moment. Best to leave it alone. Then there was Platform, Divine Shell, Senate… stuff he couldn't use, or didn't have the juice for. Like S.E.P. field and Ki Arrows. He couldn't pay the upkeep. Lastly there was Soul of Zen. He sighed, rubbing the back of his head. "That's tempting too."

He had both too many options, and not enough of them at the same time. "Alright. I need help. I have no idea what the heck is more important here. This isn't my strong suit. I need someone who is solid in minimizing weaknesses and maximizing strengths in a game system. Yvessa, is there anyone who can help?"

He pressed the prompt when it came.

Absolutely! And I allow none of them to do so much as give you a shred of advice. Figure it out by yourself, or that part of the research is meaningless. No amount of feedback from the outside is going to help you. So suck it up and be responsible for your choices!

He gasped at the audacity. "You dare use my own core messaging against me? Yvessa, you cheeky lady!"

The next prompt was an image of a lady sticking her tongue out at him. Ha! Fine. He'd take this in comical, well-meaning stride. "Oh very well. What about information on which skills matter for my second specialization? At least with my first, it was somewhat clear. Now there's no active skills or abilities. Just passive ones. I do not feel properly informed by the system, and cannot make meaningful choices."

He was laying it on thick, curbing the truth more than a little to suit his scheming needs. He tapped the prompt with glee when it came, knowing full well he could make meaningful choices with next to no information in his pocket.

Old man, you barely recover enough stamina to keep up the costs to fire that ballista. Reminder: 1,000 stamina per shot. You had to slow down the last time you flurried. That's just shooting. A normal person at this time wouldn't have nine to ten thousand stamina, and then still you don't have enough left over to do anything special. You want specialization experience? Remember how you learned to jump, and just use the siege engine. Here, take this and don't prod me about this again.

**Ding*!*
Skill gained! Successive Shots.

This skill relies on Siege Engine Mastery. Successive Shots is a passive skill that improves your chances to hit, so long as you are targeting a single opponent. If you change the opponent targeted, this bonus resets to zero. Each successful or missed projectile will add cumulative a +1% to hit bonus on the next projectile fired. The mechanics of this bonus to hit chance function identically to Luckshot. Attacks that missed, but shouldn't have if this bonus was to move that bar over the threshold, will find a way to successfully hit instead. This skill has no levels or ranks.

Artorian tapped his fingers together, and sighed after dismissing the screen. A neat 'take this cookie and be quiet'!

Though he supposed what helped him was the jumping reminder. Growth had to correlate with intent. He supposed he'd just try that line of thinking, while hoping he wouldn't forget. That was getting worse again. He mulled over his options for a while, but the choices were all starting to blur together. He didn't feel too great. He had to remind himself that sleep in Eternia did not count towards true and proper Core sleep.

That worry didn't have time to grow. The points remained unspent as Soni called out from a distance. "Sunny! This scorpion-type portal will be ready in one minute! Get over here!"

CHAPTER FORTY-FOUR

Artorian entered his Astra form and set up with Ikaruga. A fresh bolt aimed at the soon to be finished portal while Soni went through a countdown. "Thirty seconds! Ready?"

"I'm ready for the cheeeese, glorious cheese!" The bowman rolled his shoulders, pulling back on the corded string. This was, of course, exactly the point where he realized where he wanted his skill points to go. Why would things be convenient? "Yvessa. Skill points into Siege Engine Mastery and Bow Mastery. Bump them up to be even, as high as they will go!"

His remaining skill points vanished, pulling both the requested skills just barely into the Expert ranks. It would make the math easier, even if he'd realized that it was the damage bump which was going to be the lynchpin when he let this shot go. He considered using the Soul of Zen ability, but there was no point. It was stamina regeneration that mattered right now. He could currently fire six bolts a round, if his mental math was right, and he didn't want to cut into his refire potential.

"Let's see." Ammunition was limited. With only forty-eight bolts to go, he had... if he loosed six shots a round, that made for eight rounds of shots. If he *didn't* think about Flurry. So he'd expend all his ammunition after forty-five seconds, if he could sustain his fire… which was unlikely. With a regen of five-hundred, that meant after a round he recouped two thousand five-hundred stamina when starting with a pool of almost ten thousand.

Soni said nothing in response, busy preparing to open the scorpion gate. As far as he was concerned, this was a beautiful, evil tactic. Why give your opponent any chances? Why let them fight back at all? He didn't fully follow the cheese reference, but figured that a Divine may be able to talk with the Voice of the World. How convenient for him. "Three, two… Open!"

Overseer Mu was content with life.

He hadn't been prior to bovine ascension, but now he'd mellowed out. Even if he ate seven times as much grass as the next largest Cow King did. He was listlessly chewing on some reeds when the sky above warbled.

He paid it no heed. Just another oddity that would even itself out. After all, what was there to worry about as the strongest demon in the entire realm? A realm with nothing in it but bovines and bovine food. Though a lot was bovine food for Hel-cows. Being omnivorous without drawbacks had its perks.

If he ever craved some meat like the old days… well. Nobody noticed a single grain of sand missing from the desert. Similarly, nobody noticed a single cow when it went missing from the herd. There were perks to low perception and intelligence. He just didn't care about things, so he didn't worry.

Taking a black plasma crystal to the face made continuing not to worry… a touch difficult. The second one missed him, but landed in front of his face. That one he could continue blissfully not worrying about. Until they both exploded. The audacity!

How dared some minor little sky-stick fragment—why did

he feel such pain? That was unnatural. His armor was Legendary, and his damage reduction made any threats that had been present moo-t. It turned out that explosion damage didn't care for such things, even if the initial impact from the face-bedazzler had been mostly mitigated.

The crystal shrapnel was no cause for concern, regardless of the bovine herd in his immediate vicinity experiencing a live rendition of his favorite stage play: the meat grinder. Mu changed his mind and took the threat seriously when more of these spiky beams rained down. Their thunderclap explosions rocked his surroundings, changing the local bright green decor back to the blasted cragscape he was far more used to seeing. It still beat out the entropic nothingness of the abyss, but not by much.

His massive axe, named Grass Mower, cut through the ground from its resting place on a nearby hill, destroying the landscape in a straight swath as his weapon connected with his hand. It was a shame then, that after another set of explosions, his hand traveled more and more into the 'over there' region. The axe kept going, and his dismembered hand went with it.

Easily five out of six of these deadly bolts tore chunks out of his body and health over the first twenty seconds. Mu didn't understand how the threat level had—without warning—jumped from laughably peaceful to immediate limb-loss dangerous as his health pool warned him it was down to the halfway mark.

That was another thing which was impossible. He was Mu! He had fifty thousand health! There was no way he'd just lost half of it all to some random sky sticks. Not ready to tackle this problem right now, he looked up to feel his many stomachs tie up into a pretty bow knot.

So high up in the sky that it was painfully difficult to see, a portal hung open. What made the portal so difficult to see were the rapidly descending dozen or so black spires that shot down from orbit. Far enough away for their incoming waves to be visible, while close enough for him to realize he should move his feet and find some cover.

He needed to find some cover! Right now!

The fourth and fifth duo of bolts struck him in the chest at the same time, like the number four on a dotted die. So even and equal were the piercing wounds that Mu thought this was some sort of practical joke. Based on the pain, he could tell at least two of the shards were critical strikes.

The orbital bolts stabbed him in unpleasantly sensitive places. His precious stomachs! He needed those! Worse, the other two had stabbed right through him, pinning him to his current location while trapping him to the spot until these bolts destabilized as well. They, as one might surmise from past events, exploded when they rebelled against the authority of all things solid.

Mu wanted to say something clever, but didn't survive the orbital bombardment. He was dead thirty seconds after the first spire struck him. The remaining ammunition in the air bombarded the blasted battlefield to a chunked ruin. If anyone wanted to search Mu for loot, they would have to figure out which leathery scrap was him first. A difficult feat, given the collateral damage.

"How did that not level me up?" Artorian was surprised when he spent the last of his current ammunition bundle, having noted the lack of need to jump through the scorpion portal and commence mopping up. Mu was dead. Very dead. So dead. A proper 'where did he go' joke-worthy kind of dead. "I gained a specialization level, but no general level up. Oh right, I need a ridiculous amount for one hundred eighty-six. Fair, fair."

Soni's jaw hung open, eyes squinted at his own portal. When he did manage to speak, the sound was flustered. "How? *How*? How did you whittle down fifty thousand health that fast?

I didn't think his health was even that high until I saw it just now. You didn't even hit him with all of them!"

Artorian stowed Ikaruga, releasing his Astra form for relief to get that tension out of his joints. "It's a bit of an explanation. You sure you want it?"

Soni closed the portal and threw his hands to the ground, as if making some heavy statement. "Yes! In detail!"

"Alright, alright." Artorian put his hands up, wondering where to start. "Let me write some of these values in mud to help."

He found a nearby stick that pleased him, and started mud-scribing. "So. Ikaruga is a siege engine, thus does siege engine damage. One hundred flat, plus a hundred-sided die for variable damage. Maximum two hundred. I have a skill called Overdraw. It slows down my shooting, even if it sort of gets balanced out by Flurry, but let's only look at damage. Ikaruga has a maximum strain of eight hundred, meaning I can safely overdraw up to seven-fifty without concern; that's seven-fifty raw damage added to the formula. So we're at eight hundred and fifty base damage, plus randomization."

He wrote down that number and circled it. "Now for bonuses. I have an Expert rank in the corresponding mastery skill. That thing I yelled out before firing? That. This gives me a sixty percent accuracy, damage, and armor penetration bonus. Or armor ignore; I notice it gets listed differently depending on who wrote it. That needs to be streamlined."

Artorian wrote a fifty to have something listed as the dice roll to total up to nine-hundred, then added the bonus on top of it. Which came out to five-hundred and forty. Five-forty and nine hundred made one-thousand four hundred and forty damage. He circled that last number. "A decent chunk. Yes? Now we add my special trait. I do double damage to all demons… just because."

He flashed Soni a toothy smile just to unsettle him, but the bat was already holding his head, plenty unsettled from math alone. He swallowed before speaking. "That's almost three thousand. By *itself*."

Artorian nodded, making Soni shrink away as he continued writing in the formula. There was more! "Two thousand eight hundred and eighty. For one bolt. After which, there's a possibility for a critical strike, which would double my damage again. However! I have a special skill which allows it to be possible for my damage to be multiplied by five during a critical hit, rather than merely twice. Lovely facial expression you've got there."

Soni was now holding his heart, appalled and shrinking away ever further from this mathematical madness. "Tell me it… stops there."

Artorian giggled. "Of course it doesn't!"

Soni thought he had the vapors, because he was going to faint.

The human just kept scribing. "Now we can't account for criticals. They're lucky. So let's just get on with the formula. Time for weapon effects! Every bolt I fire counts for two. I'm sure you noticed them burning up and becoming those crystal-shard-looking things. Each of these spikes still deals damage normally, but I'm getting a dual hit as a freebie. If they both hit on a target with no armor to ignore, that's five thousand six hundred damage somewhere, when rounded for convenience. Then comes fun part one of three!"

Soni screeched via inhaling, wanting this to stop. He regretted ever asking. Artorian gave the bat no such reprieve. "My engine also adds explosion goodness. Now, first I thought explosion damage happened in lieu of the initial impact. You know, boom instead of stab. Well, I was wrong! The spikes deal their impact damage, and *then* explode. The text on the weapon says the spikes will explode 'on impact.' So I really thought it wasn't the case. Impact still has to be made for the explosion to trigger, and impact means hit damage. I've even noticed many of them go off after a delay. I'm expecting Pylon tweaks."

He waved that detail off. "On explosion, the total damage of the impact is considered to be the diameter. So divide by half if you prefer to think of it as a radius. Dwarven math is fun that way. So if we pretend five thousand six hundred becomes the diameter, that's a big orb of damage. The closer to the center, the more damage done, and the damage starts identical to the diameter. You're safer if farther out… sort of. Not really. It happens per independent projectile. So, big bada-booms all around."

Artorian underlined the current number, and drew the rough size of the bubble when scaled down. "Fun part two out of three. After explosion damage, Onyx Sunglass comes out to play. I think it happens at the same time as the explosion, but for the purpose of showing the formula, I just shrug and put it here. Sunglass shatters into obsidian shards. It's not actually obsidian, but, you know. Jagged, sharp, very cutty."

Soni just nodded out of sheer defeat, his heart dropped to his stomach. "Yeah. *Uh-huh.* Great. Sure."

The academic in the old man was on a roll now; there was no stopping until the end of the lecture. "This messed with me, too. Since at first, I thought it was the shards doing the explosion damage. Turns out I'm wrong. Shard damage is independent from explosion damage. Its damage just isn't listed because it's really just around one or two damage per shard. The fun bit is that this damage improves depending on sharp velocity… which… forget calculating that mess. Or how far they go. Easily twice whatever the prior explosion radius was."

Soni laid on his back, holding his own knees to gently rock himself. "That was only part two?"

The academic nodded, his finger shooting to the air as he descended into lecture mode. "Indeed, my young student. Part three was giggles on the system's end, I think. I discovered by some leisurely reading that the roiling black flame stuff inside the crystal is known as plasma. It doesn't seem to remain stable very easily, but that's not the important part. This plasma wants to disperse, causing it to cling onto the sunglass shards flying in all directions. For a reason beyond me, it coats those shards in that plasma. Adding bonus fire damage to each fragment for a second or two before the reaction fizzles out. I noticed how some of the visible injuries they caused self-cauterized. Of course, those without plasma still cause bleed damage, so no fuss."

"Is… is that finally everything?" Soni's ears hung down the sides of his head, his mind having gone blank with the horrors inflicted by Dwarven math homework. His face buried into the ground when Artorian made a so-so hand motion. Rolling over to hide himself in the grass, he was done. Absolutely done. "What does any of this have to do with *cheese*?"

"Oh! I came up with it on the fly, though I have this odd feeling that the idea isn't mine. Cheesing means to defeat an opponent or complete an event in an unfair way, manner, or method. Such as bombarding Mu when he had no chance of fighting back, or really doing any harm to us. I don't know why Eternium thinks I'm not going to resort to cheap shots. I'm here on a mission, not some enthusiastic stroll through the woods."

**Ding*!*
You have received a message from: Yvessa.

Artorian paused his chat, and pushed accept on the prompt. Which began speaking in Yvessa's voice. Though it appeared only he could hear it.

I have heard about your 'enthusiastic walks through the woods.' They're just as bad. Hurry up and head to Jotunheim. A friend of yours named Zelia has entered Eternium and mentioned she'd wait for you there. She said there's some problem with a giant snow crab named Thrymm, and that you'd know what that meant. Also, we just got the damage numbers in from your… It's being logged as a field test? We need to rebalance damage output. Don't get too attached to your siege toy.

Artorian's pleasantry fell right down from his face. He stomped his foot down on the ground, his arms flailing while his hands balled into fists. "Abyss-blast it. Why crabs! Why is it once again those cranky crabs? Do they not remember what I did to the last one!"

"Uh-uh. Crabs. Very terrible. Don't catch them. They're snappy." Soni just added commentary, having completely given up on trying to make sense out of any of this. He raised his hands up, making pincer movements at the sky. **Kchoo Kchi Kchoo Kchi**.

CHAPTER FORTY-FIVE

Artorian stopped his half-hearted outrage with a quirked brow, looking at the resting bat over his shoulder. The demon listlessly stared at the sky, speaking without energy. "You have a visitor, by the way."

He flicked a tiny finger upwards with dejected effort. A movement which the human followed to see what appeared to be a pocket-portable meteor hurl down from the sky. From the direction of: moon. It vaguely looked like an angry bear on fire, wearing some kind of strange white shirt outfit with matching black pants. Artorian thought of the word 'office.' Though he wasn't sure what it meant. The word vanished with a fleeting yeet from his mind when the meteor approached uncomfortably close.

Specifically because it veered off to arc towards his direction. Never a good sign. Artorian cleared his throat, taking his chances with a question. "Any chance it's friendly?"

Soni shrugged. "It's Urcan. So… no. He looks to be in his Garuda form. So he's already angry. I never did figure out if that was a bear with wings, or a really muscular birdman. He likes fire, procedure, proper paperwork, and applying fire to anyone who doesn't… I'm hungry."

Artorian recalled he did turn the hunger systems on, taking this moment to flicker his Sustenance effect to life, Soni included. That Pylon system was a recent development, surely it wasn't bad enough to make any big waves yet?

Urcan's impact proved him wrong on both counts. His **ker-slam** to the ground caused waves of ground, grass, and greenery to bulge upwards and swiftly roll outwards. The crater that formed, coupled with the air displacement and tons of moved Alfheim earth, was more than enough to send both Soni and Artorian catapulting away. Soni remained mostly listless on his forced flight, flicking Urcan rude gestures with both his hands as he went.

That was fine. He didn't want to be here anyway. When he hit ground again, Soni already knew he was going to start portal work to get off this soon-to-be wreck of a realm right away. Urcan was not known in his old circle for his ability to hold back. Or he would have, had Urcan not moved to snatch him out of the sky like a bacon-wrapped potato.

The fifteen-foot-tall Garuda hit Alfheim ground hard enough to create another crater. Though his attention was on the tiny bat being half-squished in his hand. His voice was surprisingly cordial and polite, given his rage. "Savant Soni? You are alive? This cannot be, we saw your darkness leave from the Devourer's chambers."

Soni didn't even bother struggling. Urcan had him beat in statistics, but Soni had beaten himself into a depressed stupor. "You know how it goes, Urcan. We get thrown around. Get punted here, get punted there. End up in pieces everywhere."

Urcan opened his bird-like talons molded in the shape of a bear claw, unsure why Soni was acting like he was dead. "This is not the mindset of a savant. Have pride in your heritage. We are almighty, undefeatable! Everlasting."

Soni sounded far from convinced. "Are we? Sure, we're

Torture Savants. So why has that stopped meaning anything? I've been where you've been, Urcan. I did the paperwork. I dressed the part. I felt the bags under my eyes become a ton of bricks, just as yours currently are. We used to hold top spots in the hierarchy, unless a True Deamon like Yasura was around. It's not like we have a lot of S-rankers. Wasn't Yasura our only one?"

Urcan roared in Soni's face, nothing sensible or meaningful being conveyed. Soni was the picture of detachment. Urcan was mad. "Speak not of the Deamons in such a cynical, disgraceful way. They are eternal."

Soni sighed, unaffected. "Are they, Urcan? Are they? When did savants become servants? When did our invulnerability become squishy flesh and soft fur? When did the lessers in our ranks lose their respect for us, the pain and fear gone from their eyes? I know you've seen it, Urcan. We are demons in name only. We have become different here. We are affected. Weakened. Malleable. So what if I speak ill of the True Deamons? Did Ghreziz return? Did Yasura? Tell me they came back, and I will go bend my knee to them this instant. Tell me where they are, Urcan. Tell me."

Another howl which became little more than a show of burning heat coursed over Soni's tiny frame. He was highly resistant to fire, and his A-ranker attributes were plenty powerful enough to ignore this. "They… they will come. They will all return with news of glorious victory. Tales of bodies torn and souls wrenched. I know they will."

Soni shook his tiny head left and right. "They lost. The difference between being defeated and being captured… Does it matter? You want to know why I vanished from the priming chamber? I lost, Urcan. I lost bad."

The tiny bat managed a saccharine smirk. "Though even before I lost, the glory of the savant was in tatters. I can't care about a title when the society that makes me believe such a thing matters is nowhere to be seen. I feel no connection to the Abyss here, Urcan. There is a membrane, a wall, a mountain unscalable, between it and me."

Soni shook his head. "There are no supplicants, no servants, no true lessers. We are all forms made of numbers. We are the lessers here, and I now know that we are the lessers out there as well. We are on the wrong side of the war, Urcan. Our summoner will lose. I see it. I hope you see it too."

Urcan threw Soni into the ground with such force that half the bat's health bar vanished in a flash. The bat mumbled a sound of pain while buried three feet deep, crawling out only to sigh and brush his now brown robes off.

Urcan raged. "You are a betrayer! A link-ripper. A summoner forsaker. You are foul even for a demon! I would destroy you here, now, if I did not have a prior entry on my carefully itemized list to write off first. I bet you are somehow responsible for our recent slew of losses."

Soni laid down on his back, holding his hands against his own chest. Speaking more with his motions than his words. "Oh sure, blame the bat, what the heck, we're easy targets. Kick me while I'm down, why don't you."

Urcan finally heard something he could agree with. "Gladly!" **Fwump**.

Soni felt another quarter of his bar salute and check out while he flew over the current edge of Urcan's impact crater, moaning **Owwww**. Change of plans; forget just escaping, the order of the day was now escaping, *plus revenge*.

A duo of Onyx Sunglass bolts bit into Urcan's feathery side when Soni left the danger zone, Urcan's plumage still on orange-yellow fire when he took the hit. Surprised, he staggered from the impact with a follow up grunt. Said grunt turned into a roaring howl when both spikes exploded point blank, the resulting sharp shards causing the pain of a hundred cuts. A particularly lucky shard cut him right across the beak, giving him a very nice battle scar. Shame about all the other injuries, of course.

Artorian drew his second shot and ducked up from his tiny, newly created hill when shard friendly fire was no longer an imminent threat. He was far too close to be using Ikaruga, but it was still his best b—

**Baf*!*

His grip on Ikaruga went limp as a strong case of disorientation walloped him in the nose. Flavored like peppery spices, physically on fire, and in the shape of a bear claw as he got decked in the schnozz. Urcan had hit him hard enough to send him skipping across the landscape like a flat stone over a lake. He bounced several times before he had a chance to get his footing, at which point a rather eagle-talon-shaped foot kicked him in the stomach to send him skywards.

Urcan didn't mess around! Artorian cursed out loud when he squeezed his hand, realizing he'd lost the grip on his specialization weapon. He'd have to go looking for it after the battle. First was halting this keister-kicking he was suddenly on the receiving end of. How was this beastie both so big and so fast at the same time?

Mid-corkscrew spin, Artorian groaned and shot an inspect at his current opponent. He badly needed to know what was going on, because that burning bear bird was already hot on his tail. The dang thing could fly! Also celestial whoppers! His health bar! "Blessed feces on a stick, what happened?"

That bash to his face cost him a thousand four hundred health, and so had the kick to the stomach. He was almost three thousand health in the hole and he hadn't even caught his footing yet! Artorian scanned the information he got before it looked like Urcan could punch him again. Which would be too soon for his liking.

Name: Urcan
Race: Garuda (Demon)
Character Level: 404. (Error. True level not found. Occlusion ability active.)
Class: Fighter
Specialization: Moonrager
Profession: Floor Manager

Hit Points: 41,038 / 56,000

Characteristics:
Strength: 1,400
Dexterity: 1,424
Constitution: 2,800
Intelligence: 726
Wisdom: 729
Charisma: 732
Perception: 727
Luck: 744

Well, that was several variations of bad. Abyss-blast that constitution score! How was he going to get through all of that without his siege engine? Urcan was already too close for comfort. Those massive eagle wings of his turned him into a fast, burning projectile. How he wished he had access to his platforms. Though… technically, didn't Urcan count as one? A thought struck Artorian like lightning, his mouth fast on the pickup. "Ad Astra!"

The pressure of Empowerment pushed out from Artorian's skin as he went super. There was no way he was winning anything in mid-air, though he did catch sight of some nearby clouds. Could… could he still? Best to unsettle the enemy first. "Hey you, big and burning! You know what you don't have? You've got *no style*!"

The pressure around Artorian flared, turning bright light blue as his martial arts actively kicked into gear via his proclamation. The Garuda roared at him, but Artorian had gotten his bearings. "Breathe the Air. Flow like Water. Focus. *Deny the Blow*. Power Launch."

Urcan lashed out with his taloned claw rather than try to punch the no-longer spinning foe. His claws were on the perfect course to tear the human's face off, but the side of the human's wrist struck his attack from the side, veering it off from its intended trajectory. The push turned into a swift grab. Not one for grappling, but for leverage and control.

Urcan's very body allowed Artorian to move freely in the air by using the Garuda as a counterweight, his leg coming down as a sharp axe kick, though the blow struck Urcan with far more force and far less injury than he expected.

Instead, the kick broke his momentum entirely, seeming to add to the human's launch as the mortal spiraled toward a set of thick-packed clouds as Urcan crashed into the Alfheim ground. This added yet another crater to the growing set. The Garuda pushed up and off from this new crater to start flight once again, barely dented from this injury in comparison to the prior ones. As if a flyer wouldn't create ability insurances against crashes. "I have plenty of style! Ant-crushing is an art of ease! No matter what that wretch Nivila says."

The Garuda's vision snapped to the sky, his wings spreading. He did not see the glowing blue creature he expected, though the human was caught soon enough. He'd ended that power-up effect in favor of some kind of blobbing cloud field around him, which rubbed Urcan in a bad way. He'd read the reports on that ethereal field, that was the over-time demon-killer. The poofening. "Too bad, human! I won't be in there long enough for a ticking effect to do me in. My health is too high! My power is maximum!"

Urcan deepened his current crater on liftoff, angling straight for the cloud-bouncing human who seemed to be running across their surface. He gradually picked up speed as he zipped and arced from cloud to cloud via long jumps, favoring the long stretches of clouds to continue to increase his velocity. The Garuda howled, not caring what the human was planning. It was just going to kill him and eat the remains before dealing with that traitor, Soni.

Artorian thought he had the luck of the heavens themselves. That or inside help. His Power Launch to the clouds had been a gamble! His foot moved to the closest one as his leg outstretched. He remembered the text on cloud-running well. It was only free if he was running! In a burst of inspired genius—or stupidity, depending on who was talking—he tapped into his Speech skill and yelled at the cloud. "I am running!"

He loved the dumb prompt that came up.

**Ding*!*
You have convinced the cloud that you are running.

When his foot touched the cloud surface, he put all his weight down on it, disbelieving that the cloud could hold that much downward force, even as it did. He ended his Astra form to flicker his Resplendence field on, wanting that lost health back pronto as he tried to put some distance between him and the flying bear-bird.

Why was Urcan even here? He didn't seem to have arrived for Soni. That was a surprise based on the quick peek Artorian stole while they were gabbing. The Garuda did seem to be hunting him down in a seething rage, but why now? Why so randomly? Did this demon come all the way from the freaking moon? With basic flight and sheer anger? Something didn't add up.

"If it was the food problem, there should be stamina penalties. Urcan was showing none of those. Though with that constitution..." Artorian would be lucky if the demon was even low on stamina. His grunt bar must have been huge! Sadly, the distance between himself and Urcan became tiny, causing Artorian to bicker at the bear. "Stop rushing me!"

Artorian tried to summon his glaive from his spatial ring, but was met with an unceremonious error sound. "What?"

Yvessa's green light hummed next to his head. Her voice did not bother to whisper since the demon had zero chance of hearing her. "Tell me you don't need that already? We're still working on it. That weapon is in system lockdown. I... *oh.* Blacklights! You do need it already! What the abyss is that one doing here? He belongs on the moon!"

"Why don't you go ask him for me?" Artorian grumbly

mumbled in turn. He didn't like having his toys taken away. Especially not when he badly needed them! "That leaves me without a weapon, Yvessa! His stats are higher than mine even if I boost myself, and that pruned piece of plumage can properly fly!"

Yvessa didn't see the problem, ignoring the stab. "So what? So can you."

His caretaker winked out while the stars bloomed in Artorian's eyes. That's right. He could fly! Just not… like this. Would it be faster than cloud running? He wasn't managing to break the sound barrier right now, and the Garuda was easily catching up.

Should he double back and go for the siege engine? He didn't exactly have aerial superiority advantage against a natural flyer. He was dabbling at best. An enticing option, but no. His dragon form was currently a cleverly disguised dead end. He needed to practice, not *Dale it* with that option. A random thought occurred that his Long was his real form, and that his human form was just an alternative. Wouldn't that explain why his attributes remained locked to the dragon age penalty?

You know what? This was a really bad time for that! Back to brass tacks! "Step one. Run away! Step two. Check options! Step three. Improvise really quickly because Celestial Feces, how did that tarry tart get in my face so fast? *Deny the Blow*!"

CHAPTER FORTY-SIX

Urcan the Torture Savant hissed at the bothersome human when his claw was knocked out of harm's way again. Except, this time, it allowed the bothersome ant to knee him in the throat and kick him in the back of the head while spinning away. Throttling a noisy gasp, the human escaped from Urcan's claws when he needed that partial moment to catch himself. That and the awful shiny field made Urcan feel as if he just took a tumble into an acid bath. It burned, and not in the way he liked.

"Where did that annoying mortal twig go?" Urcan looked below him, but saw nothing. No movement, and no flickering spec of light. Worse still, he was not yet free of this bothersome ethereal cloud! Wait… didn't that mean the human foe was still nearby? "Where would it be if it was still nearby?"

"Gotcha!" Human arms and legs wrapped around the base of Urcan's wings from behind, thieving from him the ability to fly, and turning the otherwise mobile Garuda into little more than a heavy rock currently spending time in the sky.

Urcan was going to fall. He was going to fall hard. The

blasted creature had assailed him from above! He howled as the wing-pinning nuisance spoke.

"Crackers and *toast*, that burns!"

Urcan furiously reached behind him, his Garuda form unable to reach the prized flesh that he so dearly wanted to crush between his claws as the freefall began. "Curses upon you, annoying creature! May my infernal fires scorch you to the bones, until even they are blackened and broken. I will reach you yet!"

Artorian wasn't convinced, squeezing the wings hard in an attempt to break them. He'd expected these things to be hollow, but he had no such luck. That blasted massive constitution wasn't something he was currently able to overcome. He grit his teeth while speaking. "Yeah? Well, let's see what wins first then. Your little flames, or my healing. Why are you even here, you oversized rotisserie chicken?"

Urcan screamed at the bothersome ant on his back as they fell. He knew the impact would hurt, but that it was happening at all was irritating! His clothes conflagrated to nothing as he infused himself with infernal prowess and power. The orange flames blackened before suddenly extinguishing altogether. Though not by Urcan's will. "Fire needs air to breathe, my boy! You're soot out of luck while in my field. Thanks for aligning that fire for me! Saved me some health loss."

The Garuda was still adapting, his orange feathers blackening further even if his natural burning protections were no longer active. He was taking an annoying amount of damage from that poof field he'd told himself he wouldn't be in long. Yet here the miscreant had his wings grappled! Even worse, it wouldn't shut up! "You know. I always wanted to know what would happen if I tried a weapon maneuver without having the appropriate weapon. What a fantastic opportunity!"

The human drew a fresh breath, speaking with clear purpose. "Halcyon Days, Breath Series. Starfall!"

Urcan did not like the sudden appearance of a comet-like visual effect to become visible around him as the terminal velocity which he fell to the ground with seemed to double. He couldn't be sure it actually had, but it felt like it when the duo smashed into the ground hard. Forming yet another crater in the landscape. The Garuda howled in pain rather than rage as bone crunched and his wings audibly broke.

His status sheet only confirmed the awful news. *Wing status: Broken, x2*.

At least his health hadn't taken a big hit, but whatever dumb little technique the human just applied had provided enough oomph to overcome the bonus armor value he'd applied to his very bones. Was Starfall an armor breaker? Surely not. Must have been a fluke.

Artorian did not get lucky in getting away. He was firmly grabbed by Urcan's claw and slammed to the ground four to five times, before the angry beast hurled him into the distance. Some trees broke his flight after he once again played the role of the skipped rock. Artorian coughed out a pained sputter, the lack of Astra form having made that hurt far more than it would have. Instead, his field patched him up gradually, at a slow but reasonably steady pace.

Artorian realized it wouldn't matter. His health couldn't survive the kind of damage this Garuda could clearly do. A few straight, solid hits, and he was done for. Was this the kind of problem children he would be running into in the future? Was Odin going to hit that much harder? Because even this was nearly unbearable. "One madness at a time, old boy!"

He pressed his hands to his knees, groaning as he got himself up. Heaving in a fresh breath as his active skills removed the majority of his maluses, Artorian popped his shoulders as he saw Urcan get up in the distance as well. Just to be a cheeky snoot, he started doing Flexibility exercises right there on the spot. "Had a nice fall? Seriously though, why in the abyss are you here, destroying my garden? Get off my lawn!"

Urcan's form bulged with power, and delighted in seeing the human's expression fall when his strength score doubled. So the creature could see his features? Good. Let the weak mortal tremble in its boots. Full of fear and despair at its inevitable demise. "Lawn? I care not for your realm, mortal whelp! I will break you, and pull from your flesh the truth of where the mechanism hides. That cruel contraption which causes us all to experience the pangs of hunger. It's destroying office productivity!"

There it was. That word again. What the abyss was an office, and why did it sound like a terrible place to be? What was next? Another random, awful word? He bet it would be something along the lines of 'cubicle.' Who knew? What Artorian did know was that the information network of his foes had fractured.

Urcan didn't know there was no Artifact or item creating that effect. It was literally a function of the world which had been turned on. That explained why a head honcho demon had come, but hadn't he activated that effect on Vanaheim? Had he been on Alfheim? Unimportant details. The demon was clearly gunning for him. "Well, why are you bothering *me* then? I don't have this hunger thingy you're on about. Go play with someone else. I have things to do! Like start up the grill for a buffet of cow patties I'm fixin' to make."

The Garuda was twenty bloody feet tall now, steadily approaching him with obvious confidence, as if the demon had already won. His angry voice was thick, full of bluster and certainty. "You lie! The Raven Savant divined your appearance as the soul responsible for the source of this new misery. I have tracked you, found you, gained victory over you. Now you will tell me where the Artifact is, and how to end its miserable application."

"Victory? Big words from such a tiny man." Artorian hopped in place on his toes, taking off his outer robe as his field patched up the rest of his current injuries. He loved keeping a demon talking. It bought him so much time when he got them to gloat. Worked like a charm. "Well I've got a question for you then, tiny, since you think you're going to win anyway. Consider it a curiosity. What's your favorite weapon?"

Urcan bellowed with laughter, unable to hold back when face to face with such a sudden, random, idiotic query. "Ha! Is that a clever attempt to tell me you want me to use my favorite toys to gut you? I am a Floor Manager! Pretty little quips like that are useless, though since it will bring me such gruesome joy, I may as well! My favorite weapon is this."

Reaching to his chest, Artorian felt sick when the demon plunged his claw *into* his sternum as if it was little more than an inky well, of which the surface tension was disturbed. Oh… oh, ew. *All* Demons had Soul Items that they could use here? Not fair! So not fair!

A long hilt pulled free from Urcan's chest, a longer curved blade following. Though, it was too thin and too long to be a scimitar. Artorian frowned at it, not having a clue what it was. His curiosity got the better of him "The abyss is *that* thing? Does… Does it have a name?"

The Garuda bellowed out another bout of amused laughter. The blade was as black as his current colorations, lined with yellow flames that sprouted from the tsuba handguard. "This beauty got lost in time. It's called a katana, and I don't do something as pathetic as give the weapon a name. That is a cute trick for the weak to make themselves feel better about their inferiority. A weapon is a tool. Treat it like a tool. Just like people are tools. My tools deserve no names. They must simply bend to my will, and my rigorous lean-staffing schedule!"

Artorian didn't like the look of the weapon, but he disliked the sudden focus his opponent gained far, far less. He was no longer fighting a raging beast, and suddenly sized up against a seasoned warrior as soon as that weapon wound up in Urcan's hands. The entire vibe of the fight changed, and Artorian knew at the drop of a hat that this was no longer an encounter he could talk his way through.

His bluster and anger were gone, replaced by warrior's rage and refined murderous intent. Abyss! Artorian snapped to his denial martial arts stance from the sheer terrible squeeze his stomach gave him. His Resplendence field dropped so his Astra form could coalesce and snap into activity. The slow, sustained victory was no longer in his grasp. He knew it instinctually.

Of course these overseers would have high-level tricks and techniques hidden in their sleeves. He simply hadn't been leaving them alive long enough to see them. He'd cheesed the living abyss out of Mu, tricked Pencil, and converted Soni. Urcan was an invalid target for any of these options. This was going to be a straight up tussle between experts, bound down by these annoying numbers.

Artorian didn't see Urcan launch. He just felt the blade pass through his side while a full third of his freshly replenished health bar called it quits. He barely focused Soul of Zen into activity in time to avoid the follow up blow, which would have taken off far more than another third, considering the ominous yellow edge present on that long blade.

That cursed Garuda had barely even drawn his weapon, and **fwoop**! The attack was made. What was that kind of nonsense? Artorian cranked his Zen ability all the way up, as high as it could go. This let him come to the grim realization that he was moving in a timeframe identical to Urcan, given that everything else was slow, yet they were moving at similar speeds.

Not. Good.

Artorian felt the hidden strain factor bite him right away. He likely had a little longer than last time, but a minute of real time was going to be the majority of it. Crackers. Student-ranked Soul of Zen put him on *equal* footing? Blast this under-cooked chicken all the way back to the Abyss. Oh, right. Not an option while in Cal. "*Uuuurgh.*"

Flow Like Water let him dodge the sudden third and fourth strikes of the opportunity attacks Urcan made, able to keep up now that he was on even footing. A fact that the demon greatly despised as his slicing attacks were suddenly evaded. Then blocked by the human's denial maneuvers and pushes as the twenty-one-strike combination went on. Urcan still cackled as the seventeenth strike found purchase and pierced deep into the mortal's shoulder. This took the man's entire left arm out of commission and forced him to dodge the rest of the strikes.

Artorian rolled away ungracefully, holding his limp arm with the other while gritting his teeth to cope. "Abyss, that thing hurt!"

The cut caused more pain than health damage, but *yeowch*! It was like that yellow flame was meant for causing agony rather than true harm. Given what he was up against… not an unreasonable assumption. Breathe the Air prevented him from becoming winded, so his lungs took a breath even if his brain hadn't caught up to that point yet.

He'd have been a goner without Impeccable Focus. What was his health at? Three thousand six hundred and twelve? Oof. *Big Oof.* He needed to heal his bloody shoulder, but couldn't without dropping the Astra form, and that boost in his dexterity was one of the few helpful factors in dodging.

Sweat rolled down his face and forehead. Artorian suddenly realized how much effort he'd exerted to get out of that devious set of skillful strikes. His foot moved back, and he understood he was on the losing end here. He needed to turn this around. But how. *How*? That cut on his side didn't stop bleeding, and twelve health vanished from his pool when he glanced again. "A bleed effect? *Fantastic*."

CHAPTER FORTY-SEVEN

Artorian had a terrible idea. Terrible *not* because of how dumb it was, nor how utterly foolish and impractical the attempt would be… it was just something that even a seasoned warrior like Urcan would never see coming. "Oh, I am going to regret this…"

The human shook his head, snapping himself out of that mentality as Urcan toothily smiled and circled. Also knowing he was heavily favored to win this matchup, even with the human's power boosts. "I regret nothing. I take the actions I can live with. Even if those actions would receive the greatest fool award. Yes… that's right. Choices I can live with."

He drew breath, exhaling strongly enough to cause the wind to visibly move before him in the slowed sense of time they both shared. "It's just like that raider… in the Fringe. So long ago. Why do I remember and know your name, Alphas?"

"Going senile, little warrior?" Urcan barked at him. His voice warbled from the dilation while the readied circling continued. "Worry not. I know how to carve you up so you can still tell me what I wish to know."

Artorian repeated himself, the words from a memory ancient by current standards. He whispered his words exactly as he remembered doing so the first time. Though today they were directed at another creature he could not find a shred of love for. "Hush now. I'm knowingly and willingly doing some awful things. I must thank you for the opportunity you've provided me. In truth, I've been *dying* to know how this interaction worked."

His eyes were cold when they locked with his veteran of a foe. "You know… today, I am not a good man. I had hoped never to be back at this line. Or scooch so much as a toe across it. Yet here I am again. I am sorry… Urcan. Even *you* do not deserve this."

That steady last comment made the Garuda freeze on the spot, his circling ended so he could take a defensive stance, even if the tip of his blade pointed straight at the strange human. "Demons are immune to threat, and fear."

Artorian's pose and posture relaxed, his expression turning solemn. As he resigned himself to stray from the path of good. This was a terrible idea. A cruel idea. When stoic strength filled his face for Urcan to clearly see, the Garuda hesitated no more. The demon struck!

The blade did not strike its mark as Artorian pushed forward during his move. His hands overlapped Urcan's massive claws as they brought the blade down toward him. He had denied the blow, but was now in progress of doing something truly awful.

Urcan's bluster returned when he saw the human's last-ditch effort to prevent his own death. The creature had evaded the blade, but initiated a contest of strength by pushing against its hands. Better still, the human had made some kind of critical mistake! A mistake which caused Urcan to stretch his demonic smile from ear to ear. The human was giving him stamina! Using some odd, gentle pink glow to do it.

A powerful strength filled him, and Urcan paused his desire

to crush the human beneath the sheer weight of his fists. He felt mighty! More capable than ever as might from the mortal surged into him! The Garuda bellowed with amused, self-righteous laughter. The human's little trick had gone awry, and now Urcan was absorbing the power! Except it was *true* power! Not the cheap little number-trick variant available here.

"No. This is Mana! *Real Mana*!" Where Urcan had initially been cautious, now he threw it to the wind. The opportunity for true gain had presented itself, and the demon drew on it greedily and deeply, commencing a 'pull' where Artorian invoked a 'push.' The smiling demon bared his fangs, looking down at the mortal he was going to drain entirely dry of might.

The human's face was wrenched in agony. Wet streaks running down his cheeks. Too late did Urcan realize that the human was not in physical pain, but suffered emotional injury. Drawing a staggered breath, Artorian whispered his feelings out into the open. "I'm sorry. I'm so, *so sorry*."

Before he was a summoned creature in the place known as Eternia, Urcan had been an abyss-proper A-ranked demon. He had been summoned during countless wars, in countless civilizations, over countless eras. Each one had grown his power. Each one had increased his might.

Yet this? This was the easiest power gain he'd ever felt or witnessed. He was a proud A-rank six. Seven now. Soon to be eight as his sixth-tier **Law** ate up the energy he offered it. A rocking roar of power coursed through his form, and now it was rank nine that was soon approaching. The **Law**-tier of the Mage making foolish choices was high. So high! The trade-in to Mana of his tier turned mere drops into burdened oceans. Soon, he would reach the apex! He would be a True Deamon! "Your tears are succulent to my woes, mortal! What are you sorry for? Your mistake in empowering me? Ha! I shall make your end swift for this gift!"

"It is you who are mistaken… little demon. I know this might be hard to grasp, but…" Artorian spoke in words too soft for Urcan's comfort. "I was not talking… to you."

Becoming an A-rank nine, Urcan ignored the discomfort. He was unstoppable! He had won! "You jest, little Mage! Were we in the true world, I would have possessed you for your body! There is nothing you can do to me now!"

Artorian no longer felt the pressure push down against his hands. The demon was no longer trying to crush him. The demon was letting him win, via Urcan's own greed for power. The demon pulled Mana, and that gave Artorian plenty of time to shift where his hands were.

"Nothing? Little demon. I'm afraid you've forgotten where you are. You see, you are holding a weapon. A weapon that the system recognizes enough for you to use it as a normal item without problems. And… any unaltered item with the weapon tag, any at all, is subject to…" Artorian finished moving his hand, reaching far enough to allow a single finger to touch and make contact with the tsuba. The hand guard. "*Artifacting.*"

Artorian's' DE points hit the negatives, and Urcan could not stop his sudden screaming. He had no hope of stopping. The item of his very soul had just been rent apart so far past the point of cohesion that the demon's mind was on the verge of fracturing. Urcan's soul was ripped open, laid bare for alteration.

The gentle pink energy suffusing Urcan gave Artorian full control of everything he did, or tried to do. That energy might reside in Urcan, but it didn't belong to him. That same pink hum allowed Artorian to fill information into the empty fields he saw in the prompts that appeared before him, allowing him to do in seconds what could otherwise take minutes or hours.

Here, in the system, everything was numbers. Everything was Eternia. Nothing was exempt. Not even cheating remained free-floating for long, as Eternium would undoubtedly allot the Pylons for it to fit. In a fashion he approved of. Perhaps not immediately, but eventually. Artorian could get away with every new trick once. Though only once.

The unaltered katana did not remain so, but every minor alteration was a major twist and tear in Urcan's soul. The full breadth of his personal Liminal energy was ravaged by otherworldly factors, performed by the might of **Laws** that punched high above the tier six's weight. Each addition to a prompt forced Urcan to experience horror and pain beyond words, and only sometimes within understandable concepts.

The process of Artifacting was easy. The process where Artorian finished his terrible ploy and ripped Urcan's mind from his Eternia-provided body, slotting it into the Soul Item weapon like a falsified incarnation gone wrong, was easier still. His Mana made it a breeze. The energy bent to his every intent as he ripped the demon to proverbial pieces, reforging him into something else entirely via methods Artorian would rather have never touched.

Unfortunately for the Garuda, Artorian was a devious old man. One who would not be stopped from reaching his goal. One who would not pause or look twice at the atrocities he needed to commit if they allowed him to continue. This was a terrible love. The knowledge that Urcan needed to not be in his way, for the world to be turned back upright. For a family long sought to once again become whole.

Urcan's soul was ground down to its most base of components, until Urcan's lowest mental level came face to face with Artorian's as the changes began to culminate. Urcan's lowest, deepest, most primal feature of the self was fear. The demon was afraid. He performed all his other actions stemming from a basis of that fear.

That small demon looked at the other it now observed, and faltered upon taking in the sight. Where Urcan stood fearful, Artorian remained unyielding. The unswayable figure reached out to Urcan, his voice once more that of gentle whispers. "*I'm sorry*. One day, I wish you a fluffy dream. For now, I must bid you… silence. Dream no more, little demon. Dream no more."

The unyielding aspect placed its hand over the eyes of unmoving fear, causing Urcan to see only darkness. Though, he also no longer felt the fear. Instead he fell into a deep and dreamless slumber, suffering no more. Urcan's mind left the

Eternia body entirely. Whole only in the reforged item of its soul, with which it was now one.

Artorian opened his eyes in Alfheim as he accepted the finalization of the prompt without needing to look, when it asked him if he was done. His pink energy diffused, along with his upkeep for Soul of Zen, his Astra form, and his monk skills.

He was silent as he returned to real time, watching the lifeless body of a twenty-foot-tall Garuda topple and lean backward before finally falling into a crumpled heap. The shell was empty. Devoid of life, mind, and soul.

Instead, Artorian caught the katana by the grip as gravity took hold, his fingers taking it from the Garuda's failing grip. It was mundane no more, and his own grip tightened on the hilt, unwilling to let go. The black blade with its sharp yellow edge wreathed itself in constant pink fire the moment he gripped it. That true Mana had needed to go somewhere, and the only place for it to go had been the weapon. Artorian currently didn't want to recoup anything stained with demon connections. No matter how infinitesimally small the risk.

He exhaled slowly as he noticed how the world wasn't quiet. The wind blew. The clouds moved. The grass waved. The leaves bristled against one another. His heart pumped. His side bled.

As he covered himself in his Resplendence field, he saw his health had dropped down all the way to the one-thousand range. His field would patch him up, but it didn't diminish the sorrow he currently carried. What a fitting name… "I suppose I'll name you that, then. You are Sorrow."

He lifted the blade to properly look at it, but found he could not inspect it at all. The notice that came up read a cryptic message.

Weapon Locked. Reason: Legendary ranked item. Creator is formally requested to give up the object to comply with system needs.

Artorian said nothing while solemnly nodding in reply. His words were rather breathy when he did call out. "Yvessa."

He didn't have the energy or heart to be surprised when it was Oberon who showed up. Though after he managed to look up and glance to see a crowd, he noted Yvessa was there as well. Just further in the back.

A clear hierarchy was present in the light orbs near him, and he noted a little late that they were in some kind of triangle formation. A formation that did not have Oberon at the front. That honor went to someone he knew better. "Hello, Dani. I want to say that… it's nice to see you. But could you please take this out of my hand? My fingers won't open. My mind won't let go."

Yvessa stirred to motion, but several other Wisps enclosed around her space, telling her without words that it was not her place to move. It was Dani who hovered forwards. To the surprise of the Wisps behind her, she adopted a human form that reminded Artorian suspiciously much of Danielle the Detailed.

Dani's hand enclosed Artorian's free hand, rather than the one currently holding the black weapon wreathed in active pink flames. Her voice was soft, gentle, caring. Not at all the lambasting Artorian had been expecting given all the abyss he'd caused. "Are you alright?"

The man closed his eyes, slowly moving his head to tell her no. "I'm… a terrible thing, Dani. I just learned. I just learned that I could do this to anyone. Outside of Eternium. Outside of Cal. I know *how* now. I will always know how. This will follow me forever. This victory has scarred me."

Dani gently patted the back of his hand. "We… we know. There's a crack in your Seed Core. In the Silverwood Tree. Your guardian flame told us right away, and we came as soon as we could. I did not expect to find you in such a stable state. Changing the soul of another… it… it hurts your own. Are you… you?"

Artorian blinked at the question. He wondered what she meant, but thought about it as he looked at that lovely, overly bright Alfheim cloudscape. The majority of that awful luminance currently blocked out. "I… I am Artorian. A man who stood new in the Fringe. Who took hold of values and identities that have seen me to this day; the day I found out that, even though it is my desire for all others to choose their own path in life, by their own volition, I would stoop so low as to rip it from another. Yet I can't bring myself to regret it, because I know I'm going to do it again."

Dani squeezed him to provide comfort, and she was glad to see how such a little thing helped so much. "Barry?"

He slowly nodded, paining himself. "I am going to turn him into a blasted dessert fork."

The humanized Wisp laid her arm around his shoulders, pulling him close. "We can heal your Seed Core by… undoing what you just did. That demon is never going to be the same, but Eternium always had plans for…"

Artorian frowned hard, his posture straightening as his eyes bored into Dani's. The implications of what she just said ran deeper than his current debacle. "You… you wouldn't… have had plans to do this to others?"

She cocked her head to the side to motion 'not really' while fully understanding it very well could be used for the same purpose Artorian just managed all on his own. "It's called Soul Forging. Cal wanted a method that would allow… people *without* a center… to retain powers gained in his Soul Space, or dungeon, if they were ever to leave it afterwards. While Cal is still unconscious, he has some… long reaching plans you don't know about. There is a way the world is going to be, when we can finally let the current occupants leave."

Dani's tone softened. "Cal thought he figured out the one way those conditions could end up, and Soul Forging was the contingency plan. In Eternia, Soul Forging is going to be little more than the combinations of abilities or skills, to make entirely new things, so the game can remain fresh. Though, I believe you have just discovered what it is that we are actually changing."

This was too much information for a frazzled, emotionally wounded, and soul-wrenched Artorian to handle right now. "Dani... I... I currently can't—"

Shshsh. She shushed him, like a baby. "I know. I just want you to know that what you did to Urcan is no longer something that would otherwise be permanent. We can separate his mind from his soul. We can ease those back into a body. Cal has long been able to do that in the S-ranks. Eternium never blinked twice at it either. That's probably why it was so easy to do."

Artorian found some light in the darkness. "So... this horrible thing I just did. I can... undo it? Make proper reparations?"

Dani smiled and gave him a big hug. "I'm glad you're smart. Yes, old man. Yes, you can. This doesn't have to be some permanent wound or scar on your being. It only will be, if you think of it as such. The mind in that weapon is not dead. You put it to sleep. Remember that your soul is kind."

The old man inside the Eternia body was already shaking his head no. The relief building regardless as the realizations came that in Eternia, Soul Forging as he did it was not a permanent fate. A warmth filled him. He could suddenly see the network of support he had, as his eyes finally took in the details.

The Wisp crowd Dani had with her were all healers of a sort. Oberon was here because he had to be a direct representative of Eternium, but even he was holding a medical kit with his light-tendrils. Dawn was with his Seed Core. She was always looking out for him. That big sweetheart.

His death-grip on the katana felt tingly as he felt the blood resurge in his gray fingers, the color stolen entirely from his hand. He barely lifted the fallen arm that had previously been inert from a now-healed shoulder stabbing. Slowly opening his digits between Dani's, he allowed the hilt of the weapon to fall free from his other, though it hovered in mid-air when Dani took control of it. She moved the newly formed concept of

Sorrow safely behind her, into the waiting team of Wisps who would handle the katana from that point.

He sounded weak when he spoke, feeling awfully tired when the full weight of the burden lifted, his form fully slumping against her. Dani held him as if he weighed little more than a paperweight. “Thank you.”

EPILOGUE

Only three Wisps stayed with Artorian while the rest saw to other tasks. Dani was the first to need to go, given her attention was in heavy, constant demand. She did tell Artorian she'd fix that Iridium weapon issue of his. Also, that the old worry of where all of the original Iridium was had been… resolved.

Everything not taken by Barry had been recovered, and not always through fair play. Artorian didn't expect much fair play from Wisps these days. He just counted his current company as pleasant exceptions.

Oberon had to go next. He had been there just to provide Eternium a personal account, since the dungeon had ended his personal feud and attacks on the man. Now whatever Artorian did just went in the log. It would be addressed, categorized, filed, and Pyloned like any other problem. The nicest thing Oberon told Artorian was that Eternium wasn't mad at him. The dungeon was more disappointed in itself rather than blaming Artorian for the childish things he'd done.

Yvessa stayed for a while, just sitting with him in her human form. To be company while he slowly healed, and came to terms with his actions. "Dani is sweet. Isn't she, Yvessa?"

His caretaker nodded, but cut the chaff from the conversation right away. "You could tell she lied to make you feel better?"

"Oh, you are a *beauty*. That mind of yours..." Artorian smiled, the edges of his lips curling up at her genius. He kissed his fingers and let them fly. "Exquisite. I always had the feeling you were something special. To see it slowly come to bloom, now that is something that heals my heart. Yes... I knew she was lying, yet I needed it in the moment, and I believed her in the moment. The only thing that's going to fix my Seed Core is the only thing that seems to fix anything in Cal. Nap time. Give it to me straight. How badly did I extend my timer?"

Yvessa loved how he could compliment her and yet cut to the chase at the same time when he realized she didn't want to babble. "Tenfold. That crack increased your sleep requirement tenfold. If you Soul Forge again, especially without more direct system help from Eternium, that's going to compound. You probably won't shatter, but there's a chance your Seed Core might. I didn't want to tell you, but you're happier when you know."

He firmly agreed. "I am, and I sort of figured. I'm going to do it again. Though just once. I can't throw that trick around like it's nothing. That hurt me on the inside and I think one is all I have left before I am more than just 'not okay.' Please find that abyss-burned gazebo. If I don't get out after the next time I need to do this... I might shatter myself on principle. I cannot become that person, Yvessa. I cannot become so similar to a demon that I cannot distinguish myself from one."

"You won't." She held his shoulder, giving it a squeeze. "You honestly won't. Your heart's just not in it. Not like theirs. You have this powerful, important feature about you. You see when you've gone too far. You know where the line is, and if not, you draw one anyway. You might cross it, but I know you look over your shoulder and make a mental tally to make it up to someone. Your mouth couldn't stop itself from letting slip you wanted to pay that demon reparations. A demon, Artorian. You included a demon in your big spider web of a care plan. Even Soni has a spot."

Artorian weakly shrugged. "Soni is… walking the path. Even if he doesn't see it. I hold out hope in one hand, and poison in the other. In the likely event that I am wrong."

"Would it be so bad?" she asked, nudging him. "To be right?"

Artorian didn't want to admit that that was the more frightening of the two options. "I just… I want to see it, Yvessa. I want to badly see that I was wrong. I want to see one. Just *one*. A *good* demon. Proof that I was wrong. That every soul had a chance, no matter how far gone. That every soul still had that tiny, empty box, where some love could go."

She nodded along with his words, finishing the sentence for him. "Because if a demon can do it. There is nothing that couldn't. Nothing."

Artorian weakly chuckled. "Heavens, you're smart. Are you reading my mind now? Are the words carved upon my heart for you to read?"

She smirked, but shook her head no. "It's… being a Wisp. Or being a Fae? I'm honestly not a very good Wisp. I'm so wily and troublesome that Oberon, of all Wisps, is the one that can't stop stealing glances at me."

She was quiet for a moment, but Artorian recognized the confusion on her face. It was like looking at a student in the lecture room. "You have a question?"

"When do people take different names? When do you know if it's the right time?" Her tone was too serious and worried for Artorian to take this as some pleasant little comment. "I'd like to know. You were someone else before you were Artorian. I'm…"

Artorian smoothly filled in. "You're approaching that point. Where the values and identities you once held are so far from the person you knew to hold them. That they are no longer… you? I heard the inflection in Dani's words. They were practiced. Luckily, the answer is easy. The answer is anytime you'd like. Anytime you think that the person who you are now is someone else. Your core values don't need to have been changed. Nor your body. If your mind steps forwards, the rest will follow. Why don't you instead tell me the name of the person you're thinking of becoming? I know that face you're making. It's on your tongue, and you just want to tell it to someone."

Yvessa smiled, a light blush on her cheeks in a darker hue of green. "Titania. The name speaks to me, even if I don't know why. It… has a flavor in my mouth when I say it. Like a flower that has bloomed, and bloomed beautifully. Not to boast, but my spirit is too large for the body of a Wisp. I trounce through their rules. I waltz through their courts. I step on their etiquette. I get in their faces and don't stop berating them because they remind me of my favorite old man, and never will I ever chance it that they become as much trouble as you."

They shared a pleasant, warm laugh, Artorian softly slapping his knee as his caretaker stood. "It's gorgeous, Titania. I'll call you that from now on, then. It was a pleasure to have known Yvessa. My most delightful, wonderful caretaker."

He stood, and extended a hand in greeting. "Just as it is wonderful to meet you, Titania. Queen of the Fairies!"

She punched him in the shoulder in jest, but a massive blush filled her cheeks. A deeper color that was far stronger than the playful one from before. She shook his hand after he stopped giggling, his smile falling when her flush did not go away. "You… oh. *Oh.* You said… Oberon can't stop stealing glances. He's… stolen more than glances."

He smirked, winking at her. "I won't tell. You just be happy. I'll be here, causing trouble like always. As love does. I suppose he perhaps wasn't in that big triangle just for Eternium them, but to be company."

Yvessa burned bright green when she looked away. "I might… fancy him. A little bit. Nothing serious!"

"*Uhu.*" Artorian enjoyed a devious bit of snickering. "You realize, of course, that now I *must* meddle."

Yvessa's spoon stabbed Artorian in the nose. "Don't you *dare.*"

Artorian pressed his innocent fingers against his chest. "What? Meeee? Never."

The spoon shook as Yvessa's cheeks became thick and pouty. She sharply narrowed her eyes at him, huffed, and vanished on the spot, leaving Artorian alone before he completely broke down in sappy, weak laughter that he just couldn't stop himself from enjoying. Oh, it was good to laugh. It was good to feel happy. It was good to know that outside of his current problems, others were finding happiness. That was how he liked it. That was how he wanted things. That was the note he wanted to go out on.

Sadly, the music had not finished playing for him just yet. One day, but not now. Not today. There were things to accomplish, regardless of the current small victories and setbacks. There was a war on, but there was always a war on. Barry still needed smiting. Demons still needed punting. His family still needed a home. His children still needed to run free. Dawn still deserved those couple centuries of his time. Or was he up to countin' in millennia now?

He smiled, shaking his head as his ears picked up a rustle in the distance. Soni was finally finishing the trek back to the battle zone. It had only taken the poor bat several hours. Not that he'd tell the human Urcan had knocked him unconscious.

When Soni crawled over the crest of the next closest crater, he saw what was left of Urcan's body. When he'd made the trek all the way to it, Soni spitefully kicked the fallen body in the shin before turning his attention to Artorian. "Alright. What went wrong? You do not have the face of a person who is happy with his victory."

Artorian chuckled, making a 'come along' motion as the duo walked to go pick up Ikaruga a small league away. Or however far the dang siege engine was. "You didn't miss much. In short, I won. Didn't level up. Am rather tired, and am not sure how I'm getting my third specialization so I can get into Jotunheim. Fairly certain that was a must have."

Soni made a **pfft** noise. "I solved that one for you. We're going to think with portals and play scry and fry, except with a ballista instead of spells. You're going to hit your tenth level in your second specialization *so fast.* Your only hiccup will be figuring out how to unlock number three. Just how many moos do you think infest the secret cow level?"

"You are willing to just... help me with that?" Artorian felt hopeful, with a twinge of surprise. "I thought you might have your own plans."

Soni threw his hands into the air. "Which would consist of what? 'Oh hello there, my old chaps. Why yes, I have betrayed you. I am also the only one with a gate ability that could conveniently assault the dot on the map we can all see at all times. Please, become aware of my continued existence'!"

He shot Artorian a look. "No. No, and thank you for more no. The only way I am getting anywhere with life is if my old 'team,' for lack of a better word, goes the way of the Dodo. Oh, wait, no. Those still exist. Or don't exist yet? I need to stop listening to diviners. Some other species that are extinct, I mean. Mind telling me how you beat Urcan?"

The human made a so-so motion with his hand, seeing the weapon he'd lost glimmer in the distance. Gosh, sunglass was easy to spot. He'd keep that in mind. "Got my hands on an item of cultural and historical interest. It turned out he was deathly allergic to historians."

Soni's eyebrow raised high. "What. You're saying you're a historian?"

"Oh yes!" Artorian confirmed, gleeful at the ancient reference. "An art historian! I'll have my own museum one day. You might even say I have a thing for... *Artifacts.*"

ABOUT DENNIS VANDERKERKEN

Hello all! I'm Dennis, but feel free to call me Floof. Credit of the name now being accumulated by the vast and powerfully cultivated viking beard, that grows ever more in potency. I'm now counting my writing experience in years, so let me say it is my great pleasure that you are reading this, and welcome back to the goodness!

I have been the designer, plotter, and writer of Artorian's Archives since its inception, and look forward to gracing your eyes with ever more volumes of the story. Indulging my dear readers in secrets otherwise forever obscure.

If you have any questions, or would like to chat, I live on the Eternium discord server. Feel free to come say hi anytime! I will keep you entertained for years to come!

Connect with Dennis:
Discord.gg/mdp
Patreon.com/FloofWorks

ABOUT DAKOTA KROUT

Associated Press best-selling author, Dakota has been a top 5 bestseller on Amazon, a top 6 bestseller on Audible, and his first book, Dungeon Born, was chosen as one of Audible's top 5 fantasy picks in 2017.

He draws on his experience in the military to create vast terrains and intricate systems, and his history in programming and information technology helps him bring a logical aspect to both his writing and his company while giving him a unique perspective for future challenges.

"Publishing my stories has been an incredible blessing thus far, and I hope to keep you entertained for years to come!" -Dakota

Connect with Dakota:
MountaindalePress.com
Patreon.com/DakotaKrout
Facebook.com/TheDivineDungeon
Twitter.com/DakotaKrout
Discord.gg/mdp

ABOUT MOUNTAINDALE PRESS

Dakota and Danielle Krout, a husband and wife team, strive to create as well as publish excellent fantasy and science fiction novels. Self-publishing *The Divine Dungeon: Dungeon Born* in 2016 transformed their careers from Dakota's military and programming background and Danielle's Ph.D. in pharmacology to President and CEO, respectively, of a small press. Their goal is to share their success with other authors and provide captivating fiction to readers with the purpose of solidifying Mountaindale Press as the place 'Where Fantasy Transforms Reality.'

Connect with Mountaindale Press:
MountaindalePress.com
Facebook.com/MountaindalePress
Twitter.com/_Mountaindale
Instagram.com/MountaindalePress

MOUNTAINDALE PRESS TITLES

GameLit and LitRPG

The Completionist Chronicles,
The Divine Dungeon, and
Full Murderhobo by Dakota Krout

King's League by Jason Anspach and J.N. Chaney

Arcana Unlocked by Gregory Blackburn

A Touch of Power by Jay Boyce

Red Mage and
Farming Livia by Xander Boyce

Space Seasons by Dawn Chapman

Ether Collapse and
Ether Flows by Ryan DeBruyn

Bloodgames by Christian J. Gilliland

Threads of Fate by Michael Head

Wolfman Warlock by James Hunter and Dakota Krout

Axe Druid,
Mephisto's Magic Online, and
High Table Hijinks by Christopher Johns

Skeleton in Space by Andries Louws

Chronicles of Ethan by John L. Monk

Pixel Dust and
Necrotic Apocalypse by David Petrie

Henchman by Carl Stubblefield

Artorian's Archives by Dennis Vanderkerken and Dakota Krout

www.ingramcontent.com/pod-product-compliance
Lightning Source LLC
Chambersburg PA
CBHW030801260626
47169CB00001B/145

* 9 7 8 1 6 3 7 6 6 0 4 7 8 *